Studies in Liturgical Musicology
Edited by Dr. Robin A. Leaver

1. Frans Brouwer and Robin A. Leaver (eds.). *Ars et Musica in Liturgia: Essays Presented to Casper Honders on His Seventieth Birthday*. 1994.
2. Steven Plank. *"The Way to Heavens Doore": An Introduction to Liturgical Process and Musical Style*. 1994.
3. Thomas Allen Seel. *A Theology of Music for Worship Derived from the Book of Revelation*. 1995.
4. David W. Music. *Hymnology: A Collection of Source Readings*. 1996.
5. Ulrich Meyer. *Biblical Quotation and Allusion in the Cantata Libretti of Johann Sebastian Bach*. 1997.
6. D. Dewitt Wasson. *Hymntune Index and Related Hymn Materials*. 1998.
7. David W. Music. *Instruments in Church: A Collection of Source Documents*. 1998.
8. William T. Flynn. *Medieval Music as Medieval Exegesis*. 1999.

Medieval Music as Medieval Exegesis

William T. Flynn

Studies in Liturgical Musicology, No. 8

The Scarecrow Press, Inc.
Lanham, Maryland, and London
1999

SCARECROW PRESS, INC.

Published in the United States of America
by Scarecrow Press, Inc.
4720 Boston Way, Lanham, Maryland 20706
http://www.scarecrowpress.com

4 Pleydell Gardens, Folkestone
Kent CT20 2DN, England

British Library Cataloguing in Publication Information Available

Library of Congress Cataloging-in-Publication Data

Flynn, William T., 1956–
Medieval music as medieval exegesis / William T. Flynn.
p. cm. — (Studies in liturgical musicology ; no. 8)
Includes bibliographical references and index.
ISBN 0-8108-3656-4 (alk. paper)
1. Church music—Catholic Church. 2. Music—500–1400—History and criticism. 3. Liturgics. 4. Bible—Criticism and interpretation—History—Middle Ages, 600–1500. I. Title. II. Series.
ML3003.F6 1999
781.71'009'02—dc21 99-15108

The paper used in this publication meets the minimum requirements of American National Standard for Information Sciences—Permanence of Paper for Printed Library Materials, ANSI/NISO Z39.48–1992.
Manufactured in the United States of America.

To Jane

CONTENTS

TABLES

EXAMPLES

EDITOR'S FOREWORD

FOLLOWING in the wake of deconstruction in philosophy and literary criticism over the past thirty years or so, other disciplines have undergone a similar process of deconstruction and reconstruction.

The preoccupation in musicology used to be focused almost entirely on the musical work, its physical manifestation in manuscript and/or printed sources, its musical text, meaning, and significance. But the "new musicology" has broadened the scope of the discipline to include contextual and philosophic studies. Thus political, economic, literary, liturgical, religious, and other contexts, instead of being regarded as incidental to the development of music, are now understood as fundamental pressures and influences that have materially affected specific changes in musical form, genre, and style. Like other deconstructed disciplines, the new musicology has adapted and borrowed methodologies, research, and conclusions from other disciplines.

Liturgical studies are similarly being deconstructed. Much of the liturgical movement of the twentieth century was committed to the premise that liturgy is text. Therefore in liturgical studies great emphasis has been placed upon the liturgical text and its subtext: the liturgical form, its sequential structure, primary elements, the words to be spoken and sung (prayer, praise, and proclamation), and the words to be observed (rubrics). But liturgy is more than text, in the same way that a play is more than its written script and an opera more than its printed libretto. It also includes sight and sound, as the seasons and celebrations indicate their changing context by the different colors of paraments and vestments and by the alternative music of celebrant, choir, and congregation, and as the liturgical order is actualized in ritual actions, processions, silences, and sometimes the visual and olfactory presence of incense. The "new liturgiology," if one may call it such, is therefore moving beyond the earlier preoccupation with textual concerns to encompass a broader, three-dimensional understanding of liturgical rite. As with other older disciplines, it is now developing interdisciplinary dimensions, rather than remaining an area of inquiry confined within its own boundaries. Indeed, the process of deconstruction and reconstruction in the established disciplines has created new disciplines which are in themselves interdisciplinary by nature.

Liturgical musicology is one of these newer interdisciplinary areas of research and inquiry, which this series is designed to promote and explore. This new study by Dr. William Flynn is particularly significant in that it pushes the interdisciplinary boundaries of liturgical musicology beyond the twin disciplines of liturgiology and musicology to embrace a wider range of investigatation that includes biblical exegesis, medieval studies, Latin linguistics, as well as ecclesiastical history. It is also a substantial work of deconstruction and reconstruction in which long-held negative assumptions regarding the nature and content of the medieval developments of the eucharistic liturgy are replaced by a fundamentally positive evaluation. Dr. Flynn has therefore produced a provocative book with conclusions that are somewhat controversial. However, his careful and integrated research in these interdisciplinary areas persuasively demonstrates that the Tridentine judgment concerning liturgical tropes and sequences failed to do justice to the exegetical and hermeneutical functions they were originally intended to supply: instead of distorting the balance and integrity of the Mass their purpose was to clarify and explain it. It is therefore somewhat ironic to observe that the Reformer Martin Luther probably understood the purpose of such troping better than the framers of the decrees of the Council of Trent. His German Sanctus, *Jesaja, dem Propheten* (1526), follows the form and structure of the typical Latin sequence, as well as being written in rhymed couplets, the primary characteristic of the Latin model. Further, rather than being confined to the liturgical text of the Sanctus, Luther's German version also provides the exegetical context of the Seraphic hymn, being based on Isaiah 6, verses 1-4, rather than on verse 3 alone. Dr. Flynn's work provides a foundation for discussing such issues, making this is an extremely important piece of research: it is not only a major contribution to liturgical musicology but one that also has significant implications for liturgical studies generally.

Robin A. Leaver, Series Editor
Westminster Choir College of Rider University
and Drew University

PREFACE

Audiences, Methods, and Scope

WHILE it is perhaps obvious that the histories of liturgy and music cannot easily be told separately, the field of Liturgical Musicology is nonetheless relatively new and emerging. Part of the reason for this is that the two disciplines of liturgics and music have specialized languages, methods, historiographies, and goals, and these differing approaches need to be negotiated, hopefully without losing potential readers in a maze of technical language and methods of argumentation specific to one or the other field. This particular book is especially wide-ranging, since it aims to engage not only musicologists and liturgists, but also biblical exegetes, ecclesiastical historians, and students of medieval Latin literature. Since these groups of readers do not share the same technical vocabularies and will necessarily approach the work from within their specialties, a large part of my task has been to provide enough of an introduction so that specialists in one area, who are perhaps novices in quite another area, may be able to follow and benefit from the whole work. About half of the book has the necessary object of providing background information, which prepares for an extended analysis of two services in chapter four. These preliminary chapters address the issue of how makers and users of musical-liturgical texts in the eleventh century were taught to make them and to evaluate them, and it is the thesis of this study that these texts were occasioned by a reflection and meditation upon memorized scripture provided by the liturgy itself, and deepened by the study of commentary. The fourth chapter's analysis shows how all of this "pre-scholastic" training—poetic, musical, liturgical, and exegetical—fed into the study of scripture and how these seemingly diverse activities were often experienced as a unified pedagogy that had its origin and its culmination in the liturgy.

Such an approach is not without risks: since large portions of the work are given over to introductory material, it may help specialist readers to skim those sections that simply summarize well-known positions for non-specialist readers and proceed more quickly to the final chapter. However, even in the introductory section, complex issues are often taken up. Hence in chapter one, a very simple introduction to the study of grammar in the Middle Ages is followed by a detailed discussion of grammatical tropes as viewed by Donatus, Augustine, Cassiodorus, and Bede. Similarly in chapter two, although musicologists will find that much of the chapter simply summarizes the work of Matthew Bielitz and Calvin Bowers on the relationships between medieval grammar and medieval music theory, mixed in with this is a detailed examination of grammatical terms that were not used in music theory as well as a new reading of perhaps the most influential work in chant theory, Guido's *Micrologus*. The third chapter provides a detailed analysis of variations in festal liturgies, based on the contents of the Autun Troper. Nevertheless, I have omitted a detailed codicological treatment of the Troper, since it is beyond the scope of this work. (Specialist readers may wish to consult my dissertation "Paris, Bibliothèque de l'Arsenal, MS 1169: The Hermeneutics of Eleventh-Century Burgundian Tropes, and Their Implications for Liturgical Theology," Duke University, 1992, pp. 19-75.)

It is my hope that I have walked the tightrope between too little and too much background information in such a way as to make the work accessible to its diverse readership without overburdening any one group with elementary material. In this way, the work as a whole may be seen to help consolidate and summarize the gains made in the interdisciplinary study of tropes and sequences most notably carried out within the past twenty years by three philologists from Stockholm University: Gunilla Björkvall, Gunilla Iversen, and Ritva Jonsson. In publishing the critical text editions of liturgical tropes and prosulas (*Corpus Troporum*, Stockholm: Almqvist & Wiksell International, 1975-), and in a multi-year project of international congresses, they have created both the standards for the study and presentation of these liturgical texts, and made it possible for me to examine liturgies of the eleventh century. While readers from the diverse specialties will no doubt be able to refine and modify the picture that has emerged here, it is my hope that this work will provide a new look at the riches and goals of eleventh-century liturgies and a starting place for more detailed collaborative work.

Presentation of Liturgical Texts and Music

The critical text editions of the tropes in this book are published by the *Corpus Troporum* and these and all of the other liturgical texts are presented here in accordance with their editorial practices: in general, the texts are given with a minimum of editorial additions; obvious contractions have been expanded silently; editorial additions are marked with angle brackets, < >; angle brackets also mark the expansions of the highly abbreviated base texts in the tropes; trope elements are given in lower case while the liturgical base texts are given in upper case; the medieval spellings of the manuscripts are retained, while standard spellings are adopted in editorial additions and expansions. Manuscript sigla are also adopted from the *Corpus Troporum* editions.

The original notation of the Autun Troper does not supply enough information about the pitches of the melodies to provide an exact reconstruction of its melodies. However, I have reconstructed the melodies by comparing the neumation of the Troper with closely concordant sources (i.e., sources which present a concordant series of neume shapes set to the same text and which therefore bear a close family resemblance to the Autun versions of the melodies). The concordant sources are indicated in footnotes within the music examples. Although it is important to keep in mind that it is impossible to speak with complete certainty about the musical content of the versions used at Autun, the close correspondence of the neumation to pitch-secure versions does make it possible to offer some suggestive musical analyses that apply both to the concordant versions and to the Autun versions so far as they can be reconstructed. Most of the analyses do not rely on the exact pitch content, but a few cases do. Although these analyses may be cautiously read as applying only to the concordances, the concordant sources are themselves representative of the kinds of musical and textual exegesis that I discuss throughout this work. For example, we can never know that the version of *Ecce adest de quo prophete* used at Autun was based on 'a' as it was in Nevers. What we do know is that the neumation of the Nevers version matches more exactly than any other concordant pitched source and therefore it is the most pertinent pitched source to choose for analysis; it represents both an analyzable version of the melody in use at a neighboring institution, and a "best guess" about what was done at Autun.

Music examples are presented in diplomatic notation printed above the edition in square notation. I based the diplomatic notation closely upon the shapes that are present in the original manuscript. So far as possible, I have used the square notation (prepared with the computer program *Chant Scribe* 2.4, available from St. Meinrad Archabbey, St. Meinrad, IN 47577) in such a way that it reflects the original notation; for example, the virga is always rendered as such and not replaced by a punctum, and equivalent square forms are supplied for several types of liquescent neumes.

Acknowledgments

This work could not have been accomplished without the help and support of many people and institutions. I would especially like to thank Emory University for a grant which enabled me to deepen my knowledge of the manuscripts formerly held by the cathedral of Autun and for a research leave that enabled me to complete the writing. My sincerest thanks go to the staffs of the following libraries: the Newberry Library (Chicago), the Bibliothèque Nationale and the Bibliothèque de l'Arsenal (Paris), the British Library (London), and the interlibrary loan staff at Emory University (Atlanta). Marie-Josette Perrat of the Bibliothèque Municipale d'Autun was especially helpful and Claire Maître, who prepared the library's catalogue of musical and liturgical manuscripts, drew my attention to many important sources. Peter Marshall kindly read the entire manuscript and gave help and encouragement. Most importantly, I would like to express my deepest thanks and appreciation to Jane Flynn, who read and commented extensively on every draft of this book.

INTRODUCTION

IN his famous series of lectures, later published as *The Love of Learning and the Desire for God,* Jean Leclercq gives a summary of the importance of the liturgy to what he termed "monastic culture" in the eleventh and twelfth centuries:[1]

> The liturgy had been the motive for the renewal of monastic culture in the Carolingian period, and was also its fruit. During the following centuries, it is in the atmosphere of the liturgy and amid the poems composed for it, *in hymnis et canticis,* that the synthesis of all the *artes* was effected, of the literary techniques, religious reflection, and all sources of information whether biblical, patristic, or classical. In the liturgy, all these resources fully attained their final potentiality; they were restored to God in a homage which recognized that they had come from Him. Thanksgiving, eucharist, theology, *confessio fidei*—all these expressions, in the monastic tradition, expressed only slightly differing aspects of a single reality. In the liturgy, grammar was elevated to the rank of an eschatological fact. It participated in the eternal praise that the monks, in unison with the angels, began offering God in the abbey choir, and which will be perpetuated in Heaven. In the liturgy, love of learning and desire for God find perfect reconciliation.

While Leclercq was correct in identifying this form of religious life as "monastic," it is perhaps an unfortunate coinage, since it suggests that monasteries were the only institutions where one could live out a commitment to a common life centered on worship. This would have been the case by the late twelfth century, but in the eleventh century, cathedral chapters were also organized by various "rules,"[2] and at cathedrals

1. Jean Leclercq, *The Love of Learning and the Desire for God: A Study of Monastic Culture,* 3d ed., trans. Catherine Mirashi (New York: Fordham University Press, 1982); originally published as *L'Amour des lettres et le désir de Dieu: Initiation aux auteurs monastiques du moyen-âge* (Paris: Les Éditions du Cerf, 1957), 250-51.

2. For example in Burgundy, the cathedral chapters were supposed to follow the rule of Chrodegang, adopted by the Council of Aix in 816. This rule, although not as strict as the Benedictine rule, required an enclosed life for the canons who took common meals, shared sleeping quarters, and celebrated the liturgy to-

where the rule was strictly applied, the features of "monastic culture" are clearly evident. This suggests that the regular and communal celebration of the liturgy may be the determinative factor in producing "monastic culture"; where the liturgy flourished, a synthesis of learning and devotion appeared which was not confined to the monastery, but more broadly representative of a "liturgical culture."

Many of the changes that occurred in the "secular" cathedral chapters during the eleventh and twelfth centuries illustrate the gradual erosion of this common liturgical culture. In the eleventh century, well-regulated and disciplined cathedrals were already the exception rather than the rule, and the Gregorian reforms of the late eleventh century arose from the myriad abuses of undisciplined chapters.[3] Even at the better regulated "secular" institutions, the Gregorian reforms had the ironic effect of weakening their rules and allowed canons who were living in community to own their own property and celebrate the liturgy privately. One of these "transitional" cathedrals (St. Nazarius at Autun in central Burgundy) is the focus of the present book:[4] it was only during the late twelfth century that the rows of private houses were built that mark the Autun close to this day—a testimony to the new status of secular clergy, and to the erosion of their common life.

gether. See Alfred Baudrillart, ed., *Dictionnaire d'histoire et de géographie ecclésiastiques* (Paris: Letouzey & Ané, 1950-53), s.v. "Chrodegang." For an edition of the rule, see Chrodegang, *Regula canonicorum*, in Patrologiae cursus completus, sive Bibliotheca universalis . . . omnium ss patrum, doctorum scriptorumque ecclesiasticum qui ab aevo apostolico ad usque Innocenti III tempora floruerunt. . . . Series [Latina], ed. J. P. Migne (Paris, 1844-64), 89:1097-1120.

3. For instance, in most of Burgundy, "cathedral chapters did not adopt a strict rule of common life. . . . Cathedral canons commanded their own property in the eleventh and twelfth centuries, rather than holding possessions in common. . . . In most sees, they had individual houses, grouped near the cathedral." (Constance Brittain Bouchard, *Sword, Miter, and Cloister: Nobility and the Church in Burgundy, 980-1198* [Ithaca, NY: Cornell University Press, 1987], 47).

4. Although there is ample evidence that the rule of Chrodegang was relaxed in much of Burgundy during the ninth and tenth centuries, it appears to have been maintained at Autun. For example, in the late ninth century, Bishop Jonas (ep. 850-865) reconstructed and expanded the communal buildings, including a dormitory, cloister, and refectory, and also increased the endowment of the chapter so that its income could support the canons. According to Chevalier Gagnare, *Histoire de l'église d'Autun* (Autun, 1774), 354, the chapter held strictly to a common life, and a document of 1014 shows that prospective canons consented to be governed by the rule.

This erosion can also be traced through the surviving liturgical books from Autun. The marvelous gradual-troper from the early eleventh century that is the centerpiece for this study is merely one of many books needed to celebrate the mass.[5] It was the cantor's book and contains only the music he specifically needed; it contains cues and incipits for other participants, and its lacunae need to be filled by the choir and clergy who used many other liturgical books. In contrast, a late twelfth-century missal from Autun shows a rite in transition, and implies a celebration that was somewhat contradictory:[6] gone are most of the special songs for the cantor, and all of the necessary texts of the mass are presented in order, including those traditionally reserved for the choir. Although the texts could be read by a single priest (celebrating the mass privately), the texts of the choral chants have music carefully entered above them. The book is clearly for an individual, but its contents imply that the mass could not simply be read: it still required musical vocalization. Later missals, which omit the musical notation entirely, suggest the practice of quiet, private reading at a side altar.[7] These books no longer imply a life focused on common worship, even if communal liturgical celebrations were still the norm for Sundays and feasts.

No doubt the history of the Autun cathedral school would show similar changes from the eleventh to the twelfth century, if it could be told as completely as the history of other more famous schools, such as Chartres.[8] Its early history clearly fits into the model Leclercq describes as monastic, and if the survivals from its library are any indication, the focus in the eleventh century was on the interpretation of scripture and celebration of the liturgy.[9] The school's more famous sisters show

5. Paris, Bibliothèque de l'Arsenal, MS 1169 (PaA 1169). This earliest layer, which constitutes the bulk of this manuscript, dates from some time between 1005-1018.

6. Autun, Bibliothèque Municipale, S 10 (8*) (Autun 10).

7. For example, Autun, Bibliothèque Municipale, S 146 (123) (Autun 146) from the fifteenth century.

8. The transformation of cathedral schools has recently been masterfully analyzed by Stephen Jaeger, *The Envy of Angels: Cathedral Schools and Social Ideals in Medieval Europe, 950-1200* (Philadelphia: University of Pennsylvania Press, 1994).

9. The following manuscripts dating from around the year 1000 were included in a list of the contents of the cathedral library made in 1717; most of them were probably added to the library at the time they were compiled: Augustine's Commentary on the Psalms, and his Enchiridion, Dialogues of Gregory, and an

that a more "scholastic" curriculum focused on training clergy for administrative tasks or higher education appeared during the twelfth century.[10]

By the twelfth century, it would be valid to classify cathedrals and monasteries as representing distinctive "cultures" or "textual communities."[11] However the monasteries were continuing a liturgical culture that is represented by many cathedral liturgies of the eleventh century. Where these liturgies flourished, a distinctive way-of-knowing appeared, and one has access to it to the extent that one can participate in or imagine its communal celebrations.

The following chapters develop a series of "links" intended to help us understand and appreciate liturgies of the eleventh century, by focusing on the liturgy itself as the *schola* that shaped the interpretive practices of the eleventh-century

---

Exposition of the Pentateuch compiled from Augustine, Ambrose, Fulgence and Gregory. (See Gagnare, *Histoire de l'église d'Autun*, 472-73). An *explicit* at the end of a manuscript Bishop Walter (ep. 978-1018) gave to the cathedral reveals that Walter commissioned some of the codices and collected the others, and that he annotated some of them; it follows with a partial list: "this and two other of the Moralia [Gregory's *Moralia in Job*]; the Homilies of Gregory on Ezekiel; Augustine's Confessions; Augustine's Words of the Lord; Expositions on the books of Kings, Daniel and Isaiah; Boethius' Consolation of Philosophy; two [codices] of the letters of Jerome; two also of canons; the exposition of the books of the parables of Solomon, that is, Ecclesiastes and the Song [of Solomon]." The entire explicit reads as follows: "Hunc librum cum caeteris Moralium qui sequuntur dedit beato Nazario suus pontifex Walte[r]us. Contulit etiam illi omnes suos codices, quos ipse aut plures scribi fecit aut nonullos dono acquisiuit, quorum quoque numerus his annotantur et tituli. Horum autem quemlibet si quis ab huius loci iure quocumque modo subtrazerit, ultione anathematis, donec restiuat, percussum se nouerit. Hunc et alios de Moralibus duos. Homelias Gregorii super Ezehihel. Augustinum de confessione. Augustinum de verbis Domini. Exposciones super libros Regum, Danihel et Eschiae. Boaetium de consolatione phylosophyae. Duos epistolarum Hieronimi. Duos quoque de canonibus. In expositione librorum Salomonis Parabolarum, videlicet Aecclesiastis et Can—." The manuscript is described in an exposition catalogue from an exhibit in the city of Autun, *Autun Augustodunum capitule des Éduens*, Exposition catalogue 16 mars-27 octobre 1985 (Autun, 1985), 354-55.

10. Works of "dialectic" such as Peter Lombard's *Sententiae* would form the basis of the new discipline of theology, and legal training would be important for both church and secular jurisdictions. For an excellent study of these changes, see G[illian] R. Evans, *Old Arts and New Theology: The Beginnings of Theology as an Academic Discipline* (Oxford: Oxford University Press, 1980).

11. The most influential recent study of the rise of "scholasticism" is Brian Stock's *The Implications of Literacy: Written Language and Models of Interpretation in the Eleventh and Twelfth Centuries* (Princeton: Princeton University Press, 1983). Stock focuses on distinctions between oral and literate uses of texts for the formation of distinctive "textual communities."

church. The aim is to recreate something of the perspective of the monks, nuns, and clerics who created (and used) new forms of musical and poetic expression to enhance their participation in the liturgy. From the perspective of a monastic or clerical worshipper, the medieval liturgy was a powerful vehicle for the practice and expression of the Christian faith. It required an impressive educational system geared towards the liturgy's intelligent performance, and, as Leclercq argues, it formed both the center and the goal of their religious life.

I have intentionally focused on the perspective of the monks, nuns, and clerics in order to redress what I take to be an imbalance in standard histories of the liturgy. This imbalance stemmed from pastoral and theological goals of an earlier generation of liturgical scholars who were concerned with recovering a sense of the centrality of worship for the modern church.[12] During the late nineteenth and early twentieth centuries,

> the Catholic liturgists sought to recover (for these things had been present in early history) the intelligent and active cooperation of the whole people in the rites. Intelligibility required at least the use of the vernacular language and a contemporary catechesis. Active cooperation required the appropriate distribution of functions among the various 'orders' within the assembly, and above all full lay participation, at the heart of which stands regular eucharistic communion.[13]

Eleventh-century liturgies seem to violate these principles, since they were performed in Latin, by clerics, monks, and nuns on behalf of patrons who were often not even present, and any nonmonastic laity who were present had little or no active role in the rite. However, from the perspective of the monastic or clerical choir, they reveal a richness both in their crafting and in the demands they make on the participant that has seldom been equaled. These liturgies were designed to produce a particularly active engagement in the rite: the participants equated the work of prayer with the work of God and thought that

12. Nicholas Lossky et al., eds., *Dictionary of the Ecumenical Movement* (Geneva: WCC Publications, 1991), s.v. "Liturgical Movement," by Teresa Berger and "Liturgical Reforms," by Balthasar Fischer.

13. Geoffrey Wainwright, *Doxology: The Praise of God in Worship, Doctrine and Life* (New York: Oxford University Press, 1980), 294.

their worship life was sufficient to represent the whole congregation and the whole world to God.

While I do not wish to deny that the clericalization of the medieval liturgy is theologically problematic, the value of liturgies that the clerics, monks, and nuns produced in the eleventh century is not solely determined by their original context. If I am correct in locating the "monastic" way-of-knowing as a peculiarly "liturgical" way-of-knowing (resulting from a life of common prayer), its texts, music, patterns, and forms have a great interest to a church which has once again placed worship in the center of its constitution, life, and mission.[14]

Interpreting Scripture within the Eleventh-Century Liturgy

The method that is employed by "liturgical culture" is *sacra pagina*: interpreting the sacred page through understanding, appropriating, and proclaiming scripture. Although *sacra pagina* is linked to the practice of exegesis, we will miss the depth and riches of what was meant by it if we look for its fulfillment in the eleventh-century homily or sermon. Eleventh-century liturgies only rarely demanded the composition of new sermons: any extended homily found its normal liturgical place within the prayer office, rather than in the mass, and while patristic examples of such sermons were studied, liturgically read, and orally imitated, they became once again a common literary form only in the twelfth century.[15] To understand *sacra pagina* in the eleventh century, one needs to look instead at a wider range of interpretive practices, which included the memorization of scripture, meditation, and the vocalization of the text.

---

14. As Robert Franklin points out, "Vatican II was important as a symbolic assent of the entire Roman Catholic Church to the liturgical movement . . ." (*Nineteenth-Century Churches: The History of a New Catholicism in Württemberg, England, and France* [New York: Garland Publishing, 1987], 512). The widespread influence of the movement on the liturgy may be traced through Max Thurian and Geoffrey Wainwright, *Baptism and Eucharist: Ecumenical Convergence in Celebration* (Geneva: WCC Publications, 1983).

15. One of Stock's premises is that the largely oral sermon became a written form as new "textual communities" were created by greater access to literacy. From this perspective, the flowering of scripture commentary can be viewed as a way of preserving the old "liturgical culture" (which required gathering face-to-face) in a new "literate" form that could be read privately. See Stock, *The Implications of Literacy*, 403-54.

These aspects of *sacra pagina* were reinforced immeasurably by the weekly singing of the Psalter in the office and the sung texts of the eucharistic liturgies. They found their written expression in the mass liturgies, which use new repertories of song (especially tropes and proses) that interact with the inherited texts and actions of the liturgy; these aid in the participants' appropriation of the scripture's imagery, language, and narrative patterns. They were specifically written for the most important feasts in a church's calendar, and at one level can be thought of as being a special ornamentation of the rite, adding weight to it by lengthening it and making it more complex. However, tropes and proses also played a role in deepening and enriching the interpretation of scripture within the rite. They borrow their language and many of their techniques from scriptural exegesis, adding to these the richness of meaning that stems from their placement in the liturgy and from their musical settings.

In order to create a context that enables us to "read" these liturgies as *sacra pagina*, we need to know something of the skills that were considered essential for their performance and interpretation. Letting the liturgies speak requires several related tasks: we have to "reconstruct" their texts and music, so that they can be experienced as sung prayer. We have also (at least imaginatively) to "flesh them out" by considering how the texts and music interact with the spaces in which they were performed and with the orientation and location of their performers. At each stage of this reconstruction we have to examine how the creators of these liturgies theorized their own work, and let their opinions shape our understanding of the material.

Chapters one through three focus on three different but related elements of the "pre-scholastic" educational system, and examine the skills that were thought to be basic for being able to understand and participate fully in the liturgy. Chapter one discusses how the study of grammar influenced the creation of new repertories of song for the eleventh-century liturgy, and shows how the songs were expected to reinforce traditions of understanding, interpreting, and proclaiming scripture. Chapter two investigates aspects of the musical style of the period and analyzes the relationships that were cultivated between music and text and between music and rite. Chapter three looks at the actions and the use of scripture within the liturgy, and discusses eleventh-century interpretations of the liturgy. The study culminates in chapter four with an analysis of the solemn Christmas and Easter masses as they might have been celebrated at the cathedral of St. Nazarius in Autun in the early part of the eleventh century.

1

Reading and Proclaiming
Interpreting Ornate Language in Grammar, Rhetoric, and Liturgy

Grammar Study and the Liturgy

IT would not be much of an exaggeration to characterize the training given to clerics and monastics in the eleventh century as essentially grammatical. Grammar study not only provided the foundation of all of the liberal arts, it provided models for liturgical poetry, as well as the aesthetic rationale for the use of verbal and musical ornament in the liturgy.[1] The influence of grammar study on the liturgy can be seen clearly in four passages from the eleventh century which discuss new liturgical compositions. While all of the passages are in some ways spurious, they are all the more valuable for our purposes, since their descriptions are not to be read as contemporary with the ninth-century popes to whom they appeal, but with the authors' own contemporary repertories.[2] In these passages, terms from the secondary study of grammar are used to describe the new repertories of liturgical song, and are presented here in the order that outlines the entire program of study for secondary grammar students.

The first passage is from a life of Notker Balbulus (ca. 840-912) written by Ekkehard IV (ca. 980-1060). Ekkehard not only commented on new repertories of liturgical song, but also contributed to them, reworking several poems of the earlier gener-

1. On grammar as the foundation of all of the liberal arts, a short history of the teaching of grammar in the Middle Ages and a short bibliography for medieval grammar, see Jeffrey F. Huntsman, "Grammar," chapter 3 in *The Seven Liberal Arts in the Middle Ages*, ed. David L. Wagner (Bloomington: Indiana University Press, 1983), 58-95. On the pervasiveness of grammar as a model for scriptural hermeneutics, see Evans, *Old Arts and New Theology*.

2. Each author claims papal approval of the new repertories, but places that approval in the reigns of consecutive popes. Furthermore, the glowing reports of council liturgies cannot be taken at face value, since they were part of a fabrication supporting the apostolate of St. Martial.

ation, and writing both sequences and *versus*.[3] Thus his concern that the musical and poetic repertory of the monastery of St. Gall be validated by papal approval is aimed to authorize the current repertory and his own contributions to it:

> And not only those [sequences] which the blessed man Notker had dictated, but truly those which his friends and brothers in the monastery of St. Gall had composed; he [Pope Nicholas I (r. 858-867)] canonized all of them, that is, hymns, sequences, tropes, litanies and all the little songs, which they had made by rhythm, meter or prose.[4]

In this passage, the types of "little songs" (including tropes and sequences) that eleventh-century writers were contributing to the liturgy are clearly connected with the secondary study of grammar by the terms "rhythm," "meter," and "prose." These were technical terms for three different ways of organizing the flow of poetic language and public speech and these topics formed the first part of secondary grammar studies—metrics.

The second passage also describes the liturgy, while referring to the next topic in secondary grammar: the study of figurative language—schemes and tropes. These grammatical traditions are specifically associated with the liturgical trope in a spurious addition to a manuscript of the *Liber pontificalis*, which was copied by Ademar of Chabannes (989-1034), whom Louis Duchesne described as a "monk of Saint-Cybar of Angoulême, and celebrated champion of the apostolate of St. Martial."[5] Ademar completely revised and rewrote the tropes for the feast of St. Martial, making him the earliest known composer to leave music in autograph, and this passage serves

3. Stanley Sadie, ed., *The New Grove Dictionary of Music and Musicians* (London: Macmillan Publishers, 1980), s.v. "Ekkehard of St. Gall," by Alejandro Enrique Planchart.

4. "Et non solum ea quae beatus vir Notkerus dictaverat, verum etiam ea quae socii et Fratres ejus, in eodem monasterio S. Galli composuerant; omnia canonizavit, videlicet hymnos, sequentias, tropos, letanias, omnesque cantilenas, quas fecerunt, rythmatice, metrice, vel prosaice" (Godefrido Henscenio and Daniele Papebrochio, *Acta sanctorum Aprilis collecta, digesta, illustrata a Godefrido Henscenio et Daniele Papebrochio: Tomus I [April 1-10], Acta sanctorum, no. 10* [Paris: Victor Palmé, 1866], 584).

5. See Léon Gautier, *Histoire de la poésie liturgique au moyen âge: Les tropes* (Paris, 1886; reprint, Ridgewood, NJ: Gregg Press, 1966), 38.

as a direct witness of what a creator of tropes thought he was doing in writing them:[6]

> In monasteries, at the major mass, for the most important solemnities [Adrian II (r. 867-872)], established not only that the interspersed hymns, which are called *laudes* are to be sung in the angelic hymn "Gloria in excelsis deo"; but also that inserted songs are to be sung in the Psalms of David which they call the Introit; which [songs] the Romans call "festival *laudes*" and the Franks call "tropes," which means "ornamental figures in praise of the Lord." He handed down also the harmonious-sounding melodies before the gospel, which they call "sequences," because the gospel follows them.[7]

Ademar's explanation of this liturgical repertory refers to two important concepts from grammar: first, these additions are "figures," i.e., they use rhetorical figures. All such figures consisted of words or phrases arranged to create poetic effects, such as assonance or rhyme, or having a variety of transferred meanings, such as analogy or metaphor. Changes in arrangement were called schemes or figures, and transferences of meanings were called tropes. Second, by calling the figures "ornamental," Ademar appeals to an aesthetic derived from the teaching of Latin poetry, which allowed poetic license for the sake of ornament (*ornatus*).

The third passage (also Ademar's) combines a use of the term "trope" in grammar with its use in music in order to comment on the liturgy of the second peace council of Limoges, 1031:

---

6. For information on Ademar as composer, see James Grier, "*Ecce sanctum quem deus elegit Marcialem apostolum*: Adémar de Chabannes and the Tropes for the Feast of Saint Martial," in *Beyond the Moon: Festschrift Luther Dittmer*, ed. Bryan Gillingham and Paul Merkley, Wissenschaftliche Abhandlungen, 53 (Ottowa, 1990), 28-74. Grier's edition of all of Ademar's texts and music is forthcoming as part of the complete works of Ademar to be published in the series *Corpus Christianorum Continuatio Mediaeualis* (Turnhout, Brepols).

7. "Hic [Adrianus] constituit per monasteria ad Missam majorem in solemnitatibus praecipuis, non solum in hymno angelico Gloria in excelsis Deo canere hymnos interstinctos quos Laudes appellant; verum etiam in Psalmis Daviticis quos Introïtus dicunt interserta cantica decantare, quae Romani 'festivas laudes,' Franci tropos appellant; quod interpretatur: 'Figurata ornamenta in laudibus Domini.' Melodias quoque ante Evangelium concinendas tradidit, quas dicunt Sequentias, quia sequitur eas Evangelium" (Louis Duchesne and Cyrille Vogel, eds., *Le Liber pontificalis*, 2d. ed. [Paris: E. de Boccard, 1955-57], 1:clxxi, note 1). No other manuscript of the *Liber pontificalis* contains this passage, which claims that Pope Adrian II (r. 867-872) formally authorized the use of tropes, *laudes*, and sequences in the principal masses at monasteries.

> For among the *laudes,* which in Greek are called by the name trope, from the conversion of a common melody when a versus [line of verse] about the Holy Trinity is exclaimed by the cantors.[8]

This passage obliquely refers to the grammatical use of trope. When the cantors exclaim a new line of verse about the Holy Trinity, the meaning of the whole work is changed because of the way a new line interacts with the previous text. In the same way, a grammatical trope changes the meaning of a sentence or saying.

In the fourth passage, Ademar again describes services connected with the council and praises additions to the liturgy as a fitting adornment or ornament:

> Meanwhile, the angelic hymn with tropes, that is, festival *laudes,* having been performed most ornately [i.e., admirably], the archbishop offered the first prayer of the solemnity of the church [dedication of the church].[9]

In describing the performance of tropes as *ornatissime,* Ademar appeals to the grammatical concept of *ornatus;* that is, what could be properly considered "ornamental" or "ornate" in language. A late thirteenth-century glossary confirms this relationship between liturgical tropes and *ornatus,* defining tropers "from trope, because tropers contain embellished language."[10]

---

8. "Inter laudes autem, quae τροπος Graeco nomine dicuntur a conversione vulgaris modulationis dum versus sanctae trinitatis a cantoribus exclamaretur" (Johannes Dominicus Mansi, *Sacrorum conciliorum nova et amplissima collectio* [Florence and Venice, 1757-98; reprint, Graz: Akademische Druck, 1960], 19: 529).

9. "Angelico interea hymno cum tropis, id est festivis laudibus, ornatissime expleto, primam orationem de solennitate ecclessiae dedit archepiscopus" (Mansi, *Sacrorum conciliorum,* 19:529). On Ademar as author of these reports see Richard Landes, *Relics, Apocalypse, and the Deceits of History: Ademar of Chabannes, 989-1034* (Cambridge, MA: Harvard University Press, 1995), 6, 14-15, 210.

10. The great dictionary of medieval Latin, Charles Du Cange, *Glossarium ad scriptores mediae et infimae latinitatis,* rev. ed., Léopold Favre (Niort, 1883-88; reprint, Paris: Librairie des sciences et des arts, 1937), s.v. "Troparius." "Troparius a Tropus, quia troparii ornatos habent sermones." The editors of the Du Cange dictionary found this definition in a Glossarium latino-gallicum from Paris, Bibliothèque Nationale, fonds latin, MS 7679—a source containing numerous medieval glossaries and grammatical treatises, some of which were attributed to the grammarian John of Garland (ca. 1195-1272).

The whole of the study of grammar was intended to provide ways of recognizing, interpreting, and imitating such language.

Taken together, these four passages show that two eleventh-century writers, each of whom contributed to the repertory of new liturgical compositions, applied concepts from the secondary study of grammar in explaining and evaluating new liturgical compositions. The secondary study of grammar began with metrics and concluded with a study of figurative language. Both parts of this secondary study were intended to teach how to interpret and appreciate the varieties of properly ornamented language.

Prosa (Sequentia) and *Tropus* as Grammatical and Liturgical Terms

The two terms *prosa* and *tropus* are not only important to the study of grammar, but are also found as rubrics in many manuscripts from the ninth to the twelfth centuries. In fact, much of the new liturgical repertory of this period can be classified as one or the other. In medieval grammar, the term *prosa* (prose) is not used to identify ordinary speech, but is the term for ornamented public speech: *prosa* occupies a place between poetry and ordinary conversation. In constructing *prosa,* one is concerned with balancing periods and defining cadences through rhythm or meter, therefore they have a natural connection with the liberal art of music, which had at its first aim the investigation of the flow of language. The liturgical rubric *prosa* has a more complicated history. Although the first two of the passages quoted above use the term *sequentia* (sequence) to refer to the melodies sung before the gospel (and it is this term that is most common in modern usage), during the tenth and eleventh centuries, in many sources, the songs sung before the gospel are marked with the rubric *prosa*. Often such songs are marked as *sequentia* when the melody alone is notated without the text, and marked as *prosa* when the text is given without music; however, this practice is not consistent.[11] For our

11. Perhaps this explains Ademar's use of the term in the passage quoted above. Since he is talking about the "harmonious-sounding melodies" and not specifically about their texts, he uses the term *sequentia*. He also gives a liturgical etymology for the term *sequentia*: they are called "sequentia" because the "gospel

purposes here, the rubric *prosa* correctly identifies the grammatical and rhetorical techniques that went into the composition of the text.[12]

The term *tropus* has an even more complex web of meanings, since it is also an important term in music theory (equivalent to mode, melody, or melodic phrase from Boethius on). Indeed, most modern authors, while noting the importance of the term in grammar, have claimed that the use of the term "trope" in music theory is ultimately the origin of the use of the term in liturgy,[13] while others have argued that the grammatical, musical, and liturgical uses are all relatively unconnected to each other.[14] However, as Jeremy Yudkin points out, the meaning of the term in grammar helps provide a good analogy for the way items marked *tropus* are often used in the liturgy:

> The word trope—*tropos* in Greek (Latin *tropus*)—means a turn of phrase or figure of speech by means of which the language is embellished. Similarly a trope in the liturgy is an embellishment of the liturgy—either by music alone, or by music and words together.[15]

---

follows them" (*sequitur eas Evangelium*). Actually, the term seems originally to have been musical, but the "false" liturgical etymology became standard.

12. Richard Crocker, among others, suggests that in modern usage, we might do well to reserve the term "prose" for the texts and the term "sequence" for the melodies; however, as Margot Fassler pointed out, this does not adequately reflect the complexities in the manuscripts. I will use the terms "prose" and "sequence" more or less interchangeably as do many French eleventh-century sources, and make further distinctions as necessary, to talk about the text alone or the music alone. See Sadie, ed., *New Grove Dictionary*, s.v. "Prosa," by Crocker, and for a different solution, see Fassler, *Gothic Song: Victorine Sequences and Augustinian Reform in Twelfth-Century Paris* (Cambridge: Cambridge University Press, 1993), 41-43.

13. See especially Gautier, *Les tropes*, 70, and Jacques Handschin, "Trope, Sequence, and Conductus," in *Early Medieval Music up to 1300*, ed. Anselm Hughes, vol. 2, The New Oxford History of Music (London: Oxford University Press, 1954), 128-74. For the limited extent to which the use of the term "trope" in musical theory had an impact on the liturgical trope, see below, chapter 2, pp. 90-101.

14. Friedrich Blume, ed., *Die Musik in Geschichte und Gegenwart* (Kassel: Bärenreiter, 1949-79), s.v. "Tropus," by Bruno Stäblein. Ruth Steiner's article in Sadie, ed., *New Grove Dictionary*, s.v. "Trope (i)," does not connect the various meanings of the term.

15. Jeremy Yudkin, *Music in Medieval Europe* (Englewood Cliffs, NJ: Prentice Hall, 1989), 206.

While this analogy is useful, the four passages with which the chapter began suggest that the relationship between grammatical and liturgical tropes was both more precise and more substantial.[16] The first passage suggests that liturgical tropes were considered embellishments not only because they were additions to the liturgy, but because they used poetic techniques to produce ornate language. The second, third, and fourth passages use the term for specific liturgical items and not others: tropes are defined as interspersed additions to the gloria (passages two and four), inserted additions to the introit (passage two), or conversions of an unspecified pre-existing song by the insertion of a new line of verse (passage three).[17] This suggests that both the elements of embellishment (addition) and of conversion (reinterpretation) were important to the liturgical repertory; theories of both grammatical schemes and grammatical tropes played a part in influencing the formation of the liturgical repertory. The grammar treatises not only supplied clerical and monastic writers of liturgical tropes with examples of ornate language, but also supplied them with practice in locating and interpreting tropes, which in turn supplied a set of expectations of how the liturgy itself might profit from interpretative interpolations as well as from ornamentation and elaboration.

---

16. Nancy van Deusen was the first to point out the importance of the connections to rhetorical theory and scripture exegesis, but did not discuss grammar treatises. Moreover, she does not treat the topic chronologically, and cites none of these eleventh-century passages. See van Deusen, *The Harp and the Soul: Essays in Medieval Music* (Lewiston, NY: The Edwin Mellen Press, 1989), chapter 4, "The Use and Significance of the Sequence," 109-164, and chapter 5, "Origins of a Significant Medieval Genre: The Musical 'Trope,'" 165-200, and below, pp. 48-56.

17. This passage (number three) is ambiguous and could be taken to refer only to musical features of tropes and *laudes*. For example, the phrase "conversion of a common melody" could refer to (1) supplying text to a preexistent melody, (2) using melodic gestures that are common to a specific repertory, (3) writing melody and text in the same style as a preexisting melody. If "common melody" (*vulgaris modulationis*) refers simply to the modal formulae that make up any melodies, the passage is merely praising "new" compositions; however, in that case the author would not need to make special reference to the subject matter of the new line. For this reason I think that *vulgaris modulationis* refers not to the new line, but to the whole of the earlier work that is being converted by the addition. Moreover, trinitarian additions were most common in tropes for the kyrie, the sanctus and the agnus dei, so it seems likely that Ademar is referring to part of the mass ordinary here.

All of the authors quoted above appeal to terms from grammar in their descriptions of liturgical tropes and proses, showing that they believed that there was a relationship between the grammatical theories, which provided them with the basic techniques for understanding and commenting on scripture, and their own poetic compositions. Since scripture was revered not simply for the beauty of the language but for its efficacy as God's word, it is very likely that clerics who wrote the liturgical tropes intentionally cultivated an interplay between the liturgy and scripture. They based their new contributions to the liturgy on the theory of ornamental language, which they encountered in their studies of both grammar and rhetoric, and which they applied in their interpretation of scripture. By investigating how these theories were taught in ecclesiastical schools, modern interpreters can become aware of the liturgical and aesthetic expectations held by the clerics who were writing and using the new liturgical repertories. A knowledge of these expectations is crucial for understanding liturgies from this period.

Grammar and the Theory of Ornamental Language

In eleventh-century monasteries and schools, clerics and monks acquired their knowledge of grammar in three stages. First, young students (starting at around the age of seven) were required to memorize vast passages of chanted scripture for use in the liturgy. This also provided them with a working vocabulary of ecclesiastical Latin.[18] Second, they studied the parts of speech and the rules of pronunciation and accent. This completed their elementary education, which equipped them to

---

18. Pierre Riché, *Écoles et enseignement dans le haut moyen âge: Fin du Ve siècle—milieu du XIe siècle*, 2d ed. (Paris: Picard Editeur, 1989), 223-24, points out that the Psalter was the basic primer of both cathedral and monastic schools, especially since it had to be memorized for the office. He suggests that this had enormous consequences for the medieval *mentalité* (e.g., "to be *psalteratus* meant to know how to read") and laments the fact that the influence of the Psalter on medieval culture has still not attracted much modern study. The history of several cathedral schools and institutions suggests that the curriculum during the eleventh century was still largely tied to the liturgical and administrative needs of the chapter. In general, the differences between "schools" and monasteries grew more marked only when the canons abandoned common living arrangements and a communally celebrated liturgy. See the Introduction above, pp. 1-4.

participate fully in the liturgy and to carry out administrative tasks. Third, at some time between the ages of fourteen and eighteen, they studied secondary grammar, including the theory of ornamental language, which provided them with a foundation for studying the other liberal arts,[19] and with a facility for understanding and appreciating more difficult and ambiguous language. The primary goal of this more advanced study was to gain a thorough knowledge of scripture, which the students acquired by directed reading of commentaries, starting with those of the book of Psalms. Finally, they could demonstrate their own mastery by adding to the scriptural glosses, by preaching, or by writing religious poetry.[20]

Both classical and medieval grammarians were greatly concerned with ornamental language, since its study could enable a student to recognize poetic devices which were considered rhetorically effective and aesthetically pleasing. Even more importantly, grammarians were concerned with the interpretive problems arising from the use of ornamental language which could disrupt normal word order, spelling, and grammatical forms, or even transfer meanings of words and phrases from their proper (ordinary) usage. Therefore, the study of ornamental language became a prerequisite for the study both of the poets and of scripture. Because the teaching of grammar consisted of both directed reading (*lectio*) and a method of explaining the authors (*ennaratio*), it provided a set of interpretive con-

---

19. See below, pp. 43-48, and chapter 2 for the influence of secondary grammar on the study of poetry (rhetoric) and music. On the goals of clerical and monastic education see Riché, *Écoles et enseignement*, 280-85. These educational goals could be described as prescholastic, but they do not antedate cathedral schools; rather the schools later changed their goals, and evolved differently from the monastic institutions by the mid-twelfth century. See Jaeger, *The Envy of Angels*, for a perceptive discussion of the evolution of cathedral schools.

20. For the basic grammar texts and curriculum see Riché, *Écoles et enseignement*, 222-25, 227-37, 246-52. Paul Abelson, *The Seven Liberal Arts: A Study in Medieval Culture*, Columbia University Teachers College Contributions to Education, no. 11 (New York: Teachers College, Columbia University, 1906), 11-20, 35-42, gives a good description of the elementary curriculum and texts and ibid., 52-58, treats schemes and tropes (not unjustifiably) as part of rhetoric. In fact, the best information on the theory of grammar in the Middle Ages is still to be found in a history of rhetoric, James J. Murphy, *Rhetoric in the Middle Ages* (Berkeley: University of California Press, 1974), 26-29, 32-42, 57-67, 71-73, 76-80, 82-88, 135-94. Murphy also emphasizes the practical aspects of rhetorical education, which became subdivided into three practical arts for (1) writing poetry, (2) writing letters, and (3) preaching (see ibid., 196-355).

ventions that became the common property of all moderately educated clerics and monks. Even the products of this process frequently became the text to be explained: "patristic" scriptural commentaries consisting largely of grammatical glosses were themselves glossed by masters, doubly inculcating both the method and its conclusions.

In grammar, the theory of ornamental language was developed in its most pedagogically influential form by Aelius Donatus. His book was modified and adapted to the needs of clerical education throughout the Middle Ages, most significantly by Augustine, Cassiodorus, and Bede. By the eleventh century, almost every center of education would use portions of the grammatical works of these four authors, or by authors influenced by them. However, the transmission of Donatus, whether intact, or with adaptations and commentaries, while widespread, was pragmatic rather than systematic. As Louis Holtz (the editor of the critical edition of Donatus) points out, grammatical codices generally contained more than one work, and Donatus could often be found relatively intact, side by side with various commentaries, expansions, and revisions, and even more often excerpted and adapted to make a manuscript suited to the state of knowledge and pedagogical interests of the institution where the manuscript was copied.[21] Nevertheless, the

21. See Louis Holtz, *Donat et la tradition de l'enseignement grammatical* (Paris: Centre national de la recherche scientifique, 1981), 340-441. Holtz describes a particularly interesting eleventh-century manuscript (Oxford, Bodleian Library Addit. C. 144) from Monte Cassino, which shows the type of adaptation that occurred, and although it is unusually complex, its method is typical. Holtz's inventory show that it follows the form of Donatus' complete manual, but that it expands the elementary manual with additions by Isidore, Maximus Victorinus, and Peter the Deacon; the *Ars maior* 1 and 2 follow with marginal commentary (perhaps by Paul the Deacon); *Ars maior 3* is expanded and adapted in a similar way to Bede's revision in *De arte metrica*, and *De schematibus*; the theory of vices of language is taken either from Donatus or from Servius; this is followed by extensive additions on syllables compiled from Isidore and from Bede's *De arte metrica;* Bede's *De schematibus* replaces the corresponding chapters of Donatus; and the volume concludes with a compendium of grammatical texts, including commentaries on Donatus, Servius' work on metrics, and poems which could serve as examples.

Cassiodorus may have compiled a similar compendium: in some manuscript traditions of his *Institutiones*, Cassiodorus (or his redactor) refers to a grammar compendium containing "the Art of Donatus, into which we have introduced a second treatise, On Orthography, and a third, On Etymology, and to which we have added a fourth treatise as well, Sacerdos' On Figures of Speech, in order that the diligent reader may be able to find the facts which he knows are consid-

method of teaching the theory of ornamental language in almost any medieval institution was to a large extent established by Donatus' order and the adaptations of Augustine, Cassiodorus, and Bede, and excerpts from their treatises formed the core of grammar instruction in the eleventh century.

By examining the treatment of ornamental language by each of these authors in chronological order, and by highlighting their differing concerns, I will demonstrate the important changes and adaptations of the classical theories that led medieval clerics to develop genres of liturgical poetry that derived both name and function from grammar terms.

Table 1 summarizes the topics covered by each of these four authors in their treatments of ornamental language, showing a continually evolving set of concerns and emphases.[22]

---

ered to belong to the art of grammar" (*An Introduction to Divine and Human Readings by Cassiodorus Senator*, trans. Leslie Webber Jones [New York: Columbia University Press, 1946], 148; see also Cassiodorus, *Cassiodori Senatoris Institutiones*, ed. R. A. B. Mynors [Oxford: Clarendon Press, 1937], 96).

One indication of the influence of Donatus and Bede can be seen from the number of surviving manuscripts: Holtz, *Donat et l'enseignement grammatical*, 422-23, lists sixty-two manuscripts dating from before the twelfth century which include some part or all of Donatus; Gussie Hecht Tanenhaus [sic], in "Bede's *De Schematibus et Tropis*—A Translation," *Quarterly Journal of Speech* 48 (1962): 239 lists fifty-seven medieval manuscripts containing *De arte metrica* and *De schematibus et tropis*, or *De schematibus et tropis* alone. Twenty-six of these date from before the twelfth century, and almost all are found on the continent, not in England.

22. The first and last columns of this table are adapted from Murphy, *Rhetoric in the Middle Ages*, 79, with many additions.

Table 1. Summary of topics in theories of ornamental language from Donatus to Bede

Ars maior 3 of Donatus	*De doctrina christiana* 3 of Augustine	*Institutiones* 2. 1 of Cassiodorus	*De arte metrica* of Bede
1. Barbarisms: vices of diction concerning alterations of letters and syllables (spelling, elision, accent, etc.).	1-3. Problems of interpretation caused by *male pronuntians*.	Recommends Donatus' *Ars minor* for "boys and novices" and the *Ars maior* for more advanced students. Summarizes *Ars maior* without changes until discussing figures.	(Does not include doctrines of "vices or faults of diction.") 1. Letters 2-8 Syllables
2. Solecisms: vices of diction concerning alterations of words (changes of grammatical form or word order).	4. Problems of interpretation caused by the variations in syntactical forms from language to language.		
3. Other vices: vices of diction concerning ambiguity (transferred, ambiguous, or multivalent meanings).	5-22. Problems of interpretation caused by ambiguity in scripture and a treatise on its theological and moral consequences.		
4. Metaplasms: faults concerning letters and syllables (parallel to barbarisms, chapter 1), permitted to preserve meter or for adornment.			13-14. Metaplasms (synalipha, episynalipha, diaresis) 15-16. Poetic license
			(Expands Donatus with information on scansion and meter.) 9-10. Examples of various meters 12. " 17-23. " 24. Rithmus 25. Three types of poetry

Table 1 continued

Ars maior 3 of Donatus	*De doctrina christiana* 3 of Augustine	*Institutiones* 2. 1 of Cassiodorus	*De schematibus et tropis* of Bede
5. Schemes: faults concerning word order and syntax (roughly parallel to solecisms, chapter 2), permitted to preserve meter or for adornment.		Rejects doctrine of faults of diction. Blurs distinction between figures and tropes. One term, "schemes," covers both figures of words and of thought. All of these are used for adornment and sanctioned by holy scripture. *Expositio psalmorum* of Cassiodorus Contains 338 comments on 105 different figures of words and thought. Scheme is used as a generic term covering both figures and tropes.	1. Schemes: modified word order which provides ways in which speech is "clothed or adorned."
6. Tropes: faults concerning words transferred from their proper meanings (parallel to "other vices," chapter 3), permitted for adornment or from necessity.	29-35. Recommends knowledge of tropes as an aid to identifying figurative locutions, and lists the more prominent figurative locutions in scripture which are not specifically identified as tropes. (He discusses them as the "Rules of Tychonius.")	Because of extensive treatment of ornamental speech, the lore of figures is specifically associated with the book of Psalms and with the sung liturgy (chapter 15 of the preface).	2. Tropes: transferred meanings of words for the sake of adornment or from necessity; includes a fully developed description of the "four senses" of scripture, which he equates with the most eloquent or "urbane" speech.

The following close examination of the topic of ornamental language from Donatus to Bede highlights the changing concerns of grammatical instruction which was increasingly geared to the needs of clerical and monastic institutions. These modifications of classical theory created a lore that directly influenced the creation of new poetry for use in the liturgy.

Donatus (fl. 350), the most influential classical grammarian and teacher of Jerome, provided the outline for almost every subsequent medieval work on the teaching of grammar in his four books, *Ars minor* and *Ars maior* 1, 2, and 3.[23] Donatus treated the elementary aspects of grammar in the first book (*Ars minor*), gave the same topics more extended and advanced treatment in *Ars maior* 1 and 2, and covered the theory of ornamental language in book 3 of the *Ars maior*.[24]

Donatus' central thesis concerning ornamental language was that usages which were correctly considered vices in ordinary speaking could be considered verbal ornaments in good poetry; the difference between the two was related primarily to the poetic effect. Therefore, a rule of grammar could be broken only if it contributed to some aspect of poetic language, such as preserving meter, creating a pleasing pattern of words, or creating

23. On the importance of Donatus, see Riché, *Écoles et enseignement*, 246, Abelson, *Seven Liberal Arts*, 35, and especially Holtz, *Donat et l'enseignement grammatical*. Although no one has yet written a history of the teaching of schemes and tropes, Holtz's work makes it possible to trace its broad outlines in relation to Donatus; see especially ibid., 37-46, 69-74, 245-53, 256-58, 318-22, 349. Holtz points out that no matter how much Donatus was reworked, hundreds of subsequent authors of grammatical texts applied his pedagogical structure and order.

24. According to Holtz, *Donat et l'enseignement grammatical*, all four books were intended as one work, consisting of an introductory catechism on the parts of speech, and then the three more advanced books, which treat the following topics: book 1 examines speech from the simplest components to entire sayings; vowels and consonants, syllables (classified as long or short), poetic feet (i.e., groups of two, three, and four syllables), tones (i.e., accents which consist of three- and four-syllable poetic cadences), and punctuation in writing (placing a *punctum* at the top, bottom, and middle of the letters to indicate period, colon, and comma), and distinctions in reading, where the whole sentence is called *periodos* and its parts are called *cola* and *commata*. Book 2 classifies the eight parts of speech (nouns, pronouns, verbs, adverbs, participles, conjunctions, prepositions, and interjections) in systematic detail, paying attention both to elementary syntax, and to the effects of the various forms of words on the accent and duration of words and syllables. Book 3 covers vices and permitted faults in speech (see main text for complete discussion) and was often transmitted as a separate treatise called *Barbarismus* (taken from its opening word). For a succinct discussion of the transmission of Donatus, see Murphy, *Rhetoric in the Middle Ages*, 77-80.

a vivid poetic image. For Donatus, all vices of diction ought to be corrected, and even ornaments that were considered allowable faults required grammatical commentary, since any improper usage (or any usage departing from the ordinary) always created varying degrees of difficulty in both the reading (*lectio*) and understanding (*ennaratio*) of a text.

Donatus' treatment of these interpretive problems is concise and highly systematic and demonstrates the relationship of both vices and permitted faults to grammatical problems. The six chapters of book 3 were conceived of as two sets of three chapters each: the first set deals with vices of diction and the second set deals with permitted faults. Each set treated the following types of problems: (1) alterations in single words, (2) changes of standard grammatical order or forms, and (3) transferences of meaning. The differences between Donatus' doctrine of vices and doctrine of permitted faults become clear when one compares the parallel chapters in detail: see the first column of the summary, table 1 on pp. 20-21. The first chapter on "barbarisms" and fourth chapter on "metaplasms" treat alterations of single words that create some difficulties for reading (since either the written form and/or the sound of words is different from the norm), although they have no syntactical or logical effects on the phrase in which they occur. Metaplasms are allowable because they enable a poet to preserve meter or create other pleasing effects: "A metaplasm is a certain transformation of a correct and unmetrical word to another type for the sake of the meter, or ornament."[25] Donatus lists five ways in which barbarisms and metaplasms are created: (1) by adding or subtracting a letter or syllable at the beginning, middle, or end of a word; (2) by adding or subtracting a quantity either by lengthening or shortening a single vowel or by making a diphthong into two vowels or two vowels into a diphthong; (3) by eliding a syllable; (4) by changing a letter; and (5) by reordering letters.

The second chapter on "solecisms" and the fifth chapter on "schemes" treat improper grammatical constructions or word

25. "Metaplasmus est transformatio quaedam recti solutique sermonis in alteram speciem metri ornatusve causa" (Donatus, *Ars maior*, in *Donat et la tradition de l'enseignement grammatical*, ed. Louis Holtz [Paris: Centre national de la recherche scientifique, 1981], bk. 3, chap. 4).

order that departs from the norm. These create some problems for interpretation since they obscure the syntax, making it more difficult to link the parts of the sentence together. Schemes are allowable in poetry because they are intentional reworkings of syntax or order used to maintain the meter, or for the adornment of the style. Unlike the examples in the first and fourth chapters, the examples that Donatus gives in these chapters are not closely parallel to each other: all of the solecisms are created by the substitution of one grammatical form for another, whereas the schemes are created through an intentional repetition of syntactical structures (e.g., one verb joining clauses which vary in number; various patterns of word repetitions; or poetic effects created by repetitions of words with the same grammatical forms). Unlike solecisms, schemes only rarely result in grammatical faults, although both schemes and solecisms can cause difficulties in reading.

The most profound difficulties for interpretation (*ennaratio*) are posed by the vices and allowable faults covered by the third chapter on "other vices" and the sixth chapter on "tropes." Since these faults transfer the meaning of a key word, they have an effect on the meaning of the whole phrase or sentence, rather than affecting single words as do metaplasms or affecting the connections between words as do many schemes. All of the "other vices" listed in chapter four and tropes in chapter six are potentially ambiguous, since they are created in identical ways: (1) by using terms improperly, (2) by disordering the words, (3) by being loquacious, (4) by using ambiguous (bivalent) language, and (5) by using obscure (multivalent) language. Tropes, like the other figures, are allowable because of their usefulness in poetry: "A trope is a word <or saying>, transferred from its proper meaning to one similar but not proper, for the sake of embellishment, or because of necessity."[26] The two reasons Donatus gives for the use of tropes relate to specific poetic effects which can be obtained through

26. "Tropus est dictio translata a propria significatione ad non propriam similitudinem ornatus necessitative causa" (Donatus, *Ars maior* 3, chap. 6). The word *dictio* ("word" or "saying) is ambiguous, since it can mean a larger unit of speech than just a single word, and Donatus tends to use the word *sermo* for a single word. Although most of Donatus' examples depend on a shift in meaning of a single word, the transferred meaning cannot normally be recognized without reference to the entire context; therefore, either translation is justifiable.

using metaphorical language: (1) metaphorical language would enable one to embellish poetry by creating vivid imagery, and (2) metaphorical language may be necessary to describe things which lack a proper name through poetic devices, or to obtain a wider variety of word choices which could be substituted for a metrically unsatisfying word.

Donatus' grammar was admirably suited to help a master train students to read, interpret, and appreciate the "poets," because it provided a vocabulary for discussing grammatical faults and poetic license (such as that used in the three quotes discussing liturgical tropes given at the beginning of this chapter), and it gained and retained a preeminent position in medieval pedagogy. However, it was necessary for later authors to revise Donatus in order to meet the specific needs of clerical and monastic education. In fact, all grammar instruction came under attack in the fourth and fifth centuries, when many factions within the church argued that the liberal arts were so bound up in the pagan culture that they were of no use to Christians.[27] In the end, it took a figure as influential as Augustine to argue the case for using the liberal arts, and in the four books of *De doctrina christiana,* he provided a rationale for applying what one had learned in studying grammar and rhetoric to one's interpretation and proclamation of scripture.[28]

Briefly, Augustine argued that if the "arts" of grammar and rhetoric were subordinated to the "rule of faith," they could rightly aid in interpretation of scripture and in preaching.[29] This meant that the "arts" had to be brought into an on-

27. For a lucid survey of this "major cultural debate," see Murphy, *Rhetoric in the Middle Ages,* 47-88. Arnobius, Hilary, and Titian were among those who largely rejected the liberal arts and who particularly rejected grammar and rhetoric; this was because the former was intended to awaken an appreciation of the pagan poets, and the latter tended towards verbal excess; see ibid., 47.

28. Augustine, *De doctrina christiana,* ed. William Green, Corpus scriptorum ecclesiasticorum latinorum, no. 80 (Vienna: Hölder-Pichler-Tempsky, 1963). All English translations are taken from Augustine, *St. Augustine On Christian Doctrine,* trans. D. W. Robertson, The Library of Liberal Arts, no. 80 (New York: Liberal Arts Press, 1958). Murphy, *Rhetoric in the Middle Ages,* 57-64, provides a summary of the work, especially of book 4 on rhetoric which will be discussed below, pp. 43-46.

29. Augustine supports this argument with a whole theory of communication in book 1, stating: (1) that the self-revelation of God makes knowledge of God possible, even though God, like every other reality, may be learned about only through signs; and (2) that all other realities (things) may, through God's grace, lead towards the enjoyment of God. Since people share the capability of enjoying

going dialogue with scripture, since, for Augustine, "the rule of faith" was not simply a set of doctrinal propositions but consisted of a gradual conversion to a Christian way of life. This conversion included an acknowledgment of God which led "toward a recognition of His will," and entailed a piety towards scripture, which would keep one from ignoring it when it "is seen to attack some of our vices" and when "it is not understood, and we feel as though we are wiser than it is and better able to give precepts."[30] Nevertheless, for Augustine, the process of open-ended dialogue with scripture created an important role for the "arts" in interpretation, because scripture was not always obviously internally consistent, and could even seem, at times, to violate or be irrelevant to the rule of faith.[31] Augustine argued that if one wanted to understand and proclaim scripture, one needed a method of discovering (*modus inveniendi*) its meanings; the method would mediate between the doctrinal and the literary, while leaving the interpreter open to the process of conversion.[32] Because the art of grammar had

God, they are not to be used like other things, but enjoyed in God. This basic principle is *caritas,* which is summed up by Christ's dual commandment to love God and neighbor. Augustine uses this principle as the primary test for judging interpretations of scripture: any reading which appears to disagree with this central tenet must be false. In book 3, he applies this argument specifically to the interpretation of figurative language. Part of Augustine's theory is very well summarized by Eberhard Jüngel, *God as the Mystery of the World,* translated by Darrell L. Guder (Grand Rapids, MI: Eerdmans, 1983), 4-9; originally published as *Gott als Geheimnis der Welt,* 3d ed. (Tübingen: J. C. B. Mohr, 1977). However, Jüngel does not follow the entire argument of Augustine's book, and wrongly attributes a theological *aporia* to Augustine that belongs rather to late medieval revisions of Augustine's thought. In fact Jüngel (correcting the supposed *aporia*) reinvents Augustine's basic position, which is that human words about God are made possible through the Word and in God's grace.

30. Augustine, *De doctrina christiana* 2, chaps. 9-10.

31. Ibid., bk. 1, chap. 41.

32. Ibid., bk. 1, chap. 1; bk. 4, chap. 1: "There are two things necessary to the treatment of the Scriptures: a way of discovering those things which are to be understood, and a way of expressing what we have learned." Many authors have focused on the second of these "needs," pointing out that book 4 of *De doctrina christiana* is in effect a "Christian rhetoric"; however, I would like to claim that Augustine meets the first of these "needs" by providing a fairly complete Christian grammar in books 2 and 3. Book 2 relates the study of scripture directly to the elementary topics covered in the study of grammar: first, Augustine recommends a basic familiarity with the Scriptures, which can be attained through "reading" it. "Reading" was the art of reading aloud, and included the proper pronunciation, value, and punctuation of the words, and implied a basic familiarity with the language and its forms. This would require an instructor who could help correct the vocal mistakes of a novice who had a knowledge of

as its eventual goal the "understanding" of texts, Augustine considered it ideally suited for adaptation to the needs of scriptural exegesis.

In book 3 of *De doctrina christiana,* Augustine dealt with the problems that ornamental language posed for the interpretation of scripture, using analytical tools from advanced grammar similar to that found in Donatus' *Ars maior.* (For a summary, see column two of table 1 on pp. 20-21 above.) Augustine was solely concerned with clarifying the language of scripture, and therefore shifted the emphasis from identifying "vices of diction" or appreciating "permitted faults" toward a direct confrontation with the problems in interpretation that linguistic forms could pose. Compared with Donatus, this was a change in emphasis rather than a change in method, since Donatus' classification of vices and permitted faults (based on the departure from ordinary usage) could help one to identify the most common ways in which texts could pose interpretive problems. Indeed, Augustine's treatment of interpretive problems follows roughly the same order as Donatus' grammar.

Augustine's most important modification of Donatus' method was that he placed the blame for misinterpretation on the reader or translator rather than on the grammatical faults of the text.[33] For example, Augustine pointed out that even if a

grammar roughly corresponding to the material covered in Donatus' elementary grammar. Augustine allows that this kind of "familiarity" with the Scriptures may also be obtained by the less arduous method of memorizing it. Second, he treats the beginning stages of "understanding," which consist of explaining any unknown or difficult words to the student. (Like classical grammarians, he distinguishes between "reading" and "understanding.") Book 2, chapter 9 begins with a treatment of "those obscure things which must be opened up and explained." This process consisted of clarification of two types of terms: first, the definition of unknown signs, which required learning different languages (or at the very least a vocabulary of terms from Hebrew, Aramaic, etc., that occur untranslated in the Scriptures, and a working knowledge of Greek); and second, the explanation of ambiguous or figurative signs required a knowledge of things, such as the habits of animals or the basics of mathematics, which provided insight into the ways that difficult similes might be constructed in scripture. (Book 2, in chapters 11-14, covers knowledge of languages; book 2, in chapters 15-42, covers figurative signs: Augustine suggests that the liberal arts can provide metaphorical vocabularies which are useful in understanding the figurative signs in scripture.) Book 3 moves on to more advanced grammatical topics similar to those found in Donatus' *Ars maior,* since they prove useful in dealing with interpretive problems in scripture (see main text).

33. The only "barbarism" that Augustine points out is that which results from a reader's mispronunciation (see below); the only "solecisms" and "ambiguities"

text conformed to correct grammatical principles, it might be read in two logically conflicting ways. Such problems were inherent in the written texts of Augustine's time, since they were written entirely in capital letters without any break between words and usually without any punctuation: a reader may breathe in a logical place (conforming to the grammatical rules), which was nevertheless the wrong place and one which distorted the meaning of the text.[34] Therefore, Augustine was more concerned with the process which might lead to a theologically proper reading and a faithful understanding of the "inspired" text, rather than with correcting so-called "barbarisms, solecisms or other vices." For Augustine, the interpreter's task was to understand, not correct, the scriptural text, even if certain passages were extremely difficult and ambiguous.

For the reasons outlined above, Augustine's catalogue of "vices" relating to ornamental language was very short. Indeed, he gives only one example of a barbarism and one example of a solecism. The first example demonstrates the reader's mispronunciation of the word *os* (bone), which if given a long vowel sound would mean "mouth." Such mistakes of accent have many direct parallels in Donatus *Ars maior* 3, chapters 1 and 4, since poetic language frequently changes the length of vowels in order to preserve the meter. Donatus would have called such a reading "mistake" a "barbarism," but would have named simi-

---

in the text which Augustine regards as faults are those which result from mistranslation (i.e., they can be attributed to the human translator rather than to the inspired message of the Scriptures). See Augustine, *De doctrina christiana* 2, chap. 13.

34. This is a problem of "distinctions" (i.e., punctuation) covered in Donatus, *Ars maior* 1, chapter 6. Augustine's example of *male distinguens* is of particular interest, because it demonstrates how his theory of the fault of ambiguity is governed by the rule of faith. He claims that people had made a "heretical" reading of the prologue of John's gospel by "mispunctuating" it. I am giving his examples with classical format and am indicating the punctuation that a reader might have added to the text to show how easily such an ambiguity could arise:

INPRINCIPIOERATVERBUM·ETVERBUMERATAPUDDEUM·ETDEUSER
AT.VERBUMHOCERATINPRINCIPIOAPUDDEUM.
("In the beginning was the Word, and the Word was with God, and God was. This Word was in the beginning with God."), instead of

INPRINCIPIOERATVERBUM·ETVERBUMERATAPUDDEUM·ETDEUSER
ATVERBUM.HOCERATINPRINCIPIOAPUDDEUM.
("In the beginning was the Word, and the Word was with God, and God was the Word. The same was in the beginning with God.")

lar changes "metaplasms" if they were encountered in poetry. Augustine's example of a solecism stemmed from otherwise equivalent words having a different variety of forms in Latin and Greek, so that a reading which was clear in Greek could be open to ambiguity in Latin. Augustine argued that in such cases the translator should opt for a less ambiguous reading, or consult the earlier language.[35]

Although Augustine did not need to spend much time discussing grammatical faults, he could not avoid the interpretive problems caused by scripture's use of ornamental language in which certain words were not always to be read literally, but were used with a variety of transferred meanings. But rather than classifying this language as flawed or resulting from "vices of diction," he focused on the choices that it presented to the interpreter, and the consequences of making the wrong choice. Augustine identified two ways that an interpreter could choose wrongly when dealing with figurative language: first, one might mistake the figurative or transferred meaning of a word for its literal meaning; this is the equivalent of mistaking "signs" that refer to something other than themselves for "things" which refer to themselves. At its worst, such a practice could lead to idolatry, where one worships a statue as if it were God. (Augustine argued that even if one were to point out that a statue of the god Neptune, for example, is a figure for the sea, it would still be idolatrous to worship the statue, since it does not matter whether one worships the idol or the sea.)[36]

35. Augustine, *De doctrina christiana* 3, chap. 4. His example is 1 Thess. 3:7 (in the Itala version): *Propterea consolati sumus fratres in vobis*, in which the word *fratres* is to be read as a vocative (as in the Greek), but could be taken as an accusative, altering the sense of the passage: instead of "Therefore we were comforted, brothers, in you," it could read "Therefore, we comforted the brothers among you"). Both readings are consistent with the rule of faith, and the context of the passage might not clarify it sufficiently. Furthermore, it would be difficult to render the meaning in Latin without adding something to the biblical text, so Augustine suggests that the exegete compare translations or consult the earlier language.

36. However he concedes that worshipping the works of God is slightly better than worshipping the works of an artisan. (Augustine, *De doctrina christiana* 3, chap. 7). However, since such a distinction could argue against God's using signs efficaciously, he argued (against the Manicheans) that the signs given to the Israelites (temporal and carnal sacrifices) were of a different order: they were "useful signs," which had been divinely instituted to lead them to the worship of God. Augustine explicitly relates these to the sacraments of baptism and the eucharist, which differ from the Israelites' signs only because Christians are not

The second mistake would be to take "literal expressions as though they were figurative," which could undermine the knowledge of sin, since scripture condemns only whatever is destructive of charity. Augustine called this mistake "cupidity" and defined it as the "motion of the soul toward the enjoyment of one's self, one's neighbor, or any corporal thing for the sake of something other than God."[37] Therefore, according to Augustine, even though scripture contains passages which use transferred meanings in attributing human emotions to God, one may not use the mere presence of figurative language as an excuse to ignore what the passage teaches. For example, if a passage, in condemning an action, figuratively attributes the human emotion of wrath to God, it implies that God condemns the action even though God cannot "properly" be described as having human emotions.[38] On the other hand, whenever scripture appeared to teach something contrary to the rule of faith, one ought to look for a use of ornamental language; this could suggest a way of interpreting the passage that was not inconsistent with the rule of faith. Augustine found it necessary to go into detail about specific misinterpretations, and he devoted several chapters to examples of figurative and literal use, remarking that changes in custom from the time of the Israelites could make many passages difficult and controversial.[39]

Because the ornamental language in scripture posed such frequently encountered problems for interpretation, in book 3, chapter 29, Augustine explicitly recommended a knowledge of tropes as an aid to discovering and understanding figurative language. He claimed that "all those modes of expression which the grammarians designate with the Greek word [for] tropes were used by our authors, and more abundantly and copiously than those who do not know them [the Scriptures] and

---

enslaved by them: their meaning (the reality which they make known) is understood; see Augustine, *De doctrina christiana* 3, chaps. 8-9.

37. Ibid., bk. 3, chap. 10.

38. Ibid., bk. 3, chap. 11.

39. Ibid., bk. 3, chaps. 12-32. Augustine summarizes his findings in ibid., bk. 3, chap. 32: "Although all or almost all of the deeds which are contained in the Old Testament are to be taken figuratively as well as literally, nevertheless the reader may take as literal those performed by people who are praised, even though they would be abhorrent to the custom of the good who follow the divine precepts after the advent of the Lord. He should refer the figure to the understanding, but should not transfer the deed itself to his own mores."

have learned about such expressions elsewhere are able to suppose or believe."[40] For Augustine, at almost every point at which scripture presented a problem for interpretation, one could find a use of ornamental language, which was not to be considered a fault in scripture, even though it did present a problem for understanding. Therefore he identified all figurative locutions as some kind of trope (i.e., as a permissible, ornamental usage) "even though the name of the particular trope employed is not found in the art of rhetoric."[41] In short, Augustine wanted to argue that a knowledge of how to look for figurative language was necessary not only to understand scripture, but also to appreciate the special eloquence of scripture, which did not necessarily conform to many of the classical standards for eloquence.[42]

Thus Augustine provided a rationale for the study of the liberal arts by meeting the theological objections of those who thought the arts too tied to the pagan culture. His approach allowed the study of ornamental language to remain an important part of the study of scripture. This kept the precepts of ornamental language available to later monastic and clerical authors (including writers of liturgical tropes).

Augustine's approach was dependent on students' already having acquired a background in grammar and rhetoric from studying the classical authors in secular schools. However, in the fifth century, the success of the barbarian invasions effectively eliminated secular elementary education in much of the Latin west (except for some parts of Italy); therefore, it became the task of the monastery to teach at the elementary level.[43] However, instead of teaching the arts of grammar and rhetoric exactly as they had been taught in secular schools, the curriculum was modified to suit the particular needs of the clergy and

40. Ibid., bk. 3, chap. 29.

41. Ibid. Book 3 ends with some of the more common ways that scripture uses figurative locutions, most of which are not named as specific tropes. For this purpose, in *De doctrina christiana* 3, chaps. 30-37, Augustine adapts the Donatist work *Of Rules* by Ticonius; see Francis Crawford Burkitt, *The Book of Rules of Tyconius* (Cambridge: Cambridge University Press, 1894).

42. Augustine, *De doctrina christiana* 3, chap. 29. In book 4, which will be outlined below, pp. 43-46, Augustine recommends scripture as a model for preaching.

43. See Riché, *Écoles et enseignement*, 11-46, for the effects of the invasions on education.

monks; therefore, the study of ornamental language became associated as much with the *introductory* study of scripture as with the study of poetry. One of the most influential of these adapters was Flavius Cassiodorus Senator (480-575), who retired to a south Italian monastery at the age of sixty. He wrote for his monks the first Christian encyclopedia, *Institutiones divinarum et saecularium litterarum,* which outlined their course of studies and provided a bibliographical guide to the study of the Bible and of the liberal arts.[44] Unlike Augustine, who took the secular school system for granted, Cassiodorus provided his monks with their complete educational program and a library of key works, which they were to copy for their own use and for use in other institutions.[45]

Cassiodorus influenced the teaching of figures and tropes in three important ways, all of which created a tendency to treat scripture as a model for Christian letters.[46] (See column three of the summary, table 1, on pp. 20-21 above.) First, although he recommended Donatus' *Ars maior* for the study of grammar, and summarized its contents in his *Institutiones,* he argued directly against Donatus' identification of some figures as vices or faults of diction, preferring to follow the third-century grammarian Marius Plotius Sacerdos:

> Figures of speech are transformations of words or thoughts, used for the sake of adornment; they are represented as being ninety-eight in number in the collection made by the grammatical writer Sacerdos; this number therefore includes those which are considered faults by Donatus. Like Sacerdos, I too feel that it is unfortunate to label as faults those figures which are supported by the example of authors and particularly by the authority of the divine law.[47]

---

44. Although Cassiodorus' *Institutiones* is considered to be an encyclopedia, it is really more of an annotated bibliography, intended to provide quick access to the codices of the monastic library; it was not intended to give comprehensive information on any particular topic but to outline parts of a given topic and give references to more detailed treatments.

45. Cassiodorus, *Institutiones* 1, chap. 30.

46. Ibid. 1, chaps. 15-16.

47. "Schemata sunt transformationes sermonum vel sententiarum, ornatus causa posita, quae [ab] artigrapho nomine Sacerdote collecta fiunt numero nonaginta et octo; ita tamen ut que a Donato inter vitia posita sunt, in ipso numero collecta claudantur. Quod et mihi quoque durum videtur, vitia dicere, quae auctorum exemplis et maxime legis divinae auctoritate firmantur" (Cassiodorus, *Institutiones* 2, chap. 1). In his psalm commentary, Cassiodorus

By rejecting the idea of faults of diction, Cassiodorus changed the emphasis that Donatus had given to the study of figures, replacing the doctrine of permitted fault with a doctrine of verbal ornament. Although Cassiodorus was aware that words had to be shifted from their "natural" grammatical forms or meanings to create a poetic effect, he was less concerned with analyzing the violations of grammatical rules and more concerned with appreciating the beauty of language or thought that such shifts produced. By stressing the beauty of scripture, Cassiodorus de-emphasized the primary grammatical (exegetical) concern with clarifying ambiguities (demonstrated in Augustine's *De doctrina christiana* 3). Instead, he concentrated his attention on the secondary and more rhetorical concern of appreciating literary style, which now derived its standards from the styles in scripture.

Second, Cassiodorus blurred the distinctions that Donatus had made between metaplasms, schemes, and tropes; all of these figures (when encountered in scripture) were to be considered models of ornate (i.e., pleasing) language. On the other hand, since the metrical effects of metaplasms could not apply to scripture translated into prose, they were no longer emphasized as part of the concept of ornament. Only those schemes and tropes that were based on more general poetic effects (such as rhyme, word repetitions, or poetic imagery) were retained, and since in prose the substitution of one word for another did not have any important metrical or poetic consequences, many figures of thought (tropes), which allowed transferred meanings were to be judged solely by the vividness of their imagery, or even by the theological depth hidden in their figurative language, not for their ability to expand a poet's choice of words to fit a meter.

---

specifically mentions instances where scripture uses *pleonasmos, tautologia, eclipsis, tapinosis,* and *amphibolia,* all of which Donatus considered "other vices." However, Cassiodorus treats fifty-three figures which do not appear on Donatus' list as either vices or figures. See Donatus, *Ars maior* 3, chap. 3, and Cassiodorus, *Expositio psalmorum,* ed. Marci Adriaen, Corpus Christianorum series latina, nos. 97-98 (Turnhout: Brepols, 1958), Psalm 20:3, Psalm 12; Psalm 21:7; Psalm 37:6; Psalm 51:11; Psalm 66:8; Psalm 68:6; Psalm 73:7; Psalm 74:7; Psalm 76:2; Psalm 80:16; Psalm 89:4; Psalm 101:10; Psalm 118:49; Psalm 121:5; Psalm 136:7; Psalm 144:8. See the translation by Patrick Gerard Walsh, *Cassiodorus: Explanation of the Psalms,* Ancient Christian Writers, ed. Walter J. Burghart and Thomas Comerford Lawler, nos. 51-53 (New York: Paulist Press, 1990-91).

Third, Cassiodorus unintentionally created a strong connection between the theory of ornamental language and the book of Psalms in particular, by identifying hundreds of uses of figurative language in his commentary on the Psalms.[48] Since the book of Psalms was the first book of scripture memorized by novice monks, nuns, and clerics (by about age eight), it became the introductory book for studying detailed exegesis. Cassiodorus intended his psalm commentary to introduce the novice both to the role of secular letters in interpreting scripture[49] and to the special eloquence of scripture that made the study of the liberal arts justifiable. The following passage from the preface to Cassiodorus' psalm commentary borrows its technical language from the three verbal arts of grammar, rhetoric, and dialectic (which are indicated below by my italics); for Cassiodorus, such arts were worth studying because they could lead to an appreciation of the beauties of scripture:

> It [scripture] exploits its varieties of language in sundry ways, being clothed in *definitions*, adorned by *figures*, marked by its *special vocabulary*, equipped with *syllogisms*, gleaming with *forms of instruction*. But it does not appropriate from these a beauty adopted from elsewhere, but rather bestows on them its own high status. For when these techniques shine in the divine Scriptures, they are precise and wholly without fault, but once enmeshed in men's opinions and emptiest problems, they are dis-

48. Walsh, in *Cassiodorus: Explanation of the Psalms,* appendix D, 1:591-95, lists a total of 338 comments on 105 different figures. Although no study has been done on the influence of Cassiodorus' psalm commentary, it was apparently very well known: Adriaen, the editor of Cassiodorus' *Expositio psalmorum,* lists forty-eight manuscripts dating from before the eleventh century which contain all or part of the commentary, and which have mainly French and German monastic provenances. These include manuscripts from the seventh and ninth centuries stemming from Flavigny, and a tenth-century manuscript stemming from Cluny; ninth- and tenth-century manuscripts survive from St. Gall, and the work was described by Notker in *De Interpretationibus divinarum scriptuarum* as follows: "In whose explanation [of the Book of Psalms] Cassiodorus Senator discussed, among many other things, the extent to which all secular wisdom is useful to us; that is, it makes known the most sweet variety of schemes and tropes concealed in it" ("In cuius [libri psalmorum] explanationem Cassiodorus Senator, cum multa dissereuerit, in hoc tantum videtur nobis utilis, quod omnem saecularem sapientiam, id est schematum et troporum dulcissimam varietatem in eo latere manifestat"). Furthermore, the only major psalm commentary produced in the eleventh century, Bruno of Würzburg's *Expositio psalmorum,* in Patrologiae latina, 142:1-530, is principally a compendium excerpted from Cassiodorus, supplemented by comments from Jerome and Augustine.

49. Cassiodorus, *Expositio psalmorum,* chap. 16 of the preface.

> turbed by obscure waves of argument. What in the Scriptures is unshakably true often becomes uncertain elsewhere. So while our tongues sing a psalmody, they are adorned with the nobility of truth, but once they turn to foolish fictions and blasphemous words they are cut off from the glory of integrity.[50]

The last sentence of this quote shows that Cassiodorus specifically associated the singing of psalms with an appreciation of the eloquence of scripture, and it is likely that such associations made it natural for later monks and clerics to make connections between the grammatical lore and the liturgy.[51]

Although Cassiodorus had made significant changes in the theory of ornamental language in order to adapt it to the needs of the monastery, the process of adaptation reached its apex in countries where no vernacular form of Latin was spoken. In such circumstances, the acquisition of Latin and the analytical techniques for mastering it could be acquired only through ecclesiastical schools, which stressed its cultic importance. Because of this, it became possible for these institutions to teach Latin in such a way that all Latin texts were considered to derive their authority from the Bible.[52] The Northumbrian monk Bede (673-735) took the process to its logical conclusion, rewriting the classical pedagogical texts which had been intended to teach the pagan poets, incorporating examples useful for monks. His influence on the study of ornamental language was particularly great, since his two related works *De arte metrica* and *De*

---

50. "Haec [Scripturae] multis modis genera suae locultionis exercet, definitionibus succincta, schematibus decora, verborum proprietate signata, syllogismorum complexionibus expedita, disciplinis irrutilans: non tamen ab eis accipiens extraneum decorem, bed potius illis propriam dignitatem. Haec enim, quando in divinis scripturis splendent, certa atque purissima sunt; cum vero ad opiniones hominum et quaestiones inanissimas veniunt, ambiguis altercationum fluctibus agitantur, ut, quod hic est firmissime semper verum, frequenter alibi reddatur incertum. Sic et lingua nostra, dum psalmodiam canit, nobilitate veritatis ornatur; cum ad fabulas ineptas et blasphema se verba converterit, ab honore probitatis excluditur" (Cassiodorus, *Expositio psalmorum*, chap. 15 of the preface).

51. See also ibid., chaps. 16-17 of the preface for a discussion of the particular "eloquence" of the Psalter and its connections with individual and corporate praise. Only the singing of psalms is well documented for the sixth-century liturgy; there is no evidence that any new liturgical genres called "tropes" or any other term were in use this early.

52. Patrick S. Diehl, in his introduction to *The Medieval European Religious Lyric: An Ars Poetica* (Berkeley: University of California Press, 1985) contends that the conformity to scripture was a basic goal of the medieval aesthetic, which he characterizes as an aesthetic of "identity" rather than of "opposition."

schematibus et tropis update, supplement, and rewrite book 3 of Donatus' *Ars maior*.[53] (Compare columns one and four of the summary, table 1, on pp. 20-21 above.) By following Donatus so closely, Bede was forced to deal with the effects of meter and rhythm on ornamental language, the study of which had been suppressed in treatments like those of Augustine and Cassiodorus because of their exclusive focus on scripture. However, since Bede still expected scripture to provide the basic models for eloquent language, he maintained a tension between his piety toward scripture and his desire to explain metrical, rhythmic, and figurative effects. In order to achieve these somewhat conflicting aims, Bede found it necessary to expand Donatus' treatment in three significant ways, supplying: (1) examples for understanding metrics, including sections on poetic scansion, meters, and the new rhythmic forms of poetry; (2) an explanation and apology for the lack of meter and rhythm in scripture; and (3) a demonstration that the most common uses of figurative language in scripture (all of which were related to the trope "allegory") could be equated with the most polished or "urbane" type of speech. These three expansions will now be discussed in more detail, demonstrating how the liturgy provided Bede with material that enabled him to reconcile his pedagogical aims.

Bede's first important contribution to the theory of ornamental language was his re-emphasizing the importance of metrics. In Donatus' *Ars maior* 3,[54] Bede found a framework

53. For the Latin text of both of Bede's treatises, see Bede, *De arte metrica et De schematibus et tropis*, ed. C. B. Kendall, in *Bedae Venerabilis Opera: Pars VI, Opera Didascalica, 1,* ed. Charles W. Jones, Corpus Christianorum series latina, no. 123A (Turnhout: Brepols, 1975), 60-171. This text also includes the glosses by Remigius of Auxerre (841-ca. 908), which demonstrate (along with the large number of survivals) its influence on the continent. I know of no English translation of *De arte metrica;* for a translation of *De schematibus et tropis*, see "Bede's *De Schematibus et Tropis*," trans. Tanenhaus [sic].

54. Bede was a very original writer of textbooks, and although in *De schematibus* he borrowed heavily from Donatus, his *De arte metrica* owes considerably less to that one source. Instead, he uses a variety of sources, especially that of Donatus' follower, Servius' *De finalibus* (the continuation of Donatus' chapter on *De pedibus*), and a book on metrics called *De metris* by Mallius Theodorus (consul in 399). (Both texts can be found in H. Keil, *Grammatici latini* [Leipzig, 1857-80]: Servius, *De finalibus* is in 4:449-55; Mallius Theodorus, *De metris* is in 6:585-601.) However, as Murphy, *Rhetoric in the Middle Ages*, 79, points out, Bede considered *De arte metrica* and *De schematibus et tropis* to be related works, and their order, structure, and topics are clearly derived from Donatus' *Ars maior* 3.

which enabled him to fill in the details on metrics which Donatus had not included, while emphasizing the ways in which metric organization demanded grammatical concessions. However, like Cassiodorus, Bede rejected those passages of Donatus dealing with the "vices of diction," and in discussing metaplasms, Bede avoided Donatus' doctrine of "permitted faults," simply giving examples of standard ways in which words may be changed to accommodate a poetic meter. Bede probably avoided Donatus' doctrines of "vices and faults" for the same reason as did Cassiodorus: scripture provided Bede's model for eloquence, and scripture could not contain "faults."

Bede's second contribution to the theory of ornamental language was to give scriptural authority to literature written in meter, rhythm, and rhetorical cursus. By reemphasizing metrics, Bede was in danger of undermining the authority of scripture, which Augustine and Cassiodorus had maintained ought to be the model of all eloquent language. Bede addressed this problem in the last chapter of *De arte metrica* by attempting to demonstrate that scripture (untranslated) contained every sort of eloquence, including the poetic arts of rhetorical cursus, meter, and rhythm:

> Indeed, since we have argued many things about poems and meters, it should be pointed out in the conclusion that there are three sorts of poems. Either a poem is active or imitative, which the Greeks call dramatic or mimetic; or it is narrative, which the Greeks call descriptive or reportorial; or it is common [*commune*] or mixed [*mixtum*], which the Greeks call *ceonon* or *micton* [i.e., the same names]. That poem is dramatic or active, in which speaking persons are introduced without the interruption of the poet, as in the case of tragedies and fables: for drama is called fable in Latin: in which sort is written "where are you going Moeris? Where does your path lead—to town?" [Virgil, *Eclogues,* 9:1] and in which sort, among us, the Song of Songs is written, where the voice of Christ, alternating with that of the Church without the interruption of the poet, is clearly found. It is descriptive or narrative, in which the poet himself speaks without the interpolation of another person, as in all the first three books of the Georgics and the first part of the fourth book, and likewise in the poems of Lucretius and ones similar to these. In which sort, among us, the parables of Solomon and Ecclesiastes are written, which in their own language, like the Psalter, are composed in meter. The common or mixed sort of poem is that in which the poet himself speaks and speaking per-

> sons are introduced, as the *Iliad* and *Odyssey* of Homer are written, and the *Aeneid* of Virgil, and among us the history of blessed Job, although the latter is not altogether verse in its own language, but written partly in rhetorical cursus, partly in metrical or rhythmic language.[55]

---

55. Most of the translation is from W. F. Bolton, *A History of Anglo-Latin Literature 597-1066* (Princeton: Princeton University Press, 1967), 161-62. Bolton translates the phrase *rhetorico sermone* (at the end) as "prose"; I prefer the less ambiguous reading "rhetorical cursus," which is clearly what Bede intends.

"Sane quia multa disputavimus de poematibus et metris, commemorandum in calce quia poematos genera sunt tria. Aut enim activum vel imitativum est, quod Graeci dramaticon vel micticon applelant; aut enarrativum, quod Graeci exegematicon vel apangelticon nuncupant; aut commune vel mixtum, quod Graeci ceonon vel micton vocant. Dramaticon est vel activum in quo personae loquentes introducuntur sine poetae interlocutione, ut se habent tragoediae et fabulae (drama enim Latine fabula dicitur). Quo genere scripta est:

Quo te, Moeri, pedes? An, quo via ducit, in urbem?

Quo apud nos genere Cantica Canticorum scripta sunt, ubi vox alternans Christi et ecclesiae, tametsi non in hoc interloquente scriptore, manifesta reperitur. Exegematicon est vel enarrativum in quo poeta ipse loquitur sine ullius interpositione personae, ut se habent tres libri Georgici toti et prima parts quarti, item Lucretii carmina et his similia. Quo genere apud nos scriptae sunt Parabolae Salomonis et Ecclesiastes, quae in sua lingua, sicut et Psalterium, metro constat esse conscripta. Coenon est vel micton in quo poeta ipse loquitur et personae loquentes introducuntur, ut sunt scripta Ilias et Odyssia Homeri et Aeneidos Virgilii et apud nos historia beati Iob, quamvis haec in sua lingua non tota poetico, sed partim rhetorico, partim sit metrico vel rithmico scripta sermone."

Note that Bede follows each of the secular examples with a biblical example recommended for use "among us" (i.e., within the monastic community). Similarly, at the end of his discussion of meter in *De arte metrica,* he had mentioned that although there are other meters in a book by Porphyrius, "these, we should not touch upon, because they were pagan," and followed this with a discussion of the new rhythmic poetry, which could be treated because of its use in liturgical hymns; see *De arte metrica,* chap. 24.

Note also that Bede is following Jerome and Cassiodorus in attributing classical meter to parts of the Bible; see Cassiodorus, *Institutiones* 1, chap. 6, part 2, and Cassiodorus, *Expositio psalmorum,* Psalm 118, beginning; Jerome, *Praefatio in librum Iob,* in Patrologiae latina, 28:1140. The influential encyclopedist Rabanus Maurus (776-856) adds Deuteronomy and Isaiah to Bede's list in his *De institutione clericorum,* in Patrologiae latina, 107:194-420. The whole of Rabanus Maurus' description is revealing, in that the poetic books of the Bible are directly compared to the works of Christian poets: "It is not ignoble to know the arrangement of meter, which is taught by the art of grammar, because the Psalter in Hebrew (as blessed Jerome testified) now runs with iambs, now resounds with phaleucic, now swells with sapphic, now proceeds with half-feet. Truly Deuteronomy and the song of Isaiah and certainly Solomon and Job use hexameter and pentameter verses in their composition (as Josephus and Origen wrote). Wherefore, it is not contemptible to know well as much as you will of common gentile knowledge, because many evangelical men made brilliant books with this art, and filled them abundantly with it to please God, as did Juvencus, Sedelius, Arator, Alcimus, Clemens, Paulinus, Fortunatus and many others (Metricam autem rationem quae per artem grammaticam discitur, non ignobile est scire, quia apud

Even so, Bede could not mine scripture for suitable examples, since the Latin translations were written in prose, and his knowledge of the original languages was inadequate to revise the accepted ideas regarding scripture's use of meter. Instead, all of Bede's examples in *De arte metrica* are taken either from Christian poets or from Virgil.

Perhaps the most important consequence of Bede's claiming that scripture contained examples of meter, rhythm, and prose was that it provided an implicit reason to study Latin Christian poetry; such poetry might even be perceived to make up the defects inherent in translations of scripture (by supplying the missing metrical organization), if it could be shown to have derived its themes, vocabulary, and types of figurative imagery from scripture. Perhaps this is the reason that Bede thought his examination of metrics would lead naturally to a study of schemes and tropes in scripture (i.e., the special figurative imagery of scripture), as is shown by the conclusion to *De arte metrica*:

> I have sought to excerpt these things for you, dearest son and fellow cleric Cuthbert, diligently from the works of ancient writers, and what I have collected together by long labor here and there, I have set out before you in order, so that just as I have striven to dip into divine writings and ecclesiastical statutes, even so I might carefully instruct you in the art of meter, which is not unknown in holy books. And I have thought it to the point to add on a little book about figures or modes of speaking, which are called schemes or tropes by the Greeks, and I sedulously beg your loving kindness that you especially apply yourself to the work of reading those writings in which we have the grounds for our belief in eternal life.[56]

Hebreaeos Psalterium [ut beatus Hieronymus testatur] nunc iambo currit, nunc alchaico [falleucio?] personat, nunc sapphico tamet, nunc semipede ingreditur. Deuteronomium vero, et Isaiae canticum, necnon et Salomon et Job, hexametris et pentametris versibus [ut Josephus et Origenes scribunt] apud suos composita decurrent. Quamobrem non est spernenda haec, quamvis gentilibus communis ratio, sed quantum satis est perdiscenda, quia uitque multi evangelici viri, insignes libros hac arte condiderunt, et Deo placere per id satagerumt, ut fuit Juvencus, Sedulius, Arator, Alcimus, Clemens, Paulinus et Fortunatus, et caeteri multi" [ibid., 395-96]).

56. The translation, with the exception of the word *conlevita*, is from Bolton, *Anglo-Latin Literature*, 159. Bolton translates *conlevita* inappropriately as "fellow deacon," in order to support an early date for these works; however, the more generic translation "fellow cleric" is more usual for medieval Latin and does not predetermine the dating issue. For the debate regarding dating, see George

Bede's third contribution to the theory of ornamental language was to offer a revised aesthetic for linguistic eloquence. Instead of basing his theory on the rules of grammar and the need for poetic license (like Donatus), Bede suggested that the use of transferred meanings in scripture were the most polished models for eloquence. By concentrating on the content expressed by the transferred meanings, rather than on any inherent poetic or linguistic beauty in scripture, Bede helped to continue to modify the notion of what was considered "ornate." In effect, Bede considered that scripture was most beautiful when it converted language from its ordinary use to a use intended to convey Christian content.

Like Cassiodorus, Bede believed that the use of ornamental language in the Scriptures was wholly superior to the pagan poets, and therefore deserved an especially detailed study, in which almost all of the examples were directly taken from scripture:

> But my beloved son, so that you and all who wish to read this work may know that Holy Scripture surpasses all other writings, not only by its authority, because it is divine, or its utility, because it leads to eternal life, but also by its antiquity, and by its arrangement of language [*positione dicendi*]; and therefore it has pleased me, having collected the examples of this, to show that the masters of eloquence in any age are able to put forth nothing of the schemes or of tropes of this sort, which Holy Scripture will not excel.[57]

Hardin Brown, *Bede the Venerable,* Twayne's English Authors Series, ed. George Economou, no. 443 (Boston: G. K. Hall, 1987), 35-36 and footnote 33.

"Haec tibi, dulcissime fili et conlevita Cuthberte, diligenter ex antiquorum opusculis scriptorum excerpere curavi, et quae sparsim reperta ipse diuturno labore collegeram tibi collecta obtuli, ut quemadmodum in divinis litteris statutisque ecclesiasticis imbuere studui, ita et in metrica arte, quae divinis non est incognita libris, te solerter instruerem. Cui etiam de figuris vel modis locutionum, quae a Graecis schemata vel tropi dicuntur, parvum subicere libellum non incongruum duxi, tuamque dilectionem sedulus exoro ut lectioni operam inpendas illarum maxime litterarum, in quibus nos vitam habere credimus sempiternam" (Bede, *De arte metrica,* chap. 25).

57. The translation is slightly adapted from Bolton, *Anglo-Latin Literature,* 161-62. He translates *positione dicendi* as "very use of language," which fails to catch the intended sense of the superiority of *technical poetic* that Bede is attributing to scripture.

"Sed ut cognoscas, dilectissime fili, cognoscant omnes qui haec legere voluerint quia sancta Scriptura ceteris omnibus scripturis non solum auctoritate, quia divina est, vel utilitate, quia ad vitam ducit aeternam, sed et antiquitate et ipsa praeeminet positione dicendi, placuit mihi collectis de ipsa exemplis ostendere

Bede not only provided many more examples of schemes and tropes than Donatus had done (demonstrating their abundance in scripture),[58] he greatly expanded Donatus' treatment of tropes, since he considered them to be a key to understanding the special eloquence of scripture.[59] The most important expansion was placed under a subheading of allegory called *asteismos* (urbanity), indicating that Bede considered the use of allegory to be one of the most refined uses of language. In this expansion, Bede included a comprehensive treatment of the "four senses of scripture" derived from Gregory, which would not only help the novice recognize the most common usages of allegorical language in scripture, but would also reinforce the exegetical methods taught by scripture commentaries:[60]

---

quia nihil huiusmodi schematum sive troporum valent praetendere saecularis eloquentiae magistri, quod non in illa praecesserit" (Bede, *De schematibus et tropis*, chap. 1).

58. For instance, Bede mentioned that the figure of *anaphora* (repetition of a word at the beginning of connected verses or phrases) is especially common in the psalms and gave three examples, where Donatus had given only one.

59. For much the same reasons, Augustine had discussed the *Rules* of Ticonius, which summarized the various ways scripture was considered to use transferred meaning to speak of Christ or the church; see above, pp. 30-31.

60. For an extended discussion of the development of allegorical interpretation see Henri de Lubac, *L'exégèse médiévale: Les quatre sens de l'écriture* (Paris: Aubier, 1959-61). This work is the classic exposition of the use of allegory in Christian interpretation. Lubac argues that there was a fourfold method of interpretation which treated different interpretive problems in scripture. Through the use of (1) the "literal mode," one clarified the meaning of the words and read the text in order to understand its grammatical forms and to fill in its historical context; when one used (2) the "allegorical mode," one abstracted dogmatic themes from the text and read it in order to find relationships between the Old Testament narrative and the New Testament narrative; using (3) the "tropological mode," one abstracted moral themes from the text and read it as a model for behavior; and if one used (4) the "anagogical mode," one abstracted eschatological themes from the text and read it to find out what God has revealed about the *telos* of the created order. Lubac's treatment is flawed in that it does not locate the specifically "grammatical" uses of the modes of exegesis. In all of Bede's examples of allegory, the problems of figurative language arise from scripture's unexpected uses of figurative language rather than from other difficulty with the text. For example, in the following passage, Bede was concerned to demonstrate the variety of interpretations that could be given to the phrase "the temple of God." The phrase could easily perplex a novice student of Latin who was unfamiliar with Jesus' use of the word "temple" to mean his own body, as in John 2:19, and who might therefore make the same mistake as the "Jews" in literally interpreting the saying. The biblical passage John 2:19-22 provoked Bede's extended explanation:

"Sometimes in one and the same thing, or word, the history and the mystic sense about Christ or the Church, and the tropological, and the anagogical, are

> *Asteismos* is a multiplex trope, and of numerous powers: for whatever saying is lacking in rustic simplicity and is sufficiently polished with fine urbanity is reckoned to be asteismos, such as: I would they were even cut off, who trouble you [Gal. 5:12]. It is to be noted that allegory is sometimes made with events, sometimes with words. . . . Allegory of the word or of the deed figuratively declares sometimes the historical matter, sometimes the typical, sometimes the tropological, that is, the moral concern, sometimes the anagogical, that is, the sense that leads to higher things.[61]

Bede's two works taken together consistently adapt the whole study of poetic language to the study of scripture. In short, Bede paved the way for a "monastic poetics," whose grammar and aesthetic were founded on the figurative use of language in the Bible,[62] and which provided a new basis for

---

figuratively intimated, as in: the temple of God, according to the historical sense, is the house which Solomon built; according to the allegorical, the Lord's body, of which it is said, Destroy this temple, and in three days I will raise it up [John 2:19], or His Church, of which it was said, For the temple of God is holy, which you are [I Cor. 3:17]; according to the tropological, it is each of the faithful, about whom it is said, Know you not that you are the temple of God, and that the spirit of God dwelleth in you? [I Cor. 3:16]. According to the anagogical sense, it is the mansions of eternal joy, to which he aspired who said: Blessed are they that dwell in thy house, O Lord, they shall praise thee for ever and ever. [Psalm 83:5]" (Bede, *De schematibus et tropis,* chap. 2).

The allegorical interpretation of this particular passage is uncontroversial because the "correct" interpretation occurs within the text of John. In assessing the value of Bede's (and Augustine's) idea that the Scriptures have their own eloquence based primarily upon their use of figurative language concerning Christ and the church, one would need to take into account a host of similarly uncontroversial uses of "allegory."

61. Translation from Bolton, *Anglo-Latin Literature,* 164. It is worth noting that Bede considered the "historical sense" of scripture to be a type of allegory; he did not consider the "historical sense" to be equivalent to the "literal sense." His examples of the historical sense are derived from passages where one set of historical "facts" is analogically explained by another, or where figurative language might be read as relating to history: "History is represented through history, when the creation of the first six or seven days is likened to just so many ages of the present world. History is represented through the word, when by this which the patriarch Jacob says, Judah is a lion's whelp; to the prey, my son, thou art gone up, etc. [Gen. 49:9], is understood as applying to the reign and victories of David" (Bede, *De schematibus et tropis,* chap. 2, trans. Bolton, *Anglo-Latin Literature,* 164).

62. Bolton, *Anglo-Latin Literature,* 163-66, comes to a similar conclusion: "Thus *asteismos* is "high style" not simply in the refinement of the literary surface, but in its content of higher meaning. Bede does not deny the value of polished rhetoric: he is deliberate in his use of Greek rhetorical terms, and he is at pains to demonstrate the excellence of scriptural language by rhetorical standards. But the criterion he insists on is the suitable reference of this polish to intellectual

evaluating and appreciating lyric poetry.

Rhetoric, Preceptive Grammar, and Ornamental Language

From this survey of the development in the theory of ornamental language one can conclude that the theory provided a common basis for the interpretation of scripture and Christian lyric poetry. However, it does not provide direct evidence that the theory was used prescriptively to provide rules for composing new lyric poetry (including liturgical tropes), because the art of new composition was not part of the study of grammar, but was taught instead in rhetoric. For this reason both grammar and rhetoric treatises discussed the theory of ornamental language, the former emphasizing its usefulness for interpretation, and the latter emphasizing its usefulness for poetic invention. In order to demonstrate how principles derived from the grammatical theory of ornamental language could have governed the production of new compositions for the liturgy, I will examine the ways in which some principles of classical rhetoric survived into the eleventh century. These principles, combined with preceptive grammar and imitation of models, provided a sufficient theory to shape the new repertories of tropes and proses.

Classical rhetoric underwent even more profound adaptations to the needs of ecclesiastical institutions than did grammar. The study of Latin grammar had an obvious rationale, since it was necessary for understanding scripture and the liturgy, but the need to cultivate elegant public speaking was less obvious.[63] It was again Augustine, in the final book of *De doctrina christiana,* who provided the rationale for its study, by pointing out its applicability to preaching.

Augustine's most important contribution to rhetorical theory was to subordinate the art of rhetoric to the proclamation of Christian truths. This was why he had to teach grammatical principles in the first three books of *De doctrina christiana*: the grammatical principles provided a "way of discovering" what

content, and he has little time for schemes and tropes as accomplishments in themselves." On monastic poetics, see LeClercq, *Love of Learning*, 187-308.

63. Unlike classical grammar, which was concerned with understanding a canon of texts, classical rhetoric was concerned largely with political and legal eloquence, i.e., the art of persuasion.

was taught by the Scriptures.[64] In book 4, Augustine argued that it was also necessary to find a "way of expressing what had been learned."[65] His basic argument was that as long as Christian oratory was directed toward leading people to Christian truth, the several styles of ciceronian rhetoric could be used, (1) to teach, (2) to delight, and (3) to move or persuade. Augustine equated each of these three rhetorical purposes with a rhetorical style: the "plain style" is used primarily to teach, the "measured style" primarily in order to delight, and the "grand style" in order to persuade. However, he stipulated that, while each of these three rhetorical styles was useful, Christian eloquence had an overriding goal unknown in classical rhetoric: all Christian oratory was intended to help people turn towards God.[66]

Augustine claimed that it was not his purpose to teach the principles of rhetoric; however, he wanted to prove that examples of all three styles of eloquence could be found in scripture. By devoting most of the fourth book to demonstrating the use of rhetorical devices in scripture and in the works of "men of the Church who treat the Scriptures not only wisely but eloquently,"[67] he strongly suggested that the Scriptures themselves provide models for eloquent language, which could be imitated by those wishing to speak publicly.

In his discussion of the "measured" style, which was intended to delight, Augustine treated the theory of ornamental language. The same devices of figures and tropes which aided the interpretation of poetry could also be used to achieve the "measured style."[68] According to Augustine, the "measured style" moves listeners by appealing to their ears.[69] Although

---

64. See pp. 25-31 above.

65. Augustine, *De doctrina christiana* 1, chap. 1; 4, chap. 1.

66. As a contrast, the purposes of rhetoric in some classical schools (notably that of the second sophistic) could be considered ends in themselves, the final purpose of each style being the same thing as its method. Augustine argued that both the manner of the teaching and the content of what was taught were necessary for Christian oratory; see Augustine, *De doctrina christiana* 4, chaps. 4-5.

67. His scriptural examples are largely taken from the letters of Paul; the other examples are usually taken from writings of Ambrose and Cyprian.

68. In grammar texts, the terms "prose" or "rhetorical cursus" are exactly equivalent with what Augustine means by the measured style; however, the term "measured style" is also applicable to metrical and rhythmic poetry.

69. Augustine, *De doctrina christiana* 4, chaps. 18 and 20 passim, and bk. 4, chap. 26. Augustine first mentions figurative language in a discussion of the

he was aware that the "measured style" was only rarely encountered in the Scriptures, he claimed that part of this lack was due to translators and part due to scriptural authors' avoidance of "obvious devices." However, he admitted that he used such a style in his own writings, and saw fit not only to describe ornamented speech, but also to go so far as to reorder part of Rom. 13:12-14 in order to produce a more pleasing cadence:

> And a little later on he [Paul] says, "The night is passed, and the day is at hand. Let us therefore cast off the works of darkness, and put on the armor of light. Let us walk honestly as in the day, not in rioting and drunkenness, not in chambering and impurities, not in contention and envy: But put ye on the Lord Jesus Christ, and make not provision for the flesh in its concupiscences." If someone were to arrange this last clause [et carnis providentiam ne feceritis in concupiscentiis] thus: 'Et carnis providentiam ne in concupiscentiis feceritis,' it undoubtedly please the ear more with a rhythmic cadence, but the graver translator has preferred to keep the original word order. How this sounds in Greek pronunciation, as the Apostle spoke it, those who are learned in this language even to this point may decide. To me it seems that the word order, the same as that of our translation, does not run rhythmically there either.
>
> It must be admitted that our authors are lacking in that rhetorical ornament which consists of rhythmic closings. Whether this situation was brought about by the translators or whether (as I think plausible) they themselves avoided such obvious devices, I cannot say, since I confess I do not know. This, however, I do know, that if someone skilled in this kind of ordering would arrange their endings in accordance with the law of such rhythms, a feat which could easily be accomplished either by substituting certain words which have the same meaning or by changing the order of the words already there, he would recognize that not one of those things which are so highly regarded and taught in the schools of grammarians or rhetoricians is lacking in the writings of holy men. And he will find many kinds of expression of such beauty [decoris] that they are beautiful in our own language, although especially beautiful in theirs, which are not found at all in that literature concerning which they are so vain. But caution must be exercised lest, when

"subdued style" (largely for the purpose of teaching), which explicitly avoids the writings of those "Prophets, where many things are obscured by tropes." However, his discussion makes it clear that these writings are not flawed, but are just not useful for demonstrating a clear didactic style. In fact, tropes provide the Christian orator with opportunities for using the didactic style, since "the more these things seem to be obscured by figurative words, the sweeter they become when they are explained" (Augustine, *De doctrina christiana* 4, chap. 7).

> rhythm is added to the divine writings, their gravity be impaired. However, the musical discipline, where ordering is fully learned, is not lacking in our Prophets, for the most learned Jerome observes meter in some of them as they exist in the Hebrew tongue, although he has not translated them metrically because he wished to keep the verbal accuracy of his translation. However, to speak of my own opinion, which I know better than that of others and better than others know it, although in my own expression, I do not neglect these rhythmical endings altogether in so far as they may be used moderately, it pleases me more to find them very rarely in the writings of our authors.[70]

---

70. Ibid., bk. 4, chap. 20. "Et post paululum: Nox praecessit, inquit, dies autem ad propinquavit. Abiciamus itaque opera tenebrarum et induamus nos arma lucis. Sicut in die honeste ambulemus, non in comessationibus et ebrietativus, non in cubilibus et impudicitiis, non in contentione et aemulatione; sed induite dominum Iesum Christum, et carnis providentiam ne feceritis in concupiscentiis. Quod si quisquam ita diceret: 'Et carnis providentiam ne in concupiscentiis feceritis,' sine dubio aures clausula numerosiore mulceret; sed gravior interpres etiam ordinem maluit tenere verborum. Quomodo autem hoc in Graeco eloquio sonet, quo est locutus apostolus, viderint eius eloquii usque ad ista doctiores; mihi tamen quod nobis eodem verborum ordine interpretatum est, nec ibi videtur currere numerose.

"Sane hunc elocutionis ornatum qui numerosis fit clausulis de esse fatendum est auctoribus nostris. Quot utrum per interpretes factum sit an (quod magis arbitror) consulto illi haec plausibilia devitaverint, adfirmare non audeo, quoniam me fateor ignorare. Illud tamen scio, quod si quisquam huius numerositatis peritus illorum clausulas eorundem numerorum lege componat, quod facillime fit mutatis quibusdam verbis, quae tantundem significatione valent, vel mutato eorum quae invenerit ordine, nihil illorum quae velut magna in scolis grammaticorum aut rhetorum didicit, illis divinis viris defuisse cognoscet et multa repperiet locutionis genera tanti decoris, quae quidem et in nostra, sed maxime in sua lingua decora sunt, quorum nullum in eis quibus isti inflantur litteris invenitur. Sed cavendum est ne divinis gravibusque sententiis, dum additur numerus, pondus detrahatur. Nam illa musica disciplina, ubi numerus iste plenissime discitur, usque adeo non defuit prophetis nostris ut vir doctus Hieronymus quorundam etiam metra commemoret, in Hebraea dumtaxat lingua. Cuius ut veritatem servaret in verbis, haec inde non transtulit. Ego autem ut de sensu meo loquar, qui mihi quamaliis et quam aliorum est utique notior, sicut in meo eloquio quantum modeste fieri arbitror non praetermitto istos numeros clausularum, ita in auctoribus nostris hoc mihi plus placet quod ibi eos rarissime invenio."

Since Augustine's language is highly technical, one should refer to the passage in Latin, above. The word *numerus* has no good English equivalent; in this passage it indicates the metrical cadences for rhetorical cursus, which Augustine describes as less strict than poetic meter. It should also be noted that Augustine's book *De musica* is devoted to rhythmics (which investigates whether the sound inherent in a flow of words is pleasant or not) and metrics. His reference to "illa musica disciplina, ubi numerus iste plenissime discitur" uses the generic term *numerus* which includes both rhythmics and metrics (as well as harmonics). Since he goes on to discuss metrics, this phrase might be best translated as "the musical discipline, where metrics is fully learned."

Although Augustine's discussion of metrical ornament is directed toward the art of preaching, it would not be difficult to adapt his precepts to the creation of lyric poetry based on scriptural models. By treating schemes and tropes as a topic within his discussion of the "measured style," Augustine referred to the whole tradition of analyzing poetic devices and thereby provided a rationale for creating a liturgical poetry that would have the same *telos* as all Christian eloquence—the proclamation of scripture. This tradition was not codified in the eleventh century, but by the twelfth century became known as the *ars poetica,* which developed from the grammatical tradition of poetic analysis and the preceptive influence found both in classical rhetoric and Horace's *Ars poetica.*[71] As has been shown above, the grammatical tradition tended to include rhetorical matters well before the codification of theories oriented towards the poetic composition. For example, Bede's works included not only remarks concerning syntax, but detailed studies of metrics, rhythm, and figurative language. Such a compendium, combined with Augustine's theory of rhetoric (which focused on the imitation of models, rather than on the memorization of precepts), could provide training which informed the writing of new poetry, and which would certainly have been used to analyze the new works. Augustine, by refusing to teach rhetorical precepts, while explicitly recommending *imitatio,* may have contributed to a pedagogy in which imitation of models was more important than the teaching of generalized precepts derived from models.

By the eleventh century, any student who wanted to try to write using the art of verbal ornaments would have learned from studying grammar to recognize a typical checklist of from twelve to over a hundred different varieties of ornaments. Each of them would have been illustrated with one or two lines of hexameter verse (if from a source like Donatus) or by a line or two of prose taken from the Scriptures (primarily from the Psalms, if from Cassiodorus or Bede), and such lists of examples could readily supply models for imitation. Furthermore, a student attempting to write eloquently in the ornate style would have been confronted both with the necessities of Latin metrics

71. See Murphy, *Rhetoric in the Middle Ages,* 29-32 on Horace's "treatise" and ibid., 135-42 on twelfth-century preceptive grammar.

and with the special "theological" eloquence of the figurative language contained in scripture, and would have been taught that the two were not necessarily incompatible, since much of scripture had "originally" been written in meter.

By examining the teachings concerning ornamental language in grammar and rhetoric, I have shown that the study of grammar provided a firm basis for the composition of new liturgical poetry: the new genre of *prosa* made use of elements found in rhetorical cursus (specifically called prose in the grammar books) and also of balanced couplets and rhythmic figures found in the poetic prose of the Psalms and other poetic books of the Vulgate; the new genre *tropus* could have been even more directly drawn from the examples of hexameter verse or biblical prose taken from the grammatical treatises. Since the purpose of rhetoric had been recast as the ability to comment on Christian truths, and scripture's use of allegorical language was particularly prized, the new poetry would need to find its place where it could be publicly proclaimed and serve to comment on scripture. The items marked *prosae*, *tropi*, and *laudes* in liturgical manuscripts suggest that from the ninth through the eleventh centuries, the eucharistic liturgy became the primary outlet for such poetic and musical composition. Since the grammatical tradition of analysis of figures and tropes provided a basis for composing liturgical compositions, one can assume that the liturgical compositions attempt to conform to the stylistic attributes which clerics were taught to appreciate in scripture. This in turn implies that the liturgy itself had tasks, goals, and standards adapted from the standards of clerical and monastic biblical interpretation.

Composing Festal Liturgies: *Tropus* and *Prosa* as Liturgical Genres

The quotes at the beginning of this chapter showed that eleventh-century composers of tropes and proses were consciously influenced by their study of grammar. Thus, it has become clear that when scribes used the rubrics *tropus* and *prosa*, they intended to evoke the traditional set of tools designed to aid in the understanding and interpretation of scripture.[72]

72. Although the rubrics *tropus* and *prosa* are frequently encountered in the

These rubrics give important clues as to the construction and function of the new liturgical songs, suggesting in both cases that they consist of ornate language that uses either grammatical schemes or tropes, or some combination of both. Furthermore, the rubrics signal that this part of the liturgy is intended to focus on those passages of scripture which speak allegorically—they eloquently proclaim the mysteries of faith in a poetic language modeled on the Scriptures themselves, and require a thoughtful interpretation.

The new repertories can be distinguished by their liturgical placement and function. First, the items marked *tropus* introduce and often gloss a preexisting text,[73] and the *prosa* with its placement between the alleluia and the gospel reading can be interpreted as an alleluia commentary that serves to lead to the proclamation of the gospel. These functions are essentially exegetical and show the extent to which the new repertory was shaped by the practice of scripture commentary. It is this exegetical function that is the principal innovation of the new repertories: they clarify the scriptural allegories created in the mass and strongly undergird an allegorical interpretation of the mass itself. Thus, while the new repertories (like all liturgical song) have an important function of ornamenting the rite, they are distinguished from other liturgical songs by their function of commenting on elements of the liturgy.[74] Second, the spe-

---

sources, scribes often used alternate terms: for tropes, the terms *laudes* (meaning praises) and *versus* (a line of poetry or scripture) are the most frequent alternate terms, and for proses, the term *sequentia* (suggesting the music or the liturgical placement) is common. For further information on the rubrics associated with tropes, see Eva Odelman, "Comment a-t-on appelé les tropes? Observations sur les rubrics des tropes des Xe et XIe siècles," *Cahiers de Civilization Médiévale* 18 (1975): 15-36. For sequences, see Sadie, ed., *New Grove Dictionary*, s.v. "Prosa," by Crocker, and Fassler, *Gothic Song*, 41-42.

73. Even though Crocker is correct in stressing that the music of the newer mass ordinary compositions was often written as a single unit including the tropes, medieval authors considered the tropes to be additions. See passages two through four at the beginning of this chapter. For Crocker's view, see "The Troping Hypothesis," *The Musical Quarterly* 52 (1966): 183-203.

74. Ritva Jacobsson and Leo Treitler have outlined the factors that make it difficult to classify genres of liturgical song in "Tropes and the Concept of Genre," in *Corpus Troporum: Pax et sapientia: Studies in Text and Music of Liturgical Tropes and Sequences in Memory of Gordon Anderson*, ed. Ritva Jacobsson (Stockholm: Almqvist & Wiksell International, 1986) 59-89. Nancy van Deusen's seminal works help greatly in classifying and interpreting tropes and sequences. Her articles were the first to call attention to the relevance of exegetical traditions to the repertories of tropes and sequences. Revisions of both articles appear

cific ways that composers wrote tropes and sequences were influenced by their grammatical and exegetical studies. By using recognizable verbal ornament from the grammar treatises, composers could guarantee that their works would be recognized as having both an inventive poetic content and consequently give greater liturgical *sollemnitas* to the festival masses for which they were written.[75]

The repertories of both tropes and proses share the common features of using ornamented language for the purpose of liturgical exegesis, but their specific liturgical locations gave them separate functions that caused them to develop differing characteristic forms and poetic styles. As van Deusen points out, tropes differ from other liturgical song (including proses) in that they are always interpolated within preexisting liturgical material, and this material was most often encountered as the *verbum proprium* (the enduring or strict word of scripture) which needed exegesis.[76] The trope element was thus always encountered as a kind of gloss, which like a grammatical gloss, helped to clarify the interpretation of the passage.[77] Similarly, the prose developed from an expansion of the melisma at the end of the alleluia, and always retained its purpose of commenting on the alleluia,[78] functioning to prepare

as chapters 5 and 6 in van Deusen, *The Harp and the Soul,* 109-64; 165-200. See also pp. 14-15 above. More recently, Fassler has examined liturgical change in sequences, stressing their connections to changing interpretations of the function and meaning of the alleluia. See Fassler, *Gothic Song*, especially chapters 1-6.

75. Eugenio Costa, Jr., noted the importance of the ornamentation of festal mass liturgies in *Tropes et séquences dans le cadre de la vie liturgique au moyen âge,* Bibliotheca "Ephemerides Liturgicae," "Susidia," ed. A. Pistoia and A. M. Triacca, no. 17 (Rome: C.L.V. Edizioni Liturgiche, 1979).

76. Van Deusen, *The Harp and the Soul*, 173.

77. Ibid., 174-75. Van Deusen argues that liturgical tropes were directly related to two of the four modes of scripture exegesis: (1) the function of the proper texts taken from scripture was to provide the "historical" mode; (2) the function of the tropes was "analogical" and/or "tropological," supplying a typology which connected the largely Old Testament texts with the New, and uniting the typology to "moral purpose or actionary outlets." While tropes often unite the allegorical mode with the tropological mode, the genre is both more complex and varied than this. Moreover, the distinction between the "historical" mode and the "analogical" mode is problematic, since both are examples of *allegoria facti* (allegory of deeds).

78. Fassler, *Gothic Song*, chapters 3-4. Part of Fassler's thesis is that as clerics changed philosophical and theological positions on language, their interpretations of musical melisma (wordless music) changed. This resulted in a different form and content for the late sequence, even though it remained related as

for the gospel reading.[79] However, the structural independence of the prose from the alleluia meant that its commentary could be more sustained and involved than the simpler and shorter glosses of the tropes. Prose writers found it easier to create large structures that exploited a variety of poetic devices (such as assonance, rhyme, and accent) that could not be greatly developed in short trope elements.

Liturgical tropes and proses occur specifically at those points of the liturgy where the allegorical interpretation of the rite was most prominent and might require clarification; similarly a grammatical gloss was often occasioned by those portions of scripture that used a grammatical "trope" or traditionally required an allegorical interpretation. However, liturgical tropes and proses have features that distinguish them from grammatical glosses and commentaries. Most important, unlike grammatical glosses, they themselves are part of what they are commenting on, and as part of the liturgy, they are intended to be sung (i.e., they are ornamented with music).[80] Furthermore, liturgical tropes themselves used verbal ornament (figured and allegorical language). For this reason, while liturgical tropes and proses often served to clarify, they just as often served to enrich and develop verbal and musical ornament and allegory; they not only serve to explain grammatical "tropes," but often use grammatical "tropes" themselves. Thus, they cannot be neatly classified as glosses, and do not follow any one particular form of commentary; nor do they consistently use any particular mode of scriptural exegesis. Instead, they often use more than one technique taught in grammar and rhetoric. For example, in many manuscripts, the trope to the introit of the third mass of Christmas begins:

> Ecce adest de quo profehte cecinerunt dicentes
> PUER NATUS EST NOBIS[81]

---

commentary to the alleluia.

79. Part of van Deusen's argument is that the sequence has specific features that mark its transitional function. See *The Harp and the Soul*, chapter 5 passim.

80. For an extended discussion of the relationship between medieval theories of verbal and musical ornament, see chapter 2 below.

81. The reading is taken from the Autun Troper (fol. 3r): "Behold, he is here, of whom the prophets foretold saying, UNTO US A BOY IS BORN." Other manuscripts use the singular: "as the prophet foretold," which would refer to Isaiah, who is quoted in the base text. The Autun Troper, by using the plural

This trope functions as a gloss by pointing out the allegory to be made between the passage taken from Isaiah (in uppercase) and the events of the incarnation (the boy born to us is Christ, predicted by all of the prophets). However, it also makes a historical analogy; that is, it argues that what Isaiah predicted not only occurred in Christ, but is also present at the current ritual remembrance of Christ's birth. Furthermore, it tells the choir what to do, using the imperative—"Behold!" This suggests the tropological mode of exegesis. A second example, this time from the second mass of Christmas, shows an even more subtle relationship to both the grammatical and the exegetical traditions, in that it combines the scheme *anaphora* with the same two uses of allegorical interpretation:

Iam fulget oriens
iam praecurrunt signa
iam venit dominus
visitare nos alleluia
LUX FULGEBIT <HODIE SUPER NOS
QUIA NATUS EST NOBIS DOMINUS
ET VOCABITUR ADMIRABILIS DEUS
PRINCEPS PACIS PATER FUTURI SAECULI
CUIUS REGNI NON ERIT FINIS>[82]

This trope relates the historical incarnation to the current feast through allegory, identifies the typology in the proper text, by stressing the fulfillment of prophecy, and creates a balanced six-syllable[83] rhythmic structure in its first three

"prophets," refers to the tradition in which all the Old Testament prophets were considered to have predicted Christ's birth. This tradition eventually developed into an important genre of liturgical drama: the procession of the prophets. The verb "cano, canere" has specifically musical and poetic connotations referring to an intoned metrical "song" used in prophesying.

82. Again the reading comes from Autun (fol. 2r):
Now the sun rises (shines)
Now the signs precede
Now the lord comes
to visit us, alleluia:
A LIGHT WILL DAWN TODAY OVER US BECAUSE THE LORD IS BORN TO US, AND HE WILL BE CALLED WONDERFUL GOD, PRINCE OF PEACE, FATHER OF THE WORLD TO COME, WHOSE REIGN SHALL NEVER END.

83. "Iam" is consistently notated with a single neume.

lines, through its use of the figure *anaphora* (the repetitions of the word *iam*). Thus, as one can see from these two examples, while there are clearly strong exegetical traditions that shape the choice of poetic imagery, the grammatical and rhetorical tradition of using schemes and tropes in order to persuade is equally influential; both concerns are features of the moderate (measured) style of rhetoric. (This is apparent even without taking the music into account).

Even when the original text had no allegory that needed to be clarified, it could still be artfully expanded, or molded to a specific feast by tropes; this helps to explain why authors used the terms *laudes* and *tropi* interchangeably (as in the passages two through four quoted at the beginning of this chapter). For example, the mass ordinary song "gloria in excelsis deo" arose from a New Testament text (Luke 2:14), and its liturgical form is already an expansion of that kernel.[84] While added tropes serve as a further expansion of the text and a commentary on this song, they do not need to be used for typological or allegorical exegesis, since the New Testament context of the gloria is already clear. Thus it is likely that expansions to the gloria were called tropes principally because they use the artful poetic devices of grammatical schemes and tropes for the sake of *ornatus* rather than for clarification.[85]

The liturgical placement and functions of proses give them an even more complex relationship to grammatical and rhetorical arts. Since they are placed at the end of or after the alleluia and lead to the reading of the gospel they have (as van Deusen pointed out) a transitional nature. The following features common to most proses point towards this transitional function: (1) they tend to mix the various modes of scriptural interpretation; for example, by paraphrasing the scriptural account of a feast (literal mode) and then ending with the subject of rejoicing and giving praise in heaven (anagogical mode); (2)

84. Van Deusen comes to a different conclusion, arguing that the writers of tropes did not consider tropes to the mass ordinary (including the gloria) to be part of the genre, and that the desire to ornament the liturgy was not an important part of the aesthetic of trope writers; see *The Harp and the Soul,* 183-86. However, she did not take into account any of the passages from Ekkehard and Ademar cited above.

85. See chapter 4, pp. 173-85, for an example and a discussion of a gloria with tropes.

many sequences similarly mix musical modes, most often by starting in the plagal and ending in the authentic versions of the same tone, but sometimes ending on co-finals, or even on other transpositions of a fifth; (3) the syllabic text-setting of proses makes a textural transition from the melismatic chant of the alleluia through a tuneful syllabic chant to the lightly inflected reading tone for the gospel.[86]

The formal independence of many proses from the alleluia has made them especially difficult to classify. However, Fassler has convincingly made the case that the earlier French sequences were closely related to the function of the alleluia itself. Rather than being a commentary on the text of the alleluia, they were conceived as a response to its music, which is not only shown by their probable origin from improvised melodiae attached to the last melisma of the chant, but also from their texts, which feature the relationship between angelic and human praises. Fassler argues that the texting of these melismas led to poetic topoi that attempted to express the ineffable speech of angels in an artful but obscure human language.[87] As this chapter has shown, such concerns clearly stem from grammar study: grammar students were taught not to try to correct scripture when it violated the rules of grammar, but instead learned to appreciate the limits of language, and to recognize the way the Scriptures expressed the ineffable through using grammatical schemes and tropes.

In order to find such a language, students naturally turned to the poetic books of the Vulgate, especially the Psalter. There are (as van Deusen and others have suggested) many formal relationships between psalms and proses. These relationships point to a close relationship between proses and the study of psalm commentaries even though proses never directly paraphrase complete psalms. First, their formal poetic structure shows many resemblances to the psalms, and until the later eleventh century, *prosae* were written in parallel prose stiches of varying lengths, closely approximating the style of psalms in the Vulgate. Furthermore, like psalms, their overall length

86. The first two points summarize van Deusen. Steven Plank makes this last point in *"The Way to Heavens Doore": An Introduction to Liturgical Process and Musical Style* (Metuchen, NJ: The Scarecrow Press, Inc., 1994), 101-2.

87. Fassler, *Gothic Song*, 43-47.

varies greatly from piece to piece. Second, *prosae* draw a large amount of vocabulary from the psalms and specifically make use the psalter's musical terminology, especially terminology associated with textless music (e.g., *concordia, harmonia, symphonia, modulationis, organa, cithara,* etc.). Third, they make use of a mixed range of expressive content, and are seldom confined to one emotive state. Fourth, like the psalms, they often end by invoking a time of future praise.[88]

To sum up, writers of tropes and proses used techniques that were considered appropriate for effective scripture commentary. They could assess their work by comparing it to the examples contained in grammatical treatises and scripture commentaries, as well as to the standards for Christian eloquence advocated by Augustine, and demonstrated by scripture, the liturgy, and patristic sermons. Ultimately this meant that the pieces were judged by whether they were considered to move the clergy to respond to God, through their proclamation of the Word. Furthermore, since they were intended as part of the ornamented style, they were to produce this result by delighting the ear through their arrangement of language,[89] and through evocative poetic imagery that alluded to Christian doctrine.

Although scripture, biblical commentaries, and patristic preaching provided models for the new liturgical genres, tropes and proses reveal changes during the ninth to twelfth centuries that point both to a change in standards of what was considered "ornate," and to a more structured, thoughtful, and developed use of allegorical interpretation.[90] This is reflected in the tendency to cultivate verse forms and particularly hexameter verse in later sources of tropes, and an analogous tendency to use rhythmic and rhymed structures in proses. While this may seem to indicate that composers were less interested in scriptural models, I suggest that it more likely stems from an increasingly successful grammatical and liturgical pedagogy. As clerics and monastics carefully read both Augustine and Bede (among others) they may have moved away from the direct im-

88. Van Deusen, *The Harp and the Soul*, 111-13.

89. As the next chapter will demonstrate, the music for tropes and sequences played an important role in the "arrangement of language."

90. For the development in tropes, see Jacobsson and Treitler, "Tropes and the Concept of Genre." For proses, see Fassler, *Gothic Song*, especially chapters 5 and 6.

itation of biblical "tropes and figures" toward the restoration of the "lost" metrical ornament to the songs in scripture. Furthermore, as Fassler has argued, later prose repertories show a greater concern with the use of allegorical interpretation through biblical typology; they are increasingly marked by the features of patristic interpretation and preaching.[91] It is quite possible that both of these trends helped lead to the abandonment of tropes and to a renewed interest in the prose during the twelfth century. Gains made through monastic reform movements and clerical schools made it less necessary to underpin the allegorical interpretation of the liturgy within the liturgy itself, while the organization of language in rhythm and the use of typology in the sequence created a form that reinvented and even improved upon the measured style of patristic preaching.

91. See Fassler, *Gothic Song*, chapter 4.

2

THE TEACHING OF SINGING

Medieval Music Theory as an *Ars Poetica*

Analogies between Reading and Singing

AS the last chapter has shown, medieval theories of poetics and exegesis influenced the creation and interpretation of new liturgical texts. Just as the grammar treatises gave examples of how to create ornate language, introductory music texts provided students with specific examples of how music might influence the understanding and flow of texts, and how texts ought to shape the flow and understanding of music.[1] The principal reason for this is that the teaching of grammar and rhetoric provided medieval musicians with a set of productive analogies that could be used in teaching ecclesiastical chant. Even the process of learning to read was bound up with the process of chanting: in the eleventh century, most reading was vocalized reading, and the physical pronunciation of the text was an important part of the process.[2] As the last chapter showed, students learned to read by memorizing the Psalter, and this memorization was reinforced by the weekly chanting of all 150 psalms in the office. The traces of this learning process are shown in the nuances of chant notation, which encodes a careful and accurate pronunciation of the text that reflects the rules of pronunciation found in the grammar treatises. Writers of music treatises emphasized analogies between the syntax of texts and

1. For the influence of grammatical models on the development of music notation, see Leo Treitler, "Reading and Singing: On the Genesis of Occidental Music-writing," in *Early Music History*, no. 4, ed. Iain Fenlon (Cambridge: Cambridge University Press, 1984), 135-208. For the importance of rhetorical and poetic theories, see also Fritz Reckow, "Vitium oder Color Rhetoricus? Thesen zur Bedeutung der Modelldisziplinen Grammatica, Rhetorica und Poetica für das Musikverständnis," *Forum Musicologicum* 3 (1982): 307-21.

2. On the technologies of reading in the Middle Ages, see Paul Saenger, "Silent Reading: Its Impact on Late Medieval Script and Society," *Viator* 13 (1982): 367-414. "Silent" reading may have included moving one's lips, even if no audible sound was produced; see Mary Carruthers, *The Book of Memory: A Study of Memory in Medieval Culture* (Cambridge: Cambridge University Press, 1990), 170-76.

the syntax of music,[3] demonstrating how text structures and musical structures could complement or conflict with one another. In such treatises music is often treated as an ornament that replaces meter, since it could order, proportion, and measure the length of words even though Latin had lost its quantity, and even though the traditional corpus of chant was written in prose. However, the analogy between the syntaxes of words and music had to be refined and adapted to accommodate the new repertories of tropes and proses: these emphasized verbal ornatus, creating a poetic style that was difficult to adapt to music intended to set prose. The most important result of balancing this new relationship between words and music was the creation of the new musical styles reflected in tropes and sequences. Moreover, as compositions in the new styles entered the liturgy, the liturgy's own style and aesthetic goals changed accordingly.

Notation, Pronunciation, and Memory

The musical notation of the chant manuscripts provided the minimum frame or structure that would enable a singer to reproduce the melody. During the eleventh century, it was still common for music notation to be imprecise in representing information about the music's specific pitches, but most manuscripts encode a great number of details concerning the proclamation of the words, which were intended to help a singer master and remember the details necessary for performance. Many of these details show that grammatical training influenced even the notational practices of the chant books.[4]

Although the two structural components of music which we are accustomed to thinking most important, namely, pitch and rhythm, are often imprecisely notated, this does not mean that

3. These connections have recently been examined by several musicologists in order to arrive at a better descriptive morphology for chant. The path-breaking study is Mathias Bielitz, *Musik und Grammatik: Studien zur mittelalterlichen Musiktheorie*, Beiträge zur Musikforschung, no. 4 (Munich: Katzbichler, 1977), which extensively catalogues and analyzes the use of grammatical theory throughout the early Middle Ages.

4. Treitler, "Reading and Singing," 135-208, explores the differences in the purposes of early western music notations, classifying some as principally intended to convey the details of performance, and others as principally intended to convey pitch information.

the performers were unconcerned with either pitch or rhythm, merely that its precise visual representation was not considered necessary, or perhaps (in the case of rhythm), even possible.[5] This was because the function of the notation was to help a singer to reproduce (and teach to others) a text and melody which he or she had already memorized, rather than to learn an unknown melody. The notation, along with the singer's knowledge of the mode's structural features,[6] and ability to understand a text's syntax, conveyed all of the details of proper speech-song, reinforcing the singer's memory by visually representing: (1) the text itself, which provided the main structural indicators for both text and music, (2) the general shape and direction of the melody,[7] and (3) ornamental nuances which also

5. Since the chant style was based on prosody, its rhythmic theory would have been derived from rhythmics, which analyzed the innate *flow* of words, rather than from metrics, which analyzed the poetic organization of words. This was always considered a matter open to differing judgement calls, and hence, would not lend itself to the inflexibility of visual representation. On the importance of "rhythmics," see Margot Fassler, "Accent, Meter, and Rhythm in Medieval Treatises *De rithmis*," *Journal of Musicology* 5 (1987): 164-90.

6. In order for these early notations to function as an effective mnemonic, a singer needed to know the mode of the piece which was being sung. Indeed, the first music-theoretical books were reference works which listed the standard song texts by their modal classification. For a comprehensive examination of these sources, see Michel Huglo, *Les tonaires, inventaire, analyse, comparison,* Publications de la société française de musicologie, ser. 3, vol. 2 (Paris, 1971).

7. There is a good possibility that one enduring use of the "gestural" encoding of the pitch was to provide conducting patterns, which would help both in teaching and performing the melody. One gets a glimpse of such practices from the ninth-century treatise by Aurelian of Réôme, where Aurelian, in giving "rules for discerning the density, sparseness, height, and depth of the verses of all the tones," says that the gloria patri when sung to the authentic deuterus (third tone) should be performed in the following manner: "Wisely observe, O wise singer, that if the praise to the threefold name is sung in its entirety, in two places, that is on the sixteenth syllable, and afterwards on the fourteenth syllable, you make a three-fold swift beat like the beating hand" (Aurelian of Réome, *The Discipline of Music* [*Musica Disciplina*], trans. by Joseph Ponte, Colorado College Music Press Translations, no. 3 [Colorado Springs: Colorado College Music Press, 1968], 49.) "Sagax cantor sagaciter intende, ut si laus nomino trino integra canitur, duobus in locis scilicet in decima sexta syllaba, et post in quarta decima, trinum ad instar manus verberantis facias celererm ictum" (Martin Gerbert, *Scriptores ecclesiastici de musica sacra potissimum* [St. Blasien, 1784; reprint, Hildesheim: Olms, 1963], 1:57); Gerbert omits the word *canitur* (see *Aurelian,* ed. Ponte, 63). The gloria patri for the introit in mode III in *The Liber Usualis, with Introduction and Rubrics in English,* ed. the Benedictines of Solesmes (Tournai and New York: Desclée, 1962), 14, transmits the music for the practice that Aurelian was describing; the syllable "-to" of *sancto* and the syllable "-per" of *semper* are both marked (as in early manuscripts) with a tristrophe.

indicated specific pitch complexes, or the lengthening of certain notes. All three of these notation practices also served the purposes of teaching the melody, since they indicated nuances of performance: the text's syntax indicated musical pauses of varying lengths, the melodic shape provided the text's ebb and flow, and the ornamental signs influenced the specific vocalization of both text and music. In addition, there were a large number of signs for marking places where the pronunciation of the text needed special care. The total impression conveyed by such a notation is that it would provide a completely adequate mnemonic device for a cantor who already knew the melody, and used notation both to remember the performing details and to help express them to others.

As in other manuscripts of its type, the notation of the Autun Troper is not systematic in its neumation. Rather it represents the information which was considered important to its notator, who was most likely the same person whose duty it was to perform the music or teach it to other singers; and although the general tendency to notate the nuances of pronunciation of the text is common to many manuscripts, to some extent the notation of a manuscript represents the specialized rhetoric of the institution where it was copied. The following analysis of the introit trope complex from the third (principal) mass of Christmas reveals many of the neume forms in the manuscript and their characteristic uses. (The transcription is diplomatic, in that it presents the forms in a version very close to the manuscript and preserves the heightening of the source.)[8]

8. I have made two concessions to increase the ease of reading: (1) the trope elements are presented according to sense units or poetic form (whereas the manuscript often indicates complete units with a period, but does not organize the poetry into strophes); (2) the cues to the antiphon have been expanded with their full text. Furthermore, the heightening is not quite as regular in the manuscript as it is in a computer-generated transcription. There is really no sense of specific proportional heightening in the manuscript, only a general idea of melodic direction, and even this only when there is enough room between lines for the scribe to make distinctions.

Ex. 1. Diplomatic version of the Christmas introit trope complex from PaA 1169, fol. 3r-3v[9]

Ecce adest de quo profehte cecinerunt dicentes

PUER NATUS EST NOBIS
<ET FILIUS DATUS EST NOBIS>

Quem virgo Maria gen- u-it

CUIUS IMPER<IUM SUPER HUMERUM EIUS>

Nomen eius emmanuhel vocabi- tur

ET VOCABITUR <NOMEN EIUS>
Fortis et potens deus
MAGNI CONSILII <ANGELUS>.
CANTATE DOMINO <CANTICUM NOVUM
QUIA MIRABILIA FECIT>.

Gratuletur omnis caro

in conspectu domini

et pro hortu saluatoris

deo dicat gratias

PUER NATUS EST NOBIS

In plenitudine temporum

ET FILIUS DATUS EST NOBIS

9. For a detailed analysis, reconstruction of the melodies, and translation, see chapter 4 below.

Per partum virginis hodierne
CUIUS IMPERIUM <SUPER HUMERUM EIUS
ET VOCABITUR NOMEN EIUS>
Rex regum solus potens et omnipotens
MAGNI CONSILII ANGELUS.
Glorietur pater in filio suo unigenito
GLORIA PATRI ET <. . .>
Hodie exultent iusti
natus est Christus filius dei
deo gratias dicite eya.
PUER <NATUS EST NOBIS>
Deus pater filium suum hodie misit in mundum
de quo gratulanter dicamus cum propheta
PUER <NATUS EST NOBIS>

The first thing to note is the multiple forms for many of the neumes; for instance, an ascending interval of two notes can be represented by any of the following signs:

There are even more forms of two notes descending:

However, what I give as the first shape of each series is the most common, and some of the other shapes have specific textual and musical situations (see ex. 1, above). One large category of neumes of this kind are named *notae liquescentes* or *semivocales* in medieval treatises. Heinrich Freistadt points out that these names (like the analytical vocabulary of music) were adapted from the terminology for the classification of the letters of the alphabet.[10] This can be confirmed by examining Donatus' classification of letters from *Ars maior* 1, chapter 2:[11] Donatus classified the letters into three groups, *vocales, semivocales,* and *mutae*. The letters 'a, e, i, o, and u' were called *vocales* because their sound can be prolonged, and because they can form a complete syllable by themselves. Two of these ('i and u') have numerous exceptions; for example, they become consonants when preceding another vowel. The letters 'f, l, m, n, r, s, and x' were called *semivocales,* because although their sound can be prolonged, they require a vowel to form a syllable. Of these, 'x' was called *duplex* (as in the sound 'ks'), and 'l, m, n, and r' were called *liquidae,* presumably because their sound can melt away. The letters 's and f' required a slightly different classification, because they could do away with the power of consonants in meter (presumably through assimilation). The other consonants, 'b, c, d, g, h, k, p, q, and t', were called *mutae* because they could neither be sustained nor produce a syllable. They were subdivided into three categories: *mutae* proper, 'b, c, d, g, p, and t'; *supervacuae* (superfluities) 'k and q' which could instead be represented through the letter 'c'; and the special case of the letter 'h' which would sometimes act like a consonant and at other times like a rough breath. Donatus also admitted 'y and z' from the Greek alphabet, the former being another *vocalis,* the latter another *duplex* (presumably 'ds').

It is important to note that it was the *vox* or sound of the letters that led to their varying classifications, and that the grammar text was concerned with their being properly recognized and pronounced. Such concerns with proper and clear diction seem not only to be carried over into music notation, but have a greater flexibility for accommodating the realities of sung speech. The liquescent neumes in the Autun Troper replace

10. Heinrich Freistadt, "Die liquiszierenden Noten des gregorianischen Chorals: ein Beitrag zur Notationskunde" (dissertation, University of Freiburg, Switzerland, 1929), as quoted in Treitler, "Reading and Singing," 163. See Treitler, ibid., 162-67, for the most convincing summary of the evidence concerning the interpretation of liquescent neumes: "The shift from vocalis to semivocalis coincides with a change of phonetic quality, but not enough of a change, evidently, to constitute a change of syllable . . . ; and this shift coincides with the melodic movement from the penultimate to the final note represented by the liquescent neume" (ibid., 166).

11. For information on Donatus as well as the critical edition of Donatus' treatises, see Holtz, ed., *Donat et la tradition de l'enseignement grammatical.*

angular forms with one or more rounded forms of each sign :

for and for

These mark places where a consonant or vowel is either to be voiced or assimilated. In most of these instances, at least one of the consonants is from the group of *semivocales* or their subgroup *liquidae*; this suggests that the notational practices may have been intended to help with the careful preparation of the text for its oral presentation. The vocalization or assimilation of the consonants is most likely intended to coincide in some fashion with the melodic movement which each liquescent neume indicates. In example 1 above, the liquescent podatus over *Quem* in the second trope element indicates (1) that there is a problem with coordinating the two voiced consonants (one at the end of the syllable *Quem*, and the other at the beginning of the syllable "vir-"), and (2) that the way to overcome the problem is to close to the voiced consonant sometime during the singing of the second of the two notes indicated by the podatus:

Ex. 2. Possible way of performing liquescent neumes

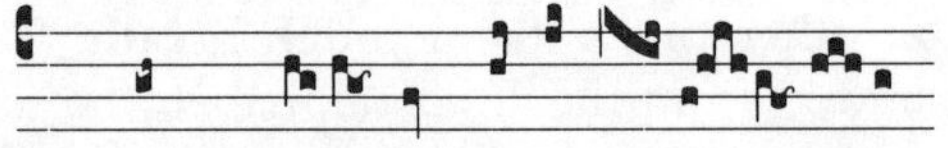

Que(m) vi-(r)go Ma-ri-a ge(n)-u-it

Interestingly, the Autun Troper shows a wide variety of liquescent neumes which seem usually to correspond with specific variants of the problem posed by enunciating a text. For example, three forms of the clivis seem to indicate differences in the way specific groups of consonants or vowels are to be vocalized or assimilated:

The sign is used only on a few liquid consonants and more often is used to indicate that the next syllable begins with an unvoiced or semi-voiced consonant (and perhaps that the consonant should be anticipated at the end of this neume so that the vowel is clearly pronounced on the next). See the last trope element in example 1, over the word *propheta*.

The sign often occurs at syllables ending either 'n or m', perhaps indicating a stronger singing through these easily voiced consonants (perhaps taking up more of the time of the second note than other liquid consonants might).

The third kind of clivis is the one commonly used to mark the occurrence of double unvoiced consonants. This probably indicates that one of the consonants is to be assimilated; however, it is also a common mark over many other pairs of double consonants and diphthongs, and may therefore indicate a lightening in voicing almost approaching the effect of assimilating a consonant, even when that is not the specific textual situation that it marks.

Other neumes in the Autun Troper have no consistent textual situation and probably indicate rhythmic nuances. For example, the remaining forms of podatus and clivis—

—could indicate some form of lengthening or accent of one of the notes of the group, rather than a specific vocal problem to be overcome. (Other neumes that thicken the normal forms, as these do, seem to serve rhythmic purposes). The modified podatus most often occurs at places where there is no need for marking liquescences. It most likely indicates a place where the notator wanted some kind of rhythmic repose or emphasis. On the other hand, the modified clivis often occurs in places that require a liquescence. Even if its purpose is to indicate a lengthening, it could also help enunciation by providing more time at problem spots.

While the liquescent and rhythmic neumes show that the largest groups of special signs were devoted to expressing the details of performance, other neumes convey pitch and performance information which is so closely coordinated that their structural and ornamental functions cannot even be distinguished. For example, the quilisma nearly always indicates the second and third notes of a rising third; they usually follow the pattern of tone, semitone, but sometimes, semitone, tone, or even tone, tone. Since the filling in of thirds is one of the most common differences to be found in variant readings of chants, one of the quilisma's purposes may be to indicate a place where such cantorial options could be taken; however, its performance is still a matter of debate. Some scholars generally cite the ninth-century cantor Aurelian, who noted that a portion of an antiphon which was usually notated with a quilisma was performed with a *tremula adclivaque vox* (a tremulous and rising sound), or argue that the quilisma is a lightly produced and perhaps shortened note.[12] Another example of a neume with both structural and ornamental meaning is the tristrophe (notated as three smaller-than-normal virgae in the Autun Troper ///), which is generally placed on the note above a semi-tone and which was probably to be performed as three lightly sung pitches. Its common function of marking the semitone could be useful in keeping a singer aware of the modal pattern, although this function is indivisibly linked with its expressing a type of ornamental vocalization.

The total impression conveyed by such markings is that public proclamation of liturgical song was considered a high art, in which the expression of minute textual and musical details was cultivated. Since so many of the signs are devoted to overcoming vocal problems which could make the text harder to hear, one may assume that the ability to recognize the words and their syntactical connections was one of the chief aims of the style and of its notation.

Musical Grammar and Rhetoric

The same convergence of language and musical arts that is reflected in the details of notation helped engender the new liturgical forms, and gave music theorists much of their analytical vocabulary and aesthetic. Since clerics and monks initially learned how to read through the memorization of the *chanted* Psalter, the teacher of the children needed to be both grammarian and musician.[13] The survivals of classical pedagogy served

---

12. Aurelian, see Gerbert, *Scriptores ecclesiastici,* 1:47, and *Aurelian,* ed. Ponte, 33. See also Eugène Cardine, "Sémiologie Grégorienne," *Études grégoriennes* 11 (1970): 126, who argues for the interpretation of the quilisma as a lightly produced shortened note, which causes a slight accent to fall on the following note.

13. For example, Bede related, "I attended to the daily singing in church" (cotidianam cantandi in ecclesia curam), in Bede, *Historia ecclesiastica gentis Anglorum*, chap. 5, line 24, in *Venerabilis Bedae opera historica*, ed. C. Plummer (Oxford, 1896). This does not mean, however, that Bede was the cantor. Most likely, he was the *magister scholae,* in charge of all parts of the children's education. (This double function of the master or mistress of choristers remained prominent into the sixteenth century.)

Guido of Arezzo, probably the most important eleventh-century music theorist, was also in charge of the musical education of the schola of children, as he stated in the prologue to his *Micrologus*: "Since both my natural disposition and

the medieval grammar master well, even though grammar treatises required adaptation to meet the needs of clerical education.[14] However, the situation regarding musical pedagogy was more complex, since the entire corpus of ecclesiastical chant arose first in opposition to, and later in isolation from, the other practical musics of Greece and Rome, and until the ninth (or possibly late eighth) century, ecclesiastical chant was transmitted in the absence of any musical notation.[15] Crocker summarizes the influence of classical theory as follows:

> The Franks started from the problems of singing and teaching chant; they were aware of, and admired, the model of rational theory in Boethius, but at first found little use for it. Consequently they either ignored it, or adapted fragments of it, sometimes in arbitrary ways; sometimes they took only terminology, or abstract formulations, which they then applied as they wished to rational structures of their own making. . . . The tension between the theoretical models of antiquity and the practicum of the chant continued for centuries; but it was the practicum that . . . provided the thrust for Western theory.[16]

---

my emulation of good <men> made me eager to work for the general benefit, I undertook among other things, to teach music to boys" ("Cum me et naturalis conditio et bonorum imitatio communis utilitatis dilgentem faceret, cepi inter alia studia musicam tradere pueris"). The Latin text is from Guido, *Guidonis Arentini Micrologus*, ed. Jos. Smits van Waesberghe, Corpus scriptorum de musica, no. 4 (Rome: American Institute of Musicology, 1955), 85; this is the critical edition. A largely reliable edition can also be found in Gerbert, *Scriptores ecclesiastici*, 2:3. The English translation is adapted from Warren Babb, *Hucbald, Guido, and John on Music: Three Medieval Treatises* (New Haven: Yale University Press, 1978), 58. See also Bielitz, *Musik und Grammatik*, 20-23.

During the eleventh century, and partly due to Guido's influence, the roles of grammarian and cantor merged even further; with the development of a musical notation that could indicate exact pitch, it became the duty of the librarian (*amalarius*) to delegate the main musical responsibilities in Cluniac monasteries. This functionary also had charge of the correct copying of both text and music of the liturgical books. See Margot E. Fassler, "The Office of the Cantor in Early Western Monastic Rules and Customaries: A Preliminary Investigation," in *Early Music History*, no. 5, ed. Iain Fenlon (Cambridge: Cambridge University Press, 1985), 29-51.

14. See chapter 1 above, 16-42, for a discussion of one aspect of grammar instruction.

15. Kenneth Levy argues for the possible existence of a neumed archetype around 800, in "Charlemagne's Archetype of Gregorian Chant," *Journal of the American Musicological Society* 40 (1987): 1-30.

16. Richard Crocker and David Hiley, eds., *The Early Middle Ages to 1300*, vol. 2, *The New Oxford History of Music*, rev. ed. (Oxford: Oxford University Press, 1990), 279.

In order to meet these practical needs, medieval music masters, who wrote treatises for the purpose of teaching ecclesiastical chant, borrowed much of their analytical terminology not from classical music treatises, but from the language arts, especially from grammar.[17] This was both practical and a particularly effective teaching strategy, since the masters taught both elementary grammar and the rudiments of chant to the same pupils.

Medieval music theorists found grammar especially suitable for providing descriptive analogies for their practical repertory, since the latter consisted entirely of music united with words. However, it is important to follow their analogies very carefully since they did not cultivate relationships between music and words that we have later come to expect, such as "word painting."[18] Instead, they developed theories to describe the practical repertory of ecclesiastical chant, which was intended primarily to ensure a rhetorically effective delivery of the text. This meant that the large structural principles of melody were closely related to the syntax of the text, and that many of the details of melodic nuance were closely related to the intelligible pronunciation of the words. For example, as Stevens points out, words which are in and of them-

17. Calvin M. Bower, "The Grammatical Model of Musical Understanding in the Middle Ages," in *Hermeneutics and Medieval Culture*, ed. Patrick J. Gallacher and Helen Damico (Albany: State University of New York Press, 1989), 135, lists twelve treatises dating from ca. 850 to ca. 1100. Such treatises were copied, circulated, used, and expanded by other music masters.

18. A modern interpreter has a set of expectations for the music/words relationships that is alien to the eleventh century, because relationships foreign to the medieval period have had a powerful imaginative effect on the subsequent history of western music. The most common pitfalls were analyzed by John Stevens, *Words and Music in the Middle Ages*, Cambridge Studies in Music (Cambridge: Cambridge University Press, 1986); see chap. 8, "Speech and Melody: Gregorian Chant," 268-307 and chap. 11, "Music and Meaning," 372-409. In brief, he demonstrates that the medieval composer "at least, patently and consistently neglects . . . the close and detailed expressive relations between words and music which we find in the songs of later periods" (409). Stevens shows that one cannot demonstrate analytically that chant displays any consistent approach to either tonic (pitch) accent or durational accent (277-83); that melismas are not consistently used to highlight "important" words (296-99); and that musical metaphor "the relation of sound to non-sound" (as in word-painting) is both rarely encountered and impossible to prove when encountered, since the primary examples (e.g., an ascending figure on *ascendit*) have numerous counter examples and do not seem to be set off from the ordinary ascending-descending melodic curve that is typical of all chant (303-7).

selves expressive (such as onomatopoeic words, or semi-onomatopoeic words like "O" used as a vocative or an exclamation) can seem to be set "expressively" because of the closeness of the relationship between the music and the delivery of the words.[19] The consequent effect has been aptly described as "speech-music" based "on the sound not the sense of the words," in which:

> the chant stylizes the 'music' of speech. The makers of chant over the centuries responded, one might say, not so much to the meaning of the words which accompany the chant as to the *sound* of that meaning.[20]

Indeed, the following inventory of musical terminology adapted from grammar shows that medieval theorists thought that the music of the liturgical repertory could be effectively described using terminology originally devised to describe speech.[21] The five paragraphs of the inventory compare and contrast the terms that were taken from grammar in order to create a musical terminology. The grammar terms come from Donatus' *Ars maior* 1 and the musical terms have been collected from the dozen sources dealing with practical music theory that have survived from the period between 850 and 1100.[22] The music theorists used the grammatical terminology in two ways: (1) adapting the grammar term to explain analogous features in melody, and (2) explaining a musical term by relating it

19. Ibid., 303.

20. Ibid., chap. 8 passim.

21. One should bear in mind that the terms are used analogously in order to describe the music's own "grammar." Only to the extent that the two grammars (of speech and music) actually coincide in practice do they confirm Stevens' claim that speech and music are closely coordinated. However, I think it is possible to detect a pattern in particular terminological choices that music theorists made in adapting the grammatical vocabulary, which indicates that the music and words were intended to coincide to an extraordinary degree, and that the grammatical theory, which was created in order to help elucidate poetry in classical hexameters, was consistently adapted by medieval theorists to help teach music which set the Vulgate-style prose of the chant repertory.

22. The musical terms in this section were collected by Bower, "Grammatical Model of Musical Understanding," 133-45. Since Bower did not discuss the use of the analogous terms in grammar, I have supplied information on (1) the grammatical use of the terms (taken from Donatus' *Ars maior* 1) and (2) grammar terms that were not considered adaptable for use in music. This reveals the places medieval theorists found no strong analogy between the structures of words and music.

to a different grammar term. Numbers 1-3 in the inventory treat the progressively smaller divisions of a sentence, or melodic unit; number 4 treats the vocabulary used to describe pauses which demarcate the various divisions; number 5 treats vocabulary used in grammar to describe the flow of poetic feet, but which was adapted in music to describe the movement of pitch. In each section, I first identify the grammar term and its use in grammar, and then describe its use or the use of analogous terms in music.

1. In grammar a whole sentence was called a *periodus*, and its two major subdivisions were called a *colon*, generally meaning a clause, and a *comma*, generally meaning a phrase. Music theorists used the same terms to describe the various divisions of a melody, the whole being called a *periodus*, and its parts *colon* and *comma*. In grammar, the *colon* was considered to have more syntactical independence than the *comma*, since a clause could form or complete a sentence, but a phrase could not. Similarly, the musical *colon* was considered to have more syntactical independence than the musical *comma*. However, music theorists sometimes reversed the hierarchy, using the term *comma* to indicate the more independent musical "clause," and *colon* to mean the musical "phrase." Some treatises substitute other terms for *periodus*, *colon*, and *comma* (often borrowed from either music or rhetoric; e.g., *diastema, systema, telesis, clausula, circuitus*); nevertheless, they always make the analogy with the grammatical divisions.

2. In grammar, the major parts of a sentence (*periodus*, *colon*, and *comma*) were collectively and generically called *distinctiones* (although the term *distinctio* was also used to specify particular divisions; for example, in Donatus, *distinctio* is equivalent with *periodus*; *media distinctio*, with *colon*; and *subdistinctio* with *comma*; Donatus consistently uses *distinctio*, *subdistinctio*, and *media distinctio* to refer to syntactical pauses in spoken discourse, and *periodus*, *colon*, and *comma* to refer to the same pauses in writing).[23] Music theorists identified as analogically equivalent any of the following terms: *distinctio*, *membrum*, *pars*, *particula*, *punctum*, or even *neuma*, which Guido considered a musical *pars*.[24] Like *distinctio* in grammar,

23. Donatus, *Ars maior* 1, chap. 6.

24. Significantly, Guido also equates *neumæ* with *pedes* (poetic feet); see below,

each of these terms could stand for a specific subdivision of the melody, although they were not often used as precisely as were the terms under number 1, above, and instead could stand for a variety of shorter units. The reason for this is that they were also used as analogies for the grammar term *pes* (poetic foot), which had only very imprecise musical analogies. In grammar, *pes* was defined as a specific number of syllables (two-to-four) which take up a specific amount of time (two-to-eight *tempora*, or units of time). Because classical Latin distinguished between long and short vowels, words of two, three, and four syllables could be classified according to the various metrical patterns of classical verse that were inherent in their patterns of long and short vowels. However, equivalent terms were generally not needed in music, since the chant repertory was created to carry prose, rather than metrical poetry.[25] Nevertheless, many of the terms above, which indicate divisions of indeterminate length (not necessarily either phrases or clauses), fill a similar middle ground, identifying musical segments that were separable (according to their musical syntax) but shorter than either a musical phrase or a clause.

3. Terms which indicate smaller units in grammar were more directly equated with analogous terms in music. Syllables (*syllabae*) in speech were considered analogous to short but identifiable melodic gestures, which were also called *syllabae*. Although there was no musical equivalent to the grammatical distinction between long and short syllables, it was the identifiability of the shape of the musical gesture, rather than the time the gesture took, which distinguished the musical *syllaba*. This meant that the musical *syllaba* did not necessarily coincide with a single verbal syllable. However, the kinds of gestures that could help define a musical syllable can be better understood by considering the analogy theorists made between letters (*littera*) and tones or pitches (*phtongi* or *vox*). Just as one or more letters might create a verbal syllable, a similar number of tones might create an identifiable melodic gesture (e.g., the decoration of a specific pitch, a melodic rise, or descent). The

---

and pp. 98 and 105. (Guido does not equate *neuma* with the marks used to notate the chant [neumes], although the marking of verbal syllables is an important function served by neumatic notations.)

25. The two important exceptions to this are hymns and tropes.

use of *vox* to indicate the building blocks of musical utterance (as letters supplied the building blocks for words) created a terminological problem for music theorists, since in grammar, *vox* means any sound whether articulate or inarticulate, and letters are the subcategory of articulate sounds. Musicians obviously felt the need for a term distinguishing pitched sound from both unorganized sound and sounds with semantic content, and therefore shifted the meaning of *vox* to fill this middle ground (i.e., organized sound without semantic content).

4. The grammar terms that indicated the pauses taken between the various *distinctiones* were adapted to indicate similar pauses in music. The terms included *tenor, mora, morula, tremula, repauso,* and *pausatio*. Some music theorists (notably Guido) thought that these pauses or holds should be of proportional durations, with progressively larger syntactical units requiring progressively longer pauses or holds. In order to differentiate between the lengths of pauses, theorists adapted the grammar terms used to mark the measurement of metrical feet to indicate the marking of time in music: *plaudo* and *metricus*.[26]

5. The vocabulary describing the flow of poetic feet was transferred in music theory to describe units of upward and downward melodic motion of varying lengths. The terms which were adapted include *arsis, thesis, levatio, elevatio, positio,* and *depositio*. Similarly, grammar terms used to describe the accentuation of syllables were adapted to indicate melodic rising and falling (e.g., *accentus, tonus, gravis, circumflexis,* and *acutus*). Their use to describe melodic movement in music rather than metrical flow of words is understandable if one keeps in mind that their function in grammar is to highlight or mark syllables. Unlike the grammatical syllable, which could be

26. Most scholars interpret these terms as indicating the proportional lengths of time that notes should be lengthened at the ends of particular *distinctiones;* they do not seem to be used to indicate a "beat" or *tactus* going throughout an entire piece. See Richard Crocker, "*Musica Rhythmica* and *Musica Metrica* in Antique and Medieval Theory," *Journal of Music Theory* 2 (1958): 2-23. Recently, Crocker's interpretation has gained a fairly wide acceptance (see, for example, Bower, "Grammatical Model of Musical Understanding," 138), and has been supported by some new evidence from medieval treatises on rhythmics which have been analyzed by Fassler, "Accent, Meter, and Rhythm in Medieval Treatises *De rithmis,*" 164-90. However, other scholars have come to different interpretations; see Jan W. A. Vollaerts, *Rhythmic Proportions in Early Medieval Ecclesiastical Chant* (Leiden: E. J. Brill, 1958), 168-72, 177-94.

distinguished by its accent or lack of accent, the musical syllable could be distinguished only by describing its shape; therefore, the terms which originally indicated accent were adapted to indicate the direction or shape of melodic syllables.

Music as Punctuation

One of the most interesting features of the adaptation of grammar terminology to musical theory was the minimal role assigned to the metrical measurement of time. Although theories of metrics were well-known, even essential in interpreting classical poetry, early Christian poetry, and the newer hexameter tropes, the only significant temporal measurements mentioned by music theorists were those between the various units of melody that they considered syntactically distinguishable. This avoidance of metrical organization of sound suggests that the essentially prosodic style of the texts for the chant repertory had profound effects on the musical structure of the repertory.

The influence of prosody on the repertory can be confirmed by examining how the music theorists related the grammar of the chant texts to the larger musical structures (i.e., those which concern the mode of the chant).[27] The theorists suggested that certain pitches could be considered structural for the mode and these could serve to mark important melodic points in much the same way that punctuation could mark syntactic units of text. Moreover, their treatises demonstrate that the important structural points in the musical syntax would generally be used to mark important structural points in the verbal syntax. Not only were musical marking and punctuation analogous, but they generally were used to achieve the same purpose of correctly declaiming the text. (This is especially true of the simpler repertories of office antiphons that theorists considered suitable for teaching music to novices).

John, an otherwise anonymous music theorist from around

27. Several authors have recently noted some of these relationships; see especially Bower, "Grammatical Model of Musical Understanding," 138-43, and Ritva Jonsson and Leo Treitler, "Medieval Music and Language: A Reconsideration of the Relationship," in *Music and Language*, Studies in the History of Music, no. 1 (New York: Broude Bros., 1983), 8-9. Both sets of authors quote the anonymous theorist John to help demonstrate their points.

1100,[28] gave the most coherent analysis of the relationship between verbal syntax and modal syntax. (Note in the following quote that John reverses the normal hierarchy of colon and comma—for John the "comma" marks an independent clause, and the "colon" marks a phrase):

> just as in prose three kinds of *distinctiones* are recognized, which can also be called "pauses"—namely, the colon, that is, "member"; the comma or *incisio*; and the period, *clausula* or *circuitus*—so also it is in chant. In prose, where one makes a pause in reading aloud, this is called a colon; when the sentence is divided by an appropriate punctuation mark, it is called a comma; when the sentence is brought to an end, it is a period. . . . Likewise, when a chant makes a pause by dwelling on the fourth or fifth note above the final, there is a colon; when in mid-course it returns to the final, there is a comma; when it arrives at the final at the end, there is a period.[29]

John goes on to give an example, which shows he intended these two syntaxes to be coordinated, so that the verbal syntax would be marked with a melodic cadence on a note which highlighted its important divisions:

> So in the following antiphon: "Peter therefore" colon "was kept in prison" comma "but a prayer was made" colon "for him without ceasing" comma "of the church unto the Lord" period.[30]

---

28. Smits van Waesberghe identifies him as Johannes Affligemensis (i.e., from Belgium), but his country of origin is still in dispute, see *Johannis Affligemensis, De musica cum tonario,* ed. Jos. Smits van Waesberghe, Corpus scriptorum de musica, no. 1 (Rome: American Institute of Musicology, 1950). Although the identity of John is unknown, there is wide agreement about the probable date of the treatise. For a summary of the *status questionis,* see Claude Palisca's introduction to the translation of the treatise by Babb, in *Hucbald, Guido, and John,* 87-95.

29. Translated by Babb, *Hucbald, Guido, and John,* 116-17. The Latin text is from *Johannis Affligemensis,* ed. Smits van Waesberghe, 79: "sicut enim in prosa tres considerantur distinctiones, quae in pausationes apellari possunt, scilicet colon id est membrum, comma incisio, periodus clausura sive circuitus, ita et in cantu. In prosa quippe quando supspensive legitur, colon vocatur; quando per legitimum punctum sententia dividitur, comma, quando ad finem sententia deducitur, periodus est. . . . Similiter cum cantus in quarta vel quinta a finali voce per suspensionem pausat, colon est; cum in medio ad finalem reducitur, comma est; cum in fine finalem pervenit periodus est." According to Babb, Smits van Waesberghe's text should read *clausula* instead of *clausura.*

30. Translated by Babb, *Hucbald, Guido, and John,* 116. "Petrus autem, colon; servabatur in carcere, comma; et oratio fiebat, colon; pro eo sine intermissione, comma; ab ecclesia ad Dominum, periodus" (*Johannes Affligemensis,* ed. Smits van

Coupled with the music of the antiphon, John's analysis shows how he intended the typical patterns of modal inflection to mark structurally equivalent units of verbal syntax. There are two closely related melodies (see example 3, a and b, below) which fit John's description, and although neither is identical with the variant described by him, either can be used to illustrate his analysis.[31] (In my version, I am replacing John's comma with a colon and vice versa, in order to preserve the ancient and modern hierarchy between clause and phrase):

Ex. 3. Two versions of the antiphon *Petrus Autem*

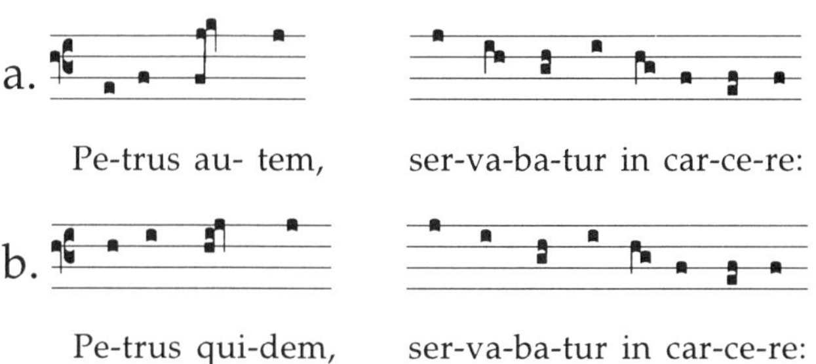
a.
Pe-trus au- tem,
ser-va-ba-tur in car-ce-re:
b.
Pe-trus qui-dem,
ser-va-ba-tur in car-ce-re:

Waesberghe, 79-80). Since John later quotes the last line of the antiphon (with music), giving the last word as *Deum*, rather than *Dominum*, Babb changed his translation of this passage to read "of the church unto God" (*Johannes Affligemensis*, ed. Smits van Waesberghe, 108; Babb, *Hucbald, Guido, and John*, 132-33).

The distinction between member and clause is difficult not only for John but also for the modern reader, who uses different standards of punctuation. However, if one reads John's analysis restoring the normal hierarchy of colon and comma, one can more easily detect that the cadence on the final is made where a longer pause would be appropriate, and that the other cadences are appropriate for shorter pauses: "Peter therefore (comma) was kept in prison (colon) but a prayer was made (comma) for him without ceasing (colon) of the church unto the Lord (period)." Although we would probably omit both the comma after the word "made" and the colon after "ceasing," John's punctuation supplies a very useful guide for where to add subtle pauses in public reading.

31. John's treatise does not give the music for the antiphon (except for the last line). However, the sources for three melodies which were used to set the text of the antiphon *Petrus autem* in the Middle Ages are listed in Alejandro Planchart's index to Babb, *Hucbald, Guido, and John*. The two which fit John's description were transcribed by Harold Powers, "Language Models and Musical Analysis," *Ethnomusicology* 24 (1980): 50.

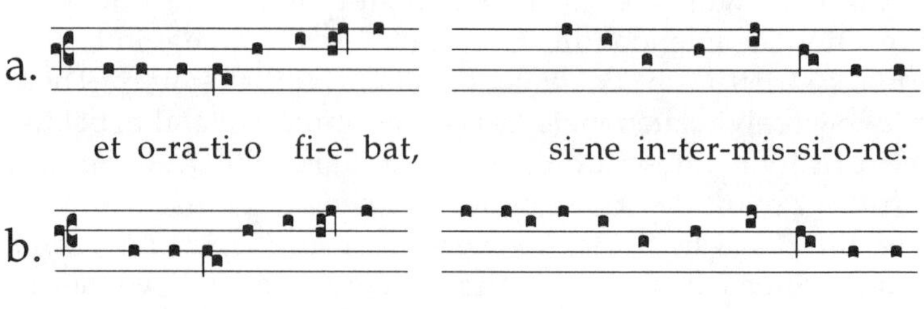
a.
et o-ra-ti-o fi-e- bat, si-ne in-ter-mis-si-o-ne:
b.

o-ra-ti-o fi-e- bat, pro e-o si-ne in-ter-mis-si-o-ne:

a. & b.

ab ec-cle-si-a ad De-um.

As John suggested, each of the syntactical units is marked by a cadence appropriate to the mode, which not only articulates the structure, but distinguishes between the syntactic units that can stand alone and those that are members of larger clauses. Those that can stand alone cadence on the final, and those that cannot stand alone cadence (in this example) on the fifth note above the final.[32] Furthermore, even though many examples of chant do not work out as clearly as this one, John has described a method of structuring melody that does indeed seem to be common in the repertory. For example, the introit for St. Stephen (also in the first mode) has the following structure:[33]

Etenim sederunt principes,	(fifth note above final)
et adversum me loquebantur:	(final)
et iniqui persecuti sunt me:	(final)
adjuva me,	(fourth note above final)
Domine Deus meus,	(fifth note above final)
quia servus tuus exercebatur	(fourth note above final)

32. As John pointed out, both the fourth and the fifth notes above the final are appropriate for cadences in the first mode. This is not the case for all of the modes; see below.

33. See *Liber Usualis*, 414-15; or *Graduale Triplex seu graduale romanum Pauli PP.VI cura recognitum & rhythmicis signis a Solesmensibus monachis ornatum: Neumis Laudunensibus (cod. 239) et Sangallensibus (codicum San Gallensis 359 et Einsidlensis 121) nunc auctum* [ed. Marie-Claire Billecocq and Rupert Fischer] (Paris: Desclée, 1979), 632-33.

in tuis justificationibus.[34] (final)

In this example, the pauses are made at the three pitches that John indicated were common for this mode. Furthermore, the pauses seem to follow a more complex hierarchical pattern which articulates some subtleties of the syntax. For example, the two pauses at the fourth above the final mark two places where the pause would not need to be very lengthy: the first occurs on the cry "Help me, O Lord my God" which could be effectively proclaimed both with or without the comma, and the second occurs after the verb in the clause "because your servant was employed in your justifications." In reading, the *incisio* "in your justifications" could be marked by a short hold on the last syllable of the verb "was employed" (although one would not use a punctuation mark to indicate this), and it appears that just such a reading is implied by the music of this antiphon. Indeed, slight pauses after the verb seem to be a typical feature of chant style. (This feature is particularly useful for a listener trying to understand the text.)

Although John's discussion was not intended to provide any kind of complete theory of cadences in chant, his example suggests that the verbal syntax and melodic syntax are so well coordinated that one may identify structurally important notes for the other modes, by attending to where the linguistic *distinctiones* are made.[35] While maintaining the idea of a hierarchical structure of cadences, different modes will emphasize different structural pitches. For example, if one were to make a habit of cadencing on the fourth note above the final, in mode V based on 'F', the tritone above the final would become a cadential point, which is melodically unacceptable, or the note 'b'

34. Translation: For princes sat, and spoke against me: and enemies have persecuted me: help me, O Lord my God, because your servant was employed in your justifications (cf. Psalm 118:23, 86).

35. Bower, "Grammatical Model of Musical Understanding," 138. John was writing for children, and he therefore gives simple and clear-cut examples from the first mode only. Furthermore, the discussion occurs as an excursus in the context of answering the question, "Why do musicians inaccurately call 'modes' tones?" See Donatus, *Ars maior* 1, chap. 5; *Johannes Affligemensis*, ed. Smits van Waesberghe, 79; Babb, *Hucbald, Guido, and John*, 116. As John pointed out, Donatus said that some *tonos* are called "accents" and others are called "holds" (*tenores*), and this comment leads to his excursus on how chant makes proper "holds."

would have to be consistently altered to 'b-flat'. Instead, mode V typically has a prominent mediant cadence on 'a' which serves to mark "commas," and avoids cadences on both 'b' and 'b-flat'.

A third medieval version of the antiphon *Petrus autem* provides a particularly good example of the way structural pitches varied from mode to mode: unlike the other two versions (see example 3), it is in mode III.[36] According to John's commentary the mode I version was often corrupted by "ignorant singers":

> They distort even the endings of chants and by false singing displace them from their proper location, as in the antiphon *Petrus autem*. Although this has the range of the protus [mode I], and the smaller and larger phrase units plainly show this, some make it end, completely out of the tone, on the hypate meson [E], singing thus:[37]

ab ec-cle-si-a ad De-um.

It should, rather, be sung in this way:

ab ec-cle-si-a ad De-um.

If either of the mode I melodies given above in example 3 were simply ended on the note 'E', the antiphon would indeed end "out of the tone" (*absone*); however, the present mode III melody (given below) prepares for the ending so that it sounds

36. *Liber Usualis*, 1577.

37. Translated by Babb, *Hucbald, Guido, and John*, 132-33; I have altered the translation of *satis absone* from "cacophonously enough" to "completely out of the tone" for precision, since John seems to be complaining about ending in the wrong mode, not about the vocal quality of the singer: "etiam fines cantuum pervertant, atque a suo statu prave canendo deflectant, ut ant. *Petrus autem*. Nam cum cursum proti habeat, idque diastemata eius, atque systemata aperte demonstrent; nonnulli eam in hypate meson satis absone exire faciunt" (*Johannes Affligemensis*, ed. Smits van Waesberghe, 108). *Absone* may be more moderately translated as "out of key."

natural, even though it bears a significant resemblance to the endings of the mode I melodies. This suggests that the mode III antiphon may be a newer version representing the final stage of a process of adaptation, which may have arisen from misclassifying or reclassifying the antiphon's mode. As the antiphon was reshaped to its new final, each *incisio* and member was recast to emphasize the proper cadential notes for mode III.[38]

Ex. 4. Mode III version of the antiphon *Petrus quidem* compared *per colon et commata* to mode I version

3.
Pe-trus qui-dem, ser-va-ba-tur in car-ce-re:
1.
Pe-trus qui-dem, ser-va-ba-tur in car-ce-re:
3.
o-ra-ti-o au-tem fi-e-bat, si-ne in-ter-mis-si-o-ne:
1.
o-ra-ti-o fi-e- bat, pro e-o si-ne in-ter-mis-si-o-ne:

38. Marie-Nöel Colette points out in "*Modus, tropus, tonus*: Tropes d'intrôit et théories modales," *Études gregoriennes* 25 (1997): 63-95, that clarifying the modal ambiguities in the less "modern" antiphon repertories may have been one of the functions served by adding tropes: in general tropes (like the simpler office antiphon repertory) show clearer correspondences to the precepts of the theorists than other repertories.

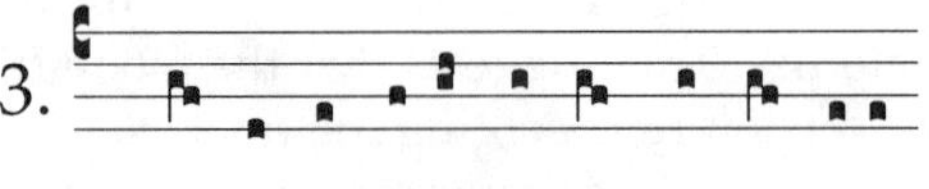

ab ec-cle-si-a ad De-um pro e-o.

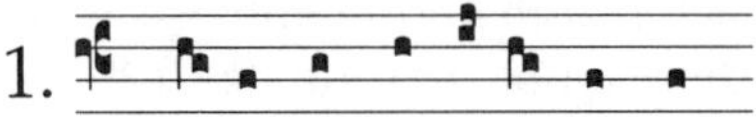

ab ec-cle-si-a ad De-um.

The mode III melody follows the outline of the mode I melody for the first two phrases, substituting the note 'c' for the comma and the note 'G' for the colon. The next two phrases taken together begin and end similarly in both versions; however, the middle part (end of the third phrase and beginning of the fourth) shows substantial differences in outline. The mode III melody marks the incisio after the verb *fiebat* with 'F' (the note above the final). This is considerably weaker than the full comma on the fifth above the final in the mode I melody, but is appropriate to the syntax which would indicate only a slight pause. The change of shape in the opening of the fourth phrase is not structurally important, and the end of this phrase gives the expected 'G' for the colon. The final phrase avoids the abrupt ending on 'E' given in John's treatise, by moving *pro eo* to the end, marking *Deum* with 'G' (another colon), and setting up the expectation for a cadence on the final of mode III. In short, the resulting antiphon is not only successful in mode III, it is more successful in articulating the syntax of the text than is the mode I "original." Such shifts in modal classification may often have prompted recomposition, and the variants can reveal structural notes for modes that the theorists do not discuss. In this instance, mode III (unlike mode I) regularly included the sixth above the final and the third above the final among its structural notes, and could use the note above the final to make a very brief pause.

The Grammar of Liturgical Song

John's treatise confirms the close relationship between verbal prosody and medieval music and demonstrates that medieval musicians used musical cadence to help deliver the text intelligibly to their listeners. However, it would be misleading to conclude from the simple examples given in such treatises that medieval musicians slavishly followed the linguistic syntax. Even in the simpler styles, theorists identified features of a musical syntax which was intended to be partially independent of the syntax of the words. The terms used to identify the relatively independent musical syntax could be applied to the repertories of chant that display complex musical structures relatively independent of the words. For example, any melismatic piece requires a singer to distinguish among sections of melodies that are not articulated by a change of linguistic syllable (in order to find an appropriate place to breathe); thus, theorists began to talk about musical syllables which did not have to coincide with linguistic syllables.

In treating the simpler styles of music, theorists identified such syllables as notes that marked the end of any significant melodic unit and reserved the term syllable, especially those which did not coincide with the larger linguistic units. (The terms that identify these "musical distinctions" are listed above under numbers 2 and 3, pp. 70-72.) As noted above (under number 4, p. 72), Guido expected every musical gesture to be clearly articulated by a short lengthening of its last note, even if the gesture did not coincide with a grammatical pause, and reserved longer lengthenings for the points which marked larger musical *distinctiones.*[39] Bower notes that (in order to expound Guido's teaching) later theorists used the first phrase of the antiphon *Dixit Dominus mulieri Cananaeae* (The Lord said to the woman of Canaan):[40]

---

39. Babb, *Hucbald, Guido, and John,* 70: "Regarding these units it must be noted that every 'part' must be written and performed correctly. A 'hold' [*tenor*]–that is, a pause on the last note–which is very small for a 'syllable,' larger for a 'part,' and longest for a phrase [*distinctio*]. It is good to beat time to a song as though by metrical feet. Some notes have separating them from others a brief delay [*morula*] twice as long or twice as short, or a trembling [*tremula*], that is, a 'hold' of varying length." Latin text: "Tenor vero, id est mora ultimae vocis, qui in syllaba quantuluscumque est. amplior in parte diutissimus vero in distinctione, signum in his divisionis existit. Sicque opus est ut quasi metricis pedibus cantilena plaudatur, et aliae voces ab aliis morulam duplo longiorem vel duplo breviorem, aut tremulam habeant, id est varium tenorem, quem longum aliquotiens apposita litterae virgula plana significat." See *Guidonis Arentini Micrologus,* ed. Smits van Waesberghe, 163-64; Gerbert, *Scriptores ecclesiastici,* 2:14-15.

40. Cf. Mt. 15:22-28.

> At the first word, "Dixit," you have a syllable, at "Dixit Dominus," a part, at "Dixit Dominus mulieri Cananaeae," a distinction. On "dixit," the ending "-xit" is stretched out a little bit. On "Dixit Dominus," the ending "-nus" is lengthened further. On "Dixit Dominus mulieri Cananaeae," the final "-ae" is extended a very long time.[41]

Bower gives the following transcription:

Ex. 5. Musical punctuation of *Dixit Dominus mulieri Cananaeae*

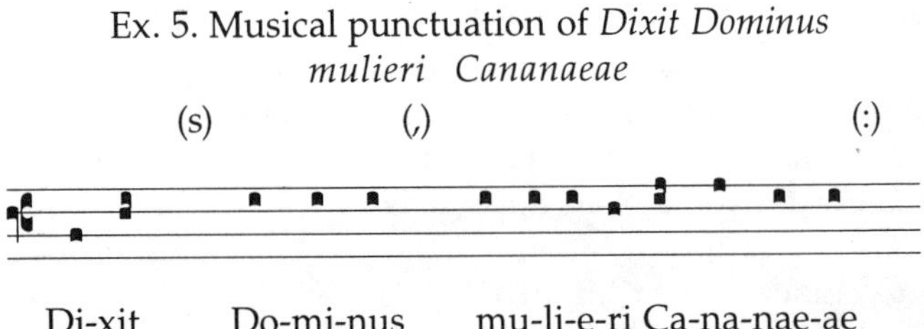
(s)
(,)
(:)
Di-xit
Do-mi-nus
mu-li-e-ri Ca-na-nae-ae

Even in this simple example, the commentator indicates three places for pauses, rather than the two places which mark the verbal syntax. Although the additional short pause on the syllable "-xit" (of *dixit*) lengthens the end of the verb, and could help with the enunciation of the double consonant between *Dixit* and *Dominus*, it seems intended primarily to mark a *musical* gesture. (In this case, the upward movement to the fourth above the final.) It is a significant point primarily because of what is happening musically. Such a concern for the special grammar of music suggests that the musical structure was considered an important organizing feature, which had rules which were to a certain extent independent of the verbal syntax. This musical syntax had the melodic "syllable" (gesture) as its basic unit and the structural notes of the mode as its grammar. While this example shows a case where a single musical syllable took place over the course of more than one verbal syllable, such a theory would be most helpful in describing melismatic chant where a number of different musical ges-

41. This analysis can be found in the anonymous *Commentarius in Micrologum*: "Illam unam dictionem 'Dixit' habeatis syllabam, 'Dixit Dominus' partem, 'Dixit Dominus mulieri Cananaeae' distinctionem. In 'dixit' finalis 'xit' intendatur aliquantulum; in 'Dixit Dominus' finalis 'nus' producatur amplius, in 'Dixit Dominus mulieri Cananaeae' finalis 'ae extendatur diutissime'" (Jos. Smits van Waesberghe, ed., *Expositiones in Micrologum Guidonis Aretini* [Amsterdam: North Holland Publishing Co., 1957], 153-54).

tures and cadential points could be used even within a single verbal syllable, as in the following example:

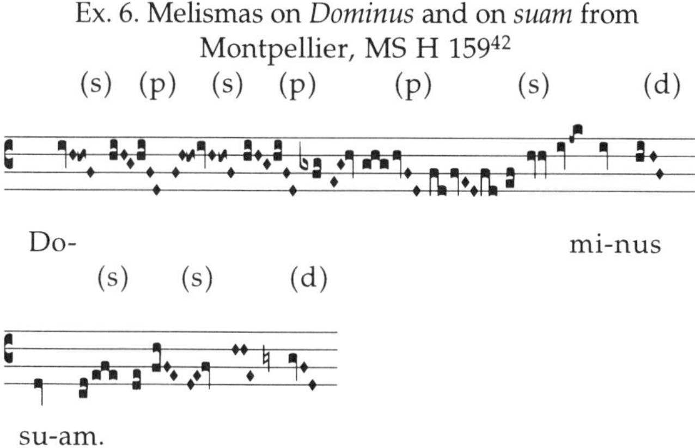

Ex. 6. Melismas on *Dominus* and on *suam* from Montpellier, MS H 159[42]

In example 6, the word *Dominus* can be divided into seven or more distinct sections, and the word *suam* can be divided into at least three. Each of the words ends a distinction in the mode V Christmas gradual from which they are extracted, and I have indicated the weight of each cadence by using Guido's terminology of syllable, part, and distinction. Although the exact divisions and the weight given to cadences is partially a matter of musical opinion, the repetitions of figures and prominence of the mode's structural pitches suggest that the analogy of musical syllables could be applied even to the most elaborate chants.[43] By distinguishing musical and verbal syllables, me-

42. Transcribed from the facsimile reproduction edited by André Mocquereau, *Antiphonarium tonale missarum (XIe siècle): codex H. 159 de la Bibliothèque de l'École de médecine de Montpellier*, Paléographie musicale: Les principaux manuscrits du chant grégorien, ambrosien, gallican, publiés en facsimiles phototypiques (Solesmes: Société de Saint Jean l'Évangeliste, 1901-5), 8: 181. This source is one of the earliest pitch-secure sources from central France, which combines an information-rich unheightened neumation with a parallel letter notation to indicate exact pitches. It was written for the monastery of St. Bénigne in Dijon in the mid-eleventh century and represents a repertory close in both date and geography to the Autun Troper.

43. Although manuscripts that indicate rhythmic pauses tend to choose slightly differing places to make them, the practice of dividing the music by pauses is common for the early period, and suggests that the marking of musical syllables was common. For examples of this gradual in a modern edition which also transcribes two early neumed versions, see *Graduale Triplex*, 48-49.

dieval theorists could account for complex relationships between the differing syntaxes of the music and of the words.

Ornamental Language and Musical Style

Since the musical style of the chant repertory had been developed to set Vulgate-style prose texts, it needed to be adapted in order to set the texts of the newer repertories of trope and sequence, which cultivated ornamental language. The Vulgate provided a norm for medieval Latin, and while the trope and sequence writers often borrowed both its vocabulary and imagery, they often reordered the words to achieve more pleasing poetic effects. Indeed, many tropes and many passages within sequences often seem to be a metrical reordering of the Vulgate text. A similar phenomenon occurred in the metrical psalmody of the seventeenth century, in which the King James version of the Bible provided similar linguistic norms. By comparing them, we can get an analogous sense of the effects of poetics on word order:

> The Lord is my shepherd; I shall not want. He maketh me to lie down in green pastures: he leadeth me beside the still waters. (King James Bible)
>
> The Lord's my shepherd, I'll not want;
> He makes me down to lie
> In pastures green; He leadeth me
> The quiet waters by.
> (*Scottish Psalter*, 1650)[44]

The poetic version contains two syntactic disruptions: "down" would ordinarily come after "lie," and "by" would ordinarily begin the last line. These alterations were not necessary for the syllable count, but were needed to retain the iambic accentual pattern in line four, and to create the rhyme between lines two and four.

Similar measures were taken in the hexameter tropes in order to preserve a proper sequence of long and short vowels and for the sake of rhyme. An example is given by Jonsson and

44. As quoted by *The Hymnbook*, Presbyterian Church (Richmond: John Ribble, 1955), 98.

Treitler, who analyzed one commonly found set of hexameter tropes (*Discipulis flammas/ SPIRITUS DOMINI*).[45] First, they noted a basic stylistic difference between the language of the trope text and of the introit antiphon; they identified this difference as syntactic "segmentation." Since Latin is an inflected language, the words of a sentence may be presented in almost any order and still "make sense" as a unit; however, the natural order of Vulgate-style prose is essentially the same as that of modern languages that have lost their inflection. In contrast, the text of a hexameter verse is likely to use a much greater variety of word order than would be encountered in prose, so that the verse can meet the requirements of the meter. The text and a translation which retains the original word order can demonstrate the kind of difference in style that Jonsson and Treitler noted. In the translation below, points of syntactic segmentation are marked with a slash /. Some of them are marked by a slash in parentheses (/) because they are weaker. For example, in the second trope element, "let us sing with our voices," taken as a unit, connects well even though it has a pause. The major syntactical problem is in connecting the adjective "clear" with its noun "songs" and identifying "songs" as the direct object of the verb:

Discipulis flammas infudit pectore linguas
SPIRITUS DOMINI <REPLEVIT ORBEM> TERRARUM
ALLELUIA
Ipsi perspicua<s> dicamus vocibus odas
ET HOC QUOD <CONTINET OMNIA SCIENTEM HABET
VOCIS ALLELUIA ALLELUIA ALLELUIA ALLELUIA>

Of the disciples / the flames / he instilled (/) into the hearts /
the tongues
THE SPIRIT OF THE LORD FILLED THE WORLD,

45. Jonsson and Treitler, "Medieval Music and Language," 12-23. In their article, they examined the trope set *Discipulis flammas/ SPIRITUS DOMINI*, a variant of which occurs in the Autun Troper (fol. 41v). In the following few paragraphs, I summarize their main points using the Autun variants of the trope set; this requires some alteration of analytical details, but does not change their basic observations, which in general are useful not only for all of the hexameter tropes, but also for any pieces in the repertory in which the requirements of ornamental language cause similar problems in the verbal syntax. As noted in chapter 1, the repertory of tropes contains prose, rhythmically organized elements, and hexameters. Sequences show a great variety of rhythmic organization, especially at cadences.

ALLELUIA,
To him / clear / let us sing (/) with our voices / songs
AND HE WHO HOLDS ALL THINGS TOGETHER HAS
KNOWLEDGE OF LANGUAGE, ALLELUIA, ALLELUIA,
ALLELUIA, ALLELUIA.[46]

In fact the syntactic segmentation is so severe, that, in the uninflected language of the translation, one must rearrange the words in order to render the sense of the trope elements: (1) "He instilled the flames, the tongues, into the hearts of the disciples"; (2) "To him, let us sing clear songs with our voices." In contrast, one need not change the original word order in order to make sense of the antiphon text. Jonsson and Treitler demonstrated that the degree of segmentation is caused by the writer's conforming to the characteristics of leonine hexameters; each line contains six quantitative feet, the first four of which are either dactyls or spondees, the fifth of which is a dactyl and the sixth a spondee. Each hexameter also has a main caesura (a word ending within the foot) after the fifth half-foot, which is emphasized by a rhyme between the syllable that marks the main caesura and that which ends each hexameter. Furthermore, the rhyme words are syntactically related to each other: in the first hexameter, the rhyme marks the two objects (*flammas* and *linguas*) which are in apposition; in the second hexameter, the adjective (*perspicuas*) and the object which it modifies (*odas*) are connected through their structural placement and the rhyme. The conventional analysis of these lines marks the divisions of feet with slashes (/), the main caesura by a double slash (//), the long syllables with a dash (¯), and the short syllables with a 'u' (˘):

```
 ¯   ˘ ˘/¯    ¯ / ¯ //¯ / ¯ ¯ / ¯ ˘ ˘/ ¯   ¯
Discipulis flammas   infudit pectore linguas
```

46. As Jonsson and Treitler pointed out, "Medieval Music and Language," 13, translating HOC QUOD, "He who," is not technically correct; however, in the Vulgate passage, Wisdom, 1:7, HOC clearly refers to "the Spirit," which was a neuter noun in the Greek, from which the Vulgate text of the antiphon was translated. (The Douay-Rheims Bible gives a literal, but not very helpful translation: "the spirit of the Lord hath filled the whole world: and that, which containeth all things, hath knowledge of the voice.")

```
 – – / –  ˘ ˘/ – // – / – – / – ˘ ˘ /  – –
Ipsi perspicua<s>  dicamus  vocibus  odas
```
[47]

However, these lines can also be analyzed in rhythmic terms as two six plus eight syllable stiches, which mimic quantitative verse, and which contain rhyme words between each half-stich. Since the music did not reflect the quantitative structure, this more minimal analysis may actually reveal what the author considered poetically important in constructing such verses. Either way, as Jonsson and Treitler point out, there is a fundamental stylistic contrast between the "old" biblical style of the antiphon and the "new" ornamental style of the hexameter tropes. This difference in style undergirds an important function of the trope elements: they create an allegory between the Old Testament antiphon and the New Testament trope.[48]

So far as the musical style is concerned, Jonsson and Treitler point out that musicians retained the basic idea of music's marking the linguistic syntax that characterizes the whole of the chant repertory.[49] Nevertheless, tenth- and eleventh-century composers tended to exploit the more independent features of musical grammar in order to set texts that cultivated ornamental language: musicians answered the syntactic segmentation with a corresponding musical segmentation, in general marking points of syntactic rupture with the endings of musical phrases on structural pitches.[50] In the following example, the entire neumation of the trope set is presented in a "diplomatic" version closely corresponding to the Autun Troper. Below the

47. Ibid., 14.
48. Ibid., 16.
49. Ibid.
50. Treitler and Jonsson demonstrate this by comparing two surviving pitch-secure versions of the trope complex for the introit of Pentecost from the Aquitanian and Beneventan repertories (Benevento, Biblioteca Capitolare, MS 34 [25]; Benevento, Biblioteca Capitolare, MS 38 [27]; Benevento, Biblioteca Capitolare, MS 40 [29]). Since the neumation of the first trope element in the Autun Troper closely corresponds with the Beneventan repertory, I can reconstruct its melody with reasonable confidence, and can securely restore the antiphon melody from the Dijon tonary (Montpellier, H 159. For a modern edition, see Finn Hansen, ed., *H159 Montpellier: Tonary of St Bénigne of Dijon* [Copenhagen: Dan Fog, 1974], and for a facsimile, see Mocquereau, ed., *Paléographie musicale*, vols. 7 and 8). These provide a version which differs in a few details from those analyzed by Jonsson and Treitler, but which reflects the use of Autun, and my analysis takes these differences into account.

Autun neumes is a realization of the first trope element (the second has no melodic concordances) and first part of the antiphon in modern pitch-secure notation:

Ex. 7. Introit trope set *Discipulis flammas/ SPIRITUS DOMINI* from PaA 1169, fol. 41v[51]

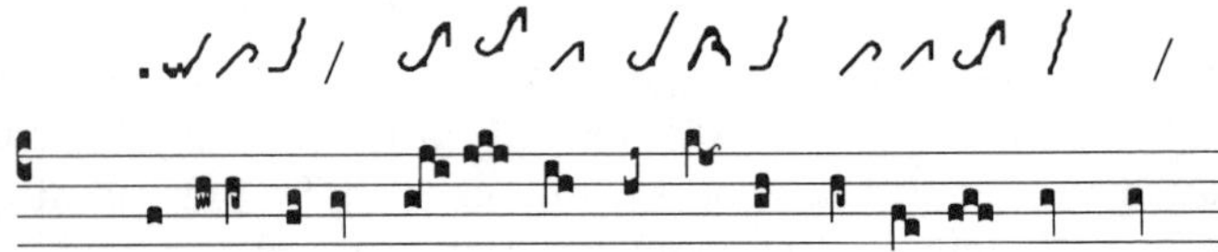

Di-sci-pu-lis flam-mas in-fu-dit pec-to-re lin-guas

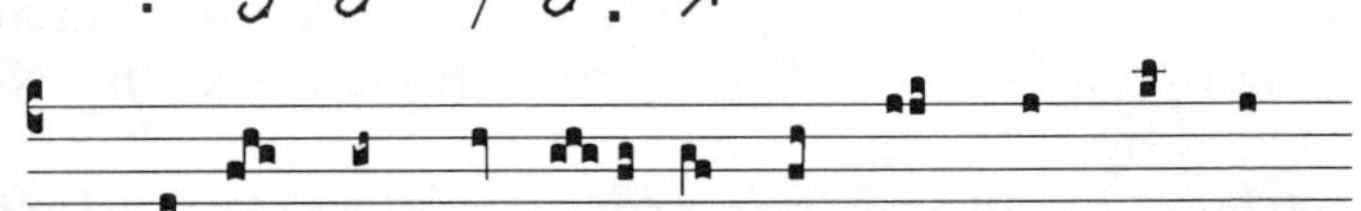

SPI-RI- TUS DO-MI- NI <RE-PLE- VIT OR-BEM>

TER- RA- RUM, AL- LE- LU- IA

Ipsi perspicua<s> dicamus vo - cibus odas

ET HOC QUOD <CONTINET OMNIA SCIENTEM HABET VOCIS>

The mode VIII melody consists of four phases, the first three setting single words: *Discipulis* cadences on the final; *flammas* and *infudit* on the flex.[52] Most importantly, the syn-

51. For an explanation of the conventions used in the modern transcription, see preface, above.

52. Since in a psalm tone the reciting note is (usually) a fourth or fifth above the final, another pitch is necessary to mark clauses effectively. This pitch (the flex of the psalm tone), was often used for secondary cadential notes in the antiphon repertory. In this mode (VIII), and in all plagal modes, making secondary cadences on the fifth above the final would put too much stress on the upper-

tactic segmentation is well reflected by the setting, although the stronger cadence on *Discipulis* suggests that the disruption was felt to be slightly more awkward between *Discipulis* and *flammas*, than between *flammas* and *infudit*.

In contrast, the last two words are set in one phrase (cadencing on the final); this phrase would have stood out, since it violates the expectations set up by the usual musical style—the two words (*pectore linguas*) do not belong together syntactically. The musical phrase provides an association here, which being contradicted by the syntax, invites interpreters to find a non-syntactical connection. The subtle association of "tongues" with the influence of the Spirit on the "heart" may well be a nuance of the text that the musical setting was intended to suggest, especially since the noun *linguas* is disconnected from the overall syntax, needing to refer back only to the verb (and not to *flammas*) to make sense.[53]

The musical setting also suggests relationships through the use of gestures of similar shape, length, and cadential formulae.[54] For example, *flammas* and *infudit* are both set to gestures that leap upward and touch on the highest note in the trope. This helps lessen the syntactic segmentation, since it suggests that the two words belong together (even if they occur in the reverse order from what one would expect). Furthermore, it cre-

---

most notes of the range. Instead, secondary cadences were most commonly made on the fourth above the final (the reciting tone for the psalm tone), the second above the final (the flex of the psalm tone), and the note below the final (the beginning note of the gloria patri of the psalm tone).

53. Both versions of the trope analyzed by Jonsson and Treitler display this feature as well, but the three versions vary linguistically, so that different words are associated in each. Of the two variants quoted by Jonsson and Treitler, even the one which is closest to the text in the Autun Troper reads differently in the last melodic phrase: *pectore blandas*, with *blandas* (gentle) modifying *flammas*. Jonsson and Treitler suggested that since *blandas* is "an adjective which is frequently used to characterize speech and song," it is appropriate to link this adjective with the empowering of special speech "within the hearts" of the disciples. The syntax of the Autun variant makes this association even more plausible; see Jonsson and Treitler, "Medieval Music and Language," 19.

54. Jonsson and Treitler also make this point, but since they are using different variants of both music and text, the specific relationships they point out differ from my examples here.

John Johnstone, "Beyond a Chant 'Tui sunt caeli' and Its Tropes," in *Music and Language*, Studies in the History of Music, no. 1 (New York: Broude Brothers, 1983), 24-37, points out a very sophisticated set of relationships between trope and base elements, which was similarly constructed by rhymes of musical phrase and figuration.

ates a relationship with the antiphon melody where *replevit* is set to a similar melodic figure. The association of two actions of the Spirit, "instilling the flames and tongues into the disciples' hearts," and "filling the world" was presumably intended by the juxtaposition of the trope element with the antiphon. However, it is made considerably more effective and precise by the use of musical similarity.

To sum up, the new repertories of tropes and sequences changed the musical style, but not the basic musical intentions of marking syntax. However, in the new repertories, structural notes could not be counted upon to mark only the larger *distinctiones*, because severe segmentation caused too many disruptions in the text. Instead, the musical "syllable" was used to create larger syntactic units by associating words or phrases which belonged together syntactically but which were separated from each other for the sake of ornament. Furthermore, by placing syntactically unrelated words within the same musical phrase and by using the musical syllable to mark words or phrases outside of the syntactical boundaries of the trope element or a sequence verse, the power of musical gesture to create associations was heightened by the new style. In short, one basic function of the musical setting of tropes was analogous to the function of linguistic tropes: creating patterns of association between words and phrases which were unusual and syntactically improper.[55]

Tropus as a Musical Term

It was within discussions of the syntax peculiar to music, particularly in chapters which dealt with the identifying characteristics of melody, that medieval music theorists treated the term *tropus*. However, during the period when liturgical tropes were composed, it gradually took on a more precise meaning. The shift in the term's meaning during the eleventh century suggests that theorists became more aware of the need to describe the construction of melodic figures in greater detail, since small distinguishable segments of melody were used to set the repertories of tropes and proses.

Eleventh-century theorists had inherited (from classical sources) such a rich vocabulary intended to describe melody

55. See chapter 1, above, pp. 16-48, for the functions of linguistic tropes.

that they had an abundance of synonymous terms. Since the sixth century, music theorists writing in Latin had three terms (*modus* [mode], *tonus* [tone], and *tropus*), which were used to indicate the specific patterns of tone and semitone, compass, tessitura, and cadential notes through which melody was classified (eventually the eight church modes). As Charles Atkinson points out, the terminological superfluity stemmed from the influential treatise *De institutione musica* of Boethius, who substituted the term *modus* (mode = measure) for the Greek technical term τροπος συστηματικος (TROPOS SYSTEMATIKOS), meaning "modulation system," while most later theorists preferred to use *tonus* (tone) from the Greek τονος (TONOS).[56] However, the term "tone" was ambiguous, since it could also indicate the specific interval of a whole tone, and theorists found it necessary to distinguish between melodic classification and the measurement of intervals, particularly when discussing organum (early polyphonic practices).[57] Moreover, the term "trope" was also ambiguous, both because of its use in the language arts and because it had other, less specific musical meanings. For example, in the sixth century, Cassiodorus (in a letter to Boethius) extolled music as "the queen of feeling embellished by its own tropes,"[58] and in the monastic *Rule of Paul* (also sixth century), the writer cautioned the monks not to sing the songs of the rite unmelodiously, as if they were lections, and not to turn the readings into "tropes with the art of song."[59] Such usages suggest that although the term TROPOS SYSTEMATIKOS was the correct Greek technical term for the

56. Charles M. Atkinson, "On the Interpretation of *modi, quos abusive tonos dicimus*," in *Hermeneutics and Medieval Culture*, ed. Patrick J. Gallacher and Helen Damico (Albany: State University of New York Press, 1989), 147-61. As the title of his article indicates, Atkinson does not treat the theorists' use of the term *tropus*, which, I argue, took on a more specific set of meanings during the eleventh century than it had previously (at least in the *Micrologus* of Guido); see below.

57. Ibid.

58. ". . . sensuum regina tropis suis ornata" as quoted in Blume, ed., *Die Musik in Geschichte und Gegenwart*, s.v. "Tropus," by Stäblein.

59. Paul and Stephen, *Regula ad monachos*, in Patrologiae latina, 66:954: "It is not proper that we change all things which are to be sung, into the manner of prose and as if readings, or that by our own presumption and with the art of song, we transform what have been prescribed to be used in the order of readings into tropes." Latin text: "Non omnio oportet ut quae cantanda sunt in modum prosae et quasi lectionem mutemus, aut quae ita scripta sunt, ut in ordine lectionum utamur, in tropis et cantilenae arte nostra praesumptione vertamus."

system of melodic classification, the term "trope" standing alone could mean the whole "art of song," that is, an art of melodic embellishment, which functioned to provide musical "ornament," and which was connected with analogous theories of grammatical and rhetorical ornamentation of words.

Because of the ambiguity of the word "tone," Frankish theorists (beginning with the anonymous *Musica enchiriadis* of the second half of the ninth century) tended to prefer the use of the word "mode" to denote the system of melodic classification, reserving the use of the word "tone" to mean the melodic interval of a tone.[60] Moreover, the term "trope" was almost always mentioned only in passing, usually simply as an alternate word for mode.[61] However, in the eleventh century, when liturgical tropes were part of the established repertory of many monastic and cathedral *scholae,* Guido refined the meaning of the term *tropus* in his treatise *Micrologus,* reconnecting the term with its use in grammar and rhetoric and defining its function within music more exactly.[62]

In order to appreciate Guido's use of the term, one must examine the overall structure of his treatise *Micrologus,* as well as his specific mentions of *tropus.* Most scholars have not considered the treatise to form a coherent whole.[63] However, by

60. Atkinson, "On the Interpretation of *modi,*" 152-55.

61. For example, see ibid., 161 and Gerbert, *Scriptores ecclesiastici,* 1:119; the author of the anonymous *Musica enchiriadis* and Hucbald both consistently use the formulation *modi* vel *tropi* in discussing modes.

62. Guido's *Micrologus* survives in more manuscripts than any other music treatise from the Middle Ages (with the exception of Boethius' *Institutiones*), making it the most widespread practical handbook for the chant repertory. Although its exact date is still in dispute, all commentators agree that it stems from the first third of the eleventh century, making it closely contemporary to the period when tropes were most widely used.

Van Deusen accurately noted that musical theorists did not make any significant connections between the terms "trope" and "mode" after the twelfth century. However, she appeared to believe that the use of the term "trope" was *entirely* an eleventh-century phenomenon, and therefore missed the significance of Guido's particular uses. See van Deusen, *The Harp and the Soul,* 176, where she states: "Writers on music draw on the term *tropus* and relate it to *modus,* during the period of musical-textual trope composition, neither before this period, nor significantly after the first generation of the twelfth century."

63. For example, Bower, "Grammatical Model of Musical Understanding," 138, in giving a description of its contents, maintained that it has two large sections: the first (chaps. 1-15) devoted to monophonic music; and the second (chaps. 18-19) devoted to polyphonic music. From this perspective, chaps. 16, 17, and 20 are considered digressions. See also Crocker, "*Musica Rhythmica* and *Musica Metrica,*"

taking Guido's penchant for analogies derived from the language arts into account, I can explain its divisions differently and more coherently. Chapters 1-13 deal with the essential grammar of melody, progressing like a grammar treatise from the smallest units (individual notes) to the largest units (the entire ambit of each mode). Chapters 15-19 cover the rhetoric of melody, offering precepts for the composition of melodic lines and for the effective use of melodic and polyphonic ornament, whether composed or improvised. Guido's remarks throughout chapters 15-19 are strikingly similar in both order and method to the later preceptive grammar tradition called the *ars poetica*.[64] He treats aspects of "invention" in chapters 15 and 17, and gives a fuller treatment of ornament than would be supplied by "grammatical" training in chapters 16, 18, and 19. Chapter 20 concludes the work with an introduction to speculative music theory that concentrates on the mathematical basis of music (proportions), just as the language arts (*trivium*) ought to lead to the mathematical arts (*quadrivium*).[65] As one would expect from the parallel to the language arts, chapter 14, which links the grammatical and rhetorical sections of the treatise, introduces the doctrine of tropes, and the topic of ornament is treated again and expanded in the following rhetorical sections.[66]

2-23. Crocker considers Guido's *Micrologus* to be even less unified than does Bower, and explains chaps. 14-20 as follows: "This 'short discourse' on music is devoted primarily to harmonics, that is, to analyses of the phenomena concerning pitch. At the end of these analyses, as adjuncts, appear several chapters devoted to other aspects of music. These include (1) a discussion of the effects of music, (2) the chapter on modulation . . . (3) an analysis of melodic progression (the *motus*-theory), (4) an exposition of the technique known to the sixteenth century as the *soggetto cavato della vocali,* (5) precepts on the performance of diaphony, and finally, (6) an account of the origins of music" (ibid., 15).

64. On the genesis of the *ars poetica,* see Douglas Kelly, *The Arts of Poetry and Prose*, Typologie des Sources du Moyen Âge Occidental, Fasc. 59 (Turnhout: Brepols, 1991), 43-60.

65. Chap. 17 is somewhat out of place. It demonstrates a semi-improvisational method of word setting, which appears to be Guido's own creation. By using this method, one can generate a "sequence-like" melody from any text. Guido appears to recommend this process principally as a spur to the musical imagination, realizing both that it lacks flexibility and that one would need to adjust cadences to fit the mode. Hence the chapter principally treats musical "invention," and would logically follow chapter 15. However, Guido may have placed it here since the method is improvisational: a chapter treating improvised melody leads smoothly to the next chapter on improvised harmony.

66. See chapter 1, pp. 16-17 and 43-45, for parallels with the language arts.

Guido's specific use of the term "trope" changes during the course of the treatise. The term is first mentioned in chapter 10, where it has its "traditional" meaning as equivalent to the word "mode": "Here are [described] the four modes or tropes, which are improperly called 'tones'. . . . These modes or tropes we name, from the Greek protus, deuterus, tritus, and tetrardus."[67] Next, in chapter 13, Guido suggests that one learn the then standard set of melodic specimens that demonstrate the characteristics of each mode and which, along with the range and tessitura, make specific modes recognizable.[68] For example, the following formula identifies the first mode:

Ex. 8. Intonation formula for mode I

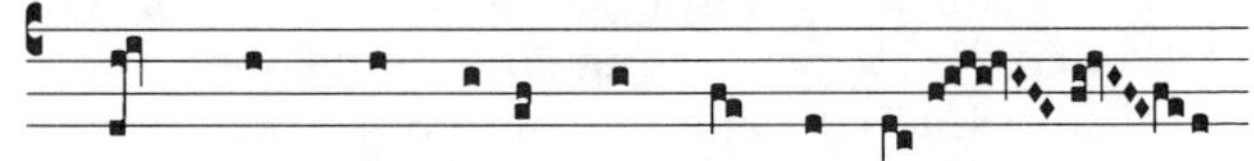

Pri- mum quae-ri-te reg-num De-i

At the end of chapter 13, Guido distinguishes between the methods of recognizing the modes from their range and from their figuration, by using the term "trope" to speak about the characteristic movement of melody, although still claiming that it meant the same as "mode":

> In studying chants new to us, we are helped chiefly by juxtaposing the aforesaid neumes [the standard formulae] and appendages [*subiunctiones*], since from the way these fit we come to see the particular character of each note through the effect of the "tropes.""Trope" is the aspect of chant which is also called

67. Babb, *Hucbald, Guido, and John*, 66; Gerbert, *Scriptores ecclesiastici*, 2:10, 11; *Guidonis Aretini Micrologus*, ed. Smits van Waesberghe, 133, 138: "Hi sunt quatuor modi vel tropi, quos abusive tonos nominant. . . . Hos autem modos vel tropos græce nominamus protum, deuterum, tritum, tetrardum."

68. The elements of "range" that were considered important were the number of notes a specific mode could go above or below its final (especially useful for determining the differences between authentic and plagal). This does not imply that a fixed pitch was used in performance, although students practised modes using fixed pitches from the monochord. One expects that the length, string materials, and therefore pitch of the monochord varied at least from institution to institution and possibly from instrument to instrument. A careful reading of the theorists suggests that one would aim at tuning the string to one's own lowest note.

"mode," and we shall now discuss it.[69]

Finally, Guido devotes all of chapter 14 to explaining how the features which give music its identifying characteristics (i.e., "tropes") also give music its power. There are three important features of this description: (1) Guido drops the term "mode" in this chapter, which suggests that he was making a distinction between this use of the term "trope" and its use as a simple equivalent to the term "mode"; (2) he relates the identifying features called trope to the characteristic movements of the melody and to other "ornamental" qualities such as "sweetness," and continues the analogy by comparing them to the way differing colors, odors, and tastes are distinguishable by eye, nose, and mouth;[70] and (3) he suggests that the power of music to delight, move, and heal was related to these identifiable characteristics of melody.

Because of its importance to the discussion, the whole chapter is given here:

> Some men who are well trained in the particular characters [*proprietates*] and, so to say, the individual features [*discretas facies*] of these tropes recognize them the instant they hear them, as one who is familiar with the different peoples, when many men are placed before him, can observe their appearance and say, "This is a Greek, that one a Spaniard, this is a Latin, that one a German, and that other is a Frenchman." The diversity in the tropes so fits in with the diversity in people's minds that one man is attracted by the intermittent leaps [*fractis saltibus*] of the authentic deuterus [mode III], another chooses the delightfulness [*voluptatem*] of the plagal of the tritus, one is more pleased by the volubility [*garrulitas*] of the authentic tetrardus, and another esteems the sweetness [*suavitatem*] of the plagal tetrardus, and so forth.
>
> Nor is it any wonder if the hearing is charmed by a variety of sounds, since the sight rejoices in a variety of colors, the sense of smell is gratified by a variety of odors, and the palate delights in changing flavors. For thus through the windows of

69. Babb, *Hucbald, Guido, and John*, 69; Gerbert, *Scriptores ecclesiastici*, 2:14; *Guidonis Aretini Micrologus*, ed. Smits van Waesberghe, 157: "in ignotorum cantuum inquisitione, prædictarum neumarum et subiunctionum appositione plurimum adiuvamur, cum talium aptitudine soni cuiusque proprietatem per vim tropicam intuemur. Est autem tropus species cantionis, qui et modus dictus est, et adhuc dicendum est de eo."

70. This analogy also was common in the later *ars poetica*, which called literary figures and tropes "colors" (*colores*).

> the body the sweetness of apt things enters wondrously into the recesses of the heart. Hence it is that the well-being of both heart and body is lessened or increased, as it were, by particular tastes and smells and even by the sight of certain colors. So it is said that of old a certain madman was recalled from insanity by the music of the physician Asclepiades. Also that another man was roused by the sound of the cithara to such lust that, in his madness, he sought to break into the bedchamber of a girl, but, when the cithara player quickly changed the mode, was brought to feel remorse for his libidinousness and to retreat abashed. So, too, David soothed with the cithara the evil spirit of Saul and tamed the savage demon with the potent force and sweetness of this art. Yet this effect is fully clear only to Divine Wisdom, thanks to which, indeed, we have gained some insight into obscure things. Since we have poured forth not a few words on the power of this art, let us now see what is requisite for shaping good melodic lines [*quibus ad bene modulandum rebus opus fit*].[71]

After chapter 14, Guido mentions the term "trope" only in chapter 18, in naming the best modes or transpositions of modes for *organum*. Although this use appears to revert to the practice of equating mode and trope, the fact that Guido uses the term "trope" to speak of both the mode and its transpositions may

71. Babb, *Hucbald, Guido, and John*, 69-70; I have added the relevant descriptive Latin vocabulary within the translation given above. Gerbert, *Scriptores ecclesiastici*, 2:14; *Guidonis Aretini Micrologus*, ed. Smits van Waesberghe, 158-61 give the Latin text:

"Horum quidam troporum exercitati ita proprietates et discreatas ut ita dicam, facies extemplo ut audierint, recognoscunt, sicut peritus gentium coram positis multis habitus eorum intueri potest et dicere: hic Graecus est, ille Hispanus, hic Latinus est, ille Teutonicus, iste vero Gallus. Atque ita diversitas troporum diversitati mentium coaptatur ut unus autenti deuteri fractis saltibus delectetur, alius plagae triti eligat voluptatem, uni tetrardi autenti garrulitas magis placet, alter eiusdem plagae suavitatem probat; sic et de relinquis.

"Nec mirum si varietate sonorum delactatur auditus, cum varietate colorum grauletur visus, varietate odorum foveatur olfactus, mutatisque saporibus lingua congaudeat. Sic enim per fenestras corporis habilium rerum suavitas intrat mirabiliter penetralia cordis. Inde est quod sicut quibusdam saporibus et odoribus vel etiam colorum intuitu salus tam cordis quam corporis vel minuitur vel augescit.ta quondam legitur quidam phreneticus canente Asclepiade medico ab insania revocatus. Et item alius quidam sonitu citharae in tantam libidinem incitatus, ut cubiculum puellae quaereret effringere dementatus, moxque citharoedo mutante modum voluptatis poenitentia ductum recessisse confusum. Item et David Saul daemonium cithara mitigabat et daemoniacam feritatem huius artis potenti vi ac suavitate frangebat. Quae tamen vis solum divinae sapientiae ad plenum patet, nos vero quae in aenigmate ab inde percepimus. Sed quia de artis virtue vix pauca libavimus, quibus ad bene modulandum rebus opus sit videamus."

indicate that he was still concerned with the characteristic figuration of each mode: specific segments of tone and semitone patterns (musical figures) can be duplicated only at selected transpositions without introducing accidentals.[72] For example, 'B and E' can only be used in parallel fourths since none of the other consonances (major second, major third, and even the fifth in the case of 'B') is notatable.

Even though Guido drops the term "trope," he continues to develop the concept of musical ornament with five chapters that serve as examples of how music uses characteristic figures: in chapter 15, Guido identifies the various units [*distinctiones*] from which melodies could be built; in chapter 16, he lists precepts for connecting various musical gestures together; in chapter 17, he gives precepts for generating simple melodies from texts, suggesting that the cadences need to be modifed to fit the characteristics of the mode; and in chapters 18 and 19, he discusses how a melody may be ornamented by doubling it at intervals where the figuration can be replicated, and again giving precepts for making a suitable cadence. Thus, in the same way that grammarians and rhetoricians taught the generic terms "figures" and "tropes," and followed them with specific examples, Guido used the term "trope" as the generic term for all musical ornament, and then gave a specific term *motus* (motion) to musical figuration, and other specific terms, *diaphonia* and *organum,* to the ornament of musical harmony. Furthermore, Guido treated these topics in exactly the same locations as did grammarians and rhetoricians; i.e., he introduced them as the final topic of his musical grammar, developing them directly

72. Babb, *Hucbald, Guido, and John*, 78: "Of the tropes, some are serviceable, others more serviceable, and still others most serviceable. Those are serviceable that provide organum only at the diatessaron, with the notes a fourth from each other, like the deuterus on B and E; more serviceable are those that harmonize not only with fourths but also with thirds and seconds, by a tone and, though only rarely, a semiditone, like the protus on A and D. Most serviceable are those that make organum most frequently and more smoothly, namely the tetrardus and tritus on C and F and G; for these harmonize at the distance of a tone, a ditone, and a diatesseron." Gerbert, *Scriptores ecclesiastici*, 2:21; *Guidonis Aretini Micrologus*, ed. Smits van Waesberghe, 202: "Troporum vero alii apti, alii aptiores, alii aptissimi existunt. Apti sunt, qui per solam diatessaron quartis a se vocibus organum reddunt, ut deuterus in B et E: aptiores sunt, qui non solum quartis, sed tertiis et secundis per tonum et semiditonum, licet raro, respondent, ut protus in A et D. Aptissimi vero, qui sæpissime suaviusque id faciunt, ut tetrardus et tritus in C F G. Hæ enim tono et ditono et diatessaron obsequuntur."

after the concept of "invention" in his musical rhetoric.

Like early treatises concerning the *ars poetica,* Guido's specific precepts for melodic rhetoric in chapters 15 through 17 are generic, vague, and idiosyncratic, and would need to be supplemented by a tutor to help a student write well. However, three key concepts emerge from considering them: (1) Musical motion (figuration) should be used to lend balance and proportion to a melody, and the various parts of a melody should be balanced in an understandable way, in which the various segments bear a "certain" yet "incomplete" resemblance to each other. (Guido made an analogy with the way in which metrical feet may be varied but are nevertheless measurable.) (2) Such figuration may be used at various pitch levels which can combine into a whole, but a melody should also contain sufficient variety in its figuration. (3) While melodic spontaneity is allowable, particular attention needs to be paid to the cadences, which must clearly be within the mode.[73] In short, Guido suggested that melodic figuration provided the balance and proportion for melody, and the primary balance and proportion for the delivery of the text, in a fashion which was analogous to the way meter can order the flow of words.[74]

Guido's narrower definition of *tropus* serves well to describe some of the specific relationships between musical syntax and the repertory of liturgical tropes and proses, especially since

---

73. Babb, *Hucbald, Guido, and John,* 70-74; Gerbert, *Scriptores ecclesiastici,* 2:14-18; *Guidonis Aretini Micrologus,* ed. Smits van Waesberghe, 162-84. The three precepts that I have derived summarize points made in chaps. 15, 16, and 17 respectively.

74. See Babb, *Hucbald, Guido, and John,* 72, where Guido states that "the parallel between verse and chant is no slight one, since neumes correspond to feet and phrases to lines of verse. Thus one neume proceeds like a dactyl, another like a spondee, and a third in iambic manner; and you see a phrase now like a tetrameter, now like a pentameter, and again like a hexameter, and many other parallels." Gerbert, *Scriptores ecclesiastici,* 2:16; *Guidonis Aretini Micrologus,* ed. Smits van Waesberghe, 173: "Non autem parva similtudo est metris et cantibus, cum et neumæ loco sint pedum, et distinctiones loco versuum, utpote ista neuma dactylico, illa vero spondaico, illa iambico metro decurreret, et distinctionem nunc tetrametram nunc pentrametram, alias quasi hexametram cernes, et multa alia."

It is important to remember that Guido was making an analogy between meter and chant, and not advocating the metrical performance of chant. It was the ability of music to give order and proportion to words that was similar to meter. For Guido, although music is concerned with proportion and measurement, it is more flexible than meter, since it can give order even to the prose which comprises most of the chant repertory.

his discussions of melodic motion provided a vocabulary for identifying melodic figuration. Moreover, two connections between musical theory and the trope manuscripts (noted by van Deusen) suggest that the changing conception of the term "trope" in music theory was known by the compilers of some manuscripts. First, the interchangeable use of the words *modus, tonus,* and *tropus* in music theory may have influenced the rubrics for liturgical tropes; the rubric *alio modo* was used to indicate proper tropes in late tenth- and early eleventh-century manuscripts from St. Gall, and the rubric *alio tono* was used for the same purpose in a manuscript now located in the Bologna library.[75] Second, the teaching of modes may have influenced the language of the trope repertory: liturgical tropes frequently use the interjection *eia* that was sometimes associated with the nonsense syllables (*noeane*), which served as mnemonic devices for remembering modal patterns.[76]

75. Bologna University Library 2824; see van Deusen, *The Harp and the Soul,* 195-96.

76. Ibid. quotes Frutolf who attributed spiritual meaning to the various syllables encountered in music theory: "*None* dicitur a graeco *vous* [presumably νοῦς (NOUS)], quod est mens vel sensus–*Noe,* flatus, *Ane,* sursum, Unde *None noeane* dicitur: sensus ad superiora ductus. Aies vel ayes interiectiones apud nos interpretari possunt 'eia'" (*None* comes from the Greek NOUS, that is mind or understanding–*Noe* is a breath, *Ane,* an upwards motion, Whence, *None noeane* is said: understanding is led to higher things. The interjections Aies or ayes, among us, can be understood as 'eia'); see Froutolf, *Breviarium de musica et tonarius,* ed. Cölestin Vivel (Vienna, 1919), 104. In the Autun manuscript, *eya* occurs thirty-one times in the original layer alone; twenty-six of these are in the proper and ordinary trope repertory and five in the proses.

Both of the connections between music theory and the repertory of tropes and proses (noted by van Deusen) are somewhat problematic: first, although the use of the rubrics *alio modo* and *alio tono,* taken together, suggest a connection with music theory, *alio modo* could simply mean "another way," and *alio tono,* "another melody," suggesting that the purpose of the rubrics was simply to indicate a replacement set of tropes, rather than making a substantive connection to music theory. Second, *eia* could be expected to occur frequently in the festal repertory without any influence of music theory, since it was a common interjection of joy or eagerness (equivalent to ha!, good!, see!, or quick!), and it could provide two syllables to fill out a rhythmic or metrical scheme without disturbing the syntax. It could have been connected with the *noeane* syllables because they were also often explained as a *vox lætantis* (cry of rejoicing); see Gerbert, *Scriptores ecclesiastici,* 1:42. Nevertheless, the convergence of terminology remains striking and gives a context for interpreting Guido's use of the term *tropus.*

Colette, "*Modus, tropus, tonus,*" 69, points out internal evidence that Guido knew tropes, citing *Micrologus,* chapter 11, where Guido states: "Deinde si eidem cantui versum aut psalmum aut aliquid velis subiungere, ad finalem vocem permaxime opus est coaptare" (*Guidonis Aretini Micrologus,* ed. Smits van

Although neither of these connections proves that a substantial convergence between the use of the term "trope" in music theory and in the liturgical repertory had taken place, they do help support the idea that the term "trope" was being associated with specifically ornamental aspects of modal theory. Guido's use of *tropus* in his *Micrologus* seems to have grown out of the need to describe the music of the newer repertory, which cultivated ornamental language, and therefore tended to isolate and distinguish musical figures from the larger musical structure.

Thus, the syntactic segmentation of "ornate" texts seems to have caused musicians to adapt the musical style to mark the texts' syntactic disruption, and to adapt musical theory, so that it could be more useful for analyzing the new style. Nevertheless, Guido's precepts demonstrate that the use of melodic ornament to control the delivery of a text was common to both the older and newer chant styles. Such use of musical ornament to give structure to a text's intonation, pacing, and proportions encoded a particular reading of the text with specific nuances and choices. In fact, the chant (to a large extent) controlled the utterance of a sung text, and therefore, in many details of delivery, the rhetoric of the text was derived from the musical syntax.

Furthermore, the musical syntax gave information that not only helped listeners understand "what was said," but, since it revealed the tone of voice and pacing, it also helped them interpret "how it was said." For example, in assessing the probable liturgical function of an elaborate chant such as a gradual or an alleluia, it may be more important to understand what effects were attributed to musical ornament than to understand the specific words of the chant. Since these short texts (one or two sentences) received such an elaborate musical setting that each syllable took several seconds to enunciate, the musical element would seem more prominent than the linguistic element, even though the syntax of the text may be marked by cadential points of the melody.

Waesberghe, 144-45). "So if you wish to attach a verse or a psalm or anything else to the same chant, you should adjust it most of all to the final note" (Babb, *Hucbald, Guido, and John*, 67). It is hard to imagine what "anything else" could mean in this context, if not tropes.

While it remains necessary to take into account the strong coordination between words and music in order to interpret the liturgy, one must also keep in mind that it is a coordination of structures that have their own grammars and rhetorics; the tensions between the two systems are just as important to take into account as their convergences. To the extent that musical syntax and textual syntax were coordinated, music could articulate the syntactical structure and therefore clarify and effectively proclaim the meaning of the texts. To the extent the musical syntax was simple or complex, music could increase or decrease the expressive importance of the verbal meaning of texts. To the extent that verbal ornament became a prominent feature, the specific use of music to mark important linguistic segments became less effective, while the associative properties of musical gesture were called upon to help make the linguistic structure clear, and to create associations between the antiphons and the trope elements. Since it was the function of most linguistic tropes to create associations between words through devices such as metaphor and allegory, it should not be at all surprising that during the period that linguistic tropes were liturgically important, at least one music theorist (Guido) gave the general term *tropus* a more specific meaning as musical ornament, which highlighted the modes' powers of association through characteristic musical gesture.

Words, Music, and the Liturgy

The analogy between words and music developed by eleventh-century theorists like Guido and John suggests that medieval musicians understood the music of the liturgy to be a form of *ornatus*, similar in function to the *ornatus* more usually associated with words themselves; musical and verbal ornament were considered equally valid ways of producing the moderate (measured) style of rhetoric that persuaded through delighting the ear. Through making an analogy with language, theorists provided a way of comparing and contrasting the ways in which the *ornatus* provided by words and music supported or contrasted with each other. Both verbal and musical syntax were considered to have four levels: (1) vocabulary, (2) parts of speech, (3) *distinctiones*, and (4) ornament. On the verbal level, the vocabulary was formed by combinations of the articulate sound of letters; the parts of speech combined to form larger syntactical units (*distinctiones*) which were articulated by pauses; ornament was achieved both by rearranging the words to achieve a measured sound and by transferring the meaning of the words through association. In music, the vocabulary was derived from the tonal content common to the compass and tessitura of the mode; the parts of speech (*syllabae*) were articulated by the modes' structural notes, which provided cadence points and melodic referents emphasizing the modes' identifying patterns of tone and semitone; the *distinctiones* were marked by cadences, which required pauses (sometimes of hierarchical length), and the ornament was supplied by musical gesture; i.e., characteristic and identifiable melodic units, to the extent that they were arranged, ordered, and associated (and made conspicuous). A further level of ornament (not generally encoded in notation) could be achieved through improvised polyphony.

If these four levels of structure were completely coordinated, musical and verbal rhetorics served exactly the same purposes; however, they were not always coordinated completely, resulting in dual readings of music and text which may modify one's interpretation. This is especially the case at level four, the bridge between grammar and rhetoric. Ornament is of syntactic importance only because it disrupts and provides exceptions to the normal syntax; however, it is of rhetorical importance because it provides measure and proportion; i.e., it provides the structure for delivery. In the style of chant inherited by the eleventh century, music was particularly apt at setting prose, and musical ornament was substituted for the ornamental level of verbal syntax, which provided the words with their measure. However, the new repertories of the ninth to eleventh centuries are marked by their cultivation of the rhythmic measurement of words, which tended to disrupt and weaken the measurement of words by units of melody.

The following two tables show the impact of these differing organizations of measure on characteristic musical and textual forms of the medieval liturgy.[77]

77. Table 3 is adapted from Joseph Gelineau, "Music and Singing in the Liturgy," in *The Study of Liturgy*, ed. Cheslyn Jones, Geoffrey Wainwright,

Table 2. Rhythmic syntax as an organizing factor in ritual forms

PROSE ⟷	POETRY
Parallel stiches[78] (psalmody, canticles)	
Rhythmic cadences (sermon, oratory)	Rhythmic stiches and prose stiches combined (tropes)
Prose stiches (most chant forms)	Parallel stiches with coordinated number and assonance (early sequence)
Prose or narrative (public reading/ cantillation)	Parallel stiches with coordinated number, rhyme, and often accent (late sequence)
Ordinary speech (conversation)	Stanzas with organization of number, rhyme, and accent (hymn)

Edward Yarnold, and Paul Bradshaw (New York: Oxford University Press, 1992), 504. My tables summarize only the eleventh-century forms, and do not purport to extend further, since to do this, one would have to account for the effects of proportional rhythmic measurement on music in later periods.

78. I am using the word "stich" (from *stichos*) as a general word indicating a verse of prose or poetry, in order to reserve the word "verse" for its normal poetic and liturgical meanings.

Table 3. Melodic syntax as an organizing factor in ritual forms

WORD ⟷ MELODY

Choir chants: e.g., introit
(syllabic and neumatic chant
including proses and tropes)

Psalmody
melodic inflection

Solo chant:
e.g., gradual
(melismatic chant)

Public reading (cantillation)
(melodic punctuation)

Acclamation:
e.g., alleluia

Ordinary speech

No ritual use:
e.g., vocalize,
jubilus[79]

The two tables reveal several interesting features about the contents of the tropers and the implied relationship between music, words, and liturgy. The parts of the service which already had the most highly developed musical rhetoric (e.g., the gradual), did not attract tropes, and the prose developed into a separate item instead of being part of the alleluia.[80] Table 2 indicates that tropes and proses are among the most poetically organized forms, while table 3 shows that they were only moderately organized musically. In effect, verbal ornament was applied only where melodic ornament was not as developed, which suggests that the two were considered to have

79. The *pneuma sequentiae* at the end of the alleluia are strictly speaking not a *jubilus*, since they are a prolongation of the last syllable of the word "alleluia" rather than being a completely textless melody. They were, however, sometimes called *jubilus* because of the relative unimportance of the text.

80. Instead, the gradual and alleluia seem to have attracted even more elaborate *musical* ornament—improvised and later written polyphony. Injunctions which specify a greater number of cantors on feasts, such as those in John of Avranches' commentary (see next chapter, p. 125) imply improvised polyphony.

similar effects. Moreover, the coordination between melodic and verbal syntax was strained in the tropes, because the neumatic style of the chants, with which the tropes interacted, was in tension with the rhythmic organization of the words. The compromise style retained the associative properties of the musical syllable, but weakened the power of cadence to indicate syntax. Although the tables indicate a similar tension in proses, which have a simple musical structure (syllabic chant) and the most sophisticated poetic structure, the musical syntax was less of a problem for the poetry. The syllabic setting of proses made the music neutral, since melismas would not disrupt the rhythmic structures implied by the words; furthermore, proses were not required to cadence on structurally important notes, except at the end of major *distinctiones* that usually coincided with the end of the proses' basic unit of a double stich.

Both tropes and proses show a change of musical style as a consequence of the increasing prominence of rhythmic organization. In the tropes, the ideal was a balance between musical and verbal *ornatus*, which undermined the rhythmic organization of texts, but generated an analogy between the associative powers of music and of words. In the proses, the generally syllabic style of the music could allow an increasing development of verbal *ornatus* (especially rhyme and rhythm). For example, as was discussed above, Guido associated setting highly organized words with strictly syllabic music. He particularly recommended a method of musical improvisation where the vowels are assigned pitches and each syllable is set to the pitch of its vowel, except at major syntactical units where the music needs to make a modal cadence,[81] and considered this musical style apt for the setting of metrical poetry:

> Thus in verse (*versibus in metris*) we often see such concordant and mutually congruous lines that you wonder, as it were, at a certain harmony of language. And if music be added to this, with a similar interrelationship, you will be doubly charmed by a twofold melody.[82]

81. *Guidonis Arentini Micrologus*, ed. Smits van Waesberghe, chapter 17.

82. The prose, although not "metrical," fits this description, as do most office hymns (which are often metrical). Babb, *Hucbald, Guido, and John*, 74; Gerbert, *Scriptores ecclesiastici*, 2:19; *Guidonis Aretini Micrologus*, ed. Smits van Waesberghe, 188: "Sicut persæpe videmus tam consonos et sibimet alterutrum respondentes versus in metris, ut quamdam quasi symphoniam grammaticae admireris. Cui si

Perhaps the compromise between musical and verbal ornamental styles represented by the tropes was yet another factor in giving them a short liturgical life. By the twelfth century, neither their heightening of the associative power of both words and music, nor their use of melodic ornament in setting metrical and rhythmic poetry would have been fashionable. The former would not support the exegetical emphasis taught in cathedral schools or in the new university, and the latter would have interfered with a musical and poetic style that was further refining rhythmic organization. In contrast, the syllabically set sequences could be developed into completely organized poems, furthering the newer artistic goals.

To sum up: eleventh-century musicians considered that verbal and musical ornament achieved similar effects, and therefore they developed verbal ornament for portions of the liturgy that were not already highly developed musically. Furthermore, the use of ornament (whether musical or verbal) was associated with the theory of ornamental language taught in grammar; those parts of the liturgy that were highly ornamented were intended to be understood as being ornate language that required an intelligent interpretation. The flourishing repertories of tropes and proses represent an intentional refocusing of both monastic and cathedral communities towards the liturgy. In an age which produced no new exegetical texts, but instead shifted the goals of these institutions towards the performance of the liturgy, the tropers stand out as unique documents of exegetical sung prayer.[83]

---

musica simili responsione iungatur, duplici modulatione dupliciter delecteris."

83. Beryl Smalley, *The Study of the Bible in the Middle Ages* (Oxford: Basil Blackwell, 1983), 44-45, points out that the liturgical revival of the tenth and eleventh centuries had seemingly adversely affected biblical scholarship: "The Cluniac and other tenth-century religious reformers emphasized the liturgy at the expense of study. As the offices multiplied, *lectio divina* moved out of the cloister into the choir." As the next chapter will show, this was quite literally true, since the structure of the liturgical day at both cathedral and monastic institutions demanded a large amount of time. However, Smalley's rather gloomy assessment should be modified in the light of the evidence of the tropers, which contain new commentary developed for use within the liturgy itself.

3

LITURGY AND SCRIPTURE STUDY
Interpreting Scripture within the Liturgy

DURING the eleventh century, the liturgy became the primary focus of those monastic and cathedral institutions that renewed their adherence to a strict rule. The intense devotion to a full celebration of the daily liturgy became a principal focus for such institutions, making the liturgy's proper celebration the focus of much of the educational system, as the last two chapters have demonstrated. Thus, the liturgy became the principal locus for the interpretation, proclamation, and appropriation of scripture; it was the natural place where one practiced all of the skills taught by the *magister scholae,* and these skills were directed toward the understanding of scripture (*sacra pagina*) through liturgical action.

The centrality of the liturgy is quite evident in the many manuscripts of tropes and sequences themselves—while only a handful of formal scripture commentaries were written during this time, over two hundred manuscripts containing tropes survive. These tropers display the nature of the gains made in the Carolingian and subsequent reforms of the ninth through the eleventh centuries: in their contents, one can trace the rising literacy of clergy and monastics, the increased sophistication in Latin expression, and a renewed attention to the principals of patristic exegesis.[1] Even though the demands of the liturgy seem temporarily to have replaced the writing down of formal commentary on the scripture, the discipline of *sacra pagina* was not lost, but on the contrary was reinforced, particularly in the festal celebrations of the rite.

This chapter examines the complex ways in which the use of scripture within the liturgy helped to reinforce the techniques of exegesis and commentary learned though the study of grammar and music. The first part examines the use of scripture in the daily round (*cursus*) of the office, in order to show how

1. David Hiley gives an excellent summary of the sources for some of the most important institutions in *Western Plainchant: A Handbook* (Oxford: Clarendon Press, 1993), 563-607.

the patterns that led to the selection and presentation of scripture readings reinforced various uses of allegorical exegesis. The second part introduces traditional allegorical interpretations of the mass itself, showing how these were derived (in part) from close readings of scripture. The last part examines how the new repertories of tropes and sequences were used within the mass, showing that the aesthetic goals of the new repertories helped differentiate the relative importance of the feasts. In these celebrations the new repertories could be more easily accepted, since their greater *ornatus* was considered a fitting way to give added solemnity to the most important celebrations of an institution or of the church year. Furthermore, the addition of tropes and sequences gave these masses different proportions from ferial celebrations, mostly by expanding those sections that concentrated on the eloquent proclamation and appropriation of scripture.

The Influence of the Liturgical *Cursus* on Scripture Study: Readings for the Festival Cycles of Christmas and Easter

The attention that monks and clerics lavished on the foremass (the present Liturgy of the Word) may come as a surprise to modern interpreters, who are, perhaps, prone to make too great a distinction between the study of scripture and the celebration of the liturgy. We tend to equate scripture study with the acts of reading a book of the Bible, or with reading or writing a commentary on a biblical pericope or book. In contrast, the principal commitment of monastics and canons was the communal celebration of the office, which took up many of their waking hours.[2] For them, memorized scripture, read and sung within

2. During the eleventh century, the commitment of canons was often less then exemplary. However, the presence of a troper may be one indication that an institution held to a strict rule for its canons. Of the two hundred tropers catalogued by the Corpus Troporum only a handful can be associated with cathedral institutions with any confidence. A significant concentration of the handful of sources connected with cathedrals is in Burgundy and Provence (the Autun Troper and two tropers from Nevers and at least the later of the two tropers associated with Apt). Two other tropers from Metz and Pistoia also stem from cathedrals. In England, since cathedral chapters were often composed of monks (as at Winchester), the distinction is not tenable for these sources. According to Gagnare, *Histoire de l'église d'Autun*, 354, the Autun chapter held strictly to a common life as is shown by a document of 1014 in which a prospective canon consented to be governed by its rule.

the liturgy itself, formed a significant source for calling to mind the text of the scripture, and in order for us to discover how eleventh-century clerics and monastics interpreted any passage of scripture, its liturgical context(s) need to be taken into account. The strict celebration of the office made a specific set of interrelationships between scripture and the liturgy available to eleventh-century monastics and clerics; these relationships can readily be demonstrated by outlining the patterns of liturgical reading of scripture during the two most important cycles of the church year—those centered around the feasts of Christmas and Easter.

The selection and presentation of scripture depended upon three basic principles: (1) The quotation of scripture by New Testament writers guided the selection of mass readings, and led to the selection of specific Old Testament books to be read continuously in the office during specific seasons. (2) The whole of the Psalter was kept present in both liturgy and memory by its sequential recitation, and its use in the New Testament was highlighted by the selection of proper psalms and psalm antiphons for the days approaching major feasts. (3) The multiple perspectives of central events in the life of Christ, which were preserved in the differing gospel accounts, were placed in the closest proximity to the days on which they were commemorated.

These principles could sometimes conflict with each other. For example, the sequential reading of books might not lead to appropriate lections for a specific feast. Therefore, the pattern of public reading of scripture was quite complex and was intended to negotiate the differing patterns implied by each principle, organizing the communal reflection and prayer of the choir.[3] This resulted in: (1) a pattern emphasizing selected

3. Although there were four overlapping patterns of worship which shaped the medieval liturgy, only the seasonal pattern (emphasizing allegory) and the daily pattern (emphasizing sequential reading) had a profound impact on the selection and presentation of scripture. The four patterns are as follows: (1) the ferial cycle consisting of a daily *cursus* encompassing the several hours of the office and one or more daily masses; (2) the dominical cycle, consisting of weekly *cursus* based on the special importance of Sundays, which usually led to a moderate amount of elaboration for some of the Sunday offices and the principal Sunday mass; (3) the temporal cycle, consisting of a seasonal *cursus*, half of which was based on the fixed date of Christmas and half of which was based on the moveable date of Easter, commemorating constitutive events for the church,

books of the Bible, which were read during the daily offices and the daily and Sunday masses, and which were intended to bring out themes and patterns found in scripture believed to have a special relevance to the season; and (2) a pattern emphasizing the weekly chanting of the complete memorized Psalter, which was in turn interpreted through scriptural commentary and the selection of accompanying antiphons.

The seasonal pattern concentrated on lections which were intended to commemorate the central events in the life of Christ, and which related events, personages, and themes from the Old Testament to the New Testament.[4] In order to achieve this, a carefully structured series of readings was adopted for each season that paid attention to the quotation of the Old Testament within the New Testament, and drew on either the Old Testament passages themselves or their interpretation in the epistles. During Advent through Epiphany, the series focused on the book of Isaiah, which was interpreted as a prophecy of Christ's coming and ministry; from Septuagesima through the Easter season, the series focused on the saving acts of God in the history of Israel as types of the saving acts in Christ's life, death, and resurrection. These different uses of Old Testament scripture (inherent already in the New Testament) gave a different liturgical emphasis to each season, since the readings during the Christmas season primarily focused on proclaiming the Old Testament prophecies that had been fulfilled by Christ's coming, and the readings during the Easter season focused on making analogies between God's salvation in the past and God's salvation in Christ.

The differing scriptural emphases of the two seasons can be best demonstrated by examining the specific series of lections

---

centered on the life, death, and resurrection of Christ; (4) the sanctoral cycle, consisting of an annual *cursus* commemorating saints, based on fixed dates, and dependent upon the temporal cycle for both its structure and its themes. For a lucid summary of the basics of the church calendar in the Middle Ages, see John Harper, *The Forms and Orders of Western Liturgy from the Tenth to the Eighteenth Century: A Historical Introduction and Guide for Students and Musicians* (Oxford: Clarendon Press, 1991), 45-57. Although necessarily oversimplified (with an emphasis on English and Anglican liturgies), this is the best available introduction to the intricacies of medieval liturgy.

4. This is true even when there is no Old Testament lection, since the epistles that were chosen used quotations from the Old Testament in interpreting aspects of Jesus' life, death, and resurrection.

for each in turn. During Advent, the Sunday mass readings focused on the New Testament writers' interpretation of the book of Isaiah, by selecting four gospel lections and one epistle lection, which were organized around a verse taken from Isaiah and applied to Jesus.[5] These readings were supported and supplemented by a focus on the sequential reading of the book of Isaiah during Advent, both in the matins office, and in the daily mass, making both Isaiah's prophecies and the theme of their fulfillment in Christ especially prominent all during the Advent season.[6] The series culminated in the readings for the Christmas vigil and the Christmas masses, which included even more texts taken from Isaiah, as well as lections which applied a verse taken from Isaiah to Christ (either implicitly or explicitly) or which spoke of all messianic prophecy being fulfilled in Christ.[7]

5. The passages and the verses quoted from Isaiah were as follows: Advent I: Mt. 21:1-11 (Is. 62:11); Advent II: Rom. 15:5-13 (Is. 11:10), and Luke 21:25-33 (Is. 13:19); Advent III: Mt. 11:2-10 (Is. 35:5, and Is. 61:1); Advent IV: John 1:19-28 (Is. 40:3).

6. The variations between uses of different institutions are determined primarily by the selection of "proper" psalms for feast days, and the specific order and structure of readings at matins. However, these differences should not be so great that the general comments I make concerning the structure of the readings are called into question. I have based my comments on the *Hereford Breviary* (a cathedral use), which was collated showing variations with the *Sarum Breviary* in the Henry Bradshaw Society edition: Walter Howard Frere and Langton Brown, eds., *The Hereford Breviary*, vol. 1, Henry Bradshaw Society, no. 26 (London: Harrison & Sons, 1904).

Both matins and ferial mass cycles for Advent follow an ascending order of lections, and supplement each other, so that a very large portion of Isaiah is read during the Advent season. Isaiah in matins: 1:1-8; 2:1-9, 10-22; 3:1-3, 10-17; 4:1-6; 5:1-14; 6:1-6, 8-11; 9:1-2; 13:1-18, 19-22; 14:1-2; 43:1-12, 20-28; 44:1-7, 21-22; 40:1-2; 52:1. Isaiah in the ferial mass: 11:1-10; 25:6-10; 26:1-6; 29:17-24; 30:19-21, 23-26; 35:1-10; 40:1-11, 25-31; 41:13-20; 48:17-19; 45:6-8, 18, 21-26; 54:1-10; 7:10-14.

7. The following lections from Isaiah were read in the Christmas vigil and the three Christmas masses at Autun: Is. 62:1-5; 9:2-7; 61:1-62:12; 52:6-10. Furthermore, the following epistle and the gospel for Christmas center around quotations from Isaiah: in the Vigil, Acts 13:16-17, 22-25 (Is. 11:1); Mt. 1:1-25 (Is. 7:14); in the first mass, Luke 2:1-14 (Is. 9:6, at least by implication); in the third mass, Heb. 1:1-12, with no specific reference to Isaiah but the lection concerns Christ fulfilling all that the prophets have spoken; John 1:1-14 (Is. 9:2, at least by implication), and continuing the idea of the words of the prophets being fulfilled in the Word of God.

The Lenten mass readings displayed a different kind of organization.[8] They were constructed according to two interlocking plans: (1) a penitential cycle which related themes of fasting, penitence, and charity in the Old Testament to the same themes in the New Testament, and (2) a prefiguration cycle which related the actions of key figures from the Old Testament (e.g., Abraham, Moses, Elijah) to Jesus' ministry. The prefiguration cycle was supported by the matins office, in which sequential selections from the books of Genesis, Exodus, Jeremiah, and Lamentations were read from Septuagesima to Good Friday.[9] However, this cycle was not directly related by New Testament quotation of the Old Testament in the gospel or epistle lessons of the mass. Part of the reason for this is that many of the gospel lections were taken from the gospel of John, which tends not to use direct quotation of the Old Testament, even though it exploits typological themes.[10] Even during Holy Week, direct quotation between the Old Testament lection and the gospel was exploited only once, and this did not undergird the typological interpretation of material from Genesis or Exodus.[11] Nevertheless, during the Easter Octave, all of the epistle readings and the gospel reading for Feria II and III either related the saving acts of God in the Old Testament to the resurrection, or quoted the passages from the Psalms and Isaiah, which were interpreted as relating to the salvation of Christ.[12]

8. For a very good summary of the intricacies of these lections, see F. Cabrol, H. Leclercq, and H. Marrou, eds., *Dictionnaire d'archéologie chrétienne et de liturgie* (Paris, 1907-53), s.v. "Épitres," and "Évangiles," by G. Godu.

9. The Lenten lections show a continual structure in matins, but not in the ferial mass, which follows the organization of the Sunday mass lections; these were thematically arranged during the first half of Lent and typologically arranged during the second half.

10. On the other hand, the gospel of John consistently portrays Christ as the new Moses, and emphasizes that Christ replaces various Old Testament institutions and feasts; see John 2:13-22; 3:14-15; 4:21-26; 5:16-47; 6:25-71; 7:14-52; 10:22-39.

11. The significant exception is on Wednesday of Holy Week, when Is. 53:1-12 and the passion according to Luke are coordinated, presumably because of the quotation of part of Is. 53:12 in Luke 22:37.

12. The readings for Feria II (Acts 10:43, Luke 24:13-35) give the primary hermeneutic principles: all the prophets bear witness to Christ, and the risen Christ teaches the disciples what the scripture says concerning him. The other relevant readings are Acts 13:16-33; Luke 24:36-47; Acts 3:12-19; 8:26-40; 1 Peter 3:18-22; 2:1-10; 1 John 5:4-10.

Although the lections for the Christmas and Easter cycles were organized with two different emphases, this does not imply that there was a fundamental difference in the interpretation of each feast. In the New Testament itself, the quotation and interpretation of the Psalter bridged the gap between these two differing patterns, bringing out the typological relationships for Christmas and the prophetic relationships for Easter; for example, certain psalms that were applied to the Christmas message were interpreted as expressing a typological relationship between David and Christ (see especially the quotation of enthronement psalms, e.g., Psalms 2, 44, etc., in Heb. 1:1-12), while other psalms were read as prophecies of Christ's passion and resurrection (see the use of Psalm 21 in Mt. 27:35, 39, 43, and 46, and the numerous quotations of Psalm 117 in Mt. 21:42; Luke 20:17; Acts 4:11; Rom. 9:33; 1 Peter 2:7).[13]

In the liturgy, the weekly sequential recitation of the entire Psalter was the most prominent feature of the offices.[14] The integrity of each psalm was respected, since (ordinarily) each psalm was chanted straight through, allowing for its own thematic development.[15] However, the liturgy shaped the use of the Psalter in two important ways, which helped reinforce the prophetic and typological interpretations. First, each psalm was prefaced by an antiphon, which was not intended to suppress the psalm's literal meaning, but rather to create a parallel structure applicable to the season.[16] For example, both

---

13. Additionally, a number of passages from Isaiah and the minor prophets were also interpreted as prophecies of the passion and resurrection by the New Testament writers.

14. The psalms would be chanted (more or less in numerical order) each week, and the typical distribution of psalms for the cathedral offices shows the influence of both daily and weekly worship patterns, following their numerical order in the matins and vespers services (with approximately the first two-thirds of the Psalter distributed amongst the weekly matins services, and the last third distributed amongst the vespers services) and a pattern based on psalms appropriate to certain times of the day at the other hours. The numerically arranged psalms were seldom repeated at any other services, while many of the others were said every day. Books were read over the course of a season; e.g., from Advent to Epiphany, or from Septuagesima to Good Friday.

15. By the eleventh century it was customary for each half of the choir to chant alternate verses.

16. The double structure undergirds all of Augustine's influential psalm commentary, which applied many psalms both to the "Head," Christ, and to the "Body," any faithful member of the church. (This is one of the rules of Ticonius

Christmas and Good Friday matins began the first nocturn with Psalm 2 ("Why have the Gentiles raged?"); the former took its antiphon from the seventh verse ("You are my son; Today I have begotten you"); and the latter took its antiphon from the second verse ("The kings of the earth stood up, and the princes met together, against the Lord, and against his Christ").[17] Each of these antiphons has a specific New Testament warrant, which connected this psalm equally well to both seasons: Psalm 2:7 was quoted by the author of Hebrews (Heb. 1:5) in the context of explaining the fulfillment of God's speaking through the prophets in Jesus. Psalm 2:2 was given the following explanation in Acts 4:27-28: "For truly they assembled together in this city against your holy child Jesus (whom you had anointed), Herod and Pontius Pilate, with the Gentiles and the people of Israel, To do what your hand and your counsel decreed to be done." This makes a clear reference to the passion, as well as providing another connection (although fortuitous) with the Christmas narrative.[18] The second way that typological and prophetic interpretations of the psalms were supported was through their special arrangement: at the culmination of the two principal seasons, the psalmody for Christmas, Good Friday, and Holy Saturday matins interrupted the pattern of sequential reading to give prominence to psalms that were either particularly heavily quoted in the New Testament, or considered especially applicable to the season.[19] These series of

that Augustine included in *De doctrina christiana*; see chapter 1, pp. 30-31, above.)

17. Psalm 2:7b: "Filius meus es tu; Ego hodie genui te"; Psalm 2:2: "Astiterunt reges terrae. Et principes convenerunt in unum. Adversus Dominum, et adversus Christum eius."

18. The Christmas connection was with Herod the Great, "who in persecuting the Lord murdered the innocents" (Cassiodorus, *Expositio psalmorum*, 42; *Cassiodorus: Explanation of the Psalms*, 59). The connection stems from (1) the Vulgate reading *puer* for παις which could be translated either "child" or "servant," and (2) the fact that both King Herod and his grandson had the same name.

Incidentally, because of the authority of this passage from Acts, Bede used Psalm 2:2 as a specialized example of the scheme *syllepsis* (nonagreement of number), pointing out that the psalmist used the plural "Kings" and "Princes" to refer to the singular "Herod" and "Pilate." Although Bede discussed this transference of meaning as a scheme, it is actually created by the linguistic trope of historical allegory.

19. Even so, some continuity with *lectio continua* was maintained, since the psalms were arranged so that they would be chanted in ascending numerical or-

psalms demonstrate how the principles of interpreting the psalms in the New Testament had been extended to the whole of the Psalter: the Christmas series features enthronement psalms, most of which have direct New Testament warrant, and supplements this with psalms stressing the theme of God's presence to creation, which were interpreted as prophecies of Christ; the Good Friday series consists almost entirely of psalms dealing with persecution and suffering, many of which were quoted in the various passion accounts; the Holy Saturday series stresses psalms which were not directly quoted, but which bring out the themes of God's promises of delivery and judgment. Clerics and monastics were thoroughly adept in reading the whole Psalter as containing prophesy and typology concerning Christ and the Church, but for us, it is often necessary to consult a contemporary psalm commentary to understand the specific connections they inferred from the use of a psalm verse in any given liturgical context.[20]

---

der: proper psalms for Christmas matins: Psalms 2, 18, 44, 47, 71, 84, 88, 95, 97; for Good Friday matins: Psalms 2, 21, 26, 37, 39, 53, 58, 87, 93; for Holy Saturday matins: Psalms 4, 14, 15, 23, 26, 29, 53, 75, 87. For the complete texts and music of these three services, see *Liber Usualis*, 368-92; 688-712; 752-73.

20. As pointed out in chapter 1 (pp. 16-17), since the book of Psalms was the first book of scripture memorized by novice monks or clerics, it became the introductory book for studying detailed exegesis. Commentaries can often explain the rationale behind the use of a psalm in a specific liturgical setting, or the selection of an antiphon; one of them, which was compiled during the first half of the eleventh century by Bruno of Würzburg (ep. 1034-45) is particularly useful, since it was compiled to help explain the psalms as they were ordinarily encountered in the liturgy itself. The work (Bruno of Würzburg, *Expositio psalmorum,* in Patrologiae latina, 142: 49-530) is a pastiche assembled from the influential commentaries of Jerome, Augustine, Cassiodorus, and Bede. However, Bruno divided the verses in a manner that corresponds with the typical divisions of the liturgical psalter, which suggests that the work was probably written for the canons, and for the cathedral school. Thus, it represents a minimal "common" knowledge of a choir in a secular cathedral in the eleventh century.

Of course, these traditional interpretations were available in many other works; for example, the cathedral library at Autun may have had a copy of Augustine's *Ennarationes in Psalmos* during the eleventh century, and Walter of Autun (ep. 978-1018) gave a copy of Gregory's *Moralia in Iob* to the cathedral during his tenure. Although Gregory's *Moralia in Iob* is not a psalm commentary, it is so wide-ranging that it serves as a commentary on the whole Bible. In the modern edition, six closely-written pages list over 660 references to psalm verses; see Gregory the Great, *Moralia in Iob,* ed. M. Adriaen, Corpus Christianorum series latina (Turnhout: Brepols, 1979), 143: 1837-44. See the introduction above, pp. 3-4, for a list of commentaries known to be in the Autun library in the eleventh century.

The third principle governing the selection and presentation of scripture in the liturgy was that of preserving the multiple perspectives of the same event narrated by the four gospels. This primarily influenced the days immediately preceding or following a major feast. For example, during Holy Week three passion accounts (Matthew, Luke, and John) were read in their entirety; Mark was left out, presumably because Luke and Matthew include the whole text of his account between them. Similarly, the lections for Christmas to Epiphany, and the Easter Vigil through its Octave, were selected in order to be as comprehensive as possible, which helped keep the full range of scripture's narrative and imagery connected to the liturgical celebration of each feast. As table 4 shows, the Christmas lections tended to tell a continuous narrative of the infancy of Christ; this was tied together by a theology of incarnation from the prologue to John's gospel, which was given the most important place on Christmas day. In contrast, table 5 indicates that although the Easter lections have some relationship to a continuous narrative, they are not always in chronological order, and the sparsest account is given the most important liturgical place.

Table 4. Gospel lections for the Christmas season

Feast	Lection	Topic
Christmas Vigil	Mt. 1:1-25	Generations and Birth of Jesus
First mass	Luke 2:1-14	Annunciation to shepherds
Second mass	Luke 2:15-20	Birth of Jesus
Third mass	John 1:1-14	Word made flesh
Innocents	Mt. 2:13-23	Flight into Egypt; the Innocents
Christmas Octave	Luke 2:21-32	Circumcision
First Sunday after Christmas	Luke 2:33-52	Simeon's prophecy, and the boy Jesus in the Temple
Epiphany Vigil	Mt. 2:19-23	Death of Herod; Return to Nazareth
Epiphany	Mt. 2:1-12	Magi

Table 5. Gospel lections for the Easter Octave

Feast	Lection	Topic
Easter Vigil	Mt. 28:1-7	Spice-bearing Women
Easter Day	Mark 16:1-7	Spice-bearing Women
Feria II	Luke 24:13-35	Emmaus
Feria III	Luke 24:36-47	Appearance to the Apostles
Feria IV	John 21:1-14	Appearance to the Disciples
Feria V	John 20:11-18	Appearance to Mary Magdalene
Feria VI	Mt. 28:16-20	Appearances in Galilee
Sabbato	John 20:19-23	Appearance to Disciples without Thomas
Easter Octave	John 20:23-31	Appearance to Disciples with Thomas

The Interpretation of the Liturgy: Mass Commentaries, Tropes, and Proses

The same types of allegorical exegesis that shaped the selection and presentation of scripture lections also shaped the gregorian repertory of mass songs themselves.[21] In the ninth century, when the Carolingian reforms imposed the Roman rite on the Frankish church, a new genre of commentary arose, which discussed the allegorical meaning of the scripture passages that had inspired the songs of the rite and which helped liturgical commentators discuss the meaning and purpose of the rite itself. The most influential commentator was Amalar of Metz, a student of Alcuin's and prominent figure in the reforms.[22] His

21. A detailed discussion of selected mass songs follows in chapter 4.

22. See Josef Jungmann, *The Mass of the Roman Rite*, 2 vols., trans. Francis A. Brunner (New York: Benziger Brothers, 1951-55), 1:89-91, and Allen Cabaniss, *Amalarius of Metz* (Amsterdam: North Holland Publishing Company, 1954), 43-106, for the influence of Amalar's commentaries. Fassler, *Gothic Song*, 18-37, gives a helpful introduction to the use of commentaries for musicologists with an emphasis on studying the shifts in attitude that point to liturgical change. My purpose here is to call attention to the traditional allegories made by commentators that help in interpreting both the old and the new repertories of mass chants.

methods of interpretation clearly stem from the same grammatical and exegetical lore that later inspired the repertories of tropes and proses. Amalar's works have extensive quotes from exegetical works of Augustine, Isidore, and Bede, and he shows familiarity with the works of Ambrose, Jerome, and many others.[23] As the summary of his shorter commentary shows, Amalar considered that both the texts and the actions of the mass should be interpreted as figures (tropes) that point to the mysteries revealed by scripture:

> The things we celebrate in the mass up to the gospel reading allude to the time of the Lord's first advent up to the time when he was hastening to Jerusalem to die. The *introit* alludes to the choir of the Prophets [who announce the advent of Christ just as the singers announce the advent of the bishop] . . . ; the *kyrie eleison* alludes to the Prophets at the time of Christ's coming, Zachary and his son John among them; the *gloria in excelsis Deo* points to the throng of angels who proclaimed to the shepherds the joyous tidings of our Lord's birth [and indeed in this manner, that first one spoke and the others joined in, just as in the mass the bishop intones and the whole church joins in]; the *prima collecta* refers to what our Lord did in his twelfth year . . . ; the epistle alludes to the preaching of John, the *responsorium*[24] to the readiness of the Apostles when our Lord called them and they followed him; the alleluia to their joy of heart when they heard his promises or saw the miracles wrought by him or else by his name; the gospel to his preaching. . . . The rest of what happens in the mass refers to the time from the Sunday when the children greeted him up to his Ascension or to Pentecost. The prayer which the priest says from the *secreta* to *Nobis quoque peccatoribus* signifies the prayer of Jesus on Mount Olivet. What occurs later signifies the time during which Christ lay in the grave. When the bread is immersed in the wine, this means the return of Christ's soul to his body. The next action signifies the greetings offered by Christ to his Apostles. And the breaking of the offerings signifies the breaking of bread performed by the Lord before the two at Emmaus.[25]

---

23. Cabaniss, *Amalarius of Metz*, 15.

24. By Amalar's day, the responsorium was more or less identical to the gradual, although it is possible that the responsorium included repetitions of the antiphon, and additional psalm verses.

25. The translation is based on the one by Jungmann, corrected and slightly expanded from Hanssens' edition; see *Roman Rite*, 1:89. Jungmann also supplied the clarifying summaries from the full chapters in the work (given in square brackets in the translation only). "Quae celebramus in officio missae usque lectum evangelium, respicientia sunt ad primum adventum Domini usque ad illud

Jungmann characterizes this kind of allegory as predominantly rememorative (equivalent to Bede's "historical" allegory); it is principally concerned with relating elements of the present celebration to events of salvation history.[26] While this emphasis is apparent, Amalar's commentaries use the full array of medieval exegesis: Amalar makes remarks about the origins of various texts and practices (literal interpretation); shows a concern with relating the Old Testament to the New (allegorical interpretation); suggests what responses various parts of the liturgy ought to call forth (tropological interpretation); and relates elements of the present celebration to the eschaton (anagogical interpretation).

Amalar's focus on rememorative allegory is not so much a result of his exegetical methods, but rather a result of the fact that he, in contrast to some of his contemporaries, believed that not only the words, but also the actions of the liturgy deserved extensive allegorical treatment. While the practice of interpreting liturgical action allegorically was not new with Amalar, his thoroughness and his propensity to make up his own interpretations that had no patristic warrant caused great controversy.[27] Amalar's main adversaries were based in

tempus quando properabat Hierusalem passurus. Introitus vero ad chorum prophetarum respicit . . . ; *Kyrie eleison* ad eos prophetas respicit, qui circa adventum Domini erant; de quibus erat Zacharias, necnon et filius eius Iohannes; *Gloria in excelsis Deo* ad coetum angelorum respicit, qui gaudium nativitatis Domini pastoribus adnuntiaverunt; Prima collecta ad hoc respicit quod Dominus agebat circa duodecimum annum . . . ; Epistola ad praedicationem Iohannis pertinet; Responsorium ad benevolentiam apostolorum, quando vocati a Domino et secuti sunt; *Alleluia* ad laetitiam mentis eorum, quam habebant de promissionibus ejus, vel de miraculis quae videbant fieri ab eo, sive per nomen ejus; Evangelium ad suam praedicationem. . . . Deinceps vero quod agitur in officio missae, ad illud tempus respicit, quod est a Dominica, quando pueri obviaverunt ei, usque ad ascensionem ejus sive pentecosten. Oratio vero quam presbiter dicit a secreta usque *Nobis quoquo peccatoribus*, hanc orationem designat quam Iesus exercebat in monte Oliveti. Et illud quod postea agitur, illud tempus significat, quando Dominus in sepulchro iacuit. Et quando panis mittitur in vinum, animam Domini ad corpus redire demonstrat. Et quod postea celebratur, significat illas salutationes quas Christus fecit discipulis suis. Et fractio oblatarum illam fractionem significat quam Dominus duobus fecit discipulis in Emmaus" (Amalar, *Eclogae de ordine romano*, ed. Jean-Michael Hanssens, *Amalarii episcopi opera liturgica omnia*, Studi e testi, 138-40 [Vatican City: Biblioteca Apostolica Vaticana, 1948-50], 3:229-31.)

26. Jungmann, *Roman Rite*, 1: 89-90.

27. There is, of course, a close connection with any notion of sacramentality and allegory—for example, the actions of the eucharist are intended to represent

Lyons;[28] the most effective of these was the deacon Florus, who not only wrote numerous works attacking Amalar's writings, but also contributed a lengthy commentary of his own. As the following excerpt shows, Florus' objections were to Amalar's innovations, not to the methods of medieval exegesis (in fact he faults Amalar for his imperfect knowledge of *De doctrina christiana*):

> Now, concerning the sacred vestments of the priests and ministers, the vessels of the holy mysteries, the tablets of the cantors, the bells, the colors and kinds of clothing and sandals, the sacred offices, and the distribution of the psalms, he has something unsuitable, foolish, and ridiculous to say, as if it had been given to him alone (after the law and the prophets, and after the gospels and the apostles) to establish archetypal and mystical things in the church, so that anyone who presumes to celebrate anything with simple and customary practice would be deemed a falsifier of the mysteries. He says he follows the authority of Saint Augustine in such imaginative fantasies. . . . But he does not consider (being entirely blinded by a lust for novelty) the things transmitted by him [Augustine] concerning the investigation of meaning in the Holy Scriptures.[29]

Christ to the assembly (allegory), but Christ has also promised to be present through them (sacrament).

28. See Cabaniss, *Amalarius of Metz*, 79-93, for a good summary of the political and theological controversies. As Cabaniss points out, much of the controversy was political rather than strictly theological: Lothair, the eldest son of Louis the Pious, had fled to Italy in disgrace after an ill-fated rebellion; one of Lothair's most ardent supporters had been the archbishop of Lyons, Agobard, who thought it prudent to join Lothair in exile. Amalar, appointed by Louis to fill Agobard's job, found that the clerics were loyal to Agobard. Not only did Agobard write works from exile condemning various of Amalar's positions, but even in Lyons, one of Agobard's deacons, Florus, wrote numerous works attacking Amalar's commentaries, and was instrumental in bringing charges of heresy in 838.

29. "Jam de sacerdotum et ministroum sacris vestibus, de vasis divini ministerii, de cantorum tabulis, de signis aereis, de ipsis etiam indumentorum et calceamentorum fimbriis, coloribus et speciebus, de officiis quoque sacris, et psalmorum distributionibus, quam inepta et fatua et omni risu digna contingit, quasi ei soli licuerit post legem et prophetas, post Evangelia et apostolos, res typicas et mysticas in Ecclesia statuere, ita ut mysteriorum ejus praevaricator habeatur, qui usu et consuetudine simplici aliud quid celebrare praesumpserit. Cicit se in talium phantasiarum adinventionibus sancti Augustini auctoritatem sequi. . . . Nec considerat, nimia novitatum cupiditate caecatus, haec illum de sacrarum Scriptuarum indagandis sensibus tradidisse" (Florus of Lyons, *Opuscula adversus Amalarium*, in Patrologiae latina, 119:75).

Although Florus was successful in having six propositions from Amalar's writings condemned at the Synod of Quiercy in 838, as early as 853 all of Amalar's liturgical writings were again in widespread use, and they remained influential throughout the Middle Ages.[30] For example, most of the interpretive remarks in John of Avranches' *ordo* (dating from ca. 1060) can be traced to Amalar, and an important commentary by Jean Beleth (dating from 1165) contains over two hundred substantial quotations from Amalar.[31] One of the reasons for this is that Amalar always tried to find a scriptural passage from which he fashioned his allegories: in fact all of Amalar's allegories are some form of "historical" allegory that either relates the Old Testament to the New, or relates passages from scripture to the present celebration of the mass.

So far as supplying a context for tropes and proses is concerned, what is most striking about Amalar's summary is his division between the liturgy of the word and the liturgy of the eucharist. Amalar states that the whole of the mass makes two historical allegories: the time of the prophets until the time of Christ's preaching is recalled through the liturgy of the word and the time from Holy Week through Pentecost is recalled through the liturgy of the eucharist. It is important to note that the allegories are not made haphazardly, but stem from a knowledge of the types of texts which were used in the (still newly inherited) Roman rite, which had occasioned the commentary. Although Amalar's propensity to make allegories of the most minute details of the mass provoked controversy even in his own day, his opponents attacked only those aspects of his commentary that had no clear scriptural basis.[32] Most of his comments would have been generally accepted, and did reflect

30. However, one may conjecture that the school of Lyons remained conservative in adopting allegories for mass actions that were not well-attested in either scripture or patristic tradition, and this may be of great importance in explaining why a few institutions (notably Cluny) seem never to have used tropes extensively.

31. See Johan Beleth, *Iohannis Beleth Summa de Ecclessiasticis Officis*, ed. Herbert Douteil, Corpus Christianorum Continuatio Mediaevalis (Turnhout: Brepols, 1976), 41:345-46.

32. Florus' own commentary, *De expositione missae*, in Patrologiae latina, 119:15-72, is a careful and scholarly compilation of the scriptural texts that form the basis of the mass ordinary, with extensive interpretations of the same texts compiled from Cyprian, Ambrose, Augustine, Jerome, Gregory, Fulgentius, Severianus, Vigilius, Isidore, and Bede.

the common interpretation of the rite, based upon allegorical exegesis. For example, at a textual level, the introit evokes the prophets first and foremost because most of the introit texts are taken from the prophetic books of scripture.[33] The kyrie reminds Amalar of Zechariah because of his canticle (Luke 1:68-79) sung at lauds every day, which treats themes related to the kyrie stating that God "has raised up a mighty savior" and has "promised to show mercy." (Similarly, the kyrie evokes John the Baptist because it was John's task to "give people knowledge of salvation by the forgiveness of sins," and it was John's task in both scripture and iconography to point to the Lamb of God, who takes away the sins of the world.) The gloria text itself could be considered a trope to the angel's song at the birth of Jesus, and Amalar's responsorium consisted of texts chosen from psalms that were traditionally interpreted as having an allegorical relationship to the proper feast.[34] His comments on the alleluia are first of all a response to the text (or more precisely the lack of text and abundance of music), which invokes angelic praise of Christ (see Rev. 19), and is therefore fittingly related to both Christ's promises and miracles.[35] Finally, Amalar's comments on the relationship of the gospel both to Christ's preaching and to the preaching of Christ is a commonplace even today.[36] In contrast, Amalar's allegories for the liturgy of the eucharist are principally occasioned by liturgical action rather than text; the secret was said silently, and it is the action of prayer that occasions the comment rather than the content of the text. The rest of Amalar's comments are

33. In the Middle Ages (and roughly until modern times) the book of Psalms was considered a book of prophecy. David was considered a particularly effective prefigurement of Christ, since he was pastor (shepherd), prophet, priest, and king.

34. See James McKinnon's "The Fourth-Century Origin of the Gradual," *Early Music History* 7, ed. Iain Fenlon (Cambridge: Cambridge University Press, 1987), 105-6, where he discusses the relationship between the gradual psalm and the creation of mass lectionaries.

35. Fassler, *Gothic Song*, 30-57, thoroughly establishes the relationship between alleluia commentary and the early *pneuma sequentiae* and proses. The theme of the alleluia as "angelic praise" stems from the book of Revelation, chapter 19, where it forms the refrain to an epithalamium (marriage song) of the lamb.

36. The one interpretation within Amalar's introductory remarks on the liturgy of the word that did not have a specific textual significance was the idea that the first collect alluded to Christ's first public appearance at the age of twelve. Interestingly, this interpretation seems not to have been taken up by subsequent commentators.

clearly occasioned by specific actions rather than texts, but other commentators, such as Florus, wrote extensively about the texts of the liturgy of the eucharist (including the sanctus and the agnus dei), locating their scriptural models and summarizing their traditional interpretations.[37]

In short, the context given to tropes and sequences through standard interpretations of the liturgy reinforce their relationship to grammatical and rhetorical training: (1) Tropes and sequences are more closely related to the full range of techniques of exegesis, since they are occasioned textually; i.e., "allegory" is not first and foremost imposed on a text, but rather it is used as a tool to make sense of the metaphors which arise from the text. (2) Tropes are likely to attract historical and/or moral allegory, since the texts that they exegete are taken from the prophetic books of the Old Testament. (3) Tropes tend to support interpretations of the liturgy where the actions of the liturgy are interpreted allegorically—making a connection between the liturgy and the present assembly. (4) Ordinary chants attract historical allegory particularly when they occur in a feast that alludes to their scriptural texts. (5) Proses are likely to attract anagogical allegory, since the text that they exegete is the alleluia, which is identified with angelic praise. (6) Moreover, since proses are transitions from the alleluia to the gospel, they are also clearly tied to techniques of preaching and are prone to be changed or replaced as understandings of the function of preaching changes.[38]

Liturgical *Sollemnitas* and *Ornatus*: Tropes, Proses, and *Ordines*

Since tropes and proses extended the types of verbal and musical ornamentation that were already present in the liturgy, it is in some sense tautological to say that tropes and sequences are additions to festal mass liturgies.[39] Indeed, during the eleventh

37. See Florus, *De expositione missae*, in Patrologiae latina, 119:34-43, and 71-72. The traditional interpretations are discussed in the following chapter.

38. For this reason, an examination of the new rhetorical genre of "arts of preaching" (the *ars praedicandi*) in the twelfth century may have great relevance in further understanding the development of late sequences.

39. Van Deusen makes this point in *The Harp and the Soul*, 186. See also Costa, *Tropes et séquences*, for the work which established the connections between tropes and festal liturgies.

century, at a major monastery or cathedral, it would have been unusual for a festival to lack these songs. However, a close correspondence can be found between the liturgical rank of a feast and the number of items that a festal liturgy would contain. By comparing eleventh-century liturgical commentaries that were intended to regulate the celebrations of specific institutions (*ordines*), such as that by John of Avranches,[40] with the contents of the tropers themselves, one can establish that the use of tropes and proses was indeed linked to the solemnity of the day, and that they helped create a hierarchy of festal celebrations. This suggests that the more important feasts would have greater musical and poetic *ornatus*. The tropers reveal a much fuller version of what mass commentaries and *ordines* summarize, and therefore tropers reveal subtler distinctions that are not brought to the fore in commentary. On the other hand, the more general information of the commentaries is important because commentaries give information both about how the ritual was to be enacted, and also about its interpretation. Particularly helpful are the distinctions that John makes between the daily mass and festal masses. His description of the daily (ferial) mass gives a simple order of service that can then be compared with the festal elaborations in both his commentary and in the tropers themselves. Furthermore, John's commentary identifies many ritual actions and their festal elabo-

---

40. John of Avranches, *Liber de officiis ecclesiasticis*, in Patrologiae latina, 147:27-62; see also the extensive editorial notes in ibid., 63-116. John of Avranches' commentary has the structure of an *ordo*, in which he first describes the entire daily round of services, both office and mass. The second part of the commentary focuses on exceptions to the daily pattern, and the third and fourth parts give specific instructions for feasts within the Christmas and Easter cycles respectively.

John became Bishop of Avranches (Normandy) in 1061 and later became Archbishop of Rouen in 1069; his commentary was most likely written between 1061 and 1067, when Mabilius (John's addressee) was at Rouen. The introduction to his commentary clearly indicates that his motivation in writing it was to renew the liturgical life of both his canons and the clerics in the archdiocese, and he directed the commentary both to Mabilius, the Archbishop of Rouen, and to his own chapter (ibid., 27-28).

Other important eleventh-century *ordines* stem from Cluny; see especially Ulrich of Zell, *Consuetudines cluniances*, in Patrologiae latina, 149:633-778. While the Cluniac sources confirm the general trend of celebrating feasts with more elaborate music and words, they do not seem to have used proper tropes; see David Hiley, "Cluny, Sequences and Tropes," in Claudio Leonardi and Enrico Menesto, eds., *La tradizione dei tropi liturgici* (Spoleto, 1990), 125-38.

ration, helping one to determine what actions may have accompanied the additional texts and music of a troper.

According to John's commentary, the principal means of distinguishing the festal mass from its daily celebration is the creation of a greater *sollemnitas* through the expansion and elaboration of the rite. For example, John specifies that the deacon and subdeacon wear chasubles on ferial days, but at feasts the deacon wears a dalmatic and the subdeacon wears a tunicle.[41] This has the effect of helping to distinguish and highlight their particular offices, as well as providing variety in the ornamental vesture. Even the ringing of the bells is to be done more festively: "At Prime, on ferial days let two bells be rung, on feast days all."[42]

The tendency towards liturgical fullness reaches its amplest expression in the elaboration of the chants, which on the more important feasts were to be celebrated "festively" with *laudes* (most likely a technical term for gloria tropes) and sequences.[43] Because of the prominence given the expanded mass songs, John pays special attention to the role of the cantor, which was made liturgically more significant during feasts in the following ways. First, on festive days, the cantors of the gradual and alleluia were to sing from the pulpit, rather than from its steps.[44] Second, additional cantors were required for special feasts: whereas on normal days the two acolytes, who doubled as lucifer and thurifer, would have sung the gradual and alleluia respectively,[45] at all feasts (including Sundays) there were to be two cantors for each of these chants.[46] Third,

41. John of Avranches, *Liber de officiis ecclesiasticis,* in Patrologiae latina, 147:38.

42. "In Primis in ferialibus diebus duæ campanæ pulsentur, in festis omnes" (ibid., 32).

43. For example Christmas is to be celebrated "cum laudibus et sequentia" (ibid., 41), and the Invention of the Cross, "cum laudibus et sequentia festive celebretur" (ibid., 57). Similar language is used to describe the feasts of the Ascension (ibid., 57), Pentecost (ibid., 58), all feasts of Mary (ibid., 60), and many other saints' feasts (ibid., 61). For the use of *laudes* to designate tropes (especially gloria tropes), see chapter 1, pp. 11-12, above.

44. "Cantores gradualis et *Alleluia,* in festivis diebus in pulpitum ascendant" (John of Avranches, *De officiis ecclesiasticis,* in Patrologiae latina, 147:34).

45. "Duo acolyti, unus qui cantet graduale, et deferat candelabrum; alter qui *Alleluia,* et ferat thuribulum" (ibid., 3).

46. "In omnibus festis induantur duo ceroferarii. Graduale, *Alleluia,* vel tractum bini et bini cantabunt clerici" (ibid., 38; see also ibid., 62, for Sundays). One assumes that one of the additional cantors carried the extra candle. All four cantors take part in the invitiatory of the office; see ibid., 40, 53.

the cantor takes the place of the acolyte at the offertory during feasts; John's explanation of this third point is worth quoting in full, since it not only confirms the prominence of the mass songs at feasts, but also suggests that its effect on the people was both positive and popular:

> At feasts, the cantor gives the water covered with a linen cloth to the deacon, which the deacon mixes with wine: for by the sweet music [*modulatione*] of the cantor, the people are inflamed with pious devotion and divine love, and thus run to the Lord, and one body in Christ is made. By the wine, Christ [is signified]; by the water, the people; by the linen covering the water, the labor of singing [*modulationis*] of the cantors, through which the people are freed from their private thoughts: for by weaving labor is expressed. The water mixed with wine [signifies] the people joined with Christ; the wine without the water is Christ, the water without the wine, the people without Christ. On other days, let the acolyte serve it.[47]

As John's interpretation of the melisma of the alleluia suggests, it was not necessary for the people to understand the words: "The notes of the *sequentia* which are sung after the alleluia signify praise in eternal glory, where the pronouncing of words will no longer be necessary, but always and only pure and intent contemplation of God."[48] John even describes the cantor's

47. "Cantor aquam linteo coopertam in festis diacono deferat, quam diaconus vino misceat: dulci enim cantoris modulatione, populus pia devotione et divine amore accenditur, et sic ad Dominum currit, et unum corpus in Christo efficitur. Pervinum Christus, per aquam populus, per linteum cooperturam aquae labor modulationis cantoris, quo liberatur populus a cogitationum pravitate: lino enim labor exprimitur. Aqua mista vino, populus adunatus Christo; vinum sine aqua Christus est; aqua sine vino, populus sine Christo. Aliis diebus ministret eam acolythus" (ibid., 35). Although much of this passage is derived from patristic commentaries, it is remarkable in concentrating entirely on the positive musical effects, which would be accessible to people who could not understand Latin. For a more classical viewpoint, see Augustine's *Confessiones,* bk. 10, chap. 31, pars. 49-50, in Corpus Christianorum series latina, no. 27, ed. Martinus Skutella and Lucas Verheijen (Turnhout: Brepols, 1981), 27:181-82, in which Augustine (reluctantly) stated that singing in church should be allowed, since "by the pleasure of hearing, the weaker soul might be elevated to an attitude of devotion." However, he also makes clear that the "thing which is sung" (i.e., scripture) ought to be the cause of the devotion rather than the song itself.

48. "Pneuma sequentiae, quod post *Alleluia* cantatur, laudem aeternae gloriae significat, ubi nulla erit necessaria verborum locutio, sed sola pura, et in Deo semper intenta cogitatio" (John of Avranches, *De officiis ecclesiasticis,* in Patrologiae latina, 147:34). This passage does not refer to the prose (sequence

book, giving it a symbolic meaning: "By the bone [ivory] tablets, which cantors hold in their hands, steadfastness of strong good works is designated, with which (steadfastness) it is proper to engage deeply in divine praises."[49]

Variations among Festal Liturgies

Although John of Avranches' commentary demonstrates that feasts required musical and textual elaboration, the tropers themselves supply more precise information regarding the variations such liturgical elaboration could take. These variations create a hierarchy that not only distinguishes feasts from feria, but also helps rank the feasts themselves. For example, at Autun each feast varied in the choice and number of chants that were expanded or added. Furthermore, each item was expanded a different amount depending on the feast—a gloria might have as few as five and as many as eighteen trope elements added, or an introit could include tropes for up to four repetitions of the antiphon.

Table 6 below demonstrates how such variations could create an increasing degree of elaboration.

---

with a text) but to the more ancient practice of adding a melisma on the final vowel of "alleluia," which could be considered to be pure music, without words.

49. "Per tabulas osseas, quas cantores tenent in manibus, fortis bonorum operum perseverantia, qua divinis opertet inhaerere laudibus, designatur" (ibid., 34). This description dates back to Amalar's commentary of ca. 820, and the term *tabulae* is often taken to mean the *cantatorium,* which would have contained the gradual and alleluia, which were soloists' songs. However, even for Amalar, the term *tabulae* could not refer to an ordinary *cantatorium,* since he himself states that these songs were included in the normal mass antiphonary; see Amalar, *Liber officialis,* book 3, chapter 16 "De tabulis," in *Amalarii episcopi opera liturgica omnia,* ed. Hanssens, 2:303-4, and Amalar, *Prologus antiphonarii a se compositi* in *Amalarii episcopi opera liturgica omnia,* ed. Hanssens, 1:361-63. Most likely, the *cantatorium* took on new life as the troper-proser, making it possible to retain the interpretation of the ivory covers symbolizing the good works of praise. For example, at Autun, the Troper (whose ivory cover certainly fits the description) would have been prominently displayed at the point of the rite which John is describing in this passage (just after the alleluia), especially if the cantor sang from the pulpit on feast days.

Table 6. Variations in elaboration of medieval masses[50]

Ferial mass	Festal mass 1	Festal mass 2	Festal mass 3
			Processional antiphon
	Liturgy of the Word		
Introit	**Introit (1-3)**	**Introit (3-9)**	**Introit (9-23)**
Kyrie	Kyrie	**Kyrie**	**Kyrie**
(Gloria)	**Gloria (5-12)**	**Gloria (7-13)**	**Gloria (9-18)**
Oratio	Oratio	Oratio	Oratio
			Laudes regiae
Epistle	Epistle	Epistle	Epistle
Gradual or (Alleluia)	Gradual or (Alleluia)	Gradual or (Alleluia)	Gradual or (Alleluia)
Alleluia or (Tract)	Alleluia or (Tract)	Alleluia or (Tract)	Alleluia or (Tract)
	Prose (Sequence)	**Prose (Sequence)**	**Prose (Sequence)**
Gospel	Gospel	Gospel	Gospel
	Credo	**Credo**	**Credo**
	Liturgy of the Eucharist		
Offertory	Offertory	**Offertory (1-6)**	**Offertory (3-4)**
Secret	Secret	Secret	Secret
Preface	Preface	Preface	Preface
Sanctus	Sanctus	Sanctus	**Sanctus**
Canon	Canon	Canon	Canon
Pater noster	Pater noster	Pater noster	Pater noster
Pax domini	Pax domini	Pax domini	Pax domini
Agnus dei	Agnus dei	Agnus dei	**Agnus dei**
(Communion)	Communion	**Communion (1-3)**	**Communion (3)**
Post-communion	Post-communion	Post-communion	Post-communion
			Episcopal acclamations
Benedicamus domino	Ite missa est, or Benedicamus domino	Ite missa est	Ite missa est

50. Numbers in parentheses indicate the range in the number of trope elements that might be added.

Column 1 (ferial mass) is an ordo for the ferial mass derived from the description in John's commentary;[51] the gloria and communion antiphon are in parentheses, since the former was optional and the latter is not mentioned in the commentary. Column 2 (festal mass 1) represents the simpler forms of the festal mass at Autun. The items in bold-face are either added (for example, the prose and credo)[52] or expanded (for example, the introit or gloria). Any mass for a feast of some importance would have at least one added or expanded item, and many had all four. Column 3 (festal mass 2) represents a slightly more elaborate feast at Autun. Most (but not all) feasts at this level of complexity would incorporate the four additions from the previous column and would add one or more of the following items: a troped kyrie, offertory, and communion. Column 4 (festal mass 3) represents Autun's most elaborate feasts. For these, most of the additions of the previous columns would be incorporated, to which several other items might be added, such as the various acclamations added to the Easter feast, or the sanctus and agnus dei tropes for Christmas.

Of the twenty-two feasts found in the Autun Troper's two earliest layers (excluding two gatherings inserted later and miscellaneous items at the end of last gathering), fourteen can be classified as festal mass 1 (Christmas I, Christmas II, St. John, Innocents, Epiphany, Common of Confessor, Feria II, two other Easter ferial days, Ascension, John the Baptist, Dedication of a Church, St. Maurice, and St. Michael); six fit the slightly more elaborate plan of festal mass 2 (St. Stephen, St. Vincent, Purification, All Saints/Common of martyr, SS. Peter and Paul, and possibly Pentecost); and only two feasts clearly fall into the category of festal mass 3 (Christmas III and Easter).

Even within these three broad categories there was a great deal of variety and flexibility. The reasons for this often depended upon several liturgical factors. First, certain chants were excluded at various times in the church year; for example, during Advent and Lent, the gloria was not sung, and the

51. John of Avranches, *De officiis ecclesiasticis,* in Patrologiae latina, 147:32-37.

52. John of Avranches identifies the credo as a festal addition (see ibid., 38), and one can probably assume that it was used at Autun for all Sundays and major feasts. At Pentecost, it was sung in Greek.

manuscript contains no glorias for any feasts within these seasons. In addition, the feast of the Innocents probably was not intended to have a gloria. According to Bernhold of Constance's mass commentary, *Micrologus*, the gloria and alleluia were omitted from this mass because the innocents initially went to hell, because Christ had not yet completed his redeeming work; both items are restored at the octave of this feast.[53] John of Avranches mentions this tradition, but suggests that it no longer be observed in his diocese; however, it appears that it was still observed at Autun, since there is no gloria trope specified for the feast.[54]

A second indication of liturgical flexibility was the practice of using the same chants for several feasts. Tropes to the ordinary texts were likely to have multiple uses, if their texts did not evoke a specific biblical story. It may be for this reason that there is a relative paucity of ordinary tropes (kyrie, gloria, sanctus, agnus dei)[55] in the original layer of the Autun manuscript; in fact, only one feast (Christmas III) seems to have been initially planned to contain a complete troped ordinary. However, the texts of all of the remaining ordinary tropes in the collection (except a few of the glorias) tend to be very formulaic and generic.[56] The sanctus tropes tend to invoke the persons of the Trinity, and the agnus dei tropes rely on a standard set of acclamations to Christ; the kyrie and most of the gloria tropes follow one or the other of these schemes. Because of this, there are no clear reasons for assigning them to specific feasts, so it is possible that the Christmas tropes would have been

53. Bernhold of Constance, *Micrologus*, in Patrologiae latina, 151:1006.

54. John of Avranches, *De officiis ecclesiasticis*, in Patrologiae latina, 147:42. On the other hand, a generic gloria trope could have been supplied from elsewhere in the manuscript.

55. The credo, although part of the stable or ordinary texts for feasts, has a different liturgical function from the other parts of the ordinary; it was intended as an affirmation of faith rather than a song of praise. Because of this, it never attracted tropes.

56. To some extent this applies to gloria tropes as well, but those for major feasts, such as Christmas or Easter, do have a number of acclamations specific to the day. Furthermore, in other manuscripts containing numerous ordinary tropes, their generic nature is still evident, suggesting that they play a slightly different role from proper tropes.

used again at Easter and any other feast deemed important enough to have a troped ordinary.[57]

A third indication of the repertory's flexibility and variety is the presence of a larger number of items than would be needed for specific feasts: additional repertory might be included for closely related feasts, such as a feast's octave, or for accommodating repetitions of a chant, but it may also have created options of using different configurations *ad libitum*. For example, several of the feasts in the Autun Troper have two proses. This might indicate that the feast serves a dual purpose; for example, two texts are given for the Common of Martyrs, one of which is suitable for one martyr and the other for several martyrs. Other extra proses could be used as alternates, at octaves, or other feast days dedicated to the same themes or saints.[58] For example, in the Autun manuscript, the two proses at Pentecost supply texts that could also have been used for the Octave of Pentecost (which may have developed the trinitarian themes implicit in Pentecost) and votive masses to the Holy Spirit or Trinity.[59] The use of seemingly superfluous repertory at a feast's octave or for related feasts might also explain the varied number of trope elements for the introit.[60] The

57. The practice of using items for multiple feasts may also explain why all of the additions of sanctus and agnus dei tropes occur within gathering 6 of the Autun manuscript. Since they were not specifically tied to any particular feast, they were simply entered all in one place when the additional sanctus and agnus dei repertory became available. Similarly, there are several gloria tropes entered without any main rubric in gatherings 4 and 5; any of these more generic glorias could have been used for a feast lacking gloria tropes (for instance the feast of SS. Peter and Paul). Since there is no gloria trope specifically mentioning this feast in their repertory, they would use a generic gloria trope such as *GLORIA/ Prudentia prudentiam*. This trope is found in the Autun manuscript under the feast of St. Stephen, but is associated with SS. Peter and Paul in the Nevers repertory. See Nancy van Deusen, *Music at Nevers Cathedral: Principal Sources of Mediaeval Chant*, 2 vols., Musicological Studies, 30, nos. 1 and 2 (Stroudsburg, PA: Sun Press, for the Institute of Medieval Music, 1980), 1:40.

58. At Autun the multiple proses for feasts of St. John and of SS. Peter and Paul would suit these purposes.

59. Trinity Sunday did not become an official part of the temporale until 1364; however, the octave of Pentecost could have been used to develop either the theme of the gift of the Spirit, or trinitarian themes.

60. John's commentary is very reticent about any additional music other than the *laudes* and *sequentia*. However, one reference makes it clear that other tropes were not unknown. John writes that the mass of the day is to be celebrated without tropes, *laudes*, and the gradual, but with two alleluias and the sequence for the ferial days following Easter: "Officium diei sine tropis, et laudibus, et gradali, cum duobus Alleluia, et sequentia celebretur" (John of Avranches, *De of-*

normal practice in the Autun manuscript was to provide one set of introit tropes consisting of an introduction and from two to five trope elements interspersed with the antiphon. However, a few feasts (Christmas, St. Stephen, St. John, Innocents, Epiphany, Easter, Pentecost, and SS. Peter and Paul) include multiple sets, some of which could have been used as alternates or at the octave of important feasts, in order to provide variety even when the same antiphons were to be sung. However, some introits may have been done with three or even more sets of tropes; if Autun followed the practice common at Cluny and many other institutions, they sang the introit antiphon three times at important feasts (twice before the gloria patri and once after it).[61] Such a pattern fits well with the material the Autun manuscript provides for Christmas: the introit starts with a four-element set including an introduction; this is followed by another four-element set including a trope to the gloria patri; next come two further introductions, one of which is marked *Item.* One of these could have introduced a third untroped antiphon following the gloria patri. Similarly, Easter and Pentecost have sufficient trope sets to cover at least a triple singing of the introit antiphon.[62]

Each addition or expansion of a chant had an effect on the ritual action, depending upon whether the chant was intended to stand alone or provide accompanying music and text for an action. Those which were intended to stand alone were the troped kyrie and gloria, sanctus, and possibly the prose; those intended to cover actions were the introit, offertory, agnus dei,

---

ficiis ecclesiasticis, in Patrologiae latina, 147:56). This accords fairly well with the Autun manuscript, which provides a troped introit and gloria as well as a prose for Feria II, but only a prose for two other days, and space sufficient only for three more proses after that. John's commentary cannot provide as much information about festival services as a troper, since he was merely trying to describe the basic patterns of festival services, rather than listing their complete contents. When confronted with something with as many additions and exceptions as the Easter services, he confined himself only to the most obvious changes of order, and simply recommended that the mass be accomplished with great solemnity: "Officium diei celeberrime compleant" (ibid., 54).

61. Jungmann, *Roman Rite,* 1:326.

62. The Easter service has six complete sets. If one discounts the set which is marked *Alia* (suggesting that it could be an alternative set) and the set added in the margin, there are still enough for four repetitions of the introit antiphon. This possibly indicates that an additional psalm verse was included as yet another festal addition.

and communion. The chants which were intended to stand alone had only a few accompanying actions, all of which call attention to the person(s) singing the chant. For example, the celebrant would turn to the east to intone the gloria,[63] and this could be made even more dramatic by several of the glorias in the Autun Troper, which contain introductions to the intonation, inviting the celebrant (in this case, the bishop) to sing. Similarly, the cantor for the prose would enter the pulpit (taking a prominent place) to sing.

The prose might also have been used to accompany ritual action, namely, the gospel procession. At feasts the procession could consist of a crucifer, thurifer, two lucifers, the subdeacon and the deacon, who took the evangelary off the altar, received the blessing of the celebrant, and preceded by the other ministers, mounted the pulpit.[64] However, a later liturgical commentary (Durand's *Rationale* of the thirteenth century) states that the deacon started singing an antiphon and the *Benedictus omnia* when he wanted to start the gospel procession for the principal feasts. It seems probable that at some point such a practice was established at Autun, since the canticle appears in the inserted pages of this manuscript.[65] In this case, the prose would have functioned purely as musical and poetic embellishment of the liturgy.

Both the introit and offertory chants were intended to cover liturgical action. The introit would normally be sung during the procession of the presiding ministers (the choir would be in place before the start of the service). However, it is difficult to discover what kind of ritual activity any of the expanded versions of the introit were supposed to cover. John of Avranches' commentary suggests that normally the ministers would not approach the altar until the gloria patri of the introit was begun.[66] This would indicate that the procession of ministers did not usually take a substantial amount of time, since it would be covered only by the repetition of the introit's antiphon. On the

63. John of Avranches, *De officiis ecclesiasticis,* in Patrologiae latina, 147:38.
64. A short description of the procession can be found in ibid., 34.
65. Guillaume Durand, *Guillelmi Duranti Rationale Divinorum Officiorum I-IV*, ed. Anselme Davril and Timothy Thibodeau, Corpus Christianorum Continuatio Mediaevalis 140 (Turnhout: Brepols, 1995), 341-42. The antiphon and canticle appear on fol. 29v of the Autun Troper.
66. John of Avranches, *De officiis ecclesiasticis,* in Patrologiae latina, 147:32.

other hand, the rite described by John seems too elaborate to have taken such a short time. It included a procession by the bishop, preceded by deacon, subdeacon, lucifers, and thurifer, after which the deacon placed the evangelary on the altar, and the subdeacon and deacon and bishop said (silently?) the prayers of confession; then the deacon and subdeacon greeted the bishop with a kiss, and the bishop and other ministers went behind the altar and prayed briefly (presumably silently); after this, the bishop bowed to the deacon, the deacon bowed to the subdeacon, and the subdeacon bowed to the choir; finally the deacon bowed to the altar, the bishop kissed the altar, the deacon kissed the altar, and the deacon and then the bishop sat down. Moreover, the great number and variety of expanded introits in the trope manuscripts suggest that the processional rite was even more elaborate and extended. The rite described by John could be expanded at many points, especially by lengthening the time for private prayer and confession (which was common during this period), as well as by increasing the number of ritual actions, such as censing the altar and ministers.[67] Presumably the solemnity of the feast dictated how much the rite would be lengthened.

In contrast to the extensive number of tropes for the introit, only a few tropes for the offertory are found in most tropers. It is difficult to explain this lack of offertory tropes by examining the ritual, since the function of the offertory chant is still open to debate. Jungmann claimed that the offertory chant was for the sole purpose of providing music for the offertory procession of the people; however, this has been seriously questioned by more recent scholarship, and there is no evidence that this was originally the purpose of the offertory chant.[68] Presumably the chant filled in the time allotted for the celebrants' preparation of the altar, silent prayers, and censing. However, a procession did become part of the rite in the liturgies of medieval France

---

67. See Jungmann, *Roman Rite,* 1:290-320. John of Avranches attests to one censing of the altar at the offertory, but does not mention censing at the introit. However, the thurifer is expected to lead the procession, and this would lead naturally to a censing of the altar; see *De officiis ecclesiasticis,* in Patrologiae latina, 147:32, 38.

68. See Jungmann, *Roman Rite,* 2:22, 27-29. The best summary of the debate can be found in Joseph Dyer, "The Offertory Chant of the Roman Liturgy and Its Musical Form," *Studi musicali* 11 (1982): 3-30.

and Germany, first described by Amalar, and dying out by the thirteenth century, as chronicled by Durand.[69] Therefore it is possible that the few offertory tropes in the Autun manuscript were used at feasts that required a procession consisting of the people offering primarily gifts of money, while the clergy possibly brought bread and wine. Even if a procession did not take place, one may assume some expansion in the rite, such as an extension of the silent prayers said by the celebrant, perhaps coupled with an extended censing of the altar.

The ritual use of the agnus dei and communion tropes is liturgically much more complex, since both of these mass chants had lost their original functions. The agnus dei had originally been intended as a fraction anthem,[70] but by this period, it was acquiring a number of different possible uses. The two most prominent of these were to accompany the kiss of peace, or to accompany the communion of the nonpresiding clergy and congregation, as a communion song.[71] Interestingly, in the one feast of the Autun manuscript which specifically requires an agnus dei trope (Christmas III), there is no communion trope provided. Furthermore, none of the agnus dei tropes in this manuscript ends with the prayer *dona nobis pacem*, but rather each repeats *miserere nobis* for a third time.[72] This may indicate that these tropes were intended to be used as communion songs rather than as an accompaniment to the peace.

The communion rite could also be extended by adding tropes to the communion antiphon itself. There are four feasts in the Autun manuscript where this is done. The antiphons for the feasts of SS. Peter and Paul and St. John have only one introductory element added; those for St. Vincent and Easter have three each, and those for Easter are lengthier than those for St. Vincent. Easter would require a significantly lengthened communion antiphon, since it was obligatory for all the faithful to take communion on that day; however, it is not at all clear why any of the other feasts would require ritual elaboration of the communion rite. On the other hand, if both the agnus dei tropes and the communion tropes were intended to extend the length of

69. See Dyer, "Offertory Chant," 11-12.
70. I.e., an anthem to be sung during the fraction, or breaking of the bread.
71. See Jungmann, *Roman Rite*, 2:332-43.
72. In contrast, the St. Martial, Winchester, and even the Nevers Tropers do contain the words *dona nobis pacem*.

the distribution of communion, their presence may provide evidence that a more regular reception of communion was being encouraged at least among the canons themselves. Perhaps this was part of the climate of reform in the stricter cathedral chapters of Burgundy; during this period, a regular Sunday communion was the rule at Cluny for all the monks, and daily communion was the practice in some other reformed institutions.[73] It is possible that even if only the canons and ministers were to receive, the rite might need to be extended somewhat, in which case the slightly lengthened agnus dei might suffice to cover it. When even more time was desired, the communion antiphon could also be lengthened by tropes.

Liturgical Shape and Purpose

Troped festal masses such as those represented in the Autun Troper were ornamented with both great complexity and freedom, but the basic patterns that were created through ornamentation were carefully constructed. They not only help identify the relative importance of each feast by the number of expansions, but also show an overall pattern of expansion that concentrates on ornamenting the first part of the mass. Kyrie and gloria tropes (as well as the gradual and the alleluia)[74] had no ritual activity associated with them, and provided two additional musical and poetic high points within the liturgy of the word. The introit and the prose, although functioning to provide music for the entry of the celebrant and possibly for the gospel procession, were expanded far beyond what would normally be necessary to cover these actions; furthermore, if a canticle were used for the gospel procession, the prose would occur without ritual movement. In short, the liturgy of the word at feasts became a liturgy of poetry and music which attempted to underline the special character of the day, and which was also summed up in the gospel lection. Only on the most important feasts (festal mass 3) did the second part of the mass attract some elaboration; however, this was very rare, and never extensive even when it did occur. The connections of the new repertory with canons of exegesis suggest that this reticence

73. Jungmann, *Roman Rite*, 2:362.
74. See table 6, above, p. 128.

stems from the nature of the chants themselves, which do not give as many opportunities for allegorical interpretation. Regardless of the function of the offertory chant, its text is only rarely well-connected to the feast.[75] Similarly, the communion chant was intended to provide time for the reception of communion, and was not always well related to the themes of the feast. Furthermore, this chant had lost much of its purpose except at Easter, and possibly two or three other feasts when the laity were supposed to take part. The ordinary chants emphasized generic praise, which might have festal significance, especially when the feast related to their scriptural origins (e.g., the gloria at Christmas, the agnus dei at Easter, or St. John the Baptist), but in general, the texts of ordinary chants were not closely connected with the specific event being commemorated. The "tropes" that they implied could be easily standardized and they were consequently never greatly developed or emphasized.[76] Thus, even though a large part of the impetus behind using tropes and proses was to provide a suitably ornate and elaborate service, an equally important element was essentially exegetical; the new repertories reinforced an interpretation of scripture that was shaped by the canons of medieval exegesis filtered through the celebrations of the liturgical year.

Although tropes and proses use all of the techniques found in scripture commentary, unlike scripture commentary (which was intended to provide a better understanding of the text), tropes and proses were geared towards the effective and eloquent proclamation of scripture-based songs (the "Gregorian" repertory), which were themselves chosen for their allegorical richness. In the eleventh century, both liturgy and scripture commentary shared the goal of appropriating the sacred text,

75. See Jungmann, *Roman Rite*, 2:27-31.

76. However, it is important to take into account the fact that one of the most venerable items of the ordinary, the sanctus, had already attracted a set of official introductory "tropes"—the preface, sung by the celebrant, which was part of the mass proper. Before any items called *tropus* were written, this chant already served the allegorical function of evoking "angelic praise" (cf. Is. 6:1 and Rev. 4:4), as well as serving the tropological function of naming the reasons for the feast and inviting all to join with the cherubim and seraphim in song. See Gunilla Iversen, "On the Iconography of Praise in the Sanctus and Its Tropes," in *De musica et cantu: Studien zur Geschichte der Kirchenmusik und der Oper: Helmut Hucke zum 60. Geburtstag*, ed. Peter Cahn and Ann-Katrin Heimerg (Frankfurt: Hochschule für Musik und Darstellende Kunst, 1993), 275-311.

but the liturgy provided a particularly effective setting where the same types of exegetical methods taught in scripture commentary could be corporately embodied and acted out, making the whole of the liturgy "tropological," i.e., a kind of morally influential allegory where the themes of salvation could be rehearsed and brought to corporate expression.

4

LITURGICAL *SACRA PAGINA*
Christmas and Easter Services at Autun in the Early Eleventh Century

AS Leclercq points out in the quote which began this book, "it is in the atmosphere of the liturgy and amid the poems composed for it, *in hymnis et canticis*, that the synthesis of all the *artes* was effected."[1] The central focus and goal of this synthesis was *sacra pagina*—the active interpretation of scripture, which included its memorization, vocalization, and expression. The new repertories of tropes and proses were designed both to display this synthesis and to reinforce it, and a close examination of the function of tropes and proses within patterns of inherited texts and music will show how the liturgy became a primary locus for the interpretation of scripture in many eleventh-century religious institutions.

The Autun Troper contains the two services that form the extended examples for this chapter. It was most likely copied at the Autun scriptorium between 1005-1018; some or all of its repertory was used there at least until 1079.[2] Its contents have concordances with a wide number of traditions, which probably reflect Burgundy's importance as a crossroads for much of Europe during the eleventh century. Even though each troper documents the liturgy of a particular institution, the Autun Troper's repertory is representative, if not "typical." Since the central feasts of the church's year often contain a large amount of common repertory with other institutions, I have chosen to examine the feasts of Christmas and Easter.[3] The source's most unusual feature is that it stems from a cathedral, not from a monastery, and so its principal festal liturgies would have been public—

1. Leclercq, *Love of Learning*, 250.

2. For a codicological examination, consideration of the repertory, date, and provenance, see William T. Flynn, "Paris, Bibliothèque de L'Arsenal, MS 1169: The Hermeneutics of Eleventh-Century Burgundian Tropes, and Their Implications for Liturgical Theology" (Ph.D. dissertation, Duke University, 1992), 19-52.

3. In fact, only by comparing the manuscript's notation with other manuscripts can its music be reconstructed.

attended by nonliterate laity. As is the case with monastic liturgies, the priest and choir had the most functionally active roles in the rite (and most of the rite was designed with them in mind), but the presence of the public did have an impact on the manuscript. (Their reception is one of themes taken up in the conclusion.)

In this chapter, the themes and discussions of each of the preceding chapters are applied to the specific texts and music for the principal masses for Christmas and Easter at Autun. The first part of the chapter examines the specific liturgical *cursus* for Christmas, demonstrating aspects of the use of scripture in liturgy that were discussed in chapter 3. This provides the liturgical setting for analyzing the troper's festal additions. Then in the second part of this chapter, each song of the third mass of Christmas is discussed in order, beginning with a discussion of the festal shaping of its base text (inherited from the Roman rite), followed next by a discussion of the festal additions (tropes, or the prose), and concluded with a consideration of the music. The discussion of texts demonstrates their connections with grammar and scripture study (outlined in chapter 1), and with festal shaping, liturgical *cursus* and ritual (outlined in chapter 3), while the discussion of music demonstrates the richer reading of the texts indicated by the musical syntax (outlined in chapter 2). The third part of this chapter applies the same kinds of analyses to the portions of the Easter mass which had proper texts that were particularly difficult to explain, and which consequently attracted festal additions that relied directly on the language of patristic scripture commentaries. In the fourth part of the chapter, the Christmas and Easter services are briefly compared, highlighting the similarities and differences of their liturgical shape and contents. The chapter concludes with a short assessment of the impact of the services on their participants.

Christmas at Autun

Cursus of services and scripture lections

The third mass of Christmas was the center and high point not only of Advent, but of a whole liturgical round that had started with the vespers service on Christmas eve. The eleventh-century commentary by John of Avranches describes a liturgical *cursus* similar to the one which would have been followed at Autun, as shown in table 7:

Table 7. The liturgical *cursus* for Christmas

Office[4]	Scripture and other "Readings"[5]
1) Vespers, festively led by two cantors	Psalms: 112, 116, 145, 146, 147; Chapter: Romans 1:1-3; *Magnificat*
2) Matins, led by four cantors	Invitiatory: Psalm 94 1st Nocturn: Psalms: 2, 18, 44 Lections: Isaiah 9:1-2; 40:1-2; 52:1 2nd Nocturn: Psalms: 47, 71, 84 Lections: taken from a sermon by Pope Leo the Great, which quotes Luke 2:14[6] 3rd Nocturn: Psalms: 88, 95, 97 Lections: taken from sermons on the following gospel verses: Luke 2:1; Luke 2:15; John 1:1[7]
At the end of matins the Bishop (if he were present) processed to the "principal church," read a gospel lection, and intoned the *Te Deum*	Gospel lection: Mt. 1:1-16
3) The first mass (with *laudes* and a sequence) led by the sacristan[8]	Lections: Isaiah 9:2-7; Titus 2:11-14; Luke 2:1-14

4. The term "office" was commonly used to mean both the prayer office and the mass, i.e., all of the daily "work." This column summarizes John of Avranches, *Liber de officiis ecclesiasticis*, in Patrologiae latina, 147:40-41. For a discussion of the commentary, see chapter 3, pp. 123-36 above.

5. The office readings may vary slightly from what was given here, but the psalmody is accurate, and the mass readings come from a twelfth-century missal from Autun, 10.

6. Sermon 1 *In Nativitate Domini*, 1-3, in *Liber Usualis*, 381-84.

7. Cf. *Liber Usualis*, 389-91, which gives one of the possible sermon selections.

8. John of Avranches uses the verb "celebrate" to describe the roles that the sacristan, "true" cantor, and praesul take in the mass, but the context makes it

Table 7 continued

Office	Scripture and other "Readings"
4) Lauds	As on Sundays: Psalms 92, 99, 62 with 66, *Benedicite*, 148-50
5) A Marian antiphon led by a cantor, and a prayer commemorating Mary	
6) The second mass (with *laudes* and sequence) led by the "true" cantor at dawn	Lections: Isaiah 61:1-62:12; Titus 3:4-7; Luke 2:15-20
7) [Prime]	As on Sundays: Psalms 21-25, 53, 117, 118:1-32
8) Terce	Psalm 118:33-80
9) The third "principal" mass (with *laudes* and sequence) led by the *praesul* [precentor?] or the deacon	Lections: Isaiah 52:6-10; Hebrews 1:1-12; John 1:1-14

The number and placement of the three masses (during the night, at dawn, during the day) is not common for any other feast, and shows the influence of the scripture lections on the liturgy (Is: 9:2-7; Luke 2:1-14; Luke 2:15-20). As John's commentary demonstrates, these lections could presumably be most effectively proclaimed at specific times of the day:

> Pope Telephorus instituted the mass to be sung in the night of the angels: because in it [the night] the Savior of the World was born, and because he himself was offered a holy sacrifice for the whole world's salvation, and in it, the angels, in his praise singing *Gloria in excelsis Deo,* announced to the shepherds the Virgin's delivery. . . . Beginning at daybreak, another mass is celebrated in the same manner as the first. The other is sung with a true exordium of light, because, in accordance with the prophecy of Isaiah, this day new light has dawned on a people sitting in darkness, or else in accordance to the visitation of the shepherds to the manger of the Lord, in which they came upon the bread of angels by which the souls of the saints are refreshed.[9]

---

clear that they are not the celebrants of the mass, which was the Bishop's own prerogative (at least at the third mass); rather, John is concerned throughout this description of festival services with who is to lead the singing of the choir, and he places this function in increasingly experienced hands; this also supports the institutional hierarchy.

9. "In nocte angelis missam cantare Telesphorus papa instituit, quia in ea natus est Salvator mundi, et quia seipsum erat oblaturus hostiam sanctam pro totius

The Autun Troper reveals a similar *ordo* and interpretation; all three masses have festival elaborations of the gloria as well as sequences and the rubric *Oriente* (with the dawn) and introit tropes for the second mass, which provide an "exordium to the true light."[10] John's placement of the third mass of Christmas after terce is normal for a principal mass, and since this was the celebration that was specifically open to the laity, it needed to be at a convenient time.[11]

Festal shaping of base texts: The Christmas introit antiphon

The principles guiding the selection of scripture in the liturgy that were discussed in chapter 3 (pp. 108-17) profoundly influenced the way the songs of the mass were interpreted, selected, and edited. By providing a context in which every scriptural allusion could be mined for its festal implications, even a relatively stable liturgical text such as the gloria (which was sung at every major feast) could be brought into prominent festal focus. Thus the gloria was particularly prominent at Christmas, since it paraphrases part of the Christmas story (Luke 1:14) in its opening line. Furthermore, the selection of psalm stiches, which had festal significance, to serve as antiphons for the recitation of psalms in the office had a counterpart in the selection and adaptation of stiches from the Bible to serve as proper songs for the mass (introit, offertory, communion). However, since the mass was intended to hold together the whole range of imagery presented during the course of the season, the texts derived from the Bible were highly selective and often were changed to help bring out their specific themes.[12] For example, the antiphon text of the introit for the

mundi salue, et in ea partum Virginis, in eius laude *Gloria in excelsis Deo,* cantantes, nuntiaverunt pastoribus angeli.. . . . Incipiente diuculo altera missa eodem modo celebretur, ut prima. Lucis vero exordio altera canitur, quia, juxta Isaiae vaticinium, ipsa die lux orta est nova populis sedentibus in tenebris, seu propter visitationem pastorum ad praesepe Domini, in quo invenerunt panem angelorum, quo reficiuntur animae sanctorum" (John of Avranches, *Liber de officiis ecclesiasticis,* in Patrologiae latina, 147:40).

10. However, the differences are significant as well. For example, the interesting allegory of Jesus in a manger (eating trough) = the bread of angels on the altar (*praesaepio* could figuratively mean table) is not developed in the Autun Troper.

11. A rubric in a twelfth-century sacramentary, Autun, Bibliothèque Municipale, S 11 (9) (Autun 11), fol. 7, identifies this mass as *missa publica;* this is a clear indication that the laity were expected to attend.

12. Although divergence from the Vulgate does not in itself indicate an intentional change, there is substantial evidence of festal shaping of Vulgate texts.

third mass of Christmas, based on Is. 9:6, shows several interesting discrepancies with the Vulgate reading:[13]

Introit:

Puer *natus est nobis, et filius datus est nobis: cuius imperium super humerum eius: et vocabitur nomen eius,* magni *consilii* Angelus.

A boy *is born to us, and a son is given to us: whose authority* [will be] *upon his shoulders: and his name shall be called* Angel of great *counsel.*

Vulgate:

Parvulus enim *natus est nobis, Et filius datus est nobis*; et factus est principatus super *humerum eius; Et vocabitur nomen eius*: Admirabilis, *Consilarius*, Deus, Fortis, Pater futuri saeculi, Princeps Pacis.

For a child *is born to us, and a son is given to us*; and the government is *upon his shoulder: and his name shall be called,* Wonderful *Counselor,* God the Mighty, the Father of the world to come, the Prince of Peace.

There are two striking differences between the texts, showing how the introit has been shaped to be more suitable for Christmas: (1) the introit reads "whose authority [will be] upon his shoulders," while the Vulgate reads "and the government is founded upon his shoulders"; and (2) the names given in the second half differ significantly from each other: "Angel of great counsel," for "Wonderful Counselor, God the Mighty, the Father of the world to come, the Prince of Peace."[14] The first of these changes can be supplied by the *Commentarium in Isaiam,* by Hervé of Bourgdieu (after 1100), which like many early commentaries, summarizes the earlier patristic exegesis, and strengthens the traditional Christological interpretation by making a reference to the cross:

> This is the child himself, who "is a little lower than the angels," who comes "not to be ministered to, but to minister." For secular Kings wear their royal insignia not on their shoulder, but on their head. But only our King lifts up the glory of his power on his shoulder.[15]

13. Throughout this chapter, I have highlighted words and phrases in texts in italic type to help in showing the relationships between scripture passages and song texts and between related song texts. Unless otherwise stated, these italics are always my additions.

14. The commas are editorial. The line can also read "Wonderful, Counselor, God, Mighty," etc. I prefer a sequence of four names with modifiers, although the modern oral tradition in English, which is based on memories of Handel's *Messiah,* conflicts with this.

15. "Hic est enim parvulus ille, qui 'minoratus est paulo ab angelis' (Heb. 2:9) qui 'non venit ministrari, sed ministare' (Mt. 20:28). Reges autem saeculi non in

Hervé's commentary supplies the traditional interpretation of the Vulgate text, not the antiphon text. Thus, the changes in the liturgical antiphon, which strengthen the traditional interpretation, should not be considered *eisegesis* in themselves, but rather a way of communicating the traditional interpretation tersely and effectively. Although *imperium* and *principatus* are basically equivalent terms, the antiphon text specifies that they refer to the Son's specific "authority."[16] Furthermore, by omitting the verb "to be" from this phrase, the antiphon resolves the problem of tense created by the Vulgate's too literal rendering of the "prophetic perfect."[17]

The second change in the antiphon text tends more towards obscuring the sense as conveyed by the Vulgate. Perhaps there was a reluctance to call Christ "Father," although the name "Father of the world to come" would be appropriate for Christ.[18] It is also very rare to find Christ called an angel; most likely the extensive reading of Isaiah during Advent brought verses 63:8-10a to mind:

> And he [the Lord] said: Surely they are my people, children that will not deny: so he became their savior. In all their affliction he was not troubled, and the *angel of his presence* saved them: in his love, and in his mercy he redeemed them, and he carried them and lifted them up all the days of old. But they provoked to wrath, and afflicted the spirit of his Holy One.

Since the theme of God's presence to creation through Christ's incarnation is extensively developed throughout the Christmas season, the selection, adaptation, and perhaps alteration of this verse from Isaiah reinforced its Christological interpretation, connecting the incarnation with elements of a kenotic Christology.

---

humeris sed in capite portant insigne regiam. Sed solus Rex noster gloriam potestatis suae in humeris extolit" (Hervé of Bourgdieu, *Commentarium in Isaiam*, in Patrologiae latina, 181:122).

16. *Imperium* could also have been preferred because of its greater authority: Christ as "emperor" rather than "prince."

17. See Fredrick L. Moriarty, "Isaiah 1-39," in *The Jerome Biblical Commentary*, ed. Raymond Brown, Joseph Fitzmeyer, and Roland Murphy (Engelwood Cliffs, NJ: Prentice Hall, 1968), 272: "Perfect tenses are used by Isaiah [9:1-6], but they are 'prophetic perfects' expressing the certainty of a future event."

18. In fact, many tropers, although not the Autun Troper, reinstate this epithet as a trope element.

Such a highly selective process of festal shaping can only be understood within the whole liturgical *cursus* of the medieval church; the *cursus* ensured that many texts from scripture were available in memory and this explains some features of the services that have baffled modern commentators. For example, Jungmann notes that around the beginning of the eleventh century, the introit psalm was reduced in almost every institution to one verse (usually the first, or second, if the first served as the antiphon);[19] he points out that this curtailment seems to obscure the relationship of the psalm to the feast, and gives as an example the psalm verse which accompanied the Christmas introit: *Cantate Domino canticum novum, quia mirabilia fecit* ("Sing to the Lord a new song, for he has done marvelous things"). As he points out, this verse has only a generic connection with the feast, while portions of the second and third verses are particularly appropriate: *Notum fecit Dominus salutare suum,* and *Viderunt omnes fines terrae salutare Dei nostri* ("The Lord has made known his salvation," and "All the ends of the earth have seen the salvation of our God"). However, Jungmann does not take into account the context of the clerics and monks who were the principal participants in the services. As I show in chapter one and three above, this context included their reading of seasonally appropriate books of the Bible in the offices, their celebration of weekly and even daily masses, their weekly chanting of the complete memorized Psalter, and their knowledge of the Psalter's interpretation in commentary. Within this context, the selection of Psalm 97:1a for the introit verse of the third mass for Christmas was not arbitrary (as Jungmann suggests); the specific highlighting of the first line carries on the important theme of naming the Boy, Son, Angel, who is proclaimed in the antiphon text. Jungmann is correct in realizing that the text alone does not provide the necessary context for understanding how the antiphon is appropriate to Christmas; the theme of "naming" in the Christmas introit cannot be easily discerned from its text alone, but would have been a commonplace in the eleventh century. A modern interpreter needs to consult a psalm commentary for the traditional interpretation of the psalm and its first verse. Bruno of Würzburg summarizes the whole of the

19. Jungmann, *Roman Rite*, 1:324-27.

psalm as follows: "The prophet urges the people of Christ to rejoice with exultation of the new song, since the marvelous advent of Christ has been granted," and gave the following interpretation of the Psalm 97:1a:

> For the new man ought to sing the new song, not the old man, who, not putting off the sins of Adam remains in them. The *new song* is to tell or to sing of the Lord's Incarnation. *New,* because the world has heard nothing like it. *Done marvelous things,* when he gave light to the blind, and [the power of] walking to the lame.[20]

The term "new song" had acquired a strong association with the incarnation from its traditional interpretation in this psalm and others (Psalms 32:3; 95:1-2; 149:1), making it unnecessary for the introit verse to make explicit reference to the whole psalm. Moreover, the term "new song" was intended to refer to the whole saving life, death, and resurrection of Christ, and was therefore a "name" for Christ which acted as a shorthand not only for the incarnation, but for its consequences for salvation.[21] Within the context of the interpretive commonplaces that they were intended to support, the "truncated"

---

20. Bruno of Würzburg, *Expositio psalmorum,* in Patrologiae latina, 142:355: "Propheta commonet populum Christianum cantici novi exultatione laetari, quando mirabilis est Christi concessus adventus." " Novus enim homo cantare debet canticum novum, non ille vetustus, qui necdum Adae peccata deponens in eis perseverat. Novum canticum est de Domini Incarnatione narrare vel cantare. Novum, quia nunquam aliquid simile mundus audivit. Fecit mirabilia, quando caecis lumen, claudis gressum donavit."

Incidentally, although the whole of Bruno's explanation is derived from Cassiodorus, Bruno's editing emphasizes the Advent readings. For example, his explanation of "marvelous things" refers to Is. 35:5-6, which Cassiodorus explicitly connects to the miracles of Jesus in the gospels, and not to the birth of Christ.

21. For the origins of this interpretation, see Clement of Alexandria, *Protrepticus,* as translated in James McKinnon, *Music in Early Christian Literature* (Cambridge: Cambridge University Press, 1987), 29-30. This tradition was transmitted to the west through the commentaries of both Augustine and Cassiodorus. Augustine equated the "new song" with the New Testament (Augustine, *Enarrationes in psalmos,* ed. D. Eligius Dekkers and Johannes Fraipont, Corpus Christianorum series latina [Turnhout: Brepols, 1956], 40:2178), and Cassiodorus equated the "new song" with "the secret of the holy incarnation, the wondrous nativity, the saving teaching, the suffering which is the mistress of endurance, the resurrection which is the most certain proof of our hope, the seat at the right hand of the Father which denotes strength and unique power" (Cassiodorus, *Expositio psalmorum,* Psalm 149:1; *Cassiodorus: Explanation of the Psalms,* trans. Walsh, 3:458). Interestingly, both interpretations imply that the use of "new song" in these psalms is an example of the linguistic trope of *antonomaisia,* by which a person is named through epithet.

psalm verses to the introit functioned both as a reminder of the whole text and as a reminder of the traditional interpretation of the psalm. In the context of the liturgy, which not only juxtaposes them with highly evocative antiphons but also (significantly in the eleventh century) includes trope elements that explicitly develop and refine the themes they imply, they are part of a surprisingly rich interpretive context, and the use of only one verse should not be considered a diminution of this context.[22]

Perhaps the curtailing of the chanting of the introit psalm during the eleventh century was intentional, since the space which was opened up in the introit could be used for tropes which alluded to a greater diversity of imagery and symbol. At any rate, the introit and to a lesser extent the other proper texts are both the most festally developed texts of the mass liturgy, and attracted the greatest number of tropes; these display a similar degree of festal development and allusion.[23]

Trope sets for the introit

At first glance, the introit trope complex as a whole can seem to be somewhat arbitrary and random, making it difficult to determine which items in the manuscript were intended to form any one particular service at Autun. As pointed out in chapter 3 above (pp. 131-32), it is unlikely that the Christmas mass could have accommodated more than three repetitions of the introit antiphon, and therefore requires at most three trope sets, yet the manuscript contains four. Although it would seem that the most likely candidate for omission is the trope element *Hodie exultent iusti,* which has no musical notation, one should bear in mind that the absence of notation does not necessarily indicate that this trope was not performed; the cantor may simply have had its music memorized. Instead, it is probably best to assume that all of the repertory in this manuscript was intended to be performed either on Christmas day or within the

22. A similar phenomenon can be seen in the *capitulum* (chapter) of the prayer offices. It usually consisted of only one line from the beginning of a chapter from scripture, and that particular verse is not always well-related to the celebration. Similarly to the introit verse, the *capitulum* was intended to remind the participants of the whole chapter, which could be brought to mind via one's memory, or even read or recited aloud from memory, if time and the institution's tradition permitted.

23. See also chapter 3, pp. 117-23 and 127-32.

twelve days of Christmas, and that was intended to create some set of specific rhetorical effects as a whole.[24] In the following analysis, the texts and music (if reconstructible) of each set of introit tropes are first presented in musical notation, accompanied by a translation in which each element is numbered for reference. A discussion of the texts follows and then of the readings implied by the music. The discussion of the introit concludes with an assessment of how the several sets were intended to be related to each other.[25]

Ex. 9. First introit trope set for Christmas *Ecce adest/ PUER NATUS* from PaA 1169, fol. 3r-3v

Ecce ad-est de quo profehte cecinerunt dicentes PUER NATUS

24. Some tropers have both an encyclopedic organization and a comprehensive repertory. In contrast, the Autun Troper is extremely concise and presents the repertory in the order in which it would be performed in an actual service. Moreover, it shows signs of extensive use over a long period of time.

25. A diplomatic version of the original Autun notation is given either above the modern notation (if the pitches can be reconstructed from a concordance) or directly above the words. The musical pitches have been reconstructed from the following sources: (1) The antiphon melody is based on the pitches in Montpellier H 159, a tonary, which stems from eleventh-century Dijon. The numbering of the melodies is taken from Hansen's edition, which serves as the thematic catalogue for this manuscript; this antiphon is Dij 568. (2) The pitches for the first trope element (*Ecce*) are reconstructed from the later of the two Nevers manuscripts: Paris, Bibliothèque Nationale, nouvelles acquisitions des fonds latins, MS 1235 (PaN 1235), fol. 183v, and collated with a second reading from Pistoia, Biblioteca Capitolare, MS C 121 (Pistoia 121). The Nevers manuscript (PaN 1235) has been transcribed by van Deusen, in volume two of *Music at Nevers Cathedral.* (3) The pitches for the next two trope elements (*Quem virgo* and *Nomen eius*) are also based on PaN 1235, fol. 183v, but are collated with Paris, Bibliothèque Nationale, nouvelles acquisitions des fonds latins, MS 1871 (PaN 1871), fol. 4v (an eleventh-century troper from Moissac). Parts of PaN 1871 have been transcribed in Günther Weiss, ed., *Introitus-Tropen,* vol. 1, *Das Repertoire der südfranzösischen Tropare des 10. und 11. Jahrhunderts,* Monumenta monodica medii aevi, ed. Bruno Stäblein, no. 3 (Kassel: Bärenreiter, 1970), as well as in Charlotte Roederer, *Festive Troped Masses from the Eleventh Century: Christmas and Easter in the Aquitaine,* Collegium Musicum: Yale University, 2d ser., vol. 11 (Madison, WI: A-R Editions, 1989).

EST NOBIS <ET FILIUS DATUS EST NOBIS> Quem vir-go

Maria gen- u-it CUIUS IMPER<IUM SUPER HUMERUM

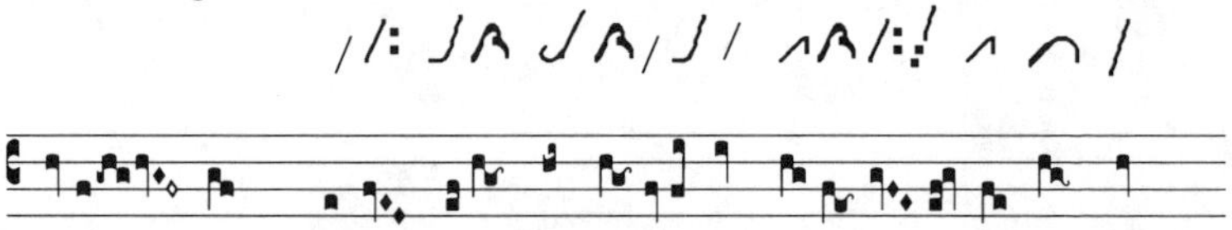

E- IUS> Nomen eius emmanuhel vocabi- tur ET VO-

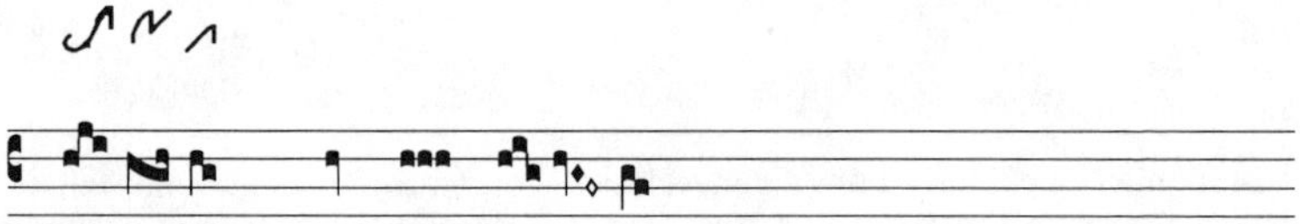

CABITUR <NOMEN E- IUS> Fortis et potens deus

MAGNI CONSILI-I <AN- GELUS.> CANTATE DOMINO

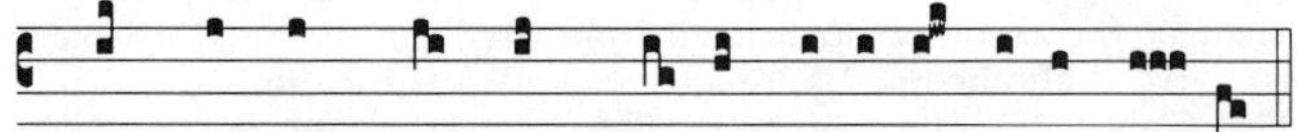

<CANTICUM NOVUM QUIA MIRABI- LIA FECIT.>

1) Behold, He is here, of whom the prophets sang saying:
A BOY IS BORN TO US, AND A SON IS GIVEN TO US,
2) whom the Virgin Mary bore,
WHOSE AUTHORITY [WILL BE] UPON HIS SHOULDERS.
3) His name shall be called Emmanuel,
AND HIS NAME SHALL BE CALLED

4) strong and mighty God,
ANGEL OF GREAT COUNSEL.
Ps. SING TO THE LORD A NEW SONG, BECAUSE HE HAS DONE WONDERFUL THINGS.[26]

The first trope element, *Ecce adest*, is a tightly compact summary of the Old Testament and the epistle lections that will be read later in the service. (For complete texts of these lections, see Is. 52:6-10; Heb. 1:1-12.) The first verse of each of the lections provides important vocabulary, imagery, and the context which are developed in the trope and introit:

Isaiah 52:6:	
Propter hoc sciet populus meus nomen meum In die illa: Quia ego ipse qui loquebar, *ecce adsum.*	Therefore my people shall know my name in that day: for I myself that spoke, *behold I am here.*
Hebrews 1:1:	
Multifariam, multisque modis olim Deus loquens patribus in *prophetis*	God, who, at sundry times and in divers manners, spoke in times past to the fathers by the *prophets*
Trope:	
Ecce adest de quo *profehte* cecinerunt dicentes	*Behold, He is here,* of whom the *prophets* sang, saying

The allusion to the Isaiah passage may explain why none of the elements for the entire introit complex gives the name "Jesus," and only the penultimate, unnotated element gives the title "Christ"; i.e., the Lord's people will know his name, when he comes. Thus, the whole trope complex develops the linguistic trope of *antonomasia*,[27] which supplies epithets in the place of a "proper" name. The Hebrews text has influenced the construction of the trope element by suggesting the use of the

26. In each reconstruction, the Latin texts are presented in a very lightly edited format. Tropes are in lowercase, while base texts are in uppercase, and there is no editorial punctuation. The reader may wish to consult my translations of the texts, which follow each example. In the translations, I have numbered the trope elements for reference, and have supplied punctuation based on the "musical punctuation" that I discuss in the following analyses. See the preface for a fuller discussion of the editorial procedures.

27. All information on specific linguistic tropes is derived from Bede's *De schematibus et tropis*; see chapter 1, pp. 35-42, for an assessment of its importance.

plural *prophets;* instead of *prophet.* Since the introit text is taken from Isaiah, the use of the singular would have suggested an allusion only to his prophecy; by using the plural, all the prophets are invoked as pointing to what Christ has fulfilled by being present; this follows not only the language, but the pattern of thought in the Hebrews lection.[28] The trope element makes it clear that the antiphon text is a quotation ("the prophets sang, saying . . ."), providing the kind of contextualization that grammar students would be familiar with from the *accessus ad auctores.*[29] Furthermore, the use of the verb *cano, canere* (to prophesy, sing, incant) to describe prophetic speech is correct according to classical usage, but rare in the Vulgate, and a reference to the imperative verb of the following psalm verse *Cantate Domino* may be intended; i.e., all the prophets (but especially David and Isaiah) have set an example by singing of the messiah's birth, which can be followed by those in the choir. In combination with the first section of the antiphon, the first trope element also brings the current feast of Christmas into continuity with the predictions of the prophets, giving the choir the double role of quoting the words of the prophet and of acknowledging that the child, the son, who is here (*adest*) is given to them *now.*

The second trope element of this complex (*Quem virgo*) and the following section of the antiphon (*CUIUS IMPERIUM*) both continue the linguistic trope of *antonomasia,* one variety of which was to replace the name with facts about a person's birth, and another of which was to replace the name with a person's office or rank. The use of the verb *geno, genere* (beget, or bear) is somewhat unusual, and is not used in Is. 7:14b (*Ecce virgo concepiet, et pariet filium*), or in the gospels (see Mt. 1:25, and Luke 2:7); instead, all three references use *pario, pariere* (to bring forth). It is possible that the author of this element

---

28. Other manuscripts transmit this trope using the singular, which creates a different set of allusions.

29. Riché, *Écoles et enseignement*, 249, gives the following description of the *accessus*: "Lorsque le maître explique une œuvre, il introduit le texte en montrant l'utilité du livre et l'intention de l'auteur, c'est ce qu'on appelle l'*accessus ad auctores.* Il peut ainsi justifier le choix qu'il fait et classer les *auctoritates* selon des critères littéraires et moraux" (When the master explained a work, he introduced the text by demonstrating its utility and the intention of the author; this is what one calls the *accessus ad auctores.* In this way, he could justify the choice which he had made and classify the *auctoritates* according to literary and moral criteria).

intended to emphasize Mary's role as *genetrix*. This would concord well with the eleventh century's growing concern with Marian devotions.

Trope elements 3 and 4 along with the antiphon segments that they introduce purport to give the "name" of the child, but instead continue giving attributes and offices. The third trope element (*nomen eius*) simply rearranges the words of the following antiphon element (based on Is. 7:14c). Moreover, it supplies the "name" Emmanuel, which actually turns out to be another epithet, since the clerics would have its translation in mind: Mt. 1:23, where Emmanuel is translated "God with us," was part of the reading for the Christmas vigil mass (see table 4, p. 116). The repetition of vocabulary between the trope *nomen eius* and the following antiphon element may seem unnecessary; instead of having a trope repeat "and his name shall be called," it would have been easy simply to add Emmanuel to the list of names following the antiphon element, which begins with exactly the same words. However, the repetition reinforces the idea of naming and helps heighten the anticipation for the "real" name. If the fourth (unnotated) trope element (*fortis et potens deus*) were sung, it could have served a double purpose: (1) it reconnects the antiphon text to the Vulgate version of its text, by supplying attributes which are close to those found in the Vulgate's rendition of Is. 9:6 (see p. 143), and (2) it is a quotation of Psalm 23:8. Psalm 23:7 had already served as the offertory song of the vigil mass on 24 December, asking the question "Who is this King of Glory?" It was perhaps considered especially appropriate to have its answer at the principal mass on Christmas day. Again the theme of supplying a name is being stressed. However, if it were not sung, the third trope element (*nomen eius*) could have served as a cue to the choir that they were to sing the last phrase of the antiphon and go on to sing the psalm verse.[30]

The music of the first introit trope set is striking for two reasons. First, if the two sources closest to the Autun Troper's neumation (PaN 1235 and Pistoia 121) are taken as models for

30. John [Gearey] Johnstone, "The Offertory Trope: Origins, Transmission, and Function" (Ph.D. dissertation, Ohio State University, 1984), 144-217, points out several such "paraphrase tropes," suggesting choral cueing as their main function.

the probable pitch (see example 9, above), then the introductory line, while using musical figuration that is modeled on the mode VII antiphon, is a whole tone higher than the antiphon, being based on 'a' instead of 'G'.[31] In other sources, the antiphon is adapted so that at least its final occurs on 'G'. This modal ambiguity separates the first line from the rest of the antiphon, and possibly makes it (in retrospect) more dramatic, since it is very similar in shape to the first antiphon element, but at a higher pitch. However, it also plays an important syntactic role, since the end of the trope needs to be open to the next line, in order to invoke what the prophets were "saying." Analyzed as a transposed mode VII unit, the trope element poses no syntactic surprises, since the trope element is in Vulgate-style prose: a leap of the fifth on *Ecce* creates its own musical syllable, since both the word and the musical gesture are dramatic; a cadence at the fourth above the final on *adest* creates a "colon" at the end of the first clause; a slight *incisio* on *cecinerunt* on the note below the final lightly marks a syntactic unit which could stand alone (but then goes on), and a cadence on the final forms a period on *dicentes*. However, if one looks at the relationship of the trope element to the following antiphon element, the modal ambiguity effects a subtle nuance that is useful for proclaiming the text: the real "period" comes on *cecincerunt* on the final of the untransposed mode VII 'G', giving closure to the thought "of whom the prophets *sang*." Then the link to the present "saying" that the choir is about to effect is musically linked by ending on a note that does not require a syntactic pause (in the "real" mode VII). In this way, the trope element is given a sense of closure and separateness, as well as a sense of forward motion. Furthermore, the idea of "quotation" is emphasized by the cadence on 'G' marking what the prophets said, and the new centering on 'G', when Isaiah is being quoted in the antiphon.

31. The Autun manuscript indicates a lengthening of the first note of the antiphon after this trope element, possibly in order to "recenter" the mode on its proper note.

For an examination of the importance of the modal ambiguity concerning questions of origin and transmission, see Ellen Jane Reier, "The Introit Trope Repertory at Nevers: MSS Paris B. N. lat. 9449 and Paris B. N. n. a. lat. 1235" (Ph.D. Dissertation, University of California, Berkeley, 1981), 1:91-106. See also Colette, *"Modus, tropus, tonus,"* 71-78.

The second striking feature of the trope element 1 is its use of musical figuration. Although an upward gesture of a fifth cadencing on a fourth above the final is common in mode VII, it is nevertheless memorable here: since *Ecce adest*; *PUER NATUS EST;* and *ET FILIUS DATUS EST* all use this gesture, it is likely that the music was specifically intended to relate the concepts "He is here," "A boy is born," and "a son is given." Thus it both strengthens the message of the antiphon (he is born, and given *to us*), and continues the rhetorical device of naming by epithet, which characterizes the whole trope set. One other phrase, *de quo prophete cecinerunt*, outlines this musical gesture, but fills in the fifth with an intervening third, and weakens the cadence at the fourth with a passing note. Nevertheless, the whole of this phrase closely mimics the shape of the antiphon element, *ET FILIUS DATUS EST NOBIS*. This creates a subtle musical association which heightens the sense of the fulfillment of a prophecy: in the trope element the prophecy occurs in the right shape and the right mode, but is hidden because of additional ornamentation and through modal ambiguity; in the antiphon, the prophecy is clearly revealed because the proper mode has been established and the musical gesture is not obscured with ornamentation.

The music of the third and fourth trope and antiphon elements (*Quem virgo* and *Nomen eius*) serves mainly to mark the expected syntactic pauses in the text. However, one relationship between the two trope elements is worth pointing out: the words of each element are carefully arranged so that the names *Maria* and *Emmanuel* are centrally located and occur on the highest notes of their respective elements. This central placement of the name *Emmanuel* was clearly intentional, since it is a rearrangement of the words of two sources (Is. 7:14; 9:6). By arranging the words of these trope elements so that they would have a parallel syntactic structure, a connection between Mary and the idea "God with us" is established, which is heightened by the use of musical range. A similar musical connection takes place between the antiphon segment that begins *CUIUS IMPERIUM* and the psalm verse: the antiphon segment is closely connected to the psalm formula, perhaps suggesting a relationship between the "wonderful things" mentioned in the psalm and the "carrying of the cross," which so strongly mark the interpretations of this verse from Isaiah in commentary and in the way the words were shaped to form the Christmas introit. This would also be completely consistent with the interpretations of the "new song" from the psalm given in contemporary commentaries.

The second trope set (apart from the trope to the doxology) is unique to this manuscript:[32]

Ex. 10. Second introit set for Christmas *Gratuletur/ PUER NATUS* from PaA 1169, fol. 3v

Gratuletur omnis caro
in conspectu domini
et pro hortu saluatoris
deo dicat gratias
PUER NATUS EST NOBIS
In plenitudine temporum
ET FILIUS DATUS EST NOBIS
Per partum virginis hodierne
CUIUS IMPERIUM <SUPER HUMERUM EIUS
ET VOCABITUR NOMEN EIUS>
Rex regum solus potens et omnipotens

32. For this reason most of its music is impossible to reconstruct; the pitches of the final trope element (to the gloria patri) are based on Paris, Bibliothèque Nationale, fonds latin, MS 903 (PaN 903); see Roederer, *Festive Troped Masses*, for a modern transcription of parts of this manuscript.

MAGNI CONSILII ANGELUS.

Glorietur pater in fili-o suo uni- ge- nito GLORIA PATRI ET

<FILIO ET SPIRITUI SANCTO SICUT ERAT IN PRINCIPIO

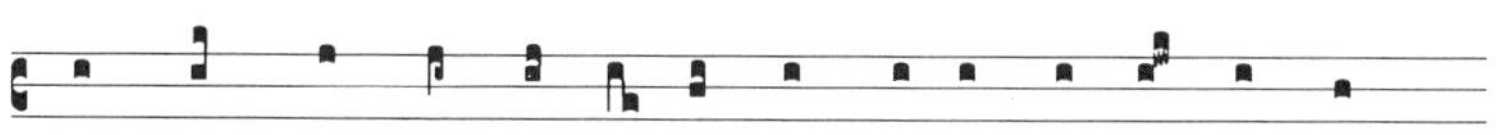

ET NUNC ET SEMPER ET IN SAECULA SAECU-LORUM

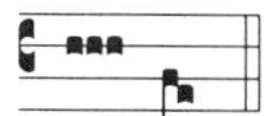

A-MEN>

1) Let all flesh rejoice
   in the sight of the Lord
   and before the dawn[33] of salvation
   give thanks to God:
   A BOY IS BORN TO US
2) in the fullness of time:
   AND A SON IS GIVEN TO US
3) through having been delivered of a virgin this day:
   WHOSE AUTHORITY [WILL BE] UPON HIS
   SHOULDERS: AND HIS NAME SHALL BE CALLED
4) King of Kings, alone mighty and all-powerful
   ANGEL OF GREAT COUNSEL.
5) May the Father be glorified in his only begotten son:[34]

33. This could be translated as "garden," since ortus = dawn, hortus = garden; however, it seems likely that an 'h' was inserted in order to create a break between the same vowels pr*o o*rtu since the more conventional image would be "dawn of salvation."

34. Literally, "May the Father glory in his only begotten son," since *glorior* is properly a deponent verb. However, it is common for verbs to lose their deponency in medieval Latin, and the sense is not seriously changed with either reading.

GP GLORY BE TO THE FATHER, AND TO THE SON, AND TO THE HOLY SPIRIT: AS IT WAS IN THE BEGINNING, IS NOW AND EVER SHALL BE, WORLD WITHOUT END: AMEN.

The second trope set carries on the development of the imagery of the lections, although instead of alluding to the Old Testament and epistle lections, it brings the important themes of the "Word made flesh" and the "light coming into the world" from the gospel lection (John 1:1-14) substantively into play for the first time in this service (see p. 142, table 7, # 9). The use of word *caro* (flesh) in the first trope element is itself an example of the linguistic trope *synecdoche,* which attributes rejoicing to a part of the human body instead of the whole. Such tropes are common in scripture, and this particular one is closely paralleled by Is. 40:5, which was the basis for the communion song of the vigil mass, and which contains much of the language of this trope element:

Revelabitur gloria *Domini*: et *videbit omnis caro salutare* Dei nostri.

The glory of the *Lord* shall be revealed, and *all flesh shall see* the *salvation* of our God.

Furthermore, the reasons that *flesh* should rejoice are to be given during this mass, especially at the end of the gospel lection (John 1:1-14):

Et verbum *caro* factum est, Et habitavit in nobis: Et vidimus gloriam eius, Gloriam quasi unigeniti a Patre Plenum gratiae et veritatis.

And the Word was made *flesh,* and dwelt among us (and we saw his glory, the glory as it were of the only begotten of the Father) full of grace and truth.[35]

The trope element further strengthens the connections with the gospel lection, since the theme of Christ as light (also prominent in the whole of the second mass of Christmas) is strongly developed in John 1, especially in verse 9:

35. The trope to the gloria patri in this set (*Glorietur pater*) also derives most of its language and context from this verse. Incidentally, Bede gives this verse for his example of the trope *synecdoche:* "*Synecdoche* is a designation allowing full understanding of a thing although saying that it is quantitatively either more or less than it is in actuality. It . . . designates the whole by means of a part, thus: 'The Word became flesh.'" (Tanenhaus, trans., "Bede's *De Schematibus et Tropis,*" 247).

Erat lux vera, Quae illuminat omnem hominem	He was the true light, that enlightens every man.

Both of the gospel lection's themes had already had an intensive development in hymns written for the office. The most readily available hymn that incorporates both the *topos* of flesh and of the dawn was sung every morning during the Christmas season to greet the sunrise at lauds: Sedelius' *A solis ortus*. This hymn combines both themes within its first two stanzas:

A solis *ortus* cardine Ad usque terrae limitem, Christum canamus Principem, Natum Maria Virgine.	From the limit of the *dawn* To the ends of the earth, Let us sing to the Ruler, Christ, Born of the Virgin Mary.
Beatus auctor saeculi Servile corpus induit: Ut *carne carnem liberans,* Ne perderet quos condidit.[36]	The Blessed creator of the world Assumed the body of a slave So by *flesh liberating flesh* That which he joined should not perish.

Another hymn (by Rabanus Maurus) seems to have provided a direct poetic model for the trope, which shares its occasion (Christmas), first line, syllable count, and accentual pattern, even if it does not combine both *topoi*:[37]

Gratuletur omnis caro *nato Christo Domino,* Qui pro culpa protoplasti carnem nostram induit. Ut salvaret, quos plasnavit Dei sapientia.[38]	*Let all flesh rejoice in the birth of Christ the Lord,* Who for the sins of "protoplasm" put on our flesh So that he may save those he formed by the wisdom of God.[39]

36. *Liber usualis*, 400-401.

37. The use of hymns as models supports my argument that the tropes grew out of a combination of educational and liturgical aims; the hymns of both Sedelius and Rabanus Maurus figured prominently in grammar treatises covering metrics; see chapter 1, p. 38, note 55.

38. See Clemens Blume, Guido Maria Dreves, and Henry Marriott Bannister, eds., *Analecta hymnica medii aevi* (Leipzig: Reisland, 1886-1922), 50:195, for the complete text of this poem, which develops themes related to other feasts in its subsequent verses.

39. Rabanus Maurus uses a more "erudite" and less liturgical language than the trope element, borrowing language from Greek, προτος + πλασμα = primordial life, and the verb πλασσω = form.

Unlike the hymn, the trope does not make a direct reference to the feast, and instead substitutes the standard phrase *in conspectu Domini* (in the sight of the Lord). This substitution served two purposes: (1) a premature reference to Christ's name was avoided, and (2) another reference to Psalm 97 was established. (This had been recited in the matins service, and the first verse was sung after the first introit set of this service.) Psalm 97:6a and 9 use the phrase *in conspectu Domini*, and could have called to mind both the whole context of these phrases and the whole interpretation of the psalm for the choir, thus emphasizing the theme of God's presence to the whole of creation:

Psalm 97:4-6a:	
Iubilate Deo, omnis terra; Cantate et exultate, et psallite. Psallite Domino in cithara; In cithara et voce psalmi; In tubis ductilibus, et voce tubae corneae. Iubilate *in conspectu regis Domini.*	Sing joyfully to God, all the earth; make melody, rejoice and sing. Sing praise to the Lord on the harp; on the harp, and with the voice of a psalm: with long trumpets, and sound of cornet. Make a joyful noise *in the sight of the Lord our King.*
Psalm 97:8-9a:	
Flumina plaudent manu, Simul montes exsultabunt *a conspectu Domini.*	The rivers shall clap their hands, the mountains shall rejoice together *at the presence of the Lord.*

Thus, trope element 1 of this set, which introduces the antiphon element "A boy is born," creates two linguistic tropes through *allegory* and *metaphor*, connecting the "boy" mentioned in the psalm verse with the "dawn of salvation," and putting the choir into the role of "all flesh" by asking them to "rejoice" by singing the antiphon.

The second and third trope elements (*In plenitudine* and *Per partum virginis*) combined with their antiphon elements paraphrase Gal. 4:4, and demonstrate that the use of scripture quotation in the trope elements could extend beyond the confines of what was read in the services leading up to Christmas. Even so, Gal. 4:4-7 was liturgically and seasonally available, since it was the epistle lection for the Sunday *after* Christmas. Its paraphrase here helps the festal mass hold together the themes that permeate the whole season. This quotation supports the theme of the incarnation as the fulfillment of time, which is important to both the epistle and gospel lections,[40] and through the interaction of the trope element and the antiphon, this fulfillment is characterized as taking place "this day"; i.e., in this service:

Gal. 4:4:	
At ubi venit *plenitudo temporis, misit Deus Filium* suum *factum ex muliere,* factum sub lege	But when the *fullness of the time* was come, *God sent his Son, made of a woman,* made under the law
Trope and antiphon:	
PUER NATUS EST NOBIS In *plenitudine temporum*: ET *FILIUS DATUS EST* NOBIS *per partum virginis* hodierne	A BOY IS BORN TO US in the *fullness of time*: AND *A SON IS GIVEN* TO US *through having been delivered of a virgin* this day

The antiphon continues to develop its thought in parallel to Gal. 4:4, since the antiphon element *CUIUS IMPERIUM* was considered to be a reference to the cross, which was a consequence of Christ being "made under the law."

Trope element 4, *Rex regum*, continues the process of naming through epithet; it provides the most exalted titles and attributes given so far, including an unusual use of the word *omnipotens* (all-powerful) applied to Christ. This can be explained partly by the continuation of the thought from Gal. 4, which appears to have structured the rhetorical development of this whole trope set. Gal. 4:7 reads, "Therefore now he is not a servant, but a son. And if a son, an heir also through God." (Insofar as trinitarian relationships are concerned the attributes accorded to God may be accorded to the Son.)

Aside from the word *omnipotens*, the rest of the trope element closely paraphrases 1 Tim. 6:15. Although this particular passage is not read in the mass during the Christmas season, 1 Tim. 1:15-17 is read on the second Sunday after Epiphany, and it is directly parallel to the later passage, except that it expands the epithets and unambiguously applies them to Christ (rather than God the Father). Furthermore, the whole context of the passage alludes to themes from the gospel of John (e.g.,

40. Cf. Heb. 1:1-3 and John 1:1-4.

life, light, and "no man has seen the Father"), also developed throughout the service:

1 Tim. 1:15-17:	
. . . Christus Iesus venit in hunc mundum peccatores salvos facere, quorum primus ego sum. Sed ideo misericordiam consecutus sum: ut in me primo ostenderet Christus Iesus omnem patientiam ad informationem eorum, qui credituri sunt illi, in vitam aeternam. *Regi* autem saeculorum *immortali, invisibili, soli* Deo honor et gloria in saecula saeculorum. Amen	. . . Jesus Christ came into this world to save sinners, of whom I am the chief. But for this cause have I obtained mercy: that in me first Christ Jesus might shew forth all patience, for the information of them that shall believe in him unto life everlasting. Now to the *King* of ages, *immortal, invisible,* the *only* God, be honor and glory for ever and ever. Amen
1. Tim. 6:14-16:	
. . . serves mandatum sine macula, irreprehensibile usque in adventum Domini nostri Iesu Christi, quem suis temporibus ostendet beatus et *solus potens, Rex regum,* et Dominus dominantium: qui *solus habet immortalitatem, et lucem inhabitat inaccessibilem*: quem nullus hominum vidit, sed nec videre potest: cui honor, et *imperium* sempiternum. Amen.	. . . keep the commandment without spot, blameless, unto the coming of our Lord Jesus Christ, which in his times he shall shew who is the Blessed and *only Mighty*, the *King of kings* and Lord of lords; *who only hath immortality, and inhabiteth light inaccessible*, whom no man hath seen, nor can see: to whom be honor and *empire* everlasting. Amen.
Trope and antiphon elements:	
ET VOCABITUR NOMEN EIUS *Rex regum solus potens* et omnipotens	AND HIS NAME SHALL BE CALLED *King of Kings, alone mighty* and all-powerful

Furthermore, the context of 1 Tim. 6 enriches the theme of time, by referring to the "second advent" in verse 14: "ut serves mandatum sine macula, irreprehensibile usque in adventum Domini nostri Iesu Christi, quem *suis temporibus*"; this reference is similar to the quotation from Gal. 4, which provided the language for the preceding trope element (*In plenitudine temporum*). Although this eschatological theme is not directly taken up by the trope, the striking use of the word *omnipotens* would help remind the clerics of it.

The antiphon and trope text taken together apply the name "King of kings" to Christ ("AND HIS NAME SHALL BE

CALLED, King of kings," etc.). This could refer not only to the passage from Timothy, which supplied the direct model for the trope itself, but also to the book of Revelation, since the name "King of kings" is attributed to the Lamb in Rev. 17:14, who is also named the Word of God in Rev. 19:13-16; both of these are fundamentally Johannine images for Christ, and therefore connect with the Christmas gospel.[41] Although these verses from Revelation are not read in any of the Christmas services, Rev. 19:13 is itself a "trope" on the same verse of Isaiah which provided the language for the introit antiphon itself (Is. 9:6), and thus provides three further names for the "boy"—the Lamb of God, who is also the King of kings and the Word of God. In Rev. 19:13a, the connection with the book of Isaiah is established by quoting Is. 63:1; then the following half verse (Rev. 19:13b) paraphrases Is. 9:6:

Rev. 19:13:	
Et vestius erat veste aspera sanguine: *et vocatur nomen eius Verbum Dei*	And he was clothed with a garment sprinkled with blood; *and his name is called, The Word of God*

The tendency of this set of trope elements is finally made explicit in the trope to the gloria patri:

Glorietur pater in filio unigenito	May the Father be glorified in his only begotten son:
GLORIA PATRI	GLORY BE TO THE FATHER

It evokes the language and thought of the last line of the gospel lection (John 1:14) and of Is. 40:5 (see above, p. 158). Thus, the whole of this trope set starts by proclaiming the salvation of all flesh, and then progressively reveals the Son's glory through more and more explicit allusions to his relationship to the Father, and to his heavenly majesty.

Although the music of most of this trope set cannot be reconstructed, some of its musical features are discernible from examining its poetic organization and neumation; these show a careful construction that helps with the delivery of the text (see example 10, pp. 156-57, above). The four lines of trope element 1

41. Rev. 17:14 ". . . the Lamb shall overcome them, because he is Lord of lords, and King of kings." Rev: 19:16: "And he hath on his garment, and on his thigh written: King of kings and Lord of lords."

form a short rhythmic poem of two units of eight plus seven syllables. Its first three lines use only one neume per syllable (for a maximum of two notes per syllable) which makes it a simple matter to bring out something of the rhythmic structure of the text in performance. (Although on the word *deo* the pattern is broken by two three-note groups, there is still only one neume per syllable throughout.) This relationship between the music and the poetic organization strengthens the possibility that the two hymn texts quoted above could have been secondary sources for this trope element (see p. 159). Furthermore, there is some indication that the syllable counting extended into the other trope elements of this set. For instance, the last line of the first trope element (seven syllables) is answered by the seven syllables of the first antiphon element; the next trope is nine syllables and is answered by nine syllables of antiphon. This pattern breaks down somewhat later, but the organization of units into the same or approximately the same number of syllables is a feature prominent in the trope repertory in general. The use of exactly equivalent syllable counts is more common in the proses, which set mostly one note per syllable and which do not have to accommodate the prose rhythms of fixed antiphon texts. The music of the trope element 5 can be fully reconstructed (see example 10, p. 157 above). It contains the same musical figure (setting the phrase "May the Father be glorified") that was developed thoroughly in the first trope set (see example 9, pp. 149-51 above). In the first trope set, this figure suggested a relationship between the action of "being present" and the actions of "being born," while in this setting it establishes a relationship between "being given" and the action of "glorifying the Father." Thus, the associations suggested by the musical figure help to strengthen the focus on the gospel lection that is developed by the whole complex of trope and antiphon elements.

The third and fourth trope sets for the introit contain only one element each. These could be used either for the final repeat of the antiphon or for an introductory trope on the Christmas Octave or on a Sunday within the Christmas season.[42] The text of the third trope set (which has no music nota-

42. The repertory of the manuscript implies three repetitions of the introit antiphon, since it contains both a psalm verse and the gloria patri.

tion) provides a fitting culmination to the whole introit, since it finally names "the boy" as well as looks forward to the feasts of Stephen, John, and the Innocents, within the Octave, by invoking "the just":

Hodie exultent iusti	Today, let the just rejoice!
natus est Christus filius dei	Christ, the son of God, is born!
deo gratias dicite eya.	Give thanks to God eia!
PUER <NATUS EST NOBIS>	A BOY IS BORN TO US

The language of this trope evokes Psalm 67:4: "Et iusti eplentur; et exultent in conspectu Domini" ("And the just shall feast, and rejoice in the sight of the Lord"). Although this psalm was not a part of the Christmas liturgy, it was connected with Christ's advent in the psalm commentaries; for example Bruno of Würzburg summarizes the whole psalm as follows: "The prophet announces the advent of Christ, his restraining the pride of enemies, and of his assumption into heaven."[43] Furthermore, its allusion to "feasting" helps to tie the introit to the liturgy of the eucharist. The language also echoes Psalm 32:1: "Exultate, iusti, in Domino, Rectos decet collaudatio" ("Rejoice in the Lord, O ye just: praise becometh the upright"). Again Bruno gives a helpful summary of the whole psalm: "The prophet warns the just to be glad in the Lord, and calls them blessed, who have deserved to lead his cult."[44] Since this psalm was used in the third nocturn of matins, celebrating the Holy Innocents, it can be connected even more substantively with the Christmas Octave than can Psalm 67, and provides a link forward to the celebration of the first martyr, Stephen, on the following day.

The final introit trope set also comprises one element. It consists of two hexameter couplets, and the music can be reconstructed from the close concordance in PaN 1235, fol. 184:

43. Bruno of Würzburg, *Expositio psalmorum,* in Patrologiae latina, 142:248: "Propheta Christi adventum annuntiat, inimicorumque ejus superbiam comprimendam, et de eius assumptione in caelos."

44. Ibid., 140: "Propheta in Domino gaudere admonet iustos, beatosque appellat, qui ad eius meruerint pertinere culturam."

Ex. 11. Fourth introit trope set for Christmas *Deus pater/ PUER NATUS* from PaA 1169, fol. 4r

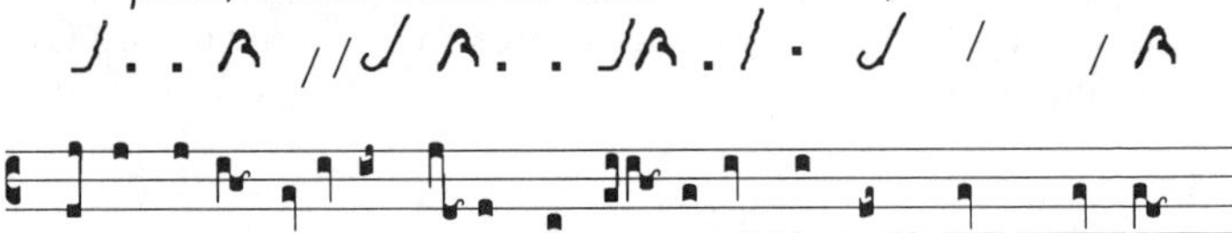

Deus pater filium suum hodie misit in mundum de quo

gratulanter dicamus cum propheta PUER <etc.>

1) Today, God the Father sent his Son into the world, of whom we say, rejoicing with the prophet:
A BOY IS BORN TO US <etc.>

The trope and its music seem to be a rewrite of the opening trope of the Christmas mass *Ecce adest*. It recasts the trope in hexameters and adds language from Gal. 4:4a (which was not used in the earlier quotation from Galatians) and echoes John 3:16:

Ecce adest *de quo profehte* cecinerunt *dicentes*

Deus pater filium suum hodie misit in mundum,
de quo gratulanter *dicamus* cum *propheta*

Even beyond the level of exact quotation *Ecce adest* and *hodie misit* have similarly placed dramatic words (*Hodie* is the first word after the hexameter's main caesura), followed by an action that stresses the "son's" presence. Another parallel is provided by the use of double verbal constructions: *cecinerunt dicentes* and *gratulanter dicamus*. Unlike the trope *Ecce adest,* the trope *Deus pater* does not evoke the lections of the Christmas mass, since it omits the quotation of Is. 52:6 and uses the singular "prophet," instead of the plural "prophets" from Heb. 1:1. Instead, it begins with a quotation from Gal. 4:4, which is the epistle lection for the Sunday after Christmas, and identifies Christ as God's Son; this echoes the principal theme of the gospel lection for the same day,[45] suggesting that the trope supplies repertory for the Christmas Octave, rather than for Christmas day.[46] (Both feasts had the same introit antiphon in this period.)

Since the trope is written as a hexameter couplet, there is some degree of "syntactic segmentation" in the text. A rendering which preserves the segmentation demonstrates that it does not cause severe problems:

> God the Father / his son / today / sent into the world:
> of whom / rejoicing / we say / with the prophets:

Nevertheless, the music (which, like the text, appears to be adapted from the music for *Ecce adest*) marks many of the points of segmentation: if it is intended to be a transposed mode VII, *suum, de quo,* and *propheta* have cadences on the final, *gratulanter* has a cadence on the fourth, and *dicamus* has a weak cadence on the note below the final; if analyzed in mode VII proper, *hodie* has a comma on the fourth, *gratulanter* has a comma on the fifth, and the verb *dicamus* has a strong colon on the final. This musical marking suggests two places that the music of the trope creates a commentary on the text. One of these occurs between the words *hodie* and *gratulanter,* which analyzed in mode VII proper, have similar upward gestures, and form cadences on notes above the final. This association of joy with the present feast is commonplace, but here is orna-

---

45. The gospel lection for the Sunday after Christmas (Luke 2:33-52) contains the story of Joseph and Mary losing Jesus in Jerusalem. Verses 48-50 contrast Jesus' responsibility to his earthly parents with his responsibility to God: "And seeing him, they wondered. And his mother said to him: Son, why hast thou done so to us? Behold thy father and I have sought thee sorrowing. And he said to them: How is it that you sought me? Did you not know, that I must be about my father's business? And they understood not the word that he spoke unto them."

46. This is also suggested by the fact that the first drawings in the Autun Troper separate this last trope and antiphon element from the rest of the complex, possibly suggesting a distinction between them. (Incidentally, through these drawings, the manuscript achieves yet another level of uniting the whole cycle of feasts of Christmas: the first drawing depicts the events in the gospel of the first and second masses of Christmas within the introit complex of the third. See Flynn, "Paris, Bibliothèque de l'Arsenal MS 1169," 402-19, for a discussion of the function of the drawings. For an art historical consideration, see Eric Palazzo, "Le tropaire d'Autun, le MS Paris, Bibliothèque de l'Arsenal 1169: sa place dans le groupe des tropaires du haut moyen âge," *Mémoires de la société Éduenne* 14, no. 5 (1985-87): 405-520.

mented through the musical emphasis. The other suggests that the first four words of the trope element belong together, because they are set in one musical phrase (whether the trope is analyzed in transposed mode VII or in mode VII proper). This is interesting for three reasons: (1) The same musical figure that marked the many "names" of Christ in the first trope set (an upward leap of a fifth) is no longer separated by a cadence from the rest of the phrase; this weakens the figure so that Christ cannot be musically *named* God Father. (2) Even more strikingly, a relationship between Father and Son is musically suggested by the fact that the syntactically disjunct words are enclosed within one musical phrase, and (3) a trinitarian relationship of identity *as well as* difference is expressed by an almost exact musical palindrome; i.e., the pattern of notes setting *Deus pater* is reversed to set *filium suum*.

The larger pattern and intentions of the entire introit trope complex can be summarized as follows: first, the tropes intensively gloss the three readings for the mass celebration, through their quotation of related texts of the Old and New Testaments. This technique is very similar to those employed in the New Testament and in patristic exegesis and commentary. Second, the tropes use the associations inherent in the antiphon text as well as those supplied by the traditional interpretation in commentary of the sources for both the antiphon and psalm verse. Third, they literally make the readings come to life by relating them directly to what the choir is doing, namely singing and celebrating a service, and by encouraging them to appropriate what the readings communicate by ritually enacting them. Fourth, the entire complex does all this with great rhetorical mastery, developing a linguistic trope of *antonomasia* throughout its length, in a particularly effective way: the words of Is. 52:6 are in fact prophetic in the present celebration; i.e., the choir does know "his name." Fifth, the music is effectively used as a device that paces the delivery and proportion of the texts, and also adds a level of association that supports the development of the linguistic tropes, creates relationships between the trope element and the antiphon, and creates relationships between the trope elements themselves that cross syntactic boundaries; all of this gives a richer reading of the text than can be supplied by the words alone.

Kyrie

Although it is a beautiful and expressive piece of music, and certainly fits into the general category of rhetorically effective utterance, the kyrie trope/prosula does not have any specific festal relationships to Christmas.[47] However, it does form a natural link with the introit trope complex. Since the latter ends with the naming of Christ, the kyrie trope is a very appropriate place in the service for the cantor to identify Christ as the redeemer and to invite the choir to join in an acclamatory litany to him. Moreover, this particular kyrie is especially suitable since, unlike many kyries from the eleventh century, all but one of the epithets within its prosulae are clearly addressed to Christ:

Ex. 12. Diplomatic version of kyrie trope *Christe Redemptor*; kyrie prosula *Te, Christe* from PaA 1169, fol. 4r-4v

Christe redemptor miserere nobis

Ky- rie-le-i-son

eya omnes dicite

47. A prosula puts text to a melody which can also be performed without text as a melisma; in this kyrie, the prosula elements introduce a melismatic repeat on the words "Kyrie eleison" or "Christe eleison." The prosula elements are preceded by a trope (designated 'A' in the following translation), which has a different melody, and would not be performed without its text, and is followed by a second element (designated 'B'), which is a prosula element that no longer introduces its repeat in a melismatic version, and which therefore functions as a trope.

The melody (Margaretha Landwehr-Melnicki, *Das einstimmige Kyrie des lateinischen Mittelalters*, Forschungsbeiträge zur Musikwissenschaft, no. 1 [Regensburg: Gustave Bosse, 1955], 55) corresponds relatively closely to the neumation of the Nevers repertory, which can be compared with the Aquitanian sources as well. For an edition of the Nevers melody, see van Deusen, *Music at Nevers Cathedral*, 2: 41-43; for Aquitaine, see Paul Evans, *The Early Trope Repertory of Saint Martial de Limoges* (Princeton: Princeton University Press, 1970), 266-68.

Te Christe suplices exoramus cunctipotens
ut nostri digneris eleyson
KYRIE LEYSON
Te decet laus cum tripudio iugiter
qua tibi petimus decanentes eleison
KYRIE LEY SON
O bone rex qui super astra sedes et dominans
qua cuncta gubernas eleison
KYRIE<LEY>SON.
O theos agye salva vivifice redemptor noster eleyson
KRISTE LEYSON
Qui canunt ante te precibus annue
et tu nobis semper eleyson
KRISTE LEYSON
Tua devota plebs implorat iugiter
ut illi digneris eleyson
KRISTELEYSON

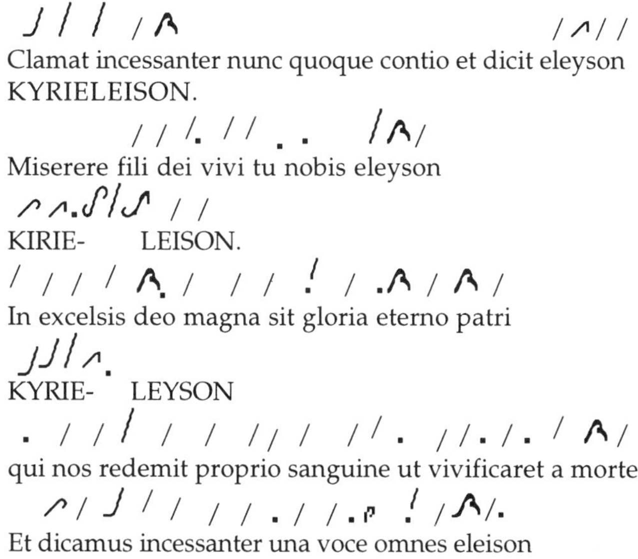

Clamat incessanter nunc quoque contio et dicit eleyson
KYRIELEISON.
Miserere fili dei vivi tu nobis eleyson
KIRIE- LEISON.
In excelsis deo magna sit gloria eterno patri
KYRIE- LEYSON
qui nos redemit proprio sanguine ut vivificaret a morte
Et dicamus incessanter una voce omnes eleison

A) Christ, redeemer, have mercy on us: Lord have mercy: all say eia!
1) O Christ we humbly entreat you, that you grant us mercy, KYRIELEYSON.
2) Praise with dancing is constantly fitting to you, through which we plead, always singing: have mercy, KYRIELEYSON.
3) O good king, you who sit above the stars and ruling what you strictly govern, KYRIELEYSON.
4) O holy God, save us, giving life, our redeemer, have mercy, KRISTELEYSON.
5) Your holy people constantly implore that you grant them mercy, KRISTELYSON.
6) We beseech those who sing before you during the year, and [we beseech] you at all times: have mercy on us, KRISTELEYSON.
7) Now the throng also unceasingly exclaims and says have mercy! KYRIELEISON.
8) Have mercy on us, you, O Son of the living God, have mercy, KYRIELEISON.
9) Great glory be to God the eternal Father on high! KYRIELEYSON.
B) Who redeemed us with his own blood, so that he may give life from death, and let us all unceasingly say with one voice: have mercy!

Like the fourth set of introit tropes, the text addresses Christ in glory surrounded by the saints (see elements 6 and 7 above), and the choir eventually joins in the heavenly praise and petition of Christ (see the last element 'B'). David Bjork (following Jungmann) has pointed to this piece as evidence of a confusion between Father and Son that was the product of a long-standing anti-arianism in liturgical prayer, and other manuscripts (which combine elements 9 and 'B' into one) show that this could happen.[48] Even as transmitted by the Autun manuscript there is potential for confusion, since the word *qui*, which begins element 'B', refers to the previous kyrie, which was itself preceded by praise to the Father. However, there are four reasons for thinking that this would be a misreading: (1) The Christmas introit trope complex (and the manuscript as a whole; see below on the Easter introit complex) suggest that the standard western interpretations of the relations between Persons of the Trinity and the Godhead were well known at Autun. (2) The text as transmitted by the Autun manuscript has a nine-fold kyrie enclosed by what may be considered two trope elements, the first identifying Christ as redeemer, the second specifying how Christ redeemed. (3) All nine petitions can easily be read as praise to Christ: the glory of the Father in element 9 would be connected with the mercy of *Christ*, who is also properly addressed as Lord (as in the acclamations ending elements 1-3, 7, and 8). This would create a petition similar to the trope to the doxology in the introit ("May the Father be glorified in his only begotten son"), which would be appropriate for the feast, since the gospel passage for the feast (John 1:1-14) develops the relationship between the Father's glory and the Son's glory. This interpretation is supported by the music, since all nine acclamations (see the neumation of the upper case texts, above) are set melismatically, and all nine prosulas are (of course) basically syllabic: the musical setting thus serves to strengthen the relationship between the acclamations.[49] (4) Element 9 is doxological and may be intended to function in much the same way as did the trope *nomen eius*, which was ex-

48. David Bjork, "The Early Frankish Kyrie Text: A Reappraisal," *Viator* 12 (1981): 16-18. See also Josef Jungmann, *The Place of Christ in Liturgical Prayer*, 2d rev. ed., trans. A Peeler (New York: Alba House, 1965): 172-90.

49. Of course, other kyrie tropes follow trinitarian patterns, where the relationship between the acclamations invites a different interpretation of their musical unity; i.e., the unity of the Godhead. It is perhaps because of the strength of the trinitarian tradition (which was carried over into Lutheran services in the reformation) that modern commentators tend to read the doxology to the Father as a defective trinitarian element, rather than as expressing a relationship with Christ, to whom *the whole* trope-prosula complex is directed.

amined in the introit complex, where it may have signaled the last choral acclamation.[50]

Thus, if one takes the music into account, it is difficult to argue that the kyrie misinterprets trinitarian relationships. However, it is clearly the case that Christ's divinity is emphasized (as in all of the texts of this Christmas mass). The emphasis stems from the larger function of this mass within the Christmas celebration. Since the two preparatory masses focused upon the narrative of the Christmas story (e.g., the gospel lections cover Luke 2:1-20), the third mass can focus on the consequences for salvation implied by the incarnation. Furthermore, it is a principal festival, not a fast: the whole effect of this kyrie (as Bjork correctly points out) is acclamatory rather than penitential;[51] it serves to keep the focus of the mass on the celebration of salvation, even though it also petitions for mercy.

Laudes

The *laudes* or gloria tropes for Christmas have a complicated structure, consisting of an introductory trope, a large series of interpolations to the gloria, two prosulas, and a wandering doxological trope to the amen.[52] Since the base text of the gloria quotes the angel's hymn at Christ's birth (Luke 2:14), it in itself is particularly appropriate to Christmas, and the length and complexity of this series is partially attributable to this. Furthermore, the special relationship to Christmas has signif-

50. See above, p. 153.

51. Bjork, "The Early Frankish Kyrie Text," 17-18.

52. Both of the prosulas are derived from the trope *Regnum tuum solidum permanebit in aeternum*, which has a lengthy melisma on the syllable "per-" of *permanebit*. Often this melisma was texted, creating prosulas within the trope element. The *Conditor* prosula in this manuscript carries the process further; it has lost its connection with the text *Regnum*, and has become a moveable refrain, creating a new element which operates more as a trope than as a prosula. See Klaus Rönnau, *Die Tropen zum Gloria in excelsis Deo: Unter besonderer Berücksichtigung des Repertoires der Martial-Handschriften* (Wiesbaden: Breitkopf & Härtel, 1967), 179-87 for a helpful description of the corpus of *Regnum* prosulae.

The doxological trope to the Amen (*Te trina*) occurs frequently in glorias. It seems to have come from the hymn *Sanctorum meritis inclita gaudia*, where it is (with different wording) a doxological last verse: see Blume, Dreves, and Bannister, *Analecta hymnica*, 2: no. 9; and ibid., 50: no. 3 (as cited in Alejandro Planchart and John Boe, eds., *Beneventanum troporum corpus*, Recent Researches in the Music of the Middle Ages and Early Renaissance [Madison, WI: A-R Editions, 1989-], vol. 2, part 2, 27); see also Rönnau, *Die Tropen zum Gloria*, 89.

icantly influenced the subject matter and imagery of the trope texts, to such an extent that it would not make sense to shift this complex to any feast outside of the Christmas season (although other sets of gloria tropes were regularly assigned to more than one feast).[53]

The opening of the gloria text invites the kind of reference and allusion to the mass lections that was found in the introit complex. The rest of the base text of the gloria functions in a similar way to the kyrie, inviting elaboration with tropes that serve to extend the gloria's own epithets and acclamations. In fact, like the tropes, the gloria itself is a stichic composition in a lyrical prose that balances various sections of similar lengths to create a larger structure. The base text of the gloria, even without tropes, already has a highly structured and rhythmic impetus, which differentiates it from the short texts of the proper: after the opening lines, quoting the angelic hymn, the gloria continues with five short acclamations starting with *laudamus te*; this is followed by praise of the Father and of the Son, and a three-fold litany to the Son (*Qui tollis—miserere nobis*, etc.); the text ends with a doxology containing three short epithets leading up to the name of Jesus Christ, to which the names of the Spirit and the Father are added. The interweaving of *laudes* within the gloria text is intended to enhance its poetic structure, and the music also suits its structured style, enabling it to accommodate poetic interpolations that are even more tightly organized than the gloria text itself.

The pitches for the melody are difficult to reconstruct, since the melody does not fall neatly into any modal categories:[54] the neumation in the Autun Troper is close both to the version

---

53. See Planchart and Boe, eds., *Beneventanum troporum corpus*, vol. 2, part 2, 29, which gives the following summary of the transmission of *Pax sempiterna*: "Planchart calls it 'one of the oldest pieces in the repertory . . . clearly an east Frankish or northern piece.' Rönnau says that its origin is uncertain although the oldest sources are East Frankish; on the other hand, Blume in *AH* 47 [*Analecta hymnica*] surmises a possible northern Italian origin on the basis of its accentual meter . . . it was almost always attached to gloria A [Bosse #39] and assigned to Christmas." See also Rönnau, *Die Tropen zum Gloria*, 73-75, on Aquitanian repertory associated with specific feasts; ibid., 76-78, on the moveable nature of trope elements and whole trope complexes for the gloria; ibid., 201-6, for information on the gloria melody, and ibid., 213-16 for the Aquitanian version of this gloria trope set.

54. See Planchart and Boe, eds., *Beneventanum troporum corpus*, vol. 2, part 2, 23-25, on the variations in notation.

transmitted from Nevers (PaN 1235) based on 'G', which contains a number of b-flats, and to a source from Benevento[55] based on 'a'. Since neither source transmits the series exactly as does the Autun Troper, the following reconstruction is a compilation from both, though it follows the Nevers source as much as possible:[56]

Ex. 13. Christmas gloria trope *Pastor bone/ GLORIA/ Pax sempiterna* from PaA 1169, fol. 4v

Pastor bone veni ante sacrum et sanctum altare
et in laude regis regum
vocem tuam prior emittere digneris
supplices te rogamus
eya dic domne:[57]

GLORIA IN EXCELSIS DEO. ET IN TERRA <PAX HOMI-

55. Benevento, Biblioteca Capitolare, MS 35 (26), from the early twelfth century (Benevento 35).

56. See PaN 1235, fol. 185, for the Nevers version of the melody. Early manuscripts do not notate the frequent b-flats of the Nevers Troper, but the transposition of the melody in the Beneventan source concurs with a regular semitone between the second and third steps. For this edition, I have used a b-flat clef, which should be considered editorial. Neither source transmits the introductory element (which is not notated in the Autun manuscript). The melodies for the first *Regnum* prosula and the trope *Te trina* are taken from the Nevers Troper (PaN 1235, fols. 188v and 192), which uses them with the same gloria melody on subsequent days of the Christmas Octave; the melody for the second *Regnum* prosula is taken from the Beneventan source (transposed down one tone) which transmits this prosula, without its enclosing trope, in the normal location for a *Regnum* prosula; i.e., between *Altissimus*, and *Iesu Christe*. The music of the Beneventan sources is transcribed and accompanied with a diplomatic version in Planchart and Boe, eds., *Beneventanum troporum corpus*, vol. 2, part 2, 110-48.

57. This is not notated in the Autun Troper.

NI- BUS BONE> VOLU<NTA-TIS.> Pax sempiterna Chri-
stus inluxit glori-a tibi pater excelse LAUDAMUS TE.
Himnum canentes hodie quem terris angeli fuderunt Christo
nascente BENEDICIMUS TE. Natus est nobis hodie
salvator in trinitate sem- per colendus ADORA-

MUS TE. Quem vagientem inter angusti antra prae-

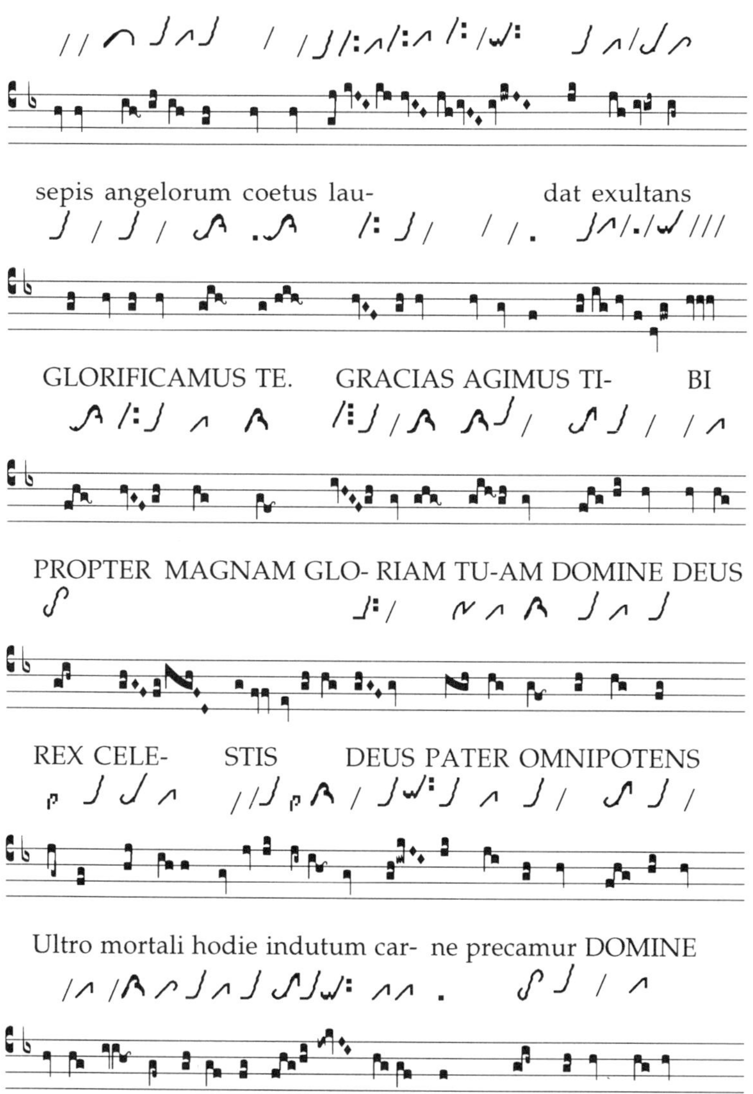
sepis angelorum coetus lau- dat exultans
GLORIFICAMUS TE. GRACIAS AGIMUS TI- BI
PROPTER MAGNAM GLO- RIAM TU-AM DOMINE DEUS
REX CELE- STIS DEUS PATER OMNIPOTENS
Ultro mortali hodie indutum car- ne precamur DOMINE
FILI U- NIGENITE IE- SU CHRISTE. DOMINE DEUS

AGNUS DEI FILIUS PATRIS Cuius ad sede lux benedicta
caliginoso orbis refulsit QUI TOLLIS <PECCATA MUN- DI
MISE-RERE NO- BIS. QUI TOL-LIS PECCATA MUN-
DI> SUSCIPE DE<PRECATIONEM NO- STRAM.>
O ineffabilis rex et admirabilis ex virgine matre hodi-e
prodisti mundo que subvenisti QUI SEDES AD DEXTERAM
PA- <TRIS MISE- RERE NO- BIS QUONIAM

TU SOLUS SANCTUS TU SOLUS DOMINUS.> TU SOLUS
ALTISSIMUS Regum tuum so- lidum Per te Christe sistit nobis
omnipotentissime Qui in cruce signum nobis dedisti vivifice
Te laudamus rex clementissime Tibi laus et onor permanebit
in eternum IE- SU CHRISTE. <CUM
SANCTO SPIRITU IN GLORIA DEI> PATRIS. Conditor
generis humani redemptor idemque ineffabilis sine fine sine

principio Salvare venisti nos Nasci dignatus de virgine Et

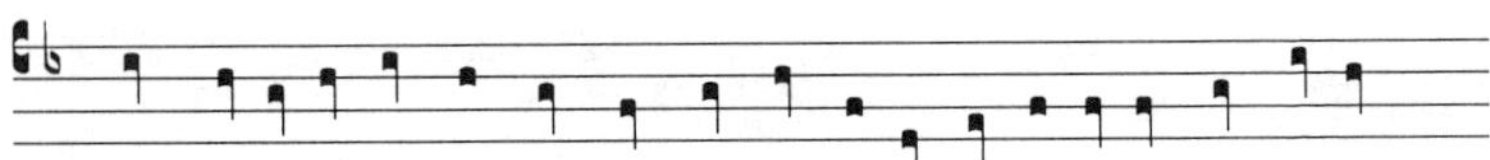

nunc deus et homo regnans O Domine dominator. Te trina

deitas et una te poscimus ut culpas aluas noxias subtrahas

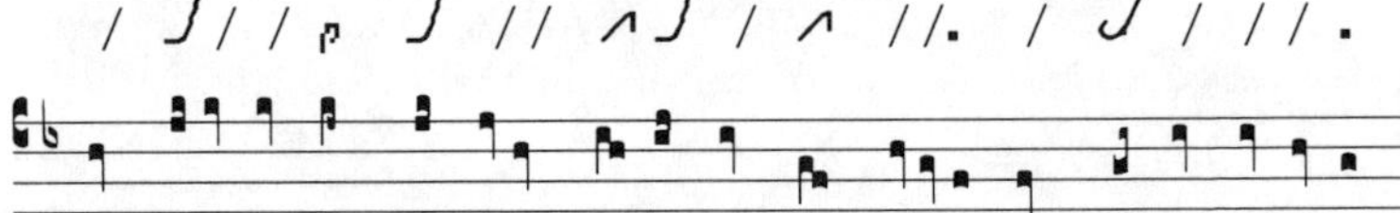

da tuis pacem famulis nobis quoque gloria per cuncta secula

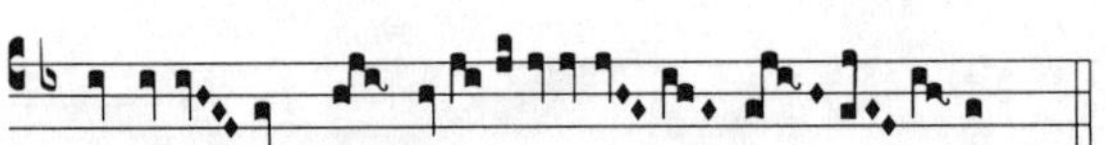

seculorum AMEN.

A) O good Shepherd:
come before the sacred and holy altar,
and in praise of the King of Kings,
you deemed worthy first to raise your voice.
We humbly ask you, say "eia" O lord:
GLORY BE TO GOD ON HIGH, AND ON EARTH PEACE TO PEOPLE OF GOOD WILL.

1) Peace everlasting, Christ has given light
Glory to you Father on high:
WE PRAISE YOU;

2) To whom the angels poured out
a hymn today on earth,
singing, for Christ was born.

WE BLESS YOU.
3) Today a savior is born to us,
always to be worshipped in the Trinity:
WE ADORE YOU;
4) Whom, crying among the hollows
of the narrow stable,
the throng of angels praise, exulting:
WE GLORIFY YOU.
WE GIVE THANKS TO YOU FOR YOUR GREAT GLORY. LORD GOD, HEAVENLY KING, GOD, THE FATHER ALMIGHTY.
5) Today, graciously
taking on flesh of a mortal
we pray:
LORD JESUS CHRIST, ONLY BEGOTTEN SON; LORD GOD, LAMB OF GOD, SON OF THE FATHER:
6) From whose throne a blessed light
has shined on the darkness of the world.
YOU WHO TAKE AWAY THE SINS OF THE WORLD:
HAVE MERCY ON US.
YOU WHO TAKE AWAY THE SINS OF THE WORLD:
RECEIVE OUR PRAYER.
7) O king ineffable, and wonderful:
Today you came forth from the virgin to the world,
which you aided:
YOU, WHO SIT AT THE RIGHT HAND OF THE FATHER:
HAVE MERCY ON US;
FOR YOU ALONE ARE HOLY,
YOU ALONE ARE THE LORD
YOU ALONE ARE THE MOST HIGH:
B) Your firm rule,
through you O Christ, is established for us all-powerfully;
You, who gave life to us through the seal of the cross:
We praise you O most merciful King.
Praise and honor will always be yours forever:
JESUS CHRIST;
WITH THE HOLY SPIRIT IN THE GLORY OF GOD THE FATHER.
C) Maker and also redeemer of humanity,
ineffable, without end, without beginning,
You came to save us deigning to have been born of a virgin,
and now, God and man reigning, O Lord and Ruler.
D) You, three and one divinity,
we pray that you yourself wash away
our faults and offenses.
Give peace through your servants
to us, and also glory[58]

58. Reading *gloriam* for *gloria*.

throughout all ages and forever
AMEN

The series opens with a trope (marked 'A' in the translation) that serves to invite the bishop to intone the gloria. Although the most frequently encountered versions of this trope (especially in France) transmit the opening as *sacerdos dei excelsi* (O priest of the highest God), the variant transmitted by the Autun Troper supports the hierarchical structure of its cathedral setting (intoning the gloria is the bishop's prerogative), while helping to connect the bishop with (1) his function as Christ's representative,[59] (2) with the shepherds who heard the angelic hymn (see the gospel lection for the first mass of Christmas), and (3) with the angels themselves who first sang the gloria.[60] The hierarchical function of the song is particularly prominent in the last line, where the cantor (representing the choir) petitions the bishop to begin. In this last line, the cantor calls the bishop "lord," using the shortened form *domne* for *domine*. This usage indicates his social location as a member of the aristocracy, although it does not indicate whether this social location comes from birth, office, or both.

The main body of the Christmas gloria consists of seven poetic interpolations of the gloria text. Although they are not completely uniform in structure, they are organized according to the rules of syllable-counting, accentual verse. The basic pattern is one of five or six syllables accented in the following manner: ∼́∼∼∼́∼ , and ∼́∼∼̀∼∼́∼ . These usually occur four times per interpolation, although elements 4 and 7 have five units, and element 5 has only three units. The third interpolation provides good examples of the basic patterns:

Nátus est nóbis // hódiè salvátor
ìn trinitáte // sémper coléndus

59. Although the title "Good Shepherd" belongs properly to Christ, the bishop carries a staff in order to emphasize his role in representing this office to the church.

60. The use of *Pastor bone* in the Autun Troper is unique outside Italy, and the *Gloria/ Pax sempiterna* trope from the Beneventan repertory is very close to the version transmitted by the Autun Troper. This may indicate some Italian influence on the Autun repertory. For a good examination of origin, function, and transmission of the introductory tropes to the gloria, see Thomas Forrest Kelly, "Introducing the *Gloria in Excelsis*," *Journal of the American Musicological Society* 37 (1984): 479-506.

Each of these interpolations takes up festally related themes, which are derived from the readings, and organize patterns of sound which make them more "ornate."

All in all the interpolations borrow heavily from the context and language of the Christmas story itself, elaborating themes from Luke, John, and Isaiah. Their primary function is to provide a measured and ornate form of the angel's hymn of praise, joining it specifically to this feast through invoking the narrative elements and bringing them into the present through remembering them. The first interpolation takes up the word "peace" from the intonation, and combines it with the theme of "light" that is prominent in the Old Testament lection (Is. 9:2-9), which accompanied the reading of Luke 2:1-14 in the first mass of Christmas. This also takes up the theme of "light coming into the world," which will be part of main gospel reading for this feast, and invites the choir to combine the differing perspectives on the incarnation offered by these readings. The second interpolation serves the role of the *accessus ad auctores*, but not only provides context for the gloria (reminding the choir who sang it and why), but encourages them to be filled with the hymn that the angels "poured out," so that the angels sing today, through the assembly. The third interpolation brings the trinitarian theme broached in the last introit tropes and in the kyrie to the foreground. The fourth interpolation has a *kenotic* element: Jesus is characterized as "crying" (literally "squalling") and has been born into poverty, yet the angels praise him through the voices of the choir. This theme is developed in the fifth element as well, and leads to the litany which addresses Christ as Lamb of God. Element 6 again quotes Is. 9:2, equating the "sins of the world" with the "world's darkness" and praising God for the "blessed light" which has come into the world; this prepares for the themes treated in the gospel lection (John 1). The series ends with a reminder of the miracle of the incarnation, which puts it firmly in the present celebration: "Today, you came forth from the virgin."

The last part of the gloria text proper contains three short acclamations to Jesus (*Tu solus . . .*), extended in this manuscript (and in many others) by a prosula (marked 'B'), which unites the message of Easter with the message of Christmas. The rhetorical effect is to make the naming of Jesus more prominent by delaying it. The *Conditor* prosula ('C') has an unusual place in this manuscript: it too would ordinarily lead up to the final naming of Jesus, but since that place has already been filled, it occurs here as an introduction to the trope ('D') to the Amen. It is (linguistically) more theologically developed than any of the trope elements that have been examined so far, borrowing language from the gospel of John, and even echoing Chalcedon: "this self-same one is actually God and actually man."[61] Presumably, the theologically developed prosula spurred the Autun scribe to add another invocation to the Trinity. The "servants" (*famulus, famulis*) referred to in the final lines are probably the angels themselves, who were the speakers of the gloria who announced "peace to people of good will."

The melody for the gloria and its *laudes* helps to identify the double structure of lyrical prose and rhythmic poetry, and makes them into a satisfying whole. Except for the two prosulas, discussed below, the melodic writing of the entire piece is in a unified style, characterized by intensively repetitive and formulaic writing. The musical figuration creates a basic contrast between the gloria elements and the *laudes*: the gloria elements primarily decorate thirds; for example, the setting of *LAUDAMUS TE* outlines the third 'G-b-flat' on the first word and decorates the third 'F-a' on the second word. The gloria melody almost never outlines a fourth, in contrast to the trope elements, which often do; for example, in trope element 3, *Natus est* outlines 'F-b-flat', and *hodie* decorates 'a-d'. The trope elements also use a wider variety of musical figures, including figures that decorate a third, although they tend to use these figures principally at the end or sometimes at the beginning of each element. This suggests that they are intentionally connected to the gloria to make a seamless melody, while their differing internal figuration provides a contrast.

The syllabic style of the gloria's two prosulas is in marked contrast with the rest of the piece. The first of these, *Regnum tuum per te Christe*, functions to lengthen the series of epithets to Christ that precedes the doxology of the gloria. Although it begins and ends with a trope in a neumatic style, it has three interior syllabic lines that cadence on rhymes (*omnipotentis-*

61. For the "definition of Chalcedon," see John H. Leith, *Creeds of the Churches*, 3d ed. (Atlanta: John Knox Press, 1982), 34-36.

sime, vivifice, clementissime); these provide the opportunity for acclamations appropriate for the choir, connecting the rule of Christ (emphasized by the gloria text itself) with Christ's giving life and mercy to the worshippers themselves. The last two elements of the gloria are both musically and textually disruptive. Since the prosula *Conditor* has lost its enclosing *Regnum* trope, its beginning contrasts strongly with the gloria melody, providing the only major disruption in an otherwise very unified piece. However, it connects well with the following trope, *Te trina,* which also begins syllabically, making the two elements into a "dogmatic" coda which affirms the orthodox belief in Christ's full divinity and humanity, and which attributes salvation to the triune God. The ending of this last element also gracefully becomes more neumatic, so that it ties into the melismatic *AMEN* of the gloria, and reconnects the coda textually to the gloria by invoking the "servants" of God who give peace.

The music of the Christmas gloria as a whole lies halfway between the types of musical procedures adopted by the introit and by the kyrie respectively. Its particularly appropriate association with Christmas and its emphasis on the Christmas narrative of the interpolated *laudes* help connect the themes of the previous two Christmas services with the third mass; however, the "dogmatic coda" of the gloria and the trinitarian shape of the gloria text itself help to strengthen the focus on the consequences of the incarnation, which marks all of the readings and music of this particular feast.[62]

---

62. The opening section of the service concluded (after the gloria) with the bishop reciting the collect for the day. The third mass of Christmas usually has this collect:

Concede, quaesumus omnipotens Deus: ut nos unigeniti tui nova per carnem nativitas liberet; quos sub peccati iugo vetusta servitus tenet. Per eundum Dominum Iesum Christum.	Grant, we pray, almighty God: that the new birth of your only-begotten in the flesh may set us free; whom the old bondage holds under the yoke of sin. Through Jesus Christ our Lord.

An early twelfth-century *collectarium,* Autun 10 gives eight additional choices for this prayer, which take up a variety of themes, praying: (1) that God's mercy be shown by the light of truth, with the birth of Christ; (2) that the glory of the Nativity be reflected by an increase in faith, hope, and charity; (3) that the new creation implied by the miraculous birth may free us from fallen creation; (4) that the new heavenly light dawn in our hearts; (5) that the people gathered at the celebration receive grace and redemption; (6) that as Christ's taking on of hu-

Gradual, alleluia, and prose

The three chants that come after the two readings and lead up to the gospel reading adopt a different set of musical and textual procedures from any of the chants discussed so far; this serves to highlight their special function.[63] While the gradual and alleluia develop a musical *ornatus*, the prose develops a verbal *ornatus*, and although the two styles contrast with each other, both were principally intended to create an aesthetically pleasing setting for the reflection on, and anticipation of, the readings. Together they form a series intended to create a musical rite that summarizes the lections and anticipates the gospel, marking the reading of the gospel as the high point of the Liturgy of the Word.

Although the texts of the gradual and of the alleluia verse were not as important as their music, they were very carefully chosen to summarize the readings (a pattern which was already extensively developed by the introit trope complex, but recapped and ornamented here). The gradual text is made up from the verses of Psalm 97 (97:3cd-4a, 2) that are most relevant to the Christmas feast, and which work well as a response for both the Isaiah passage which ends "And all the ends of the earth *shall see* the salvation of our God" (Et *videbunt* omnes fines terrae salutare Dei nostri), and also from the Hebrews passage, which concludes by proclaiming the Son's justice and work in creation. Thus, the gradual proclaims the fulfillment of the Isaiah prophecy and reinforces the message of the Hebrews lection:

---

man substance reformed it, we may conform to and partake of your divinity; (7) that the whole world know your salvation; (8) that your people be given a firm faith, liberated from adversity, and freed for joy. Presumably the choice was up to the celebrant, but most of the prayers bring the ritual remembrance of the Nativity into the present by connecting some element of the story to a prayer for present consequences.

63. During this period there were two lections as well as the gospel at the third Christmas mass; later the Old Testament lection was omitted. Autun 10, fol. 40, in a section dating from the fourteenth century lists all three readings. However, only the epistle and the gospel reading are listed in the 1556 Missal (*Sacrorum Codex (vulgo Missale nuncupatus) iuxta ritum Ecclesiae Heduensis optima ordine nunc demum multo, quam ante hac unquam catigator, in lucem emissus: In quo prater veram verborum distinctionem, orthographiam, ac prosodiam, nihil eorum, quae ac sacra peragenda pertinere videntur, desiderare polis* (Autun: apud Johannem Hamelinum, 1555/6).

Viderunt omnes fines terrae salutare Dei nostri: iubilate Deo omnis terra.
Notum fecit Dominus salutare suum: ante conspectum gentium *revelavit iustitiam suam.*

All the ends of the earth *have seen* the salvation of our God: Rejoice in God all the earth.
The Lord has made known his salvation: in the sight of the peoples, *he has revealed his justice.*

These themes are also at the heart of the standard exegetical commentaries, which equate the key nouns (salvation and justice) with Christ:

> *All have seen,* that is, all have beheld with the mind what has been effected throughout the whole world. To what vision if not to faith is it referring, so that the truth of the words may be established; truly through faith, *all the ends of the earth have seen* Jesus.
>
> *The Lord has made known salvation,* that is, the Lord, the Savior, who is rightly called salvation, because he is author of all salvation. *And he has revealed justice,* that is, Christ, who formerly was foretold by the prophets under a kind of veil. Which, having been taken away by his advent, the figure of truth itself appeared. Or [it means] the justice of life, which had been concealed by the unbelief of men.[64]

Similarly, the text of the alleluia verse evokes the theme of the gospel, which speaks of the "light coming into the world":

Dies sanctificatus illuxit nobis: venite gentes, et adorate Dominum: quia hodie descendit lux magna super terram.

The holy day has given light to us: Come, you people, adore the Lord: because today, a great light descends upon the earth.

By keeping these texts free from tropes, which tend to evoke specific responses, the choir can have time to meditate

64. Bruno of Würzburg, *Expositio psalmorum,* in Patrologiae latina, 142:355: "Viderunt omnes, id est mente conspexerunt, quod per totum mundum constat effectum. Quae visio non nisi ad fidem est referenda, ut nobis possit veritas constare verborum; per fidem enim omnes termini terrae viderunt Iesum."

"Notum fecit Dominus salutare, id est Dominum Salvatorem, qui salutaris recte dicitur, quia omnis salutis est auctor. Et revelavit justitiam, id est Christum, qui prius sub quodam velamine praedicatus fuerat a prophetis. Quo subducto in eius adventu, ipsa facies veritatis apparuit. Vel iustitiam vitae, quae incredulitate hominum fuit obsurata."

upon and appreciate the ornate music and ornate figures that they use to speak of Christ.[65] Furthermore, since the texts are placed within the context of the scripture texts which interpret them, they require little overt exegesis.

The prose contrasts with the gradual and alleluia in musical and poetic style, as well as in content. It is constructed mostly in pairs of stiches, which contain the same number of syllables, but do not have the same accentuation; this creates a form halfway between the more organized poetry of the *laudes* and the prose of the proper and scripture texts. Although most of the piece is unnotated in the Autun manuscript, it exists in many other manuscripts and versions, and I offer a tentative musical reconstruction. The text as transmitted by the Autun Troper is defective, especially toward the end, where some lines do not have a parallel syllable count. I have adapted the melody to it where necessary:[66]

Ex. 14. Prose *Christi hodierna pa<n>gamini* from PaA 1169, fol. 5v

Christi hodierna pa<n>gimini omnes una Voce simul consona

festivitatis praeclare Quod verbum caro factum exhibere se

65. For a melody for the gradual that stems from the same period and general geographic area, see Hansen, *H159 Montpellier*, 282 (Dij 833); for a contemporary alleluia melody, see Karlheinz Schlager, *Alleluia-Melodien I bis 1100*, Monumenta monodica medii aevi, no. 7 (Kassel: Bärenreiter, 1968), 118-20.

66. I have used the melody given by Richard Crocker, *The Early Sequence* (Berkeley: University of California Press, 1977), 183-88, who bases his edition on Aquitanian readings, and have collated this with the Christmas prose from the Nevers manuscript (PaN 1235, fol. 186), which has the same tune but a different text. Since only the first three and one-half lines are neumed in the Autun manuscript, my reconstruction is necessarily very tentative. However, even if the whole of the prose were notated, it would not reveal much melodic information, since it would consist almost entirely of virgas. Therefore, I have to assume that a widespread melody for this text was also the melody used at Autun. This reconstruction at least gives a melody that would have used similar patterns and similar compositional methods as the one used at Autun.

voluit. Mundo quem redemit nunc veniens de sede patris
dominus Nuntiat angelus pastoribus ingenti currunt gaudio.
Presepio puerum maria posuit in stabulum. Vagiens infantulus67
quo regitur omnis digne mundum. Vigilantes pastores exau-
riunt chorum Angelicum caelis psallentem laudem honor
decus in excelsis regi nato. Quem prophete cuncti praeconia
verunt olim Iam apparet carne quam induit dominus quem
virgo mater pannis contegit. Exiguo tegitur diversorio qui

67. The Autun Troper has no neumation after this point.

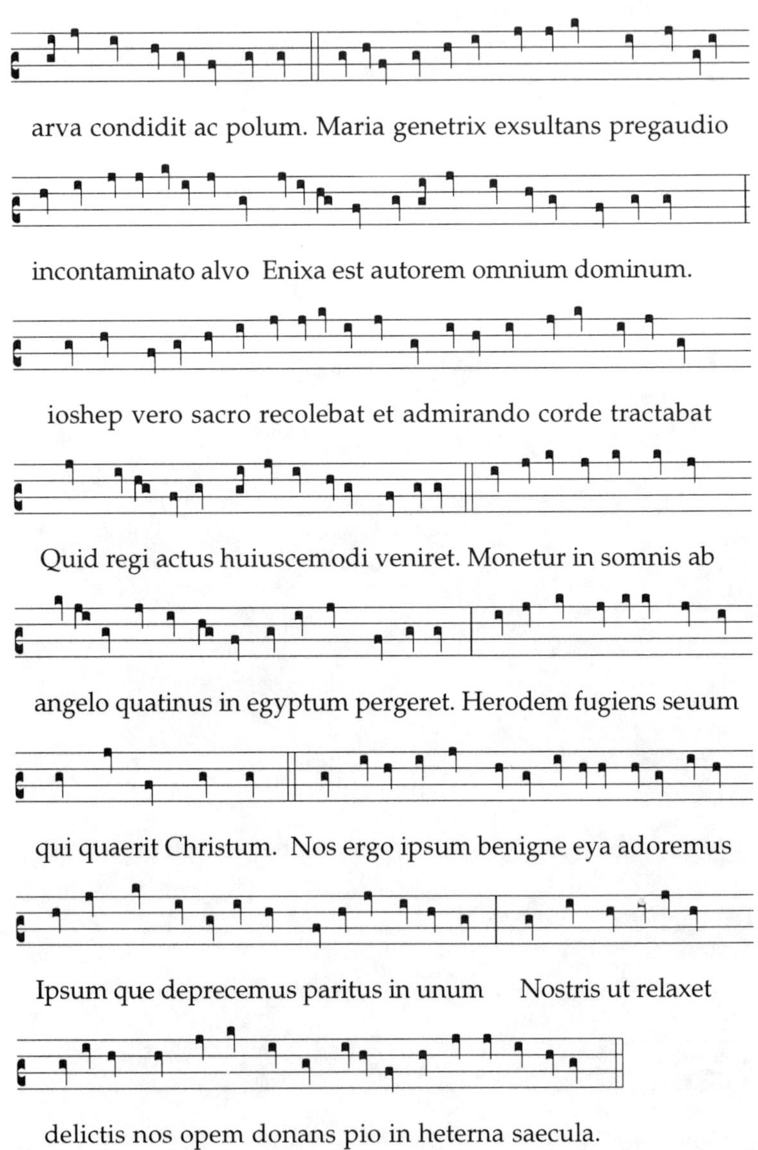
arva condidit ac polum. Maria genetrix exsultans pregaudio
incontaminato alvo Enixa est autorem omnium dominum.
ioshep vero sacro recolebat et admirando corde tractabat
Quid regi actus huiuscemodi veniret. Monetur in somnis ab
angelo quatinus in egyptum pergeret. Herodem fugiens seuum
qui quaerit Christum. Nos ergo ipsum benigne eya adoremus
Ipsum que deprecemus paritus in unum Nostris ut relaxet
delictis nos opem donans pio in heterna saecula.

1) Let all celebrate with one

2a) concordant voice this day of the magnificent festival of Christ,
2b) on which the word made flesh willed to show himself.

3a) To the world which he redeems, now, the Lord, coming from the throne of the Father.
3b) The angel tells the shepherds; they run with extraordinary joy.

4a) The boy's manger Mary placed in the stable.
4b) A squalling infant, by whom all the world is fitly ruled.

5a) And the shepherds keeping watch heard the choir of angels in heaven, singing praise, honor, glory in the highest to the newborn king.
5b) Whom the prophets of old precisely foretold, now appears, having taken on flesh, as the Lord whom the virgin mother wrapped in swaddling clothes.

6) He is sheltered in a lowly inn, who created the earth and the heaven.

7a) O Mary, genetrix, exulting with outstanding joy; by your uncontaminated womb was born the Lord and author of all.
7b) Joseph, who was recalling holy truth, and in admiration was taking to heart what a king of this sort would come to do.

8a) He is warned by an angel in a dream how to Egypt they would travel,
8b) fleeing Herod who seeks Christ.

9a) We therefore adore him with blessing *eia* and to him we pray all together,
9b) that he forgive our transgressions, giving aid to the just, for ever and ever.

Elements 1-2b, and 9ab develop themes from the readings, and contain one direct reference to the upcoming gospel ("the word made flesh") and an echo of the gradual, in the prayer for sustenance for the just at the end. However, the remainder of the text supplements the readings with the narrative elements of the Christmas story, some of which had been readings for the first two masses, and others (e.g., the flight into Egypt), which would not be read as the gospel until the feast of the Innocents in three days' time. By condensing such a large section of the narrative into a rhythmic song preceding the more abstract gospel reading, the contrast between the Christmas narrative and its more theological consequences is not only preserved, but is also made a theme in the principal mass. Moreover these passages help the prose function as a commentary on the alleluia. The theme of angelic praise is neatly woven together with the Christmas narrative starting at element 3b, which refers to the annunciation to the shepherds. Element 5a weaves together the Christmas narrative with language from one of the angels' songs to the Lamb in Rev. 5:11-13. The limits of language are explored through the use of the seeming paradox of the God of all being born as a child (see elements 4b, 5b, 6, and 7a, where Christ's divinity is contrasted with his birth).[68] All of these elements serve to reinforce the use of the prose as a commentary on the alleluia.[69] A second, less prominent refrain is that of joy at Christ's coming or even at Christ's approach (see elements 3ab, 7a). It is possible that this theme was supposed to highlight the anticipation of Christ's presence through the gospel reading itself, especially at this mass, where the image of the Word is so prominent. If the prose were used as a gospel procession, the theme of Christ's approach would have been emphasized even more by the ritual of carrying of the gospel book to the lectern.[70]

In general, the melody confirms the basic organization into repeating stiches of equal syllable counts. Furthermore, each stich is marked by a strong cadence (on either the final or the fifth of the mode), even if the syntax runs on (see especially elements 1-2a and 2b-3a). This shows the tendency of the poetic organization of words to take precedence over the marking of the syntax by melodic cadence; this violates the basic style of earlier chant, yet helps to highlight the syllable-counting structure of the verse. Most of the time, the use of parallel stiches is not too disruptive to the sense of the text, since each pair is usually constructed to create an independent syntactic unit.

The overall form of the melody displays a detailed planning of both range and tessitura; as the gospel reading approaches, the music of the prose moves into a higher range, which increases the sense of anticipation and exuberance. It is striking that the melody moves into this higher range by exploiting the same musical gesture ('G-d, e') used in the introit trope set; it is used four times in elements 5a and 5b. Moreover,

---

68. Crocker, *Early Sequence*, 187, points out some of these rhetorical gestures, but does not connect them with the larger rhetorical structure created by the liturgy itself.

69. See chapter 1, pp. 50-56 and chapter 3, p. 122.

70. See chapter 3, p. 133, on the gospel procession.

the words of element 5b even recapitulate much of the introit tropes; the melodic gesture points this out by marking the words "whom the prophets [foretold]" and "now he appears." Once the prose enters the higher range, it never returns to the original 'G' final. Instead, even the final cadence of the piece is on the co-final 'd' a fifth above. This feature (common to quite a few proses) keeps the chant open to the reading which follows. Thus, it is the reading of the gospel itself that completes the overall rite created by all three intervenient chants.

The progression of chants between the readings develops both musical and textual concepts of *ornatus*, helping to organize the communal reflection on the readings, and helping to create a sense of anticipation and excitement surrounding the gospel reading. While the gradual and alleluia offer richly ornamented summaries of the main lections, the prose maintains a closeness not only with the gospel lection but with the gospel narrative, and weaves this into a rhythmic song which would serve well for a gospel procession.

Credo

Since it was not recited at the ferial mass, the credo can be considered something of a festal addition. Although it never attracted tropes, sections of the Nicene Creed dealt with themes that were brought into a special prominence by specific seasons. For example, the relationship between the Word (the Son) and God (the Father), explained in the Credo, is a prominent theme throughout the Christmas mass. This theme had already been raised in the introit tropes, in the "dogmatic" coda of the gloria *laudes*, given rhetorical poignancy by the paradoxical refrains in the prose, and had been developed in almost creedal language in the gospel. Through the credo, these elements were collected and given a greater dogmatic precision. Furthermore, all of the subsequent tropes for songs within the eucharistic liturgy reflect either direct or indirect allusions to the credo. The relevant sections of the credo are given below:

Credo in unum deum, patrem omnipotentem, factorem caeli et terrae, visibilium omnium et invisibilium. Et in unum dominum Iesum Christum, filium dei unigenitum. Et ex patre natum ante omnia saecula. Deum de deo, lumen de lumine, deum verum de deo vero. Genitum, non factum, consubstantialem patri: per quem omnia facta sunt. Qui propter nos homines, et propter nostram salutem descendit de caelis. Et incarnatus est de spiritu sancto ex Maria virgine: et homo facuts est. . . .	I believe in one God, the Father almighty, maker of heaven and earth, and of all things visible and invisible: And in one Lord Jesus Christ, the only begotten Son of God, begotten of the Father before all worlds, God of God, Light of Light, very God of very God, begotten not made, being of one substance with the Father, by whom all things were made; who for us humans and for our salvation came down from heaven, and was incarnate by the Holy Ghost, and was made man. . . .
....	....
Et iterum venturus est cum gloria judicare vivos et mortuos: cuius regni non erit finis.	And he shall come again in glory to judge both the quick and the dead: whose kingdom shall have no end.

Offertory

The offertory marks the beginning of the eucharistic liturgy, and the ceremonial focuses on the preparation of the altar, and possibly included an offering from the laity.[71] The focus of both the offertory song and of the trope elements is on God's work in creation; this not only brings the theme of God's presence to creation into greater prominence, but connects it with the eucharist and the preparation of the eucharistic elements themselves. I have been able to reconstruct the melody of all but the first trope element from the Nevers manuscript PaN 1235, fol. 186v. Although this substitutes a different introductory trope, it retains the two internal trope elements:[72]

Ex. 15. Christmas offertory trope set *Concentu parili chorus/ TUI SUNT CELI* from PaA 1169, fol. 6r

Concentu parili chorus

71. See chapter 3, pp. 134-35, for a fuller discussion.

72. The antiphon melody is reconstructed from Montpellier, H 159; see Hansen, *Montpellier, H 159*, (Dij 903).

omnis ecclesiae psallat

mirabilia tua domine

TUI SUNT CE- LI ET TUA EST TER- RA Haec sunt etenim

prima et praecipua divine cre-a-ci-o-nis opera ORBEM

TER-RARUM ET PLENITU- DINEM E- IUS TU

FUNDASTI Omnia in sapienci- a mirabiliter condidi-sti

IUSTITI- A <ET IUDI- CI-UM PRAEPARATIO

SE- DIS TU-AE.>

1) In equal harmony, the whole choir of the church sings your wonders, O Lord:
YOURS ARE THE HEAVENS AND YOURS IS THE EARTH:
2) For these are, divinely, the first and principal works of creation.
THE EARTH AND ITS FULLNESS, YOU HAVE ESTABLISHED.
3) You miraculously founded everything in wisdom.
JUSTICE AND JUDGMENT [ARE] THE PREPARATION OF YOUR THRONE.

The base text of the offertory is taken from Psalm 88:12 and 15a, and because of its placement within the liturgy, it echoes the thought developed in the opening lines of the credo, letting the choir ascribe the creation to God. The credo, the Christmas liturgy, and the traditional interpretation of this psalm develop the theme of Christ as God's presence to creation. Moreover, the Hebrews lection, gospel lection, and the credo all ascribe creation to the Son or Word (see Heb. 1:8-10; John 1:3; credo, above). Hence, trinitarian theology becomes an explicit theme for reflection, especially God's work in creation through the Son (including the Son's judgment of creation).

Like the introductory trope to the introit, *Concentu parili* (element 1) acts as an *accessus ad auctores*, identifying who is speaking the following line from the antiphon. Bruno's commentary on this psalm serves a similar purpose; in his summary of the whole psalm, he identifies its speakers and its main topics: "The voice of the faithful praise the mercy and the power of the Lord."[73] The trope element goes further than the commentary: it identifies not only the speaker as the whole church, but makes this a substantial reality by helping the choir to join in the praise with their singing of the antiphon element. This both makes the idea of the *accessus* liturgically active and develops a theme found in a verse from the psalm that is not quoted in the antiphon:

73. Bruno of Würzburg, *Expositio psalmorum,* in Patrologiae latina, 142:327: "Vox fidelium, misericordias Domini potentiamque laudantium."

Psalm 88:6:

Confitebuntur caeli *mirabilia tua, Domine*; Etenim veritatem tuam in *ecclesia* sanctorum.	The heavens shall confess *thy wonders, O Lord*: and thy truth in the *church* of the saints.

The trope element not only uses much of the language of this verse, but also develops the idea of universal praise by asking the "whole choir of the church" to join in "equal harmony" (i.e., one accord), thus uniting the confession of the heavens with the current song. Finally, the use of the phrase "*mirabilia tua*" (your wonders) creates a connection between this psalm and the verse from Psalm 97:1 (used in the introit), where "God's wonders" referred to the incarnation itself.

While the offertory does not develop the dogmatic elements of the theme beyond what was already stated in the credo, it does explore a wider range of imagery than has been used so far, and the following two antiphon and trope elements 2 and 3 (*TUI SUNT; Haec sunt; ORBEM TERRARUM; Omnia in sapiencia*) function in a way even closer to exegetical commentary by explicitly developing elements of the psalm's traditional interpretation, as well as paraphrasing some of its other verses. The choir names the heavens and the earth as wonders of God, and then these are identified as the first and principal works of divine creation; this refers directly to Gen. 1:1: "In *principio creavit* Deus *caelum et terram*" (*In the beginning*, God *created the heavens and the earth*). The next antiphon element specifies what these works entail: the creation of the world and its fullness, which were traditionally interpreted as "the whole world of space," and "all the creatures in it."[74] Thus, the progression of thought mimics the order of the thought in the credo. If trope element 3 (*Omnia*) is read Christologically, it continues to outline the thought of the credo by attributing the foundation of everything in "wisdom," i.e., through Christ. The trope element takes some of its language from the Hebrews lection, which in quoting Psalm 44:7-8 and Psalm 101:26 relates the theme of the Son's justice to the Son's work of creation:

74. Ibid., 329.

Ad Filium autem: *Thronus tuus Deus in saeculum saeculi*: virga aequitatis, virga regni tui. Dilexisti *iustitiam*, et odisti iniquitatem: propterea unxit te Deus, Deus tuus oleo exultationis prae participibus tuis. Et: *Tu in principio Domine terram fundasti: et opera manuum tuarum sunt caeli.*	But to the Son: *Thy throne, O God, is for ever and ever*: a scepter of justice is the scepter of thy kingdom. Thou hast loved *justice*, and hated iniquity: therefore God, thy God, hath anointed thee with the oil of gladness above thy fellows. And: *Thou in the beginning, O Lord, didst found the earth: and the works of thy hands are the heavens.*

A Christological reading gains further support from the ways in which both trope elements 2 and 3, as well as the intervening antiphon element, closely parallel Psalm 103:24:

Quam magnificata sunt opera tua, Domine: omnia in sapientia fecisti: Impleta est terra possesione tua.	How great are your works, O Lord. You have made all things in wisdom: the earth is filled with your riches.

Bruno's psalm commentary makes clear the reference to Christ: "In wonder, the prophet says, 'How marvelous they are!' for this [task] is not only too difficult for men (for the work of Christ exceeds human understanding) but truly is immense for the angels themselves. This wisdom, then, is the Son of the Father."[75] The final antiphon element (*IUSTITIA ET IUDICIUM*) continues to follow the thought of both the credo and the Hebrews lection, by relating the theme of judgment to God's reign.

The trope set taken as a whole ornaments the thought of the lections using the order of the credo, and connects the poetic imagery, typology, and embellished music with the more restrained dogmatic statements. The introductory element (1) also uses poetic accent (three accents per line) to organize its words more rhythmically, and in addition, the first two lines have the same number of syllables. The music of the antiphon and trope elements 2 and 3 does not exploit musical gesture (as did

75. Ibid., 375: "Admirando enim dicit propheta, quam magnificata sunt, nam non solum hoc hominis arduum (quia excedit humanum sensum operatio Christi), verum etiam ipsis angelis probatur immensum. Ista igitur sapientia Filius est Patris."

some of the introit tropes). However, in clearly articulating the syntax of both trope and antiphon texts, it brings out significantly parallel syntactic structures between the first antiphon element and its following trope and the second antiphon element and its following trope. In the example below, I have marked the musical syllables, commas, colons, and periods that are formed by the cadential structure of the music;[76] each element of the first pairing of antiphon and trope pauses after the second word on the same verb, and has a cadence on a comma, setting off a clause which begins with the word *et*:

TUI SUNT[S] CELI, ET TUA EST[S] TERRA.
Haec sunt[S] etenim prima, et praecipua[S] divine[S] creationis opera.

Each element of the second pairing begins with the object and its modifiers, which are set off with a cadence; then each has another strong cadence before ending with the verb:

ORBEM TERRARUM, ET PLENITUDINEM[S] EIUS, TU FUNDASTI.
Omnia[S] in sapiencia, mirabiliter, condisti.

Although the musical pitches do not duplicate each other, the close duplication of syntactical structure (especially at the beginnings and ends of the stiches) and the ornamentation of each structure (through the addition of adverbs in each of the trope elements) is made clear, helping the tropes fill out and exegete the rather cryptic antiphon text.[77]

Sanctus

The Christmas sanctus has a proper preface that draws upon the gospel lection and reinforces its theme of knowing God through Christ. This is appropriate to the strong medieval sense of eucharistic presence (even before the official formulation of the doctrine of transubstantiation). It serves to empha-

76. Musical syllables are marked by a raised 's'; see chapter 2, pp. 73-84, on musical punctuation.

77. Of the prayers said silently during the offertory chant, only the secret has a festal reference: "Oblata, Domine, munera, nova Unigeniti tui Nativitate sanctifica: nosque a peccatorum nostrorum maculis emunda. Per eundem Dominum." (O Lord, sanctify the gifts we offer you, by the new birth of your only-begotten, and cleanse us from the stains of our sins. Through the same Lord.)

size the theme of seeing God in and through the eucharist, and reinforces the theme of God's presence to creation through Christ:

Vere dignum et iustum est aequum et salutare, nos tibi semper et ubique gratias agere: Domine sancte, Pater omnipotens, aeterne Deus: Quia per incarnati Verbi mysterium, nova mentis nostrae oculis lux tuae claritatis infulsit: ut dum visibiliter Deum congnoscimus, per hunc invisibiliem amorem rapiamur. Et ideo cum Angelis et Archangelis, cum Thronis et Dominationibus, cumque omni militia caelestis exercitus, hymnum gloriae tuae canimus, sine fine dicentes:[78]	It is truly meet and right, just and salutary, that we should at all times and in all places give thanks to you: O holy Lord, Father almighty, eternal God: For, by the mystery of your incarnate Word, the new light of your splendor has shone upon the eyes of our minds: that while we know God visibly, through him we may be drawn to love things invisible. And therefore, with the Angels and Archangels, with Kingdoms and Dominions, and with all the armies of the heavenly host, we sing an unending hymn of your glory, saying:

The sanctus tropes explicitly make reference to the Trinity, through short doxological interpolations which use language mostly adapted from the Nicene Creed. The trope to the benedictus is written in the margin (possibly an addition by the music scribe), but it makes clear the reference to the triumphal entry into Jerusalem that preceded the passion of Christ (which is behind the base text), and helps strengthen the theme of greeting Christ:[79]

78. This is the normal "Roman" preface, and it appears in a twelfth-century sacramentary from Autun: Autun 11, fol. 7. Other prefaces from this collection are atypical and demonstrate a tendency to include large narrative sections (especially on saints' days). For example, on fol. 8v, the preface for John the Evangelist even mentions his authorship of the fourth gospel, and quotes its opening lines to identify it. However, both Christmas and Easter prefaces are standard and restrained.

79. The closest concordance for most of the music can be found in the St. Magloire Troper, Paris, Bibliothèque Nationale, fonds latins MS 10508 (PaN 10508). The melody is identical to that on fol. 198v of the Nevers Troper (PaN 1235) until *deus sabaoth.* I have based my reading of the Autun variant on St. Magloire and have collated it with the Nevers reading. For a modern edition of the Nevers sanctus, see van Deusen, *Nevers Repertory,* 2:122. For the sanctus melody, see Peter Josef Thannabaur, *Das einstimmige Sanctus der römischen Messe in der handschriftlichen Überlieferung des 11. bis 16. Jahrhunderts,* Erlanger Arbeiten zur

Ex. 16. *SANCTUS/ Pater lumen/ Cuius in laude/ BENEDICTUS* from PaA 1169, fol. 6r

SANCTUS Pa- ter lumen heternum SANCTUS ge- nitus
ex de-o deus SANCTUS DOMINUS Spiritus maiesta- te cum
similis DEUS SABAOTH PLENI SUNT CAELI ET TERRA
GLORIA TUA <OSANNA IN EXCELSIS> Cuius in laude
voces dabant pueri regem Christum conlaudantes in altissimis
BENEDICTUS <QUI VENIT IN NO- MINE DOMINI

Musikwissenschaft, no. 1 (Munich: Walter Ricke, 1962), 203. The melody is numbered 216 in Thannabaur's catalogue.

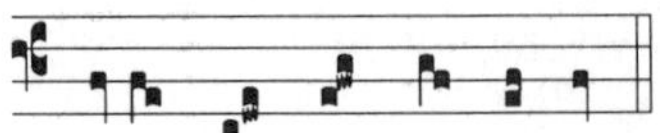

OSANNA IN EXCELSIS>

HOLY
1) Father, light eternal.
HOLY
2) Begotten from God, God
HOLY LORD
3) Spirit with a like majesty
GOD OF HOSTS HEAVEN AND EARTH ARE FULL OF YOUR GLORY. HOSANNA IN THE HIGHEST
4) In whose praise, cries rendering the children extolling the King, Christ, in the highest:
BLESSED IS HE WHO COMES IN THE NAME OF THE LORD. HOSANNA IN THE HIGHEST.

As Iversen points out, the first "trope" to the sanctus is the preface itself, which serves the purpose of naming the reasons for the feast and inviting the choir to sing with the heavenly host in praise of God.[80]

The tropes for the sanctus serve mainly to identify God as triune, while the benedictus trope element (4), *Cuius in laude*, functions as a very sophisticated gloss on the benedictus: It evokes all of the gospel accounts of Jesus' entry into Jerusalem by using more of the language from them than was provided by the benedictus itself. (I have marked with italics only those portions of the texts that are added by the trope elements; elements of the base texts can be found in all of the gospel accounts shown below):

Sanctus and Trope element:

DEUS SABAOTH OSANNA IN EXCELSIS	*GOD* OF HOSTS HOSANNA IN THE HIGHEST
Cuius in *laude voces* dabant *pueri regem* Christum *conlaudantes* in *altissimis*	In whose *praise, cries* rendering the *children extolling* the *King*, Christ, in the *highest*:
BENEDICTUS QUI VENIT IN NOMINE DOMINI OSANNA IN EXCELSIS	BLESSED IS HE WHO COMES IN THE NAME OF THE LORD. HOSANNA IN THE HIGHEST

80. See Iversen, "On the Iconography of Praise in the Sanctus and Its Tropes," 277-78.

Mt 21:

9	turbae autem quae praecedebant et quae sequebantur clamabant dicentes osanna Filio David benedictus qui venturus est in nomine Domini osanna in *altissimis*	9	And the multitudes that went before and that followed, cried, saying: Hosanna to the son of David: Blessed is he that cometh in the name of the Lord: Hosanna in the *highest*
15	videntes autem principes sacerdotum et scribae mirabila quae fecit et *pueros* clamantes in templo et dicentes osanna Filio David indignati sunt	15	And the chief priests and scribes, seeing the wonderful things that he did, and the *children* crying in the temple, and saying: Hosanna to the son of David; were moved with indignation.

Mark 11:

9	et qui praeibant et qui sequebantur clamabant dicentes osanna benedictus qui venit in nomine Domini	9	And they that went before and they that followed, cried, saying: Hosanna, blessed is he that cometh in the name of the Lord.
10	benedictum quod venit *regnum* patris nostri David osanna in excelesis	10	Blessed be the *kingdom* of our father David that cometh: Hosanna in the highest.

Luke 19:

37	et cum adpropinquaret iam ad descensum montis Oliveti coeperunt omnes turbae discentium gaudentes *laudare Deum voce* magna super omnibus quas viderant virtutibus	37	And as he was coming near the descent of the mount Olivet, the whole multitude of his disciples began with joy to *praise God* with a loud *voice*, for all the mighty works they had seen,
38	dicentes benedictus qui venit *rex* in nomine Domini pax in caelo et gloria in excelsis	38	Saying: Blessed be the *king* who cometh in the name of the Lord, peace in heaven, and glory on high!

John 12:

12	in crastinum autem turba multa quae venerat ad diem festum cum audissent quia venit Iesus Hierosolyma	12	And on the next day, a great multitude that was to come to the festival day, when they had heard that Jesus was coming to Jerusalem,
13	acceperunt ramos palmarum et processerunt obviam ei et clamabant osanna benedictus qui venit in nomine Domini *rex* Israhel	13	Took branches of palm trees, and went forth to meet him, and cried: Hosanna, blessed is he that cometh in the name of the Lord, the *king* of Israel.

All four gospels share a core of material which became the base text of the osanna and benedictus, whereas the trope element supplies variations found in one or more of the gospel accounts. From Matthew, it borrows the synonym for *excelsis* (*altissimis*) as well as the word children (*pueri*). (In Matthew the children cry hosanna in the temple, not in the procession.) From Mark, Luke, and John, the trope borrows the theme of Jesus' kingship; Mark refers to David's kingdom (*regnum*), and Luke and John name Jesus as king (*rex*). The trope blends all the accounts together by using the title Christ (Messiah) rather than the name Jesus: by using the word "king," the trope follows the language of Luke and John, but by using "Christ" instead of Jesus, the trope suggests a davidic kingship following Mark's account. By relating the theme of the "newborn king" to the passion narrative, the trope element helps to hold the larger narrative patterns of the life, death, and resurrection of Christ together, making a link between the sanctus and the canon of the mass that follows it.[81] Also from Luke, the trope element borrows the words *laudare, deum,* and *voce*. Because of the way it is constructed, the trope element can refer back to the last named noun (*Deus*) as the object of the praise it invokes at its beginning. The trope element helps to make the whole of the sanctus follow the pattern in the eucharistic prayer itself, by praising the triune God and then focusing the praise on Christ who is coming to be present in the eucharistic elements themselves.

As in many ordinary tropes, the melody and trope elements are tightly woven together in a largely unified style. This makes it difficult to find striking instances of marking the text through figuration. Nevertheless, the overall structure of the cadences suggests a very subtle reading of the text: the first *sanctus* is immediately answered with the same neumation for the word *Pater*. Both elements cadence on the piece's final ('D'), making each word into a complete unit. The next two attributes of the father ("light, eternal") move away to the weak cadence on 'C', which connects well to the next invocation of

81. The canon of the mass has only one festal variation: a specific reference to the celebration of that "most sacred day in which the undefiled virginity of the blessed Mary brought forth the savior into this world," at the *Communicantes*. It seems probable that most of the canon was said audibly, since the sanctus, even with tropes, is not long enough to cover much of it.

sanctus which ends on the weak note 'E'. 'E' remains the main cadence note throughout the invocation to the Son and the Holy Spirit, with a strong cadence on the final coming only on the words *Deus Sabaoth*, invoking the triune God. The musical setting (by giving slightly greater weight and prominence to God-Father) suggests a (proper) subordination to the Father as the "fount of deity," while the theologically exact naming of the persons of the Trinity keeps the sense of subordination from seeming arianizing.[82] Although many ordinary melodies included tropes in their original conception, it is worth noting that the sanctus melody without the tropes would have the same hierarchy of cadence points: without the trope elements the triple invocations of *sanctus* would still retain the same sense of subordination, but the type of subordinationism would be ambiguous without the orthodox language of the trope elements.

The style of the trope to the benedictus (*Cuius in laude*) is slightly different, reflecting its more fragmented syntax. The first three words ("in whose praise") cadence on the final, which separates them from the rest of the trope element. The music helps them to refer back to the God of Hosts (*Deus sabaoth*) as the recipient of the praise, but they can also refer forward to Christ (*Christum*), who is named later in this element. The music marks *Christum* with a strong cadence on the final. Furthermore, the fragmentation of the syntax is reflected in the music, which has weak cadences after *dabant, pueri, conlaudantes*, and at the end of the element on *altissimus*. These weaker cadences help separate the syntactically unrelated words, making it easier to hear the sense of the phrase. Moreover the music helps to emphasize those words that end on the stronger cadence of the final.

Agnus dei and communion

During the eleventh century, the liturgical function of the agnus dei was ambiguous, and it could occur in any of three places: (1)

82. See Wainwright, *Doxology*, 95-101, on proper and arianizing subordinationism. The trope elements seem particularly careful to be non-arian (that is, they do not imply that worship of Christ or the Holy Spirit is worship of a "creature"). Instead they name the principal difference between Christ and God (God is unengendered, while Christ is *genitus*), which dates back to Athanasius, and carefully state that the Holy Spirit is with a like majesty.

as a fraction anthem; (2) accompanying the "Peace"; and (3) as a communion song.[83] The troped agnus dei in the Autun manuscript would fit any of these situations, all of which would help to focus on the theme of Christ's presence through the eucharistic elements themselves:[84]

Ex. 17. *AGNUS DEI/ Verum subsistens* from PaA 1169, fol. 6v

AGNUS DEI QUI TOLLIS PECCA- TA MUNDI MISE-

RE-RE NOBIS. Verum subsis-tens vero de lumine lumen

MISERE-RE <NOBIS>. Optima perpetua concede gaudia

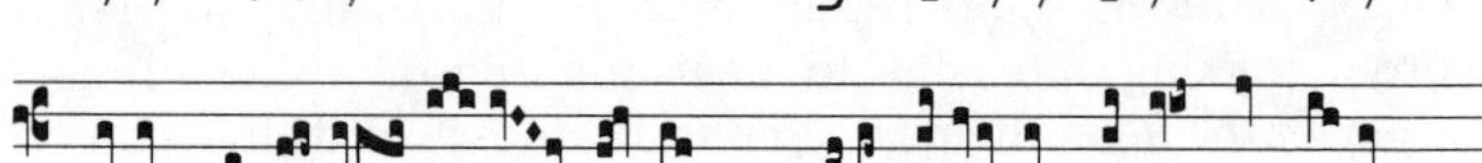

vite MISERE-RE <NOBIS>. Omnipotens e-ter-na de-i

83. See chapter 3, p. 135.

84. In other manuscripts, this trope set occurs fairly regularly with variations in the order of the three tropes. The melody in the Autun Troper appears to be close to the one listed as Melody 119 by Martin Schildbach, *Das einstimmige Agnus Dei und seine handschriftliche Überlieferung vom 10. bis zum 16. Jahrhundert* (Erlangen-Nürnberg: Josef Hogl, 1967), 112. Another version of the melody close to that in the Autun Troper can be found in PaN 1871, fols. 55r-56v.

sapientia Christe MISERE-RE <NOBIS>. AGNUS DEI

<QUI TOLLIS PECCA- TA MUNDI MI-SE-RE-RE

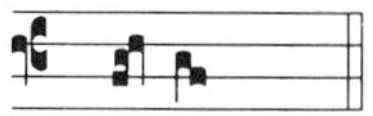

NOBIS>.[85]

LAMB OF GOD, WHO TAKES AWAY THE SINS OF THE WORLD: HAVE MERCY ON US.

1) Truth abiding in truth; from light, light:
HAVE MERCY ON US.

2) Grant the noblest perpetual joys of life;
HAVE MERCY ON US.

3) Omnipotent, eternal wisdom of God, O Christ
HAVE MERCY ON US. LAMB OF GOD, WHO TAKES AWAY THE SINS OF THE WORLD: HAVE MERCY ON US.

The trope set provides a restrained summary of the images developed during the second half of the service. The first trope is taken directly from the credo, but also echoes the language and imagery of the gospel lection. The second is a prayer asking for the full benefits of salvation, and the third makes explicit the Wisdom-Christ typology that was developed in the offertory. The exalted epithets in the trope elements strongly contrast with the sacrificial theme of the agnus dei itself, which again keeps the whole narrative of salvation present in the service. The first and third trope elements substitute other "names" for the name "agnus dei" and lead to the acclamation "miserere nobis." The musical structure supports this by provid-

85. I have not included the words *DONA NOBIS PACEM* here, since none of the agnus dei settings in this manuscript contains this phrase or a cue for it. See chapter 3, p. 135, above.

ing the same neumation for "miserere nobis" each time. In contrast, the second element adds another petition which functions more as a gloss, explaining what Christ's "mercy" entails.

The last song of the service is the communion antiphon, which was not embellished with tropes in the Autun service. It succinctly reiterates the theme of God's salvation made visible, and has the same text as part of the gradual, *Viderunt omnes fines terrae salutare Dei nostri* (All the ends of the earth have seen the salvation of our God). The communion rite itself is thereby related to the presence of God's salvation on earth.[86]

The shape and content of the third mass of Christmas

The texts and music of the third mass of Christmas at Autun confirm the basic structure for festal masses outlined in chapter 3 (see pp. 127-37, above), which demonstrated that the overwhelming weight of ornamentation and elaboration occurred in the liturgy of the word, while the eucharistic liturgy attracted more restrained elaboration. Moreover, the texts and music show that the concentration on the liturgy of the word was not simply a matter of festal elaboration, but was profoundly linked to the message of the service and its scripture lections. The trope repertory and other festal songs use musical ornamentation and poetic forms in order to develop elaborate rhetorical structures, which helped the choir assimilate the major themes of the scripture lections, and led to the gospel reading as the ritual culmination of this concentrated scripture interpretation. After the gospel reading, the theme of Christ's work in creation and the theme of trinitarian relationships implied by the development of the readings and songs remained prominent; however, the primary focus shifted to the actions of the eucharistic liturgy. The song and prayer texts supported the eucharistic liturgy by stressing the theme of salvation made "visible" through Christ's presence in creation, while keeping the narra-

86. The service ends with a prayer asking that the benefits established by Christ be extended to the worshippers. This is followed by the dismissal:

Praesta, quaesumus omnipotens Deus: ut natus hodie Salvator mundi, sicut divinae nobis generationis est auctor; ita et immortalitatis sit ipse largitor, etc.	Grant, we beseech you, O almighty God, that as the Savior of the world, born today, is the author of our divine generation, so may he also be the giver of immortality, etc.

tive structures of the scripture present, especially by linking the kenotic elements of the incarnation with elements of the passion narrative. The second half of the service came to a ritual high point with the consecration and reception of the eucharistic elements themselves, which were aided by the more restrained and more dogmatic trope elements to the sanctus and the agnus dei. Thus, the elaborate shape of festival services such as this reflects a particular attention to, and appreciation of, scripture. If one attends both to the form and to the content of this Christmas mass, it is clear that the additions either effectively proclaim the Word, using a rhetoric specifically designed for that purpose, or connect the eucharist with its larger scriptural narrative.[87] Ironically, such concerns are normally attributed to reformation liturgies as if they were lacking throughout the Middle Ages.

Easter at Autun

Since the larger picture of the way the texts and music develop themes within the festival services at Autun has been supplied by the analysis of the Christmas mass above, the analysis of the Easter mass will concentrate on those items of mass proper that attracted tropes. As in the Christmas mass, the texts of the mass proper attract the most strongly exegetical additions of the festal repertory, and in the Easter service the influence of scripture commentary on these portions of the mass is particularly strong. Two of the Easter proper texts (the introit and the offertory) are based on psalms that do not initially seem to have much to do with the Easter story, but each psalm had traditional interpretations suitable for Easter, and these interpretations were highlighted by the selection of verses that make up the introit and offertory texts.[88] The third text, the communion, is based on 1 Cor. 5:7-8, which figures prominently in the service as a whole.[89] In the following section, I discuss each of the proper items focusing first on the festal shaping of

87. Costa, *Tropes et séquences*, 440-71, deals almost exclusively with the form and not the content of such liturgies, and therefore does not attribute much significance to the elaboration of the liturgy of the word.

88. The introit is based on Psalm 138:18v, 5b, 6a, and 1-2, and the offertory is taken from Psalm 75:9b, 10a, and 2.

89. It is the epistle reading, and also is used for extra verses in the gradual.

its base text, next on the material in its tropes, and then on the music.

Proper chants as psalm and scripture commentaries: Introit

The Easter introit antiphon was based on a careful editing of Psalm 138:18, 5-6, and 1-2 that created a striking relationship to Easter that is not readily apparent when the psalm is read in its original order:

Introit antiphon: Resurrexi, et adhuc tecum sum. Posuisti super me manum tuam. Mirabilis facta est scientia tua. Domine probasti me, et cognovisti me. Tu cognovisti sessionem meam, et resurrectionem meam.	I have arisen, and am still with you. You have placed your hand upon me. A wonder has been done by your knowledge. Lord you have proved me, and known me. You have known my sitting down, and my rising up.

Psalm 138:

1	*Domine, probasti me, et cognovisti me;*	1	*Lord, thou hast proved me, and known me:*
2	*Tu cognovisti sessionem meam et resurrectionem meam.*	2	*Thou has known my sitting down, and my rising up.*
3	Intellexisti cogitationes meas de longe; Semitam meam et funiculum meum investigasti;	3	Thou hast understood my thoughts afar off: my path and my line thou hast searched out.
4	Et omnes vias meas praevidisti, Quia non est sermo in lingua mea.	4	And thou hast foreseen all my ways: for there is no speech in my tongue.
5	Ecce, Domine, tu cognovisti omnia, novissima et antiqua. Tu formasti me, et *posuisti super me manum tuam.*	5	Behold, O Lord, thou has known all things, the last and those of old: thou hast formed me, and *hast laid thy hand upon me.*
6	*Mirabilis facta est scientia tua* ex me; Confortata est, non potero ad eam.	6	*Thy knowledge is become wonderful* to me: it is high, and I cannot reach to it.
	....		....
17	Mihi autem nimis honorificati sunt amici tui, Deus; Nimis confortatus est principatus eorum.	17	But to me thy friends, O God, are made exceedingly honorable: their principality is exceedingly strengthened.

18 Dinumerabo eos, et super arenam multiplicabuntur. *Exsurrexi, et adhuc sum tecum.*	18 I will number them, and they shall be multiplied above the sand: *I rose up and am still with thee.*

Psalm 138 was primarily used in the Friday vespers service, where it had no festal interpretation, but served as a psalm of self-examination and penitence. However, the word *resurrectionem* (rising up) in the second verse no doubt suggested its festal appropriateness for Easter Sunday. The psalm commentaries reflected this double use, interpreting it (1) as containing words of Christ addressed to the Father, concerning his passion and resurrection, and (2) as a psalm about God's knowledge of, and presence to, any believer. Bruno alluded to both interpretations in his summary of the psalm: "All of this psalm ought to refer to the person of Christ the Lord, and to the Father, for it speaks of his death and resurrection, and it can truly be expounded concerning penitence."[90] The double interpretation did not cause any interpretive problems for its use in the Easter service, since as Augustine points out, even when it was interpreted as Christ speaking, it was Christ speaking in his humanity:

> Our lord Jesus Christ . . . speaks by the prophets, sometimes taking his own voice, and at other times taking our voice, because he has made himself one with us. . . . One by flesh, because he assumed flesh because of our mortality; however, not one by divinity, because he is the Creator, and we are creatures. So, whatever our lord speaks from the person of assumed flesh, pertains both to the Head, that, now has ascended to heaven, and to those members, who toil still on their earthly pilgrimage.[91]

90. Bruno of Würzburg, *Expositi psalmorum,* in Patrologiae latina, 142:496: "Totus hic psalmus, ad Christi Domini personam referendus est, et ad Patrem, quoniam de pausatione sua et resurrectione loquitur. Potest vero et de poenitente exponi."

91. Augustine, *Ennarationes in psalmos,* Psalm 139:2: "Loquitur . . . Dominus noster Iesus Christus in Prophetis aliquando ex voce sua, aliquando ex voce nostra, quia unum se facit nobiscum. . . . Una caro, quia de nostra mortalitate carnem suscepit; non autem una divinitas, quia ille Creator, nos creatura. Quidquid igitur Dominus loquitur ex persona susceptae carnis, et ad illud caput pertinet quod iam adscendit in caelum, et ad ista membra quae adhuc in terrena pergrinatione laborant." It should also be noted that this is based on Paul's metaphor, Christ as the head of his body—the church (1 Cor. 12:12-31; Eph. 4:1-16), which Augustine had taught as the first rule of Ticonius in *De doctrina christiana* 3:31.

In fact, it is this intentional double use that makes the song an effective Easter introit: what Christ has achieved, has been achieved for all flesh, and the choir can speak the words "of Christ," celebrating his victory over death; this enables them to anticipate their own resurrection.

The Easter interpretation of the psalm for use as the introit antiphon has been strengthened by the process of festal shaping, which comprised a great deal of editing and even the rewriting of the verb *exsurrexi* to *resurrexi* to make the festal significance stronger. The character of the alterations can be best assessed by comparing the intact verses (see the verses quoted above) with the selection in the introit antiphon. Not only have the verses been carefully edited to remove material that would be inappropriate for the risen Christ to speak, but the careful editing of verses 5b and 6a has created a flexible syntactic structure, which can be read as (1) a reference to the *event* of the resurrection, reading the adjective *mirabilis* (wonderful) substantively as a noun (a wonderful [thing]), and reading the feminine *scientia tua* (your knowledge) in the ablative case (by your knowledge), or (2) a reference to Christ as God's "knowledge," reading *scientia tua* in the nominative.

In the Autun manuscript, this antiphon has six complete sets of tropes. However, at the very most (if two psalm verses were performed instead of the usual one), the service could accommodate only four sets; furthermore, none of the subsequent Easter services uses the same antiphon. Therefore it would have been necessary for the cantor to make a selection from the repertory. Nevertheless, the following analysis shows that two of the sets function as alternate or substitute sets, so it is likely that a cantor would have made a selection from specific alternatives that developed the same themes in the same order.

The first set begins with the famous Easter dialogue *Quem queritis*, which clearly stands in this manuscript as an introductory trope to the introit.[92] This is followed by a set of tropes

92. Because of its importance for the "origins" of drama, this dialogue has an enormous secondary bibliography. This can be traced through Stevens, *Words and Music in the Middle Ages*, chapter 9, "Drama I: Liturgy, Ceremony and Play," passim, and especially 330, note 53, as well as through Hiley, *Western Plainchant*, 250-63.

which is unique to this manuscript, making its musical reconstruction impracticable:[93]

Ex. 18. First introit trope set for Easter *Quem queritis/ Alleluia/ hodie/ RESURREXI/ Victor triumpho potenti* from PaA 1169, fol. 18v

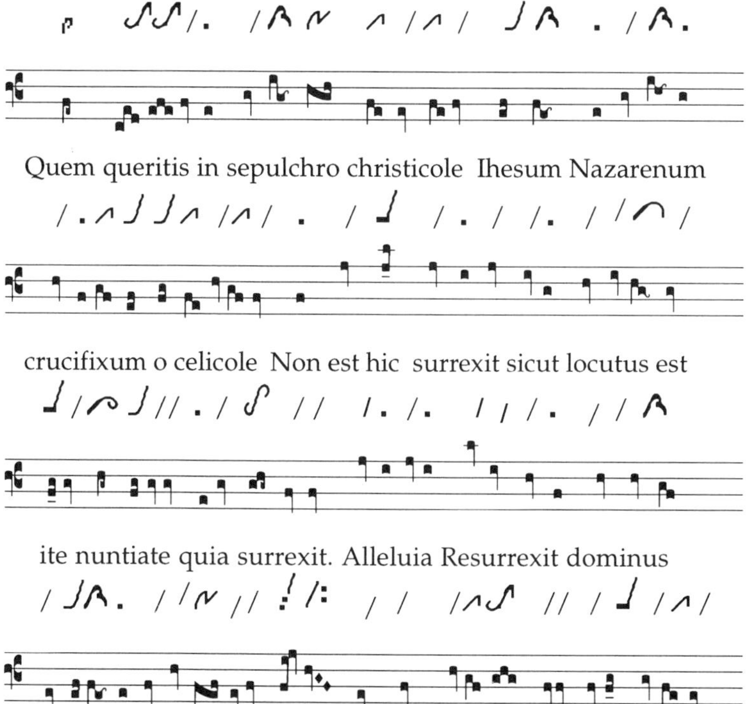
Quem queritis in sepulchro christicole Ihesum Nazarenum
crucifixum o celicole Non est hic surrexit sicut locutus est
ite nuntiate quia surrexit. Alleluia Resurrexit dominus
hodie resurrexit leo fortis Christus fili-us dei deo gratias

93. Susan Rankin, *The Music of the Medieval Liturgical Drama in France and England,* Outstanding Dissertations in Music from British Universities, ed. John Caldwell (New York: Garland, 1989), 2:4-21, has made all of the French and English versions of the melody of the dialogue available in diplomatic or modern transcriptions. I have used these to supply pitches for my reconstruction of the Autun version. For the introit melody, see example 23, pp. 228-29, below.

di-cite e-ya RESURREXI

Victor triumpho potenti

ET ADHUC <TECUM SUM ALLELUIA>

Celi terre adque maris sceptra tenes

POSUISTI <SUPER ME MANUM TUAM ALLELUIA>

Glorificasti me deifice

MIRABILIS FACTA EST

In omni virtute

SCIENCIA TUA <ALLELUIA ALLELUIA>

Qua cuncta gubernas

DOMINE PROBASTI ME <ET COGNOVISTI ME TU COGNOVISTI SESSIONEM MEAM ET RESURRECTIONEM MEAM>

1a) Whom do you seek in the tomb, O followers of Christ? Jesus of Nazareth, the crucified, O heavenly ones. He is not here: he has risen as he said. Go, proclaim that he has risen.

1b) Alleluia! The Lord has risen.

1c) Today the strong lion has risen: Christ the Son of God. Give thanks to God, eya:
I HAVE ARISEN,

2) A victor, with a triumph of power,
AND I AM STILL WITH YOU: ALLELUIA.

3) You hold the scepter of the heavens, the earth and the sea:

YOU HAVE PLACED YOUR HAND UPON ME:
ALLELUIA:
4) You have glorified me with deifying.
A WONDER HAS BEEN DONE
5) In all power,
BY YOUR KNOWLEDGE: ALLELUIA, ALLELUIA:
6) By which you strictly govern.
O LORD, YOU HAVE TESTED ME AND HAVE KNOWN ME; YOU KNOW MY SITTING DOWN AND MY RISING UP.

The Easter dialogue succinctly and dramatically summarizes the Easter gospels; however, it does not directly quote any one of them. Instead, it gathers elements from all of the varied gospel accounts to produce a liturgical enacting of the *visitatio sepulchri*. Many individual details can be traced back to specific gospel passages, but the intention seems to be to keep all of the versions in memory, and no one gospel narrative seems to be favored over another. For example, the question: *Quem queritis?* occurs only in John 20:15, where it is spoken by Jesus to Mary, and not as words of (an) angel(s) spoken to two or more women, as it is in the trope. However, Luke 24:5 also includes a question, "Why do you seek the living among the dead?" spoken by "a man," although it is rhetorical and does not instigate a dialogue. A second example concerns the number of women and angels at the tomb. The plural number of Christians implied by the word *christicole* (i.e., *christicolae*) in the Autun Troper fits with all of the synoptic accounts, but not with John. The use of a plural number of heavenly beings in the Autun version suggests a close following of the Matthew account (which was the gospel for the vigil mass of Easter). However, Matthew describes the beings as "angels," while the Troper uses the word *celicole* (heavenly ones), enabling it also to refer to the man in Mark and men in Luke, who were described as being unusual (provoking fear and wonder), if not specifically angelic. A third example comes from the words the "Christians" use in the Troper to describe the one whom they seek: both Matthew and Mark provide the closest linguistic correspondences to the description "Jesus of Nazareth, the Crucified," but this is spoken by the angels, or a man, rather than the women in the gospel accounts. A fourth example concerns the words spoken by the angels or men: all three synoptic accounts include some variation of the words "he is not here, he is risen, as he said"; however, only Luke 24:6 uses the verb *locutus est*, as in the Troper's version of the dialogue. Finally, all four gospel accounts have instructions for the women (or for Mary) to "go and tell that he is risen" to the disciples, but the Troper does not specify to whom the Christians are to tell the good news. In the Troper, the present liturgical assembly receives an Easter proclamation: "Alleluia, the Lord is risen." Moreover, this connection with the present liturgy is strengthened by the use of the word *christicole* (followers of Christ) instead of *mulieri* (women). The next element in the dialogue identifies "the Lord," and connects the current celebration not only to the Easter event, but to all of salvation history. By referring to "the strong lion of Judah," the proclamation succinctly looks all the way back to Gen. 49:9-11, and forward to Rev. 5:5-6, tying the prophecy of salvation back through Judah to Christ at Easter and forward to Christ's coming in power. The Genesis passage contains its own prophecy, which is both messianic and, in verse 11, interpretable as a prophecy of both the passion and the eucharist:

Gen. 49:9-12:

9	Catulus *leonis Iuda*: Ad praedam, fili mi, ascendisti: Requiescens accubuisti ut *leo*, Et quasi leaena, quis suscitabit eum?	9	*Juda* is a *lion's* whelp: to the prey, my son, thou art gone up: resting thou hast couched as a *lion* and as a lioness, who shall rouse him?
10	Non auferetur septrum de Iuda, Et dux de femore eius, donec veniat qui mittendus, est, Et ipse erit expectatio gentium.	10	The scepter shall not be taken away from *Juda*, nor a ruler from his thigh, till he come that is to be sent, and he shall be the expectation of nations.
11	Ligans ad vineam pullum suum, Et ad vitem, o fili mi, asinam suam: Lavabit in vino stolam suam Et in sanguine uvae pallium suum.	11	Tying his foal to the vineyard, and his ass, O my son, to the vine, He shall wash his robe in wine, and his garment in the blood of the grape.

The parallel passage from Revelation also evokes both themes by connecting the Lion of Judah with the paschal Lamb:

Rev. 5:5-6:

5	Et unus de senioribus dixit mihi: Ne fleveris: ecce *vicit leo de tribu Iuda*, radix David, aperire librum, et solvere septem signacula eius.	5	And one of the ancients said to me: Weep not; *behold the lion of the tribe of Juda, the root of David, hath prevailed* to open the book, and to loose the seven seals thereof.
6	Et vidi: et ecce in medio throni et quatuor animalium, et in medio seniorum, *Agnum stantem tanquam occisum*, habentem cornua septem, et oculos septem: qui sunt septem spiritus Dei, missi in omnem terram.	6	And I saw: and behold in the midst of the throne and of the four living creatures, and in the midst of the ancients, *a Lamb standing as it were slain*, having seven horns and seven eyes: which are the seven Spirits of God, sent forth into all the earth.

The final line of the dialogue invokes the response of the choir to the Easter *kerygma* and prepares them for speaking (1) *in persona Christi* and (2) as redeemed sinners, who can claim Christ's salvation for themselves. The tropes thus supplement and fill out the address of the antiphon by quoting short lines from various scriptural sources, which maintain the rather direct style of diction characteristic of both the introductory trope and the antiphon texts. These terse additions also maintain the traditional interpretation of the antiphon text.

The music of the Easter dialogue, like that of the introductory trope for the Christmas introit, uses a different mode from the antiphon.[94] It is in mode II, based on 'D', while the antiphon is in mode IV, based on 'E'. Since both modes are plagal modes, their range is similar, but their musical syntax is usually marked by different characteristic cadential points. Although the text of the dialogue does not demand any special treatment of cadence (its word order is straightforward), its music makes a particularly effective use of both range and cadential structure to bring out nuances of the text. Even though its first two lines are parallel, they have different syntaxes, since the first asks a question and the second answers it. In the first line, the verb (*queritis*) is marked with the strong cadence on the final; *in sepulchro* is marked with a cadence on 'F' (the tenor), and the end of the question is marked by a cadence

94. Since none of the introit sets, except for the last, is completely reconstructible, refer below, pp. 228-29, for the complete introit melody.

which rises from 'C to D', ending on the final. In the second line, the three words *Iesum Nazarenum crucifixum* are appropriately tied together within one musical phrase, and the feeling of antecedent and consequent is strengthened by the cadence of a tone descending, which answers the rising cadence (tone ascending) that marked the end of the first line. The third line of the dialogue goes dramatically outside of the normal range for mode II, ascending to 'c' at the end of *hic*, which is not a cadential note in the mode. The Autun notation suggests that the note before the 'c' ('a') be lengthened; this heightens the dramatic effect of the 'c' by providing a moment of repose on the proper cadential note to mark the colon in this mode. Furthermore, the cadence on 'c' (the "tenor" of the authentic E mode III) shifts the emphasis toward the tonal center of 'E'. This shift is confirmed by the next two clauses, which begin on 'a' and cadence on 'E' with the semitone-descending cadence that distinguishes the E modes. By (briefly) shifting the tonal center at the words "He is not here: he is risen, as he said," the dialogue makes a reference to the mode of the Easter introit itself, which speaks with the voice of Christ, and which has its major cadences on a semitone descending to 'E'. The proclamation *Alleluia, surrexit Dominus* makes a reference to the musical outline of *non est hic, surrexit,* by reversing the order of its two elements, and answering the ascending gesture (from the final to the highest note) of *non est hic* with a descending gesture (from the highest note to the final); this ties the ideas "he is not here; he has arisen" even more closely together. The two names of Christ, "strong lion" and "Christ, Son of God," are marked by similar musical gestures, which reinforce the metaphor. Finally, the invocation to the choir clearly cadences in mode II on 'D', which helps undergird the double use of the antiphon. The choir's response is invoked in mode II, and they answer in what seems like mode II, since their words "I have arisen" also cadence on 'D'. This reinforces their proclaiming these words as their own, although they apply equally to Christ. Only after the first trope element, which clearly invokes Christ ("A victor, with a triumph of power") and the following antiphon element ("And I am still with you, alleluia!") is the characteristic cadential pattern of mode IV completely established; this helps the choir celebrate Christ's victory and its consequences for them, by speaking in the mode used for Christ's voice.

The second trope set for the introit consists of only one introductory element, which is unnotated in the Autun manuscript:

Praeclara adest dies Christus qua resurgens hoste triumphato vitam dedit mundo cuius voce summo patri gratulantes cum propheta proclamemus omnes ita RESURREXI	The glorious day is here: when Christ rising, the enemy having been conquered, gave life to the world. With whose voice, to the highest Father, gratefully, with the prophets, let us proclaim thus: I HAVE RISEN.

This introit set functions as an *accessus ad auctores*, and gathers the themes of Christ's victory over death that made up the trope elements that followed the Easter dialogue. Therefore, it was probably intended to substitute for the first set.[95] It conveys the traditional (double) interpretation of the psalm upon which the antiphon is based by using the adverb "gratefully," which is appropriate to characterize the choir's proclamation of *Resurrexi*. This introduction gracefully ornaments the introit with a structured rhythmic and accentual poem, which (in this manuscript) is presented as four iambic lines of three stresses and generally six syllables each, plus three iambic lines of eight syllables with four stresses each.[96]

The next three sets of introit tropes develop both musical and verbal ornamentation to high degree. They are composed mostly in hexameters, and therefore display a fair amount of syntactic segmentation. Unfortunately, none of the sets is completely reconstructible, since many of the elements that are transmitted by the Autun Troper do not have pitch-secure con-

95. In liturgical manuscripts, a replacement normally precedes the set it replaced; therefore this set may have been superseded by the Easter introit dialogue, when it became available. However, if this set was performed, it probably substituted for the *Quem queritis* and its following tropes.

96. The editors of the *Corpus troporum* have pointed out that it may be cast in a more regular meter by shifting the word *omnes*, and creating four lines in the same pattern as the first four. This does not substantially alter the meaning:

cuius voce summo
patri gratulantes
cum propheta omnes
proclamemus ita

cordances. Therefore, I will first discuss the texts of these three sets in order, and then discuss those elements that can be musically reconstructed.

Ex. 19. Diplomatic version of the third introit trope set for Easter *Psallite regi magno/ RESURREXI* from PaA 1169, fol. 19r

Psallite regi magno

devicto mortis imperio eya

RESURREXI

Ecce pater cunctis ut iusserat ordo peractis

ET ADHUC <TECUM SUM ALLELUIA>

Victor ut ad celos calcata morte redirem

POSUISTI <SUPER ME MANUM TUAM ALLELUIA ALLELUIA>

Cla- ra dedi<t> sanctae legis documenta patere

agmina sanctorum traxi super haetera metum

MIRABILIS <FACTA EST>

Factus homo tua iussa pater moriendo peregi

SCIENTIA TUA ALLELUIA

1) Sing to the great king, having overcome the empire of death eya:
I HAVE RISEN.

2) Behold, the plan having been strictly carried out, as the Father ordered:
AND I AM STILL WITH YOU, ALLELUIA.
3) A victor, having trampled death, that I may return to the heavens.
YOU HAVE PLACED YOUR HAND UPON ME ALLELUIA
4) I gave clear proofs in order to manifest your holy laws; I led, having harvested, a multitude of your saints above the firmament.
A WONDER HAS BEEN DONE.
5) Made man, your orders, Father, by dying, I accomplished:
BY YOUR KNOWLEDGE, ALLELUIA, ALLELUIA.

The first of these sets (i.e., the third introit trope set) focuses on the work of Christ in salvation and develops the idea of Christ speaking to the Father; it uses this device to pass on a standard interpretation of the psalm from which this text is taken. The idea of Christ carrying out God's plan arises because of the foreknowledge implied by the psalm. Since the entire psalm was memorized by the choir, it was necessary for its standard interpretation to be invoked in the tropes, because portions of it could not be made to apply to Christ in his divinity; for example, Psalm 138:4-6, from which much of the antiphon was edited, has a context that emphasizes God's plan as unknowable:

> And thou hast foreseen all my ways: for there is no speech in my tongue. Behold, O Lord, thou has known all things, the last and those of old: thou hast formed me, and hast laid thy hand upon me. Thy knowledge is become wonderful to me: it is high, and I cannot reach to it.[97]

In order to explain how these verses could apply to Jesus, the trope set refers both to the incarnation (*Factus homo*) and to the Father's "plan" (*ordo*); this supports a reading of the psalm which ascribes foreknowledge to God the Father but not to Christ in his humanity. Another trope element (*Clara dedi*) even echoes some of the language and thought of Bruno's psalm commentary which deals with these psalm verses; the common language is highlighted by italics:

---

97. "Et omnes vias meas praevidisti, Quia non est sermo in lingua mea. Ecce, Domine, tu cognovisti omnia, novissima et antiqua. Tu formasti me, et posuisti super me manum tuam. Mirabilis facta est scientia tua ex me; Confortata est, non potero ad eam."

Scientia Patris est, quae per Christum ubique terrarum praedicata est. Quae est facta mirabilis per Christum, dum terrigenis *sacramenta sacrae legis narrata sunt*. Nec potero ad eam, ex humanitate et infirmitate carnis loquitur, ut in alio loco: Pater major me est: ut sit sensus: Humanam naturam, quam assumpsi, divinae substantiae adaequare non possum.[98]

"The knowledge" of the Father is what, through Christ, has been proclaimed everywhere on earth. Which was made marvelous through Christ, when the *mysteries of the holy law were recounted* to those born of earth. "I shall not be able to attain it," is spoken from the humanity and infirmity of the flesh, as in another place: "The Father is greater than I," which means, "The human nature which I assumed, I cannot make equal to the divine substance."

Much of the rest of the thought of this trope set is derived from the traditional psalm collect, which appears at the end of the psalm in Bruno's commentary:

Celi terraeque prospector, Deus, quo moriente, illuminata sunt tartara, quo resurgente, sanctorum est multitudo gavissa, quo ascendente, angelorum exultavit caterva, precamur tantae gloriae excellentem virtuem, ut directi in via aeterna.[99]

Watcher, over the heaven and earth, God, by your death, the dead were brought light, by your rising, the multitude of the saints were brought joy, by your ascending, the throng of angels exulted. We pray that by your glory exceeding all power, you lead us in the way of eternity.

The fourth set of introit tropes uses much of the language and imagery of the third set. In fact, the last trope element of the third set is probably a direct model for the first trope element of the fourth set:

Ex. 20. Diplomatic version of the fourth introit trope set for Easter *Postquam factus/ RESURREXI* from PaA 1169, fol. 19r

Postquam factus homo tua iussa paterna peregi

in cruce morte mea mortis crebrum superando

98. Bruno of Würzburg, *Expositio psalmorum,* in Patrologiae latina, 142:497.
99. Ibid.

RESURREXI <ET ADHUC TECUM SUUM ALLELUIA>

In regno superno tibi coequalis

iam ultra in eternum semper imortalis

POSUISTI <SUPER ME MANUM TUAM ALLELUIA>

Laudibus angelorum qui te laudate sine fine

MIRA<BILIS FACTA EST SCIENTIA TUA ALLELUIA ALLELUIA>

1) After having been made man, I executed your fatherly orders on the cross, by my death, death abundantly transcending.
I HAVE RISEN AND AM STILL WITH YOU, ALLELUIA:

2) In the eternal kingdom, co-equal with you. Now, beyond time, always immortal.
YOU HAVE PLACED YOUR HAND UPON ME, ALLELUIA.

3) With the praises of angels who praise you without end.
YOUR KNOWLEDGE HAS BECOME WONDERFUL, ALLELUIA ALLELUIA.

Since this set appears in the margin of the Autun Troper, it is possible that it was intended to replace the third set with slightly more elegant hexameters. However, it continues to develop the thought of the previous one, in that it focuses exclusively on the interpretation of the psalm, which explains the psalm as the risen and ascended Christ speaking directly to the Father. For example, the antiphon element (*Resurrexi, et adhuc*) and its following trope (*In regno superno*) explain the psalm verse in almost exactly the same manner as does Bruno's commentary:

"Adhuc tecum sum": non quod aliquando ab ipso divendus sit, sed qui modo nobis est invisibilis, ad dexteram Patris in coelestibus residens, omnibus postea gentibus apparebit.[100]

"I am still with you": not that he [Christ] is separated at any time from him [the Father], but who, in a manner invisible to us, residing at the right hand of the Father in the heavens, subsequently will appear to all nations.

100. Ibid.

The fifth set of introit tropes consists of only two elements, both of which use fairly obscure language. Both use images of light, blindness, and darkness, and, if applied to Christ, seem to recount either elements of the passion, or of the descent into hell. This could be developed partially from the recollections of the Easter narrative, but also could be derived in part from the whole of the introit psalm. For example, Psalm 138:7 reads "If I ascend into heaven, you are there; If I descend into hell, you are present"; and Psalm 138:12 develops the imagery of light and darkness: "darkness shall not be dark to you, and the night shall be light as the day." Again, although the tropes do not quote the exact language of the psalm, there are many rhymes of thought:

Ex. 21. Diplomatic version of fifth introit trope set for Easter *RESURREXI/ Abstuleras miserate* from PaA 1169, fol. 19v

RESURREXI <ET ADHUC TECUM SUUM ALLELUIA>
Abstuleras miserate manens michi reddita lux est
POSUISTI <SUPER ME MANUM TUAM ALLELUIA>
Ne michi tunc cecata cohors obsistere posset
Numinis atque meis lumen fuscare serenum
MIRABILIS <FACTA EST SCIENTIA TUA ALLELUIA ALLELUIA>

I HAVE ARISEN AND AM STILL WITH YOU, ALLELUIA.
1) You have swept away, with compassion remaining; to me, light is returned.
YOU HAVE PLACED YOUR HAND UPON ME, ALLELUIA.
2) The cohort, having been made blind, could not withstand me, And could not obscure the serene light of my deity.
A WONDER HAS BEEN DONE BY YOUR KNOWLEDGE, ALLELUIA, ALLELUIA.

The third, fourth and fifth sets of introit tropes have only four elements among them that can be musically reconstructed. These are the second, third, and fifth elements of the third set of introit tropes marked 'a', 'b', and 'c' in the example below and the first element of the fifth marked 'd' in the example below.[101] Their pitches are given below with their cues. (For the melodies of the antiphon cues, see the last set, below, pp. 228-29):[102]

Ex. 22. Four trope elements from the Easter introit trope complex of PaA 1169, fol. 19r

a

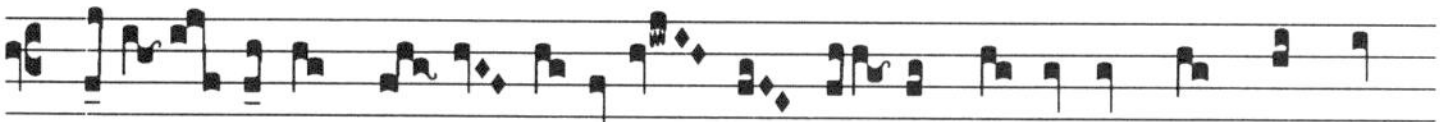

Ec- ce pater cunctis ut iusse- rat or- do peractis ET ADHUC

b

Victor ut ad celos calcata morte redirem POSUISTI

c

Factus homo tua iussa pater moriendo peregi SCIENTIA

d

Abstuleras miserate manens michi redita lux est POSUISTI

101. For their neumation and translation, see examples 19 and 21 above.

102. The pitches for trope elements *Ecce pater* and *Victor* are based on PaN 1871, fols. 13v-14. The pitches for the trope elements *Factus homo* and *Abstuleras* are based on Paris, Bibliothèque Nationale, fonds latin, MS 1119, fol. 23v (PaN 1119). For a modern transcription of parts of these manuscripts, see Weiss, ed., *Introitus-Tropen*.

The music of all four of these trope elements displays close attention to the difficulties posed by the poetic organization of the words. In fact, the syntax of the first element is so disjointed that each word has its own musical phrase, except for three words which are set in one phrase (*ut iusserat ordo*, as [he] ordered—the plan). Since these three words do not belong together linguistically, it is probable that the music is intended to suggests a relationship between them that cannot be made through its syntax alone. The whole phrase has to have *Pater* (Father) as its subject, and this creates a connection between the syntactically separate word "*ordo*" (plan) and the Father. The musical grouping suggests that the plan belongs to the Father; it could not have been known to the Son in his humanity, even though he is speaking about it having been carried out in this trope. Another striking feature of the setting is the dramatic leaping up and down a fifth on *Ecce* ("Behold"); this cadences on 'D', which sets it off from the rest of the antiphon.

All of these trope elements display the same basic structure: one short phrase cadences on the note below the final (i.e., 'D') and two longer phrases cadence on the final, 'E'. Each of them displays great subtlety in realizing this basic structure. For example, in the second element, the title *Victor* is set off from the rest of the element with a cadence on 'D'. The two remaining phrases make the same cadence of a rising tone on 'E', which gives them something of a parallel structure, especially at the end. This brings out the intended syntax, by aligning the words *ad celos* (to the heavens) with *redirem* (may I return). The liquescent consonant on "cal-" of *calcata* (having trampled) seems to have inspired the notator of the Autun manuscript to make the word slightly onomatapoeic by using another descending liquescent neume on the following syllable; coupled with the descending line down to the word "death" it makes the phrase almost seem a rare instance of word-painting. The third element (*Factus homo*) has the following structure: *Factus homo* (having been made man) is set off from the rest with a cadence on 'D'. This is followed by two parallel phrases, the first enclosing the words *tua iussa pater* (your orders, Father) and the second enclosing the words *moriendo peregi* (by dying, I accomplished). There is also a minor cadence setting off the word *moriendo* within the longer phrase. All of these cadences are on 'E', but *moriendo* and *tua iussa, pater* make a cadence from the semitone above (underlining what the "orders" entailed) and *peregi* makes a cadence from the tone below; this makes the two large phrases into an antecedent and consequent. The fourth of these elements follows the same structure, setting off the word *Abstuleras* (You have swept away), and through the use of parallel structure, equating the idea of steadfast compassion with the idea of light being given back to the Son.

The basic structure of the trope elements seems to have been derived from the antiphon itself; each antiphon element displays a tendency to cadence either on 'D' (*Resurrexi* and *Mirabilis facta est*) or on 'E' (*Et adhuc tecum suum, Alleluia* and *Scientia tua, Alleluia, Alleluia*).[103] This suggests that the antiphon elements which cadence on 'D' were intended to be related in a general way to the begining of each trope element, and that the antiphon elements ending on 'E' were intended to be related to the end of each trope element. This would line up the following combinations of words and phrases: "Behold" with "I have arisen"; "the plan having been carried out" with "I am still with you"; "Having been made man" with "A wonder has been done"; "By dying, I accomplished" with "By your knowledge"; and "You overthrew" with "I have arisen." The parallels are perhaps too close to be accidental, suggesting that the basic musical and syntactic pattern of the antiphon was intentionally duplicated in miniature by the trope elements.

The sixth (and last) trope set can be entirely reconstructed from a close concordance in PaN 1871, fols. 14v-15:

103. Colette, "*Modus, tropus, tonus,*" 91-92, points out the many features of the introit antiphon that give it an "affinity" to the plagal D mode (II). The modal ambiguity helps the music to bring out aspects of the "double-voice" that are so important to the traditional interpretation of the psalm.

Ex. 23. Sixth introit trope set for Easter *Gaudete/ RESURREXI/ Dum resurgeret* from PaA 1169, fol. 19r[104]

Gaudete et letamini quia surrexit dominus alleluia iocunde-
mus in illo dicentes e-ya RESURREXI Dum resurgeret
in iudicio de- us ET ADHUC <TECUM SUM AL-LELU-IA>
Contremuit terra Christo surgente a mortu-is POSUISTI
<SU-PER ME MANUM TUAM AL-LELU- IA> Terremotus
factus est magnus angelus domini descen-dit de ce- lo

104. The antiphon is reconstructed from Montpellier, H 159, see also Hansen, *Montpellier H 159* (Dij 465).

MIRA-BILIS FACTA EST Custodes velut mor- tui effecti sunt

SCIENCIA <TUA> Nimio terrore angeli <ALLELUIA>

AL- LELUIA

1) Rejoice and be glad, for the Lord has risen: Alleluia! Let us be glad in it, saying "eya!":
I HAVE ARISEN,
2) While God was arising in judgment:
AND I AM STILL WITH YOU, ALLELUIA.
3) The earth trembled, when Christ rose from the dead.
YOU HAVE PLACED YOUR HAND UPON ME, ALLELUIA.
4) There was a great earthquake; the angel of the Lord came down from heaven.
A WONDER HAS BEEN DONE:
5) The guards were made as if dead,
BY YOUR KNOWLEDGE,
6) By an overwhelming fear of the angel,
ALLELUIA, ALLELUIA.

This last trope set develops a narrative commentary that appears to be designed to let the antiphon serve as the voice of the choir rather than as the voice of Christ. The choir is instructed to rejoice in Christ's resurrection and does so by proclaiming that they (too) have arisen, "while God was rising in judgment." The second and third trope elements (*Dum resurgeret* and *Contremuit*) of this set are derived from Psalm 75, which deals with Israel's victories (especially the Exodus); the psalm fits well with the typological relationships between the

Exodus and the Easter story developed in the lections for the last three weeks of Lent, and especially in the Easter vigil. However, this psalm, which was also sung during the Saturday matins service preceding Easter, was interpreted not only as a prophecy of the events of Easter, but also as a prophecy of Christ's final coming in glory that the events of Easter anticipated.[105] Psalm 75:2 and Psalm 75:7-10 give the essential context of the whole psalm (and also provided the text for the offertory chant and some of its tropes; these are discussed later):

2	Notus in Iudaea Deus; In Israel magnum nomen eius.	2	In Judea God is known: his name is great in Israel.
	....		....
7	Ab increpatione tua, Deus Iacob, Dormitaverunt qui ascenderunt equos.	7	At thy rebuke, O God of Jacob, they have all slumbered that mounted on horseback.
8	Tu terribilis es; et quis resistet tibi? Ex tunc ira tua.	8	Thou art terrible, and who shall resist thee? From that time thy wrath.
9	De caelo auditum fecisti iudicum: *Terra tremuit et quievit;*	9	Thou hast caused judgment to be heard from heaven: *the earth trembled and was still,*
10	*Cum exsurgeret in iudicium Deus,* Ut salvos faceret omnes mansuetos terrae.	10	*When God arose in judgment,* to save all the meek of the earth.

The subsequent trope elements are all derived from the gospel accounts of the resurrection (cf. Mt. 28:2, 4-5; Luke 24:5). In addition, these elements could have been intended to evoke the traditional interpretation of Psalm 138 (from which the antiphon elements were derived). For example, Bruno's commentary uses language similar to many of the trope elements, and refers to the Easter narrative in exegeting Psalm 138:14:

105. See Bruno of Würzburg, *Expositio psalmorum,* in Patrologiae latina 142:285-86.

"Confiteor tibi, quia terribiliter magnificatus es; Mirabilia opera tua, et anima mea cognoscit nimis."	"I will praise thee, for thou art fearfully magnified: wonderful are thy works, and my soul knoweth right well."
Terribiliter enim magnificatus est Pater, quando in passione Christi terra tremuit, saxa disrupta sunt, sepulchra patuerunt. Necesseque fuit illum mirabilem cognoscere, quem tantorum beneficiorum piisimum largitorem cernebat Christi humanitas.[106]	For the Father was terrifyingly great, when during the passion of Christ, the earth shook, stones were split, and tombs opened. And it was necessary to know him wonderful, whom the humanity of Christ regarded the most devoted giver of such great blessings.

Finally, these pieces from the Easter narrative also continue to develop the theme of judgment, by anticipating the events of the last judgment. For example, a "great earthquake" is twice mentioned in the Apocalypse at the opening of the sixth and seventh seals (Rev. 6:12; 8:5).

The music of this trope set reflects the simple syntax of the trope elements, marking some musical syllables with a weak cadence, but generally emphasizing the larger syntactical units of comma and colon with one or two cadences per trope element. The ambiguity of mode, inherent in the antiphon itself, is also exploited in this set: the 'D' centering of *RESURREXI* is answered by a musical syllable also cadencing on 'D' on the words *Dum resurgeret*. Both of these short musical phrases rock back and forth between 'D' and 'F', marking their linguistic relationship and uniting the idea of resurrection with that of Christ's coming in judgment. While all of the trope texts of this set seem relatively independent from the antiphon, because they have an independent linguistic syntax, the music creates a tighter relationship between them. For example, the last three trope elements (*Terremotus*, *Custodes*, and *Nimio*) and their intervening antiphon elements (*MIRABILIS* and *SCIENTIA*) seem carefully sewn together through their cadential and starting notes. The trope element *Terremotus* is modally centered around 'D' and even cadences on 'C', the note below the final; the following antiphon element (*MIRABILIS*) reverses this process (starting on 'C' and cadencing on 'D'); this relates the various wonders recounted in the trope and antiphon elements to each

106. Ibid., 499.

other. A similar process manufactures syntactic unity in the last two trope elements and their intervening antiphon element: *Custodes* cadences on 'E'; *SCIENTIA* starts on 'E' and cadences on 'g'; *Nimio* starts on 'g' and cadences on 'E'. Thus, the power of God's knowledge is related to the examples of power in the trope elements.

Even though the Easter introit trope complex includes a greater number of trope sets than would have been used in any given mass, a coherent plan can be traced by examining the most likely combinations of sets. The following four series have a content and order of thematic development that make them likely alternatives for each other; each series would accommodate four repetitions of the antiphon, which was unusual, but not extraordinary, for Easter:

I	II	III	IV
1) Quem queritis	1) Quem queritis	2) Praeclara dies	2) Praeclara dies
3) Psalite regi	4) Postquam	3) Psalite regi	4) Postquam
5) Abstuleras	5) Abstuleras	5) Abstuleras	5) Abstuleras
6) Gaudete	6) Gaudete	6) Gaudete	6) Gaudete

Each of these four series develops in a similar way and all end with the same two sets. Series III and IV substitute the short introductory trope *Praeclara* for the extended *Quem queritis* and its following trope set, but both of these sets have two common functions: they proclaim the day of resurrection and stress Christ's authority and triumph over death. Series II and IV substitute the marginal set *Postquam* for the set *Psallite*; these two sets are related by their specific choice of language, by their developing the conceit of the antiphon as the voice of Christ, and by their reference to Christ's work of salvation, which had been planned by the Father. Therefore, no matter which of the four series is used, a similar order of themes unfolds: (1) the Easter story is recalled either dramatically or by recounting its effects; (2) the consequences for Christ are developed using Christ's own voice; (3) the consequences for the world are developed, still using Christ's voice; and (4) the focus shifts back to the liturgical assembly, which again relates the story. All of the series exploit trope sets that explicitly use the voice of Christ, use imagery relating to the last judgment, and use imagery of light and darkness; all of this helps undergird the traditional interpretations of the psalm upon which the antiphon is based. Unlike the Christmas trope complex, which stays very close to the context of prophecy and its fulfillment, the Easter complex attempts to explore the consequences of the resurrection for Christ and for the church, by developing the "two voices" of the psalm that were taught by the commentaries. Thus, the trope elements often exploit language and imagery that are close to that used in the commentaries themselves.

Offertory

The offertory is based on Psalm 75:9-10, which was discussed above (pp. 229-30) in relation to its use in the introit trope complex. The whole trope and antiphon set shows a high degree of unity, and the series both musically and linguistically develops the relationships among three themes: the resurrection, Christ's judgment, and the eucharist:[107]

Ex. 24. Offertory trope set for *Easter Ab increpatione/ TERRA TREMUIT* from PaA 1169, fol. 23v

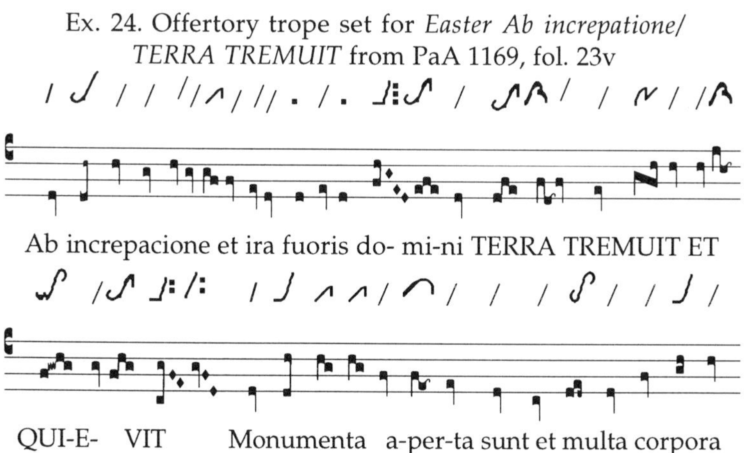
Ab increpacione et ira fuoris do- mi-ni TERRA TREMUIT ET
QUI-E- VIT Monumenta a-per-ta sunt et multa corpora

107. The pitches are reconstructed from PaN 1235, fol. 210, which have been collated with PaN 1871, fol. 15v. The antiphon melody is reconstructed from Montpellier, H 159; see also Hansen, *Montpellier H 159* (Dij 884).

sanctorum surrexerunt DUM RESURGERET Christus iudica-
turus est vivos et mortuos quando ve- ne- rit IN IUDI-CIO
DE- US Ipso resurgente a mortuis venite adoremus eum omnes
una voce pro-clamantes A- LE-
LUIA NOT<US IN IUDE- A DEUS IN IS-
RA-EL MAG- NUM NO- MEN E-
IUS AL- LE- LU-IA>

1) At the rebuke and furious wrath of the Lord:
THE EARTH TREMBLED AND WAS QUIET.
2) The tombs were opened and many bodies of the saints arose,
WHEN HE AROSE.
3) Christ will judge the living and the dead when he comes.
IN JUDGMENT GOD,
4) Himself rising from the dead: Come, let us adore him, all proclaiming with one voice:
ALLELUIA. GOD IS KNOWN IN JUDEA: GREAT IS HIS NAME IN ISRAEL.

The language of the trope elements ties together several narrative patterns and sources: (1) Exodus is linked with Easter through the trope element *Ab increpatione*; its source, Psalm 75:7-8, recounts the destruction of Pharaoh's army. (2) The wonders at Christ's death are linked with his resurrection, through the trope element *Monumenta*; its sources, Mt. 27:51, Mark 15:38, and Luke 23:45, recount the wonders at Christ's crucifixion. (3) The resurrection of Christ is linked with his coming to judge, through the trope element *Christus iudicaturus*; its source, the credo, looks forward to the final judgment. (4) Christ's presence at Christmas (Epiphany) is linked with his presence at both Easter and at this celebration of the eucharist, through the trope element *Ipso resurgente*; its sources, the story of the Magi in Mt. 2:2 ("Where is the newborn king of the Jews? We have seen his star in the east and have come to adore him") and Matthew's account of Christ's resurrection appearances in Galilee in Mt. 28:17a ("And seeing him, they [the disciples] adored him") link Christmas to Easter and supply the reference for the last half of the trope element, *venite adoremus eum* (come, let us adore him). Thus a typical Christmas refrain is used, inviting the choir to "come, let us adore him" during the preparation of the altar for the Easter communion rite, and all of these "adorations" are brought into the present. The antiphon text adds still more references to Christ's judgment through its traditional interpretation and the echoes of its language in the book of Revelation. Some of these have been explored above (pp. 230-31); another is supplied by Bruno's explanation of the offertory's psalm verse *Notus in Iudea* (Psalm 75:2). This adds the reference to Judea, which Bruno explains by using the typology of Christ as the "strong lion of Judah" (which was a prominent theme in the *Quem queritis* dialogue), and calls to mind the book of Revelation:

Iudea enim confitens interpretatur, credens in illum regem, qui per Mariam virginem ex tribu venit Iuda; Israel, vir videns Deum interpretatur.[108]	For Judea means confessing or believing in that king, who through the virgin Mary came from the tribe of Juda; Israel means a man seeing God.

The music of the offertory antiphon, like that of the introit, is in mode IV. Also like the introit, it makes frequent reference to mode II (cadencing on 'D') and does not actually cadence on its final, 'E', until the end. All of the trope elements make use of this tendency by starting and ending on 'D', and all of them make use of the rising fifth from 'D-a' to mark their openings; this gives the whole piece the feeling of a litany, which emphasizes a correspondence among each of the trope elements. Since one antiphon element (*IN IUDICIO DEUS*) also opens with a rising fifth, it seems likely that the musical gesture (a rising fifth) of the trope elements is intended to help relate the trope texts to the theme of God's judgment. Incidentally, both of the offertory antiphon elements *DUM RESURGERET* and *IN IUDICIO* use musical figures that outline a fifth and leap up to 'c'; this calls call to mind the setting of *Non est hic* in the introit dialogue *Quem queretis*, in much the same way that the figures in the sequence of the Christmas service recalled the Christmas introit tropes (see pp. 192-93). Each use of this figure is striking in its own right, and demonstrates a way that linguistic phrases can be highlighted by their interaction with the structure of the mode.

Communion

The communion antiphon is derived from the Easter epistle (1 Cor. 5:7-8), which reinforces the imagery of Passover by equating the sacrifice of Christ to the sacrifice of the paschal lamb:

108. Bruno of Würzburg, *Expositio psalmorum,* in Patrologiae latina, 142:284.

Ex. 25. Communion trope set for Easter *Laus honor/ PASCHA NOSTRUM* from PaA 1169, fol. 23v[109]

Laus honor virtus deo nostro decus et imperium regi nostro

qui precium salutas nostrae PASCHA NOSTRUM IMO-

LATUS EST Peccata nostra ipse portavit et propter

scelera nostra oblatus est CHRISTUS <ALLELU- IA

ITA- QUE EPULE-MUR IN A- ZY-MIS SINCERI-

TATIS ET> VERITATIS Le-o fortis de tribu iuda hodi-e sur-

109. The pitches are reconstructed from PaN 1235, fol. 210v.

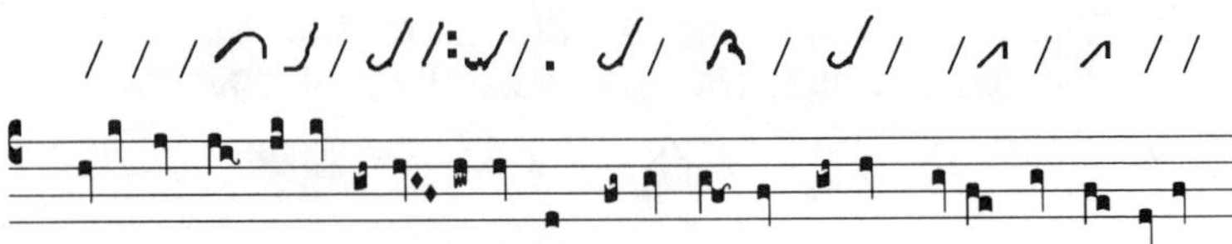

rexit a mortuis alle- luia In cuius laude celsa voce pertonate

ALLE- LU-IA <ALLE- LUIA ALLE- LU- IA>

1) Praise, honor, power, to our God; worthiness, and empire to our King, who <is> the price of our salvation:
OUR PASSOVER IS SACRIFICED.

2) Our sins, himself, he carried, and because of our evils he was offered,
CHRIST! ALLELUIA! THEREFORE LET US FEAST ON THE UNLEAVENED BREAD OF SINCERITY AND TRUTH.

3) The mighty lion of the tribe of Juda, today, rose from the dead alleluia! In whose praise with high voice thunder forth:
ALLELUIA, ALLELUIA.

Although both the introit and offertory tropes had anticipated the theme of Christ's final judgment, this trope set brings the apocalyptic imagery of the Lamb who is also the "strong lion of Judah" into its greatest prominence, by emphasizing themes of heavenly worship, found in, and borrowing language from, Rev. 4-5. The whole trope set skillfully develops the linguistic trope of epithet, by piling up attributes and actions that relate to Christ's salvation, while delaying the naming of Christ until the last possible moment. The identification of Christ with the "pascha" (Passover lamb) evokes the attributes of praise, honor, power, worthiness, and empire, which are directly taken from the songs to the Lamb in Rev. 4:11. Moreover, the language of sacrifice comes not only from the epistle, but also from the mass canon, and indirectly from Rev. 5:12 ("Worthy is the Lamb, who was slain").

The music of this set again marks the important syntactic elements. Neither the tropes nor the antiphon texts pose any severe problems of segmentation; however, the delay of

Christ's name, which is the noun for the second trope element, had to be reflected in the music. It is suitably separated from the rest of the element, since it starts and ends on the final of the mode. This helps to keep it tonally connected to the rest of the first antiphon element, *PASCHA NOSTRUM IMMOLATUS EST,* which effectively reinforces the identification of the passover lamb. Furthermore, the figure used for *PASCHA* (Passover lamb) in the antiphon is used again for *AZYMIS* (unleavened bread) and again for *VERITATIS* (truth). Lamb and Truth and Bread are all typical Johannine names for Christ, and the music helps bring out the relationships between these metaphors and the communion service itself.

The Christmas and Easter Services Compared

In the previous two sections, the complete texts and much of the music from the third mass of Christmas have been discussed in order to show the ways in which they interacted with the liturgical reading of scripture; and the Easter introit, offertory, and communion tropes have been examined in order to bring out their relationship to scripture commentary. Now the two services can be compared (filling in information on the remaining Easter texts) for their respective development of imagery and ornamentation.

Both Christmas and Easter texts of the Autun Troper display a logical and carefully planned development of imagery and ornamentation. Many of the Christmas introit tropes and some of the introit tropes for Easter focus on Christ's relationship to the Father. However, the purpose of the Christmas tropes was to reveal the name of the messiah gradually, which means that the focus is upon God's giving his Son; at Easter, the tropes concentrate on the wonder of the event itself, which brings out both the equality and difference between the Father and Son.

The extended development of the linguistic trope *antonomasia* in the Christmas service led to a kyrie that consisted of a "Christological" litany, which resolved the tension built up in the introit by its extensive repetition of the revealed "name." In contrast, the kyrie in the Easter mass is explicitly trinitarian.[110] This is a theologically satisfying and natural response to the Easter introit tropes, which raised the issue of Christ's status and the question of its consequences for believers. Furthermore, this particular kyrie trope is especially trinitarian: it quotes the triple sanctus from Isaiah in one of its elements, and it has a coda, in which the Trinity is mentioned specifically.

The texts of both the Christmas and Easter gloria tropes are festally shaped and use ornate poetic forms.[111] Both function in many of the same ways, gathering images from the readings of the service and casting them in poetic form. However, the differences in the readings for the Christmas and Easter masses result in the Easter gloria tropes connecting more directly with the eucharistic liturgy than do the Christmas gloria tropes. This is a consequence of the very specific epistle reading of the Easter service (1 Cor. 5:5-7), which mentions unleavened bread and feasting.[112] Although the Christmas gloria tropes develop the theme of Christ's presence to creation, which became a prominent theme of the eucharistic liturgy of the Christmas mass, it does not make such explicit connections with the communion rite. This difference between the Christmas and Easter glorias may reflect the particular importance of the communion rite at Easter; it was the only day of the year on which many of the laity received communion, and much of the rhetoric of the Easter service seems geared toward inviting all to partake.

Unlike the Christmas mass, the Easter mass explicitly makes a provision for the chanting of the *Laudes regiae* just before the epistle reading (see the last column of table 6 on p. 128).[113] Although this litany invokes Christ's protection of the whole secular and religious hierarchy, it is important to note

---

110. For the text see appendix, below; for closely related text and music, see David Bjork, "Early Repertories of the *Kyrie eleison*," *Kirchenmusikalisches Jahrbuch* 63 (1979): 9-43.

111. For the text of the Easter gloria see appendix below; for a related text with music, see Planchart and John Boe, eds., *Beneventanum troporum corpus*, vol. 2, part 2, 32.

112. The relevant section from the Easter gloria paraphrases the epistle: O LORD GOD, Grant that none of the tainted old leaven be mixed with us. LAMB OF GOD, true and eternal having been sacrificed for us; SON OF THE FATHER: Come! Let us feast! WHO TAKES AWAY THE SINS OF THE WORLD.

113. See appendix below for the complete text.

that it is framed within acclamations which attribute true "kingship" only to Christ; this also makes it especially appropriate to Easter Sunday, since the *Laudes regiae* acclaim the Christ who "conquers, reigns, and rules."[114]

Both Christmas and Easter proses[115] use the poetic device of paradoxical imagery: at Christmas the idea of the "squalling infant, who fitly rules the world" was developed in several parts of the prose, while the Easter prose relates the "unhappy sin of Eve" to the "happy offspring" of Mary. It is likely that the Easter vigil's prominent hymn, the exultet, provided some of the inspiration for this, with its imagery of "happy sin" (*felix culpa*). Moreover, both the Christmas and Easter proses anticipate the gospel readings in the days and weeks following their specific feasts: the Christmas prose anticipates the events of the flight into Egypt; the Easter prose looks forward to the events of the Ascension and of Pentecost. In addition, like the Easter gloria, the Easter prose also anticipates the eucharistic liturgy: (1) Christ is mentioned twice as the Lamb of God, building upon the Passover imagery, which was introduced in the gloria and developed by the epistle reading and which would lead up to the eucharistic celebration. (2) Feasting is an important theme. (3) The couplet before the transition to the higher register, *Stupens valde,* reflects upon the coming reception of the eucharist, giving thanks that one "so unworthy" may receive the "sacrament" on this day. (4) The central element of this prose marks the prose's transition to its higher register, setting the part of the text that relates the resurrection to the Lamb, whom the worshippers have seen: *Stirpe Davidica ortus de tribu Iuda, leo potens surrexisti in gloria agnus visus es eya* ("Risen from the root of David, from the tribe of Juda, a strong lion, I have risen in glory, the lamb you have seen, eya!").

Both the Christmas offertory and the Easter offertory are influenced by the credo, which immediately precedes them.

114. Herbert Edward John Cowdrey, "The Anglo-Norman Laudes Regiae," *Viator* 12 (1981): 37-78, gives an excellent liturgical and historical analysis of these texts, pointing out that they were never called *Laudes regiae* in the Middle Ages. Although they clearly invoke and support the established hierarchy, their festal appropriateness for Easter is obvious, and they put the hierarchy under the rule of Christ, who, as the rest of the texts of the liturgy declare, will come to judge.

115. See appendix below for the full text of the Easter prose, *Fulgens praeclara.*

However, the themes which are lifted from the credo for each service are appropriate to the particular feast and to the preparation of the altar for communion: at Christmas, Christ's work in creation is emphasized and connected to the idea of his presence through the created elements; at Easter, the theme of Christ's judgment is prominent, and connects this eucharist to the idea of his final coming.

While the Christmas service had no communion tropes, the communion antiphon summed up the major themes of the service, by proclaiming that "all the ends of the earth have seen the salvation of our God." Although the Easter communion antiphon (taken from the epistle) develops the Passover typology, it does not invoke Christ's judgement (even if the idea of feasting in "sincerity and truth" subtly alludes to this theme—cf. 1 Cor. 11:27-34). Instead it is the communion tropes that heighten this theme, turning the whole of the communion into an apocalyptic vision of Christ's presence. This focus on the apocalyptic feast strongly brings out the eschatological character of the eucharistic feast, which was present, but not as prominent, in the Christmas texts. Apocalyptic imagery had also occurred in the first introit trope of Easter and in the Easter prose, and was thus placed at the beginning, middle, and end of the mass, making a rhetorical refrain that always keeps the theme of Christ's coming in power present in this service.

Thus, the thematic development of the texts of both services work similarly in two general ways. First, in the form of doxology, they bring into play the entire Christian story, while emphasizing those elements which have specific festal significance and which help exegete the readings and the proper antiphons. Second, each feast has a cumulative linear progression: both start with the *kerygma* (at Christmas, in the form of a prophecy of the messiah, and at Easter, in the form of a literal relating of the narrative). These themes are recapitulated at several points in the service, often with references back to creation and forward to the apocalypse, with the prose functioning to anticipate the next installment of the gospel narrative in each case. Both services contain a second layer of texts and imagery, which becomes more prominent throughout. This second layer explores the consequences of the *kerygma*: in each case the *kerygma* implies a relationship of Christ to the Father which gives rise to praise of the Trinity and thanksgiving for the salvation of the world, and which culminates in the vision of the final victory and participation in the banquet, the eucharist.

The differences between the services are produced by the differing emphases of the seasons, lections, and ceremonial. While the anticipation of the fulfillment of prophecy marks the whole liturgy of the word at Christmas, the Easter mass uses all of the resources of biblical imagery in its attempt to proclaim the "wonder" that was accomplished in the resurrection. In order to support the different development of themes, each of the introit trope complexes develops a particular linguistic and musical conceit. The Christmas texts play upon the choir's knowledge of Christ's name, while the Easter texts play upon the choir's ability to speak in the persona of Christ and in their own persons where appropriate. The Easter mass as a whole progresses more naturally to the communion rite than does the Christmas mass (which, as was discussed above, probably stems from the Easter epistle reading and the ritual prominence of communion on that day). It is interesting that the presence of Christ was expressed primarily by visual metaphors for the Christmas mass, and by metaphors of feasting for the Easter mass. This suggests that at least some segment of the laity may have been able to follow the full textual and musical development of each rite, benefiting from the stress upon visual metaphors when they were not expected to partake.

Conclusion

"Troped" masses in eleventh-century Autun were very carefully crafted, built upon a common repertory of memorized texts and a common knowledge of the style of music to which texts were normally set. The services were constructed in such a way that their principal themes were developed and proclaimed in rhetorically effective ways, which evoked specific responses from the choir. These responses were enriched by their knowledge of how the biblical sources of the antiphons were interpreted in scripture commentary, and deepened the choir's involvement in the feast, by enabling them to enact what was being proclaimed. For the choir, the two ritual high points in the eucharistic liturgy, the proclamation of the word and the reception of the sacrament, were fully realized.

As this study has shown, the impact and purpose of eleventh-century liturgies can be most readily evaluated by adopting the perspective of a member of the monastic or clerical choir: such liturgies do have a professional element, in that they are coordinated with the educational goals and aims of the institutions that produced them. In order to participate fully as a member of the choir, one needed all of the following: (1) a clerical or monastic education that included the memorization and weekly recitation of the Psalter; (2) familiarity with a psalm commentary; and (3) a knowledge of the current style of musical setting. Typically, a child who was training to be a cleric, monk, or nun would have attained such a level of expertise after two or three years of education in a monastic or cathedral school (i.e., by about the age of ten or eleven). However, it would not be necessary for a novice to acquire a full range of linguistic and musical tools before beginning to participate: the web of biblical allusions and musical associations could be grasped at first "through a glass darkly," and only later be connected with a fuller set of interrelationships. In fact, little knowledge of the texts of the rite would be needed to understand much of the ritual enacting of the meaning of feasts demonstrated in the tropes and sequences. For example, the avoidance of the words *Iesus* and *Christus* for the first fifteen minutes of the Christmas service would be noticeable to the unschooled chorister as well as to the unlettered laity (*illiterati*), and the absence of Christ's name would be made even more noticeable by the abundance of its use in the following kyrie and gloria. Since knowledge of the rite was gained over a lifetime through its memorization and ritual contextualization, it is necessary to take seriously the medieval contention that the music of the service formed the most important link with the laity. The minimal knowledge of the rite that was available to the unlettered, through repetition of simple responses and oral instruction, is focused and strengthened in seasonally appropriate ways in every troped mass.

Sacra pagina (study of the sacred page) was not just something acquired in school, but was a set of practices that was consistently applied to eleventh-century liturgies. The tropes and sequences display how monastic and clerical composers used their command of biblical and liturgical texts and their exegetical and rhetorical finesse, in order to find connections between the Old and New Testaments, and how they used ornamental language and music in order to enrich and adorn the rite. Moreover, the meaning of the tropes and sequences is not tied solely to their words; a novice member of the choir would learn the traditional interpretations of the texts by rehearsing them within the liturgy itself. As we have seen, instead of "explaining" that Psalm 138 can be interpreted as Christ speaking to the Father of his passion and resurrection, or alternatively, as the sinner speaking to God, the choir speaks the words as Christ's words and also as their own in celebration of the ritual remembrance of the passion and resurrection. In the Christmas service, the texts which proclaim "the presence of the Lord" to creation have liturgical incarnations, as the gospel book is taken from the altar and read, and as the eucharistic elements are consecrated. All of the tropes are "tropological," not because they explain what the choir should do about their faith, but because they help them actually do it. For the principal participants, the choir, these liturgies could be expected to continue to reveal their riches as the clerics, monks, or nuns probed the mysteries of advanced Latin grammar and applied this knowledge to their daily celebrations. Moreover, all of the participants in these eleventh-century services could be expected to gain more insight into both the scripture and the services through repetition, memorization, and reflection. While a commonly accessible core remained unchanged, the liturgies were constantly deepened, renewed, and adapted to local traditions as cantors exchanged manuscripts containing their local repertories and improvised or wrote their own contributions. In short, eleventh-century liturgies engaged the participants at their varying levels of expertise, opening the treasury of the sacred page in ways that could be appreciated by all.

APPENDIX
Additional Texts for Easter from PaA 1169

Kyrie (fol. 19v-20r)

Kyrie O theos crithis dicheos in sephrros che athanatos ymas eleison
KYRIELEISON
O pater alme sedens super alas cherubin hac seraphin quibus nitentes clamantes sanctus sanctus sanctus Dominius
KYRIELEISON
Te decet sol imnus melos carmen symphonie enesis vox omnigenarum linguarum
KYRIELEISON
Kriste patris unice tuam in nobis naturam refove
CRISTELEISON
Pro quibus arborem subisti stayros unda purpurantis sanguinis dans
KRISTELEISON
Tu sanctae spiritus nostris te ohdis velis admisceri dignater
KRISTELEISON
Duo qui simul iungis vivum hac moribundum fingis homullum fragilitati eius tu miserere culpas abluendo
KYRIELEISON
Omnes vocibus altis te laudamus rex bone trine et une cuius bonitas cuncor parque in trinitate vivit et regnat Nunc et in pro infinita secula seculorum amen semper

Gloria (fol. 20r-21r)

Cives superni hodie suam simul et nostram nuntiant mundo festivitatem gloriam deo resonemus omnes
GLORIA IN EXCELSIS DEO ET IN TERRA PAX HOMINIBUS BONE VOLUNTATIS
Christus surrexit dulcibus imnis omnipotenti modulemur eya
LAUDAMUS TE
Rerum creator qui pietate motus immensa unicum dedisti mundi pro salute
BENED<ICIMUS> TE
Obtime rector generis humani qui voluisti vulnera curare fili cruore
ADOR<AMUS> TE
Iam liberati mortis a vinc<u>lo et libertate reddita vera
GLORIFICAM<US> TE
Trinitas sancta gratis honostra miserata nece

GRATIAS AGIMUS TIBI PROPTER NOSTRAM GLORIAM TUAM
Qua diminutos angelorum coros hodie restaurans multos inferno abstais funesto
DOMINE DEUS REX CAELESTIS DEUS PATER OMNIPOTENS DOMINE FILI UNIGENITE IESU CHRISTE
Protege verum pascha celebrantes Iesu Christe
DOMINE DEUS
Praesta ne nobis veteris fermenti imacula con misceatur
AGNUS DEI
Verus et aeternus nobis immolatus
FILIUS PATRIS
En epulemur
QUI TOLLIS PECCATA MUNDI
Fingens illa cruci
MISERERE NOBIS QUI TOLLIS PECCATA MUNDI
Misericors et clemens
SUSCIPE DEPRECATIONEM <NOSTRAM QUI SEDES AD DEXTERAM PATRIS MISERERE NOBIS> QUONIAM TU SOLUS SANCTUS
Pius hac benignus
TU SOLUS DOMINUS
Serenus hac severus
TU SOLUS ALTISSIMUS
A<d>que clementissimus
IESU CHRISTE CUM SANCTO SPIRITU IN GLORIA DEI PATRIS
Te residente tuere celebrantes semper et ubique una conclamemus
AMEN

Prose (fol. 21r-22r)

Fulgens preclara
Rutilans per orbem hodie dies in qua Christi lucide narrantur ovanter proelia
De hoste superbo quo Ihesus triumphavit pulchre castra illius permens teterrima

Infelix culpa eve qua caruimus omnes vita
Felix proles marie qua epulamur modo una

Benedicta sit celsa regina illa
Generans regem spoliantem tartara

Pollentem iam in aethera
Rex in aeternum suscipe benignus preconia nostra sedula tibi canencia
Patris sedens ad dexteram
Victor ubique morte superata atque triumphata polorum possidens gaudia

O magna o celsa o pulchra clemencia Christi luciflua o alma
Laus tibi honorque hac virtus qui nostram antiquam leviasti sarcinam

Roseo cruore agni benignissimi empta florida micat haec aula
Potenti virtute nostra qui lavit facinora tribuit dona fulgida

Stupens valde in memet iam miror hodiherna
Tanta indignus pandere modo sacramenta

Stirpe davidica ortus de tribu iuda leo potens surrexisti in gloria agnus visus es in eya
Fondens olim arva regna petens supera iustis reddens praemia in saecula dignanter ovantia

Dic impie zabule quid valet nunc fraus tua
Igneis nexus loris a Christi victoria

Tribus lingue admiramini quis audivit talia mysteria
Ut mors mortem sic superaret rei perciperent talem gratiam

Iudaea incredula cur manens ad<h>uc inverecunda
Pespice christicola qualiter laetis candunt inclita

Redemptori carmina ergo pie rex Christe nobis laxans crimina Solve nexorum vincula
Electorum agmina Fac tecum resurgere ad beatam gloriam Digna rependens merita

Paracliti sancti consolacionem piam
Exspectamus secundum promissionem tuam

Peracta ascensionis sancta sollemnia
Qua est regressus in celum nube tectus clara pollens laude aeterna
Amen

Laudes Regiae (fol. 22v-23r)

Christus vincit Christus regnat Christus imperat
Exaudi Christe
Illi summo pontifici et universali pape vita
Sancte Petre
Tu illum adiuva
Sancte Paule
Tu illum adiuva
Sancte Gregorii
Tu illum adiuva
Exaudi Christe
Rodberto magno et pacifico rege vita et victor<e>m

Sancte Dionisu
Tu illum adiuva
Sancte Cornelii
Tu illum adiuva
Sancte Medarde
Tu illum adiuva
Exaudi Christe
Wualterio huis aeclessiae ponticifi et omni clero et populo sibi conmisso salus et vita
Sancte Nazarii
Tu illos adiuva

<Sancte Ger>vasii
Tu illos adiuva
Exaudi Christe
Schola omnibus iudicibus
Regibus et principibus et cuncto excercitui Christianorum vita et victoria
Sancte Mauricii
Tu illos adiuva
Sancte Martine
Tu illos adiuva
Sancte Sebastiane
Tu illos adiuva
Rex regum
Christus vincit Christus regnat
Gloria nostra
Christus vincit Christus regnat
Misericordia nostra
Christus vincit Christus regnat
Spes nostra
Christus vincit Christus regnat
Auxillium nostrum
Christus vincit Christus regnat
Fortitudo et victoria nostra
Christus vincit
Lux et vita nostra
Christus vincit Christus regnat
Liberacio et redemcio nostra
Christus vincit
Arma nostra invictissima
Christus vincit
Murus noster inexpugnabilis
Christus vincit
Defensio et exultacio nostra
Christus vincit
Ipsi soli gloria et potestas per imortalia secula seculorum amen
Ipsi soli virtus et victoria per omnia secula seculorum amen
Ipsi soli laus et iubilacio per infinita secula seculorum amen

BIBLIOGRAPHY

Manuscript Sources

Autun, Bibliothèque Municipale, S 10 (8*) (Autun 10).
Autun, Bibliothèque Municipale, MS 11 (9) (Autun 11).
Autun, Bibliothèque Municipale, S 146 (123) (Autun 146).
Benevento, Biblioteca Capitolare, MS 35 (26) (Benevento 35).
Montpellier, Bibliothèque Universitaire, Section de Médicine, MS H 159 (Montpellier H 159; *see* Mocquereau).
Paris, Bibliothèque de l'Arsenal, MS 1169 (PaA 1169).
Paris, Bibliothèque Nationale, fonds latins, MS 1119 (PaN 1119).
Paris, Bibliothèque Nationale, fonds latins, MS 10508 (PaN 10508).
Paris, Bibliothèque Nationale, nouvelles acquisitions des fonds latins, MS 1235 (PaN 1235).
Paris, Biliothèque Nationale, nouvelles acquisitions des fonds latins, MS 1871 (PaN 1871).

Printed Sources

Abelson, Paul. *The Seven Liberal Arts: A Study in Medieval Culture.* Columbia University Teachers College Contributions to Education, no. 11. New York: Teachers College, Columbia University, 1906.

Adriaen, M. *See* Cassiodorus and Gregory the Great.

Amalar. *Prologus antiphonarii a se compositi.* Edited by Jean-Michel Hanssens, in *Amalarii episcopi opera liturgica omnia,* 1:361-63. Studi e testi 138-40. Vatican City: Biblioteca Apostolica Vaticana, 1948-50.

________. *Liber officialis.* Edited by Jean-Michel Hanssens, in *Amalarii episcopi opera liturgica omnia,* 2:19-580. Studi e testi 138-40. Vatican City: Biblioteca Apostolica Vaticana, 1948-50.

________. *Eclogae de ordine romano.* Edited by Jean-Michel Hanssens, in *Amalarii episcopi opera liturgica omnia,* 3:225-65. Studi e testi 138-40. Vatican City: Biblioteca Apostolica Vaticana, 1948-50.

Analecta hymnica medii aevi. See Blume, Clemens.

Atkinson, Charles M. "On the Interpretation of *Modi, quos abusive tonos dicimus.*" In *Hermeneutics and Medieval Culture,* ed. Patrick J. Gallacher and Helen Damico, 147-61. Albany: State University of New York Press, 1989.

Augustine. *Enarrationes in Psalmos.* Edited by D. Eligius Dekkers and Johannes Fraipont. Corpus Christianorum series latina, nos. 38-40. Turnhout: Brepols, 1956.

________. *St. Augustine on Christian Doctrine.* Translated by D. W. Robertson. The Library of Liberal Arts, no. 80. New York: Liberal Arts Press, 1958.

________. *De doctrina christiana.* Edited by William Green. Corpus scriptorum ecclesiasticorum latinorum, no. 80. Vienna: Hölder-Pichler-Tempsky, 1963.

________. *Confessiones.* Edited by Martinus Skutella and Lucas Verheijen. Corpus Christianorum series latina, no. 27. Turnhout: Brepols, 1981.

Aurelian of Réome [Réôme]. *The Discipline of Music* (*Musica Disciplina*). Translated by Joseph Ponte. Colorado College Music Press Translations, no. 3. Colorado Springs: Colorado College Music Press, 1968.

Aurelian. *See* Gerbert.

Autun, *Autun Augustodunum capitule des Éduens.* Exposition catalogue 16 mars-27 octobre 1985. Autun, 1985.

Babb, Warren. *Hucbald, Guido, and John on Music: Three Medieval Treatises.* New Haven: Yale University Press, 1978.

Baudrillart, Alfred, ed. *Dictionnaire d'histoire et de géographie ecclésiastiques.* Paris: Letouzey & Ané, 1950-53. S.v. "Chrodegang."

Bede. *Historia ecclesiastica gentis Anglorum.* Edited by C. Plummer. Chap. 5 in *Venerabilis Bedae opera historica.* 2 vols. Oxford, 1896.

________. "Bede's *De Schematibus et Tropis*—A Translation." Translated by Gussie Hecht Tanenhaus [sic]. *Quarterly Journal of Speech* 48 (1962): 237-53; reprint, under the name 'Tannenhaus', in *Readings in Medieval Rhetoric,* ed. Joseph M. Miller, 96-124. Bloomington: Indiana University Press, 1973.

________. *De arte metrica et De schematibus et tropis.* Edited by C. B. Kendall, in *Bedae Venerabilis Opera: Pars VI, Opera Didascalica, 1,* ed. Charles W. Jones, 60-171. Corpus Christianorum series latina, no. 123A. Turnhout: Brepols, 1975.

Beleth, Johan. *Iohannis Beleth Summa de Ecclesiasticis Officis.* Edited by Herbert Douteil. Corpus Christianorum Continuatio Mediaevalis, nos. 41-41A. Turnhout: Brepols, 1976.

Bernold of Constance. *Micrologus.* In Patrologiae cursus completus, sive Bibliotheca universalis . . . omnium ss patrum, doctorum scriptorumque ecclesiasticum qui ab aevo apostolico ad usque Innocenti III tempora floruerunt . . . Series [Latina], no. 151, ed. J. P. Migne, 973-1022. Paris, 1844-64.

Bielitz, Mathias. *Musik und Grammatik: Studien zur mittelalterlichen Musiktheorie.* Beiträge zur Musikforschung, no. 4. Munich: Katzbichler, 1977.

Bjork, David A. "Early Repertories of the *Kyrie eleison.*" *Kirchenmusikalisches Jahrbuch* 63 (1979): 9-43.

________. "The Early Frankish Kyrie Text: A Reappraisal." *Viator* 12 (1981): 9-35.

Björkvall, Gunilla, ed. *Les deux tropaires d'Apt, MSS 17 et 18.* Corpus Troporum, no. 5. Stockholm: Almqvist & Wiksell International, 1986.

Björkvall, Gunilla, Gunilla Iversen, and Ritva Jonsson. *Tropes du propre de la messe: 2 Cycle de Pâques.* Corpus Troporum, no. 3. Stockholm: Almqvist & Wiksell International, 1982.

Blume, Clemens, Guido Maria Dreves, and Henry Marriott Bannister, eds. *Analecta hymnica medii aevi.* 55 vols. Leipzig: Reisland, 1886-1922.

Blume, Friedrich, ed. *Die Musik in Geschichte und Gegenwart.* Kassel: Bärenreiter, 1949-79. S.v. "Sequenz (Gesang)," and "Tropus," by Bruno Stäblein.

Bolton, W. F. *A History of Anglo-Latin Literature 597-1066.* Princeton: Princeton University Press, 1967.

Bosse, Detlev. *Untersuchung einstimmiger Mittelalterlicher Melodien zum "Gloria in Excelsis Deo."* Forschungsbeträge zur Musikwissenschaft, no. 2. Regensburg: Gustav Bosse, 1955.

Bouchard, Constance Brittain. *Sword, Miter, and Cloister: Nobility and the Church in Burgundy, 980-1198.* Ithaca, NY: Cornell University Press, 1987.

Bower, Calvin M. "The Grammatical Model of Musical Understanding in the Middle Ages." In *Hermeneutics and Medieval Culture*, ed. Patrick J. Gallacher and Helen Damico, 133-45. Albany: State University of New York Press, 1989.

Brown, George Hardin. *Bede the Venerable.* Twayne's English Authors Series, ed. George Economou, no. 443. Boston: G. K. Hall, 1987.

Bruno of Würzburg. *Expositio psalmorum.* In Patrologiae cursus completus, sive Bibliotheca universalis . . . omnium ss patrum, doctorum scriptorumque ecclesiasticum qui ab aevo apostolico ad usque Innocenti III tempora floruerunt . . . Series [Latina], no. 142, ed. J. P. Migne, 1-530. Paris, 1844-64.

Burkitt, Francis Crawford. *The Book of Rules of Tyconius.* Cambridge: Cambridge University Press, 1894.

Cabaniss, Allen. *Amalarius of Metz.* Amsterdam: North Holland Publishing Company, 1954.

Cabrol, F., H. Leclercq, and H. Marrou, eds. *Dictionnaire d'archéologie chrétienne et de liturgie.* 30vv. Paris, 1907-53. S.v. "Épitres," and "Évangiles," by G. Godu.

Cardine, Eugène. "Sémiologie Grégorienne." *Études Grégoriennes* 11 (1970): 1-158.

Carruthers, Mary. *The Book of Memory: A Study of Memory in Medieval Culture.* Cambridge: Cambridge University Press, 1990.

Cassiodorus. *Cassiodori Senatoris Institutiones.* Edited by R. A. B. Mynors. Oxford: Clarendon Press, 1937.

________. *An Introduction to Divine and Human Readings by Cassiodorus Senator.* Translated by Leslie Webber Jones. New York: Columbia University Press, 1946.

________. *Expositio Psalmorum.* Edited by Marci Adriaen. Corpus Christianorum series latina, nos. 97-98. Turnhout: Brepols, 1958.

________. *Cassiodorus: Explanation of the Psalms.* Translated by Patrick Gerard Walsh. Ancient Christian Writers, ed. Walter J. Burghart and Thomas Comerford Lawler, nos. 51-53. New York: Paulist Press, 1990-91.

Chrodegang. *Regula canonicorum.* In Patrologiae cursus completus, sive Bibliotheca universalis . . . omnium ss patrum, doctorum scriptorumque ecclesiasticum qui ab aevo apostolico ad usque Innocenti III tempora floruerunt . . . Series [Latina], no. 89, ed. J. P. Migne, 1097-1120. Paris, 1844-64.

Colette, Marie-Nöel. "*Modus, tropus, tonus:* Tropes d'intröit et théories modales." *Études grégoriennes* 25 (1997): 63-95.

Costa, Eugenio, Jr. *Tropes et séquences dans le cadre de la vie liturgique au moyen âge.* Bibliotheca "Ephemerides Liturgicae," "Susidia," ed. A. Pistoia and A. M. Triacca, no. 17. Rome: C.L.V. Edizioni Liturgiche, 1979.

Cowdrey, Herbert Edward John. "The Anglo-Norman Laudes Regiae." *Viator* 12 (1981): 37-78.

Crocker, Richard L. "*Musica Rhythmica* and *Musica Metrica* in Antique and Medieval Theory." *Journal of Music Theory* 2 (1958): 2-23.

________. "The Troping Hypothesis." *The Musical Quarterly* 52 (1966): 183-203.

________. *The Early Sequence.* Berkeley: University of California Press, 1977.

Crocker, Richard, and David Hiley, eds. *The Early Middle Ages to 1300.* Vol. 2, *The New Oxford History of Music.* Rev. ed. Oxford: Oxford University Press, 1990.

Diehl, Patrick S. *The Medieval European Religious Lyric: An Ars Poetica.* Berkeley: University of California Press, 1985.

Donatus. *Ars minor.* In *Donat et la tradition de l'enseignement grammatical,* ed. Louis Holtz, 585-602. Paris: Centre national de la recherche scientifique, 1981.

________. *Ars maior.* In *Donat et la tradition de l'enseignement grammatical,* ed. Louis Holtz, 603-74. Paris: Centre national de la recherche scientifique, 1981.

Douay-Rheims Bible. *The Holy Bible translated from the Latin Vulgate.* Baltimore: John Murphy Co., 1914.

Du Cange, Charles. *Glossarium ad scriptores mediae et infimae latinitatis.* Revised edition by Léopold Favre. 10 vols. Niort, 1883-88; reprint, Paris: Librairie des sciences et des arts, 1937.

Duchesne, Louis, and Cyrille Vogel, eds. *Le Liber pontificalis.* 2d ed. 3 vols. Paris: E. de Boccard, 1955-57.

Durand, Guillaume. *Guillelmi Duranti Rationale Divinorum Officiorum I-IV.* Edited by Anselme Davril and Timothy Thibodeau. Corpus Christianorum Continuatio Mediaevalis, no. 140. Turnhout: Brepols, 1995.

Dyer, Joseph. "The Offertory Chant of the Roman Liturgy and Its Musical Form." *Studi musicali* 11 (1982): 3-30.

Evans, G[illian] R. *Old Arts and New Theology: The Beginnings of Theology as an Academic Discipline.* Oxford: Oxford University Press, 1980.

Evans, Paul. *The Early Trope Repertory of Saint Martial de Limoges.* Princeton: Princeton University Press, 1970.

Fassler, Margot. "The Office of the Cantor in Early Western Monastic Rules and Customaries: A Preliminary Investigation." In *Early Music History,* no. 5, ed. Iain Fenlon, 29-51. Cambridge: Cambridge University Press, 1985.

________. "Accent, Meter, and Rhythm in Medieval Treatises *De rithmis.*" *Journal of Musicology* 5 (1987): 164-90.

________. *Gothic Song: Victorine Sequences and Augustinian Reform in Twelfth-Century Paris.* Cambridge: Cambridge University Press, 1993.

Florus of Lyon. *De expositione missae.* In Patrologiae cursus completus, sive Bibliotheca universalis . . . omnium ss patrum, doctorum scriptorumque ecclesiasticum qui ab aevo apostolico ad usque Innocenti III tempora floruerunt . . . Series [Latina], no. 119, ed. J. P. Migne, 15-72. Paris, 1844-64.

________. *Opuscula adversus Amalarium.* In Patrologiae cursus completus, sive Bibliotheca universalis . . . omnium ss patrum, doctorum scriptorumque ecclesiasticum qui ab aevo apostolico ad usque Innocenti III tempora floruerunt . . . Series [Latina], no. 119, ed. J. P. Migne, 71-94. Paris, 1844-64.

Flynn, William T. "Paris, Bibliothèque de L'Arsenal, MS 1169: The Hermeneutics of Eleventh-Century Burgundian Tropes, and Their Implications for Liturgical Theology." Ph.D. dissertation, Duke University, 1992.

Franklin, R. W. *Nineteenth-Century Churches: The History of a New Catholicism in Württemberg, England and France.* New York: Garland Publishing, 1987.

Freistadt, Heinrich. "Die liquiszierenden Noten des gregorianischen Chorals: ein Beitrag zur Notationskunde." Dissertation, University of Freiburg, Switzerland, 1929.

Frere, Walter Howard, and Langton Brown, eds. *The Hereford Breviary,* vol. 1. Henry Bradshaw Society, no. 26. London: Harrison & Sons, 1904.

Froutolf. *Breviarium de musica et tonarius.* Edited by Cölestin Vivel. Vienna, 1919.

Gagnare, Chevalier. *Histoire de l'église d'Autun.* Autun, 1774.

Gallia Christiana in provincas ecclesiasticas distributa. 16 vols. Paris, 1716-1864.

Gautier, Léon. *Histoire de la poésie liturgique au moyen âge: Les tropes.* Paris, 1886; reprint, Ridgewood, NJ: Gregg Press, 1966.

Gelineau, Joseph. "Music and Singing in the Liturgy." In *The Study of Liturgy,* ed. Cheslyn Jones, Geoffrey Wainwright, Edward Yarnold, and Paul Bradshaw. New York: Oxford University Press, 1992.

Gerbert, Martin. *Scriptores ecclesiastici de musica sacra potissimum.* 3 vols. St. Blasien, 1784; reprint, Hildesheim: Olms, 1963.

Graduale Triplex seu graduale romanum Pauli PP.VI cura recognitum & rhythmicis signis a Solesmensibus monachis ornatum: Neumis Laudunensibus (cod. 239) et Sangallensibus (codicum San Gallensis

359 et Einsidlensis 121) nunc auctum [Edited by Marie-Claire Billecocq and Rupert Fischer]. Paris: Desclée, 1979.

Gregory the Great. *Moralia in Iob.* Edited by M. Adriaen. 1 vol. in 3. Corpus Christianorum series latina, no. 143. Turnhout: Brepols, 1979.

Grier, James. "*Ecce sanctum quem deus elegit Marcialem apostolum*: Adémar de Chabannes and the Tropes for the Feast of Saint Martial." In *Beyond the Moon: Festschrift Luther Dittmer,* ed. Bryan Gillingham and Paul Merkley. Wissenschaftliche Abhandlungen, no. 53. Ottowa, 1990.

Guido. *Guidonis Arentini Micrologus.* Edited by Jos. Smits van Waesberghe. Corpus scriptorum de musica, no. 4. Rome: American Institute of Musicology, 1955.

Handschin, Jacques. "Trope, Sequence, and Conductus." In *Early Medieval Music up to 1300,* ed. Anselm Hughes, 128-74. Vol. 2, *The New Oxford History of Music.* London: Oxford University Press, 1954.

Hansen, Finn, ed. *H159 Montpellier: Tonary of St Bénigne of Dijon.* Copenhagen: Dan Fog, 1974.

Harper, John. *The Forms and Orders of Western Liturgy from the Tenth to the Eighteenth Century: A Historical Introduction and Guide for Students and Musicians.* Oxford: Clarendon Press, 1991.

Henscenio, Godefrido, and Daniele Papebrochio. *Acta sanctorum Aprilis collecta, digesta, illustrata a Godefrido Henscenio et Daniele Papebrochio: Tomus I* (April 1-10). Acta sanctorum, no. 10. Paris: Victor Palmé, 1866.

Hervé of Bourgdieu. *Commentarium in Isaiam.* In Patrologiae cursus completus, sive Bibliotheca universalis . . . omnium ss patrum, doctorum scriptorumque ecclesiasticum qui ab aevo apostolico ad usque Innocenti III tempora floruerunt . . . Series [Latina], no. 181, ed. J. P. Migne, 17-592. Paris, 1844-64.

Hiley, David. "Cluny, Sequences and Tropes." In *La tradizione dei tropi liturgici,* ed. Claudio Leonardi and Enrico Menesto, 125-38. Spoleto, 1990.

________. *Western Plainchant: A Handbook.* Oxford: Clarendon Press, 1993.

Holtz, Louis. *Donat et la tradition de l'enseignement grammatical.* Paris: Centre national de la recherche scientifique, 1981.

Huglo, Michel. *Les tonaires, inventaire, analyse, comparison.* Publications de la société française de musicologie, ser. 3, vol. 2. Paris, 1971.

Huntsman, Jeffrey F. "Grammar." Chapter 3 in *The Seven Liberal Arts in the Middle Ages,* ed. David L. Wagner, 58-95. Bloomington: Indiana University Press, 1983.

Husmann, Heinrich. *Tropen- und Sequenzenhandschriften.* Répertoire international des sources musicales, no. B/V1. Munich: G. Henle, 1964.

The Hymnbook. Presbyterian Church, USA. Richmond: John Ribble, 1955.

Iversen, Gunilla, ed. *Tropes de l'Agnus Dei.* Corpus Troporum, no. 4. Stockholm: Almqvist & Wiksell International, 1980.

Iversen, Gunilla. "On the Iconography of Praise in the Sanctus and Its Tropes." In *De musica et cantu: Studien zur Geschichte der Kirchenmusik und der Oper: Helmut Hucke zum 60. Geburtstag*, ed. Peter Cahn and Ann-Katrin Heimerg, 275-311. Frankfurt: Hochschule für Musik und Darstellende Kunst, 1993.

Jacobsson, Ritva, and Leo Treitler. "Tropes and the Concept of Genre." In *Corpus Troporum: Pax et sapientia: Studies in Text and Music of Liturgical Tropes and Sequences, in Memory of Gordon Anderson*, ed. Ritva Jacobsson, 59-89. Stockholm: Almqvist & Wiksell International, 1986.

Jaeger, Stephen. *The Envy of Angels: Cathedral Schools and Social Ideals in Medieval Europe, 950-1200*. Philadelphia: University of Pennsylvania Press, 1994.

Jerome. *Praefatio in librum Iob*. In Patrologiae cursus completus, sive Bibliotheca universalis . . . omnium ss patrum, doctorum scriptorumque ecclesiasticum qui ab aevo apostolico ad usque Innocenti III tempora floruerunt . . . Series [Latina], no. 28, ed. J. P. Migne, 1137-42. Paris, 1844-64.

John. *Johannis Affligemensis, De musica cum tonario*. Edited by Jos. Smits van Waesberghe. Corpus scriptorum de musica, no. 1. Rome: American Institute of Musicology, 1950.

John of Avranches. *De officiis ecclesiasticis*. In Patrologiae cursus completus, sive Bibliotheca universalis . . . omnium ss patrum, doctorum scriptorumque ecclesiasticum qui ab aevo apostolico ad usque Innocenti III tempora floruerunt . . . Series [Latina], no. 147, ed. J. P. Migne, 1-116. Paris, 1844-64.

Johnstone, John [Gearey]. "Beyond a Chant: *Tui sunt caeli* and Its Tropes." In *Music and Language*, 24-37, *Studies in the History of Music*, no. 1. New York: Broude Bros., 1983.

________. "The Offertory Trope: Origins, Transmissions, and Function." Ph.D. dissertation, Ohio State University, 1984.

Jonsson, Ritva, ed. *Tropes du propre de la messe: 1 Cycle de Nöel*. Corpus Troporum, no. 1. Stockholm: Almqvist & Wiksell International, 1975.

Jonsson, Ritva, and Leo Treitler. "Medieval Music and Language: A Reconsideration of the Relationship." In *Music and Language*, 1-23, Studies in the History of Music, no. 1. New York: Broude Bros., 1983.

Jüngel, Eberhard. *God as the Mystery of the World*. Translated by Darrell L. Guder. Grand Rapids, MI: Eerdmans, 1983. Originally published as *Gott als Geheimnis der Welt*. 3d ed. Tübingen: J. C. B. Mohr, 1977.

Jungmann, Josef. *The Mass of the Roman Rite*. 2 vols. Translated by Francis A. Brunner. New York: Benziger Brothers, 1951-55. Originally published as *Missarum Sollemnia: eine genetische Erklärung der römischen Messe*. 2d ed. Vienna: Herder, 1949.

________. *The Place of Christ in Liturgical Prayer*. 2d rev. ed. Translated by A. Peeler. New York: Alba House, 1965. Originally published as *Die Stellung Christi im liturgischen Gebet*. 2d ed. Münster: Aschendorff, 1962.

Keil, H. *Grammatici latini.* 8 vols. Leipzig, 1857-80.

Kelly, Douglas. *The Arts of Poetry and Prose.* Typologie des Sources du Moyen Âge Occidental, Fasc. 59. Turnhout: Brepols, 1991.

Kelly, Thomas Forrest. "Introducing the *Gloria in Excelsis.*" *Journal of the American Musicological Society* 37 (1984): 479-506.

King James Bible. *The NIV/KJV Parallel Bible.* Grand Rapids, MI: Zondervan, 1983.

Landes, Richard. *Relics, Apocalypse, and the Deceits of History: Ademar of Chabannes, 989-1034.* Cambridge, MA: Harvard University Press, 1995.

Landwehr-Melnicki, Margaretha. *Das einstimmige Kyrie des lateinischen Mittelalters.* Forschungsbeiträge zur Musikwissenschaft, no. 1. Regensburg: Gustave Bosse, 1955.

Leclercq, Jean. *The Love of Learning and the Desire for God: A Study of Monastic Culture.* Translated by Catherine Mirashi. 3d ed. New York: Fordham University Press, 1982. Originally published as *L'Amour des lettres et le désir de Dieu: Initiation aux auteurs monastiques du moyen-âge.* Paris: Les Éditions du Cerf, 1957.

Leith, John H. *Creeds of the Churches.* 3d ed. Atlanta: John Knox Press, 1982.

Levy, Kenneth. "Charlemagne's Archetype of Gregorian Chant." *Journal of the American Musicological Society* 40 (1987): 1-30.

The Liber Usualis, with Introduction and Rubrics in English. Edited by the Benedictines of Solesmes. Tournai and New York: Desclée, 1962.

Lossky, Nicholas, et al., eds., *Dictionary of the Ecumenical Movement.* Geneva: WCC Publications, 1991. S.v. "Liturgical Movement," by Teresa Berger and "Liturgical Reforms, " by Balthasar Fischer.

Lubac, Henri de. *L'exégèse médiévale: Les quatre sens de l'écriture.* 2 vols. in 4. Paris: Aubier, 1959-61.

Mansi, Johannes Dominicus. *Sacrorum conciliorum nova et amplissima collectio.* 31 vols. Florence and Venice, 1757-98; reprint, with supplement, 53 vols. Graz: Akademische Druck, 1960.

Marcusson, Olof, ed. *Prosules de la messe 1 Tropes de l'alleluia.* Corpus Troporum, no. 2. Stockholm: Almqvist & Wiksell International, 1976.

McKinnon, James. "The Fourth-Century Origin of the Gradual." In *Early Music History,* no. 7, ed. Iain Fenlon, 91-106. Cambridge: Cambridge University Press, 1987.

________. *Music in Early Christian Literature.* Cambridge: Cambridge University Press, 1987.

Mocquereau, André, ed. *Antiphonarium tonale missarum* (*XI*[e] *siècle*): *codex H. 159 de la Bibliothèque de l'École de médecine de Montpellier.* Paléographie musicale: Les principaux manuscrits du chant grégorien, ambrosien, gallican, publiés en facsimiles phototypiques, nos. 7 and 8, ed. A. Mocquereau and J. Gajard. Solesmes: Société de Saint Jean l'Évangeliste, 1901-5.

Moriarty, Fredrick L. "Isaiah 1-39." In *The Jerome Biblical Commentary,* ed. Raymond Brown, Joseph Fitzmeyer, and Roland Murphy, 265-82. Engelwood Cliffs, NJ: Prentice Hall, 1968.

Murphy, James J. *Rhetoric in the Middle Ages.* Berkeley: University of California Press, 1974.

Odelmann, E. "Comment a-t-on appelé les tropes? Observations sur les rubriques des tropes des Xe et XIe siécles." *Cahiers de civilisation médiévale* 18 (1975): 15-36.

Palazzo, Eric. "Le tropaire d'Autun, le MS Paris, Bibliothèque de l'Arsenal 1169: sa place dans le groupe des tropaires du haut moyen âge." *Mémoires de la société Éduenne* 14, no. 5 (1985-87): 405-20.

Paul and Stephen. *Regula ad monachos.* In Patrologiae cursus completus, sive Bibliotheca universalis . . . omnium ss patrum, doctorum scriptorumque ecclesiasticum qui ab aevo apostolico ad usque Innocenti III tempora floruerunt . . . Series [Latina], no. 66, ed. J. P. Migne, 949-58. Paris, 1844-64.

Planchart, Alejandro Enrique. *The Repertory of Tropes at Winchester.* 2 vols. Princeton: Princeton University Press, 1977.

Planchart, Alejandro, and John Boe, eds. *Beneventanum troporum corpus.* Recent Researches in the Music of the Middle Ages and Early Renaissance, nos. 16-28. Madison, WI: A-R Editions, 1989-.

Plank, Stephen. *"The Way to Heavens Doore": An Introduction to Liturgical Process and Musical Style.* Metuchen, NJ: The Scarecrow Press Inc., 1994.

Powers, Harold. "Language Models and Musical Analysis." *Ethnomusicology* 24 (1980): 1-60.

Rabanus Maurus. *De institutione clericorum.* In Patrologiae cursus completus, sive Bibliotheca universalis . . . omnium ss patrum, doctorum scriptorumque ecclesiasticum qui ab aevo apostolico ad usque Innocenti III tempora floruerunt . . . Series [Latina], no. 107, ed. J. P. Migne, 194-420. Paris, 1844-64.

Rankin, Susan. *The Music of the Medieval Liturgical Drama in France and England.* 2 vols. Outstanding Dissertations in Music from British Universities, ed. John Caldwell. New York: Garland, 1989.

Reckow, Fritz. "Vitium oder Color Rhetoricus? Thesen zur Bedeutung der Modelldisziplinen Grammatica, Rhetorica und Poetica für das Musikverständnis." *Forum Musicologicum* 3 (1982): 307-21.

Reier, Ellen Jane. "The Introit Trope Repertory at Nevers: MSS Paris B. N. lat. 9449 and Paris B. N. n. a. lat. 1235." 3 vols. Ph.D. dissertation, University of California, Berkeley, 1981.

Riché, Pierre. *Écoles et enseignement dans le haut moyen âge: Fin du Ve siècle—milieu du XIe siècle.* 2d ed. Paris: Picard Éditeur, 1989.

Roederer, Charlotte. *Festive Troped Masses from the Eleventh Century: Christmas and Easter in the Aquitaine.* Collegium Musicum, Yale University, 2d ser., vol. 11. Madison, WI: A-R Editions, 1989.

Rönnau, Klaus. *Die Tropen zum Gloria in excelsis Deo: Unter besonderer Berücksichtigung des Repertoires der Martial-Handschriften.* Wiesbaden: Breitkopf & Härtel, 1967.

Sacrorum Codex (vulgo Missale nuncupatus) iuxta ritum Ecclesiae Heduensis optima ordine nunc demum multo, quam ante hac unquam catigator, in lucem emissus: In quo prater veram verborum distinctionem, orthographiam, ac prosodiam, nihil eorum, quae ac sacra peragenda pertinere videntur, desiderare polis. Autun: apud Johannem Hamelinum, 1555/6.

Sadie, Stanley, ed. *The New Grove Dictionary of Music and Musicians.* London: Macmillan Publishers, 1980. S.v. "Ekkehard of St. Gall," by Alejandro Enrique Planchart; "Prosa," by Richard Crocker; "Trope (i)," by Ruth Steiner.

Saenger, Paul. "Silent Reading: Its Impact on Late Medieval Script and Society." *Viator* 13 (1982): 367-414.

Schildbach, Martin. *Das einstimmige Agnus Dei und seine handschriftliche Überlieferung vom 10. bis zum 16. Jahrhundert.* Erlangen-Nürnberg: Josef Hogl, 1967.

Schlager, Karlheinz. *Alleluia-Melodien I bis 1100.* Monumenta monodica medii aevi, no. 7. Kassel: Bärenreiter, 1968.

Smalley, Beryl. *The Study of the Bible in the Middle Ages.* Oxford: Basil Blackwell, 1983.

Smits van Waesberghe, Jos., ed. *Expositiones in Micrologum Guidonis Aretini.* Amsterdam: North Holland Publishing Co., 1957.

Stevens, John. *Words and Music in the Middle Ages.* Cambridge Studies in Music. Cambridge: Cambridge University Press, 1986.

Stock, Brian. *The Implications of Literacy: Written Language and Models of Interpretation in the Eleventh and Twelfth Centuries.* Princeton: Princeton University Press, 1983.

Tanenhaus [sic Tannenhaus]. *See* Bede.

Thannabaur, Peter Josef. *Das einstimmige Sanctus der römischen Messe in der handschriftlichen Überlieferung des 11. bis 16. Jahrhunderts.* Erlanger Arbeiten zur Musikwissenschaft, no. 1. Munich: Walter Ricke, 1962.

Thurian, Max, and Geoffrey Wainwright. *Baptism and Eucharist: Ecumenical Convergence in Celebration.* Geneva: WCC Publications, 1983.

Ticonius. *De regula (Of Rules). See* Burkitt.

Treitler, Leo. "Reading and Singing: On the Genesis of Occidental Music-writing." In *Early Music History,* no. 4, ed. Iain Fenlon, 135-208. Cambridge: Cambridge University Press, 1984.

Ulrich of Zell, *Consuetudines cluniances.* In Patrologiae cursus completus, sive Bibliotheca universalis . . . omnium ss patrum, doctorum scriptorumque ecclesiasticum qui ab aevo apostolico ad usque Innocenti III tempora floruerunt . . . Series [Latina], no. 149, ed. J. P. Migne, 633-778. Paris, 1844-64.

van Deusen, Nancy. *Music at Nevers Cathedral: Principal Sources of Mediaeval Chant.* 2 vols. Musicological Studies, 30, nos. 1 and 2. Stroudsburg, PA: Sun Press, for the Institute of Medieval Music, 1980.

________. *The Harp and the Soul: Essays in Medieval Music.* Lewiston, NY: The Edwin Mellen Press, 1989.

Vogel, Cyrille. *Medieval Liturgy: An Introduction to the Sources.* Translated, revised and edited by William Storey and Niels Rasmussen. Washington DC: Pastoral Press, 1986.

Vollaerts, Jan W. A. *Rhythmic Proportions in Early Medieval Ecclesiastical Chant*. Leiden: E. J. Brill, 1958.

Vulgate Bible. *Biblia Sacra juxta Vulgatam Clementinam*. Edited by Alberto Colunga and Laurentio Turrado. 5th ed. Biblioteca de Auctores Cristianos, no. 14. Madrid: La Editorial Catolica, 1977.

Wainwright, Geoffrey. *Doxology: The Praise of God in Worship, Doctrine and Life*. New York: Oxford University Press, 1980.

Walsh, P. G. *See* Cassiodorus.

Weiss, Günther, ed. *Introitus-Tropen*. Vol. 1, *Das Repertoire der südfranzösischen Tropare des 10. und 11. Jahrhunderts*. Monumenta monodica medii aevi, ed. Bruno Stäblein, no. 3. Kassel: Bärenreiter, 1970.

Yudkin, Jeremy. *Music in Medieval Europe*. Englewood Cliffs, NJ: Prentice Hall, 1989.

INDEX

About the Author

WILLIAM THOMAS FLYNN holds a joint appointment in the Candler School of Theology and Emory University's Department of Music. He has published articles on music and theology in the *Music Review*, *Reformed Liturgy and Music*, *The Dictionary of the Ecumenical Movement*, and *Liturgy and Music: Lifetime Learning* and has received awards and commissions for compositions from the American Guild of Organists, the Wieniawski competition, Washington National Cathedral, Montreat Conferences on Music and Worship, and the Presbyterian Association of Musicians. His edition of Hildegard von Bingen's *O frondens virga* is published by Treble Clef Press, N.C. Dr. Flynn's *Western Chant Practicum* regularly presents reconstructions of medieval services during the spring semester at Emory University. Past reconstructions have included services from fourteenth-century Salisbury, tenth-century Winchester, and Hildegard von Bingen's *Lauds for the Feast of St. Ursula and the XI Thousand Virgins.*

Assistant Professor of Music and Liturgy, Emory University. B.Mus., Eastman School of Music (University of Rochester), 1978; M.Mus., Edinburgh University, 1979; M.A., Duke University, 1988; Ph.D., Duke University, 1992.

ABOUT THE AUTHOR